ADDITIONAL PRAISE FOR ROSENEATH

"*Roseneath* grabs you from the first page and pulls you deeply into its world of miracles and terrors. Dana McSwain deftly weaves together genres while delivering shocks that land with the force of a punch to the chest. The pacing is intense, the characters are richly developed, and the dread is palpable. It's a modern gothic horror that is impossible to put down, even after you've finished reading it." —David Genzen, host of the *"Little House on the Scary"* podcast

"McSwain is a vibrant new voice in gothic horror, exploring old-world themes of good and evil with a modern, paranoiac twist. Her prose is at once lush and sinister, a love letter to language, and it often had me swooping between nostalgic lows and giddy, terrified highs within the same paragraph. I feel equally in love with tensile Georgia Pritchard and her shadowy husband, Nathan, and wished there was a way I could have witnessed their story unfold through my fingers like I was watching the very best horror movie. *Roseneath* made me gleefully afraid of many, many things, including: basements, mirrors, flowers, ghosts (which...fair), childbirth, greenhouses, and my own spouse. I can't wait to see more from this author!" —Sydney Kalnay, young adult fantasy author

"Georgia and Nathan Pritchard, desperate to outrun their grief after a heartbreaking loss, place all their hopes and dreams into a gorgeous but neglected old Victorian home called Roseneath. What they could not know is that Roseneath is the site of an ongoing battle between good and evil and the Pritchard's dream home soon becomes a waking nightmare. Georgia finds secret solace in a little ghost girl named Edie whose body was hidden in the attic. Below, Nathan has claimed the basement and greenhouse as his domain. That is, until he is called away for work. Alone in the house, Georgia's reality becomes something of a fever dream in which time is meaningless. As her situation becomes more desperate, Nathan is trapped in his own nightmare, lost to both himself and Georgia. Can they save each other or are they destined to be lost to the darkness that dwells deep within Roseneath? With writing so lush, lyrical, and reminiscent of fairy tales and epic adventures, the horror of the story sneaks up on you at times, catching you off guard while reminding you of the evils lurking in the basement of Roseneath. *Roseneath* will lure you in, enchant you, and leave you wary of basements and unable to ever look at a rose bush the same way again."   —Megan Alabaugh, librarian

"From the moment we are plunged into the mysterious and intriguing prologue of *Roseneath*, it's clear that this novel will be something else entirely - if you want a breezy beach read, you've come to the wrong place. The curtain is pulled back just long enough to reveal a glimpse of death, ancient betrayal, the literal forces of good and evil clashing behind it before snapping back to introduce the reader to Georgia Pritchard. Having suffered tremendous and unspeakable loss, we meet her as a haunted shell of the bright and hopeful mother-to-be she had been just weeks before. Her devoted and equally heartbroken architect husband, Nathan, struggles to find a way to lift her from her despair and build a bridge across the chasm that has formed between them. He thinks he may have found the answer in Roseneath, a sprawling and long-neglected Victorian estate just begging to be restored to its original beauty. And at first it seems to work - each of them discover something secret and compelling within their new surroundings that takes their mind off their sorrow and hints at a fresh start, a viable and promising future. But not all that glitters is gold, and as Georgia and Nathan plunge blindly ahead on the paths that have opened before them, the darker forces manifesting those paths begin to make themselves known. But is it too late for them to turn back? Sometimes the only way out is through, and never is that more true than in *Roseneath*. A breathless and exhilarating ride that takes the reader through time, space, hell and high water; we discover that the bonds of love can never be too strong, and the fire can never be hot enough."

—Lindsey Emery, bookworm and cereal aficionado, insurance agent by day, dope and powerful witch by night.

"From the very first page of *Roseneath*, I wanted to know more of the Pritchard's story, rooting and fearful for them at the same time. I caught myself speaking to them as if I was watching this gothic horror tale unfold right before my eyes and was so swept up that I was not able to put the book down. If you enjoy gorgeous prose, being surprised by the unexpected, and fearful that good will not overcome evil, pick this up and read *Roseneath* immediately. Also . . . there's some David Bowie."

—Jeanne Lady, literary aficionado

"Roseneath is a gorgeous, crumbling, old mansion in Ohio and the setting for a story of young lovers, archangels and demons, and a little ghost girl from the past. McSwain paints a vivid picture, building immediate suspense in this story that references architecture, Lewis Carroll, and fun slang from a bygone era. We may delight in time spent with a ghost in the attic, but make sure to avoid Roseneath's creepy greenhouse. And most definitely do not go down into the basement where Evil dwells. *Oh frabjous day! Calloo Callay!*"

—Kristin Schrader, book lover

Roseneath

ROSENEATH

DANA MCSWAIN

Webb House Publishing

Roseneath by Dana McSwain
Copyright © 2020 by Dana McSwain

Published by Webb House Publishing, L.L.C.
Lakewood, OH 44107
www.WebbHousePublishing.com

Cover and interior by Timm Bryson, em em design, LLC

ISBN: 978-1-7352860-4-4 (print)
ISBN: 978-1-7352860-5-1 (eBook)

www.danamcswain.com

FOR WINSTON

Heaven is a place on Earth with you.

PROLOGUE

IN THE BASEMENT OF ROSENEATH, AN ARCH-
ANGEL WEPT.

*He knelt in the damp earth, heedless of the mire
that splattered his tarnished armor, and gathered the little girl
into his arms. She had been beautiful in life. Hair the color of
burnished sorrel, rose petal lips, skin like fresh cream cast with
an uneven dusting of cinnamon freckles. In death, her sweet
features were twisted into a gruesome mask by the blasphemy
that had been done to her. He ran his hand over her bloodstained hair, gingerly touched her face and arms where the
blood had congealed around each vicious thorn. A vain hope
caused him to shed one glove and lay his hand upon her small,
still chest—reaching, feeling, searching for some spark of life
that might yet linger in an effort to coax it back to her. But it
was too late. He was too late.*

Again.

*The problem, as ever, was time. The disconnect, the shift,
from his world to this was inconstant. For him, it was mere
seconds from the moment her screams shattered the stillness
of his solitary post. An impossible feat that woke him from
his reveries, shocking him to hear the faint strains of his own*

angelic lilt and the tiniest measure of the language of the stars reaching out to him from some unknown place. And layered through the plaintive cries like broken glass and gravel, a voice he knew well. His own brother, damned and Fallen to Earth. The archangel had raced, sword drawn, from Eden to Earth, wild with hope that whatever this new . . . anomaly was, it might put his feet on a path toward the end of his solitary watch and his brother's reign. But by the time he arrived in this house, in this time, in this place, the girl who had cried out to him had been dead for hours, perhaps days. Only the smallest traces of his brother's presence still saturated the earth she died in, no clue beyond her broken body that Lucifer had ever even been there, or where he had fled once his mysterious task had failed. That this was his brother's work he had no doubt. But what Lucifer had done to her, what twisted alchemy he'd tried to work on this child, and why, was unclear.

The archangel climbed the stairs, carrying the dead girl out of the foul lair his brother had built. The child was wholly human, he was certain of it; he could feel her fragile humanity threaded through every inch of her still form, and yet there was something there, something more. A glimmer in the light stroking her pallid face, how her hair did not lie quite still. If he opened her dead eyes, might he see a flicker of the angelic even there, too? The last time he'd seen a glimmer such as this it hadn't been a flicker. It had been a flood, pouring out of his beloved's eyes, saturating the earth she walked on. He'd drowned in its forbidden familiarity for too short a time. But this child, no matter how precious, was not of his kind. She was something more. Something outside Creation.

Impossible. But the evidence was in his arms.

What was she? What had his brother done?

He paused in the living room. She'd fought, however futilely, to escape this fate. Broken lamps, chairs overturned, small handprints of blood and mud mapped her struggling path to the basement. He gazed into the large mirror recessed over the mantel. He wished, for a brief moment, to take her through to his world, to Eden, to lay her innocent body in the earth under the great sycamores, safe inside the ring of sentinel pines. An unsullied place where the air smelled of incense and time, where the earth was loamy and fertile. A sacred rest for so precious a child.

He knew it was impossible. However 'other' she might be, her fragile human form could not traverse the great divide between this world and his own and he knew he would arrive in his solitary garden empty-handed, her corpse scattered by the journey. He looked down at her again, this impossible child, and was reminded of another day long ago when the impossible seemed possible. The day he had allowed himself to hope that he too might build an impossible thing, the one thing in all of Creation denied to him.

A family.

But Lucifer had taken that hope from him ages ago. In the blink of an eye, his brother had burned that hope from existence.

The archangel turned away from the mirror and began climbing the steep staircase. A family. In this world, such a small thing to want, but in his world a literal impossibility. He paused on the landing and allowed himself a moment to remember. Thousands of years had passed, yet he could still feel her skin on his lips, her hot breath in his ear.

"Galliana," he whispered. The name echoed in the stairwell like a prayer, shook the house with the weight of his memory.

Laying the child gently in the deep clawfoot tub, he bathed her, tenderly washing his brother's putrescence from the little girl's translucent skin, his deft fingers plucking each cruel thorn from her flesh. Then he dried her body, wrapped it in a clean white sheet and climbed the last flight of stairs, the shrouded child cradled in his arms. The stair treads scorched under his boots as he let slip the tight reins that held his temper in check. The air around him crackled, the paint on the walls bubbled and burst, the joists above him groaned as an oppressive density surged out from every molecule of his body, the ruinous deluge a mere fraction of his raw nature. The archangel, in a fit of rage, had forgotten how fragile this plane was. His lips peeled back in a snarl at the very idea of placing the child in the ground. That was the true blasphemy, he thought, as he fought to control the righteous anger inside him. Earth was cursed, sickened with the foul soul of his Fallen brother, and yet these fragile, ignorant humans buried their dearly departed in that very soil, sacrifices to an uncaring God and a Devil, offerings to the very ones who were the cause of all their sorrow.

The scene he found in the attic set his flame-filled eyes to white hot. His hands burned through his gloves and singed the simple shroud around the young corpse. A tattered rug littered with the child's playthings. A lofty sanctuary, a playhouse the child in his arms must have made for herself in the gloomy attic. He laid her down on the rug and studied the meager pile of trinkets. A stack of well-worn books, a blanket, a sleeve of heavy phonograph discs, and a scattering of black feathers. A toy sword and a red ball with a lamb on it. A smudged sketchbook and charcoal. Finally, a small roll of parchment that revealed a cunning painting of a silver ship made of feathers in a *storm-tossed sea. Without knowing exactly why, the archangel reached into his surcoat and withdrew a clutch of artifacts from his home—sycamore leaves and rose hips— and placed them on the rug with the child's toys. He then rolled the child up in the rug, tucking her under the eaves with her small assortment of earthly delights as close to the stars and their mournful unending song as he could. It was not the eternal rest he wished for her, but as with every other thing in this damned Creation, the lesser of two evils. Better, certainly, than placing her in the ground.*

He made his way slowly back down the stairs, through the house, listening, feeling, trying to understand what had happened here and why. Whatever it was, he could be certain of two things. First, that Lucifer had conjured some new evil— aborted, failed, yes—but new and filled with an unknown but undeniable portent. And, second, the path that he and his brother were doomed to travel for eternity had been altered forever in this house with the death of this mysterious child. Before him stretched a now unfamiliar road, his journey once again intersecting with his brother and ultimately— hopefully—with his beloveds.

I must remember this place, this time, *he thought as he waved one gloved hand, the air in front of him parting into a swirl of clouds, enveloping him in a damp treacle and pulling him through to his home, his prison, his paradise. Eden. I* must mark this grave and return to it. And next time I cannot be late. Something began here today, and, one day, I fear it will end here as well.

Decades of solitude passed for the deserted old house known as Roseneath before the archangel reappeared. The home no longer smelled of new wood but of rot. It had become a ghostly relic, hollow and haunted. He paused in the living room, listening. A small voice sang in the attic, a child's verse, that same small lilt of the heavens she'd had in life. And somewhere, below, deep below, the familiar smell that accompanied his Fallen brother. Decay. The coppery scent of blood. He reached out further with his preternatural senses, deep into the tainted earth and felt his brother's rabid glee, a twisted delight that only the slender hope of his beloved's return could generate. The slam of a door at the back of the house sent the archangel striding to the window in time to see a man, disheveled and covered in dry earth, an insidious dusting of his brother's dominion, climb quickly into a battered old truck and leave as if chased. The brief glimpse he was granted of the young human's bewildered, vacant expression was a haunting, all-too-familiar hallmark of his elusive, foul brother's handiwork. Lucifer. He closed his eyes and listened, feeling with his unearthly senses for a trace of the beast himself, catching little more than a tantalizing, sulfurous wisp that was gone as soon as he detected it.

The floor under his feet smoldered, his hand gripped the hilt of his sword tight, the air around him sparked. Upstairs, the child's song cut off. She, too, was listening.

Whatever had taken place before, it was happening again. Here. Now. After all this time. With a wave of his hand, the archangel conjured the cloud-drenched portal to his own world. Once through, he drove his sword into the mossy ground at his feet and knelt, his gaze fixed squarely on Roseneath.

ONE

GEORGIA SLIPPED OUT OF BED AND CREPT TO the window, her posture that of a schoolgirl balancing books, careful to keep her eyes locked forward. She separated the curtains to watch over her husband while he slept in his truck. Before, Nathan's schedule had always been unpredictable—sixteen-hour shifts, eight-hour shifts, half days that transformed mid-afternoon into late nights.

She could set a clock by him now.

He would park his truck in the street just before sunset and sleep, arms crossed tightly across his chest, for exactly sixty minutes, as she kept vigil over him. It was a strange sort of togetherness—her chin propped on the windowsill, his head slumped against the side door. Her finger slid against the window as if she could smooth his furrowed brow from her mournful eyrie. The hour was all too brief a communion before he would uncoil and awaken, his expression lost in the dying light of the setting sun, to make his way into their home like a condemned man. Wide-eyed in bed, she would count the minutes . . .

Three of them,

as he stood at the bottom of the steps. She would imagine the tightening of his jaw as he gathered the strength to deal with her. Then he would walk into their room . . .

Three steps,

wrap her in his arms and ask,

"Are you all right now, Georgia?"

His patient tone slipping each day closer to pleading.

She was starting to hate him for it.

Nathan woke then, his arms stretching to span the truck cab. Not today. She couldn't bear his patience today. She hurried to the bathroom,

Chin up, don't look down. Never look down.

her path a zigzag hopscotch to avoid the carpet, the last step into the bathroom a Double Dutch hop,

Step on a crack, break your mother's back,

then she slammed the door and locked it. The mewling chorus in her head rose and fell in pitiful, needful waves.

No, no, no, please not again.

Running the water as hot as it would go, she shed her gown and studied the ceiling. The steam billowed around her, wreathing her naked body in a shroud, erasing her, the rushing water drowning out the doleful notes of a newborn weeping. She raised her arms and swirled them, making patterns in the mist until the air condensed on her in tear-shaped drops.

"Georgia? Everything all right in there?" Nathan's worried voice broke through her pleading reverie.

No, everything is not all right. It will never be all right again. What do you expect me to say? She hugged herself, digging her fingernails into her arms until she felt the skin break, until she felt blood well up under her nails, until the pain became a refuge she could hide in. "Everything is fine, Nathan. I just want a shower. Then I'll go back to bed. The doctor said I should rest, so I'll do that."

She heard the heavy thud of his shoulder against the locked door. "Georgie? Can I come in?"

She dug her nails in deeper, barely able to rein in her furious voice. "No, Nathan, you can't. I don't want you to see me like this. Just leave me alone. Please."

The refuge vanished as the pain she was hiding from returned, pooling back to her as if drawn by her outburst. She pulled her nails from her arms and examined them. Rosy little half-moons. A heavy rasp as Nathan's shoulder slid down the door. A thump, keys jangling, boots sliding out as he slumped against the door. She could hear his breathing low in the hallway.

Don't look down. Whatever you do, do not look down. Focus on your hands, that's a good girl.

"Georgie, please. Maybe you don't want me, but I need you. Please. Let me in. Just let me hold you for a minute. Baby, I am so sorry."

Georgia's mouth filled with a million bitter replies, but she choked on each one. Her bloodstained fingertips vanished as the steam shifted around her. Who cared what he needed? She needed to be alone. She needed time

We were supposed to have time.

to scratch and pick at this pain, methodically extract every fragment of glass she could find. She needed to memorize each shard, catalogue them, and then put each precious piece back together inside her where they belonged. Where *she* belonged. Hers. Forever.

Closing her eyes, she breathed deeply

In

Out

In

Out

until she found what she was looking for. There it was. No matter how hard he'd scrubbed, no matter how much bleach he'd used, she could still smell it in the dank humidity of the bathroom. A delicate, coppery perfume, like spoiled fruit, like rotting flowers.

Georgia stood wrapped in the rising steam, breathing in her daughter's last moments, moments she could never regain, cataloguing every nuance of bleach and blood and fluid and locked it away inside her, the man on the other side of the door forgotten until his voice floated under the door, "Fine, Georgia. It's fine. I understand. I'm going to run out and get some food. You need to eat. I'll be back soon. Okay?" After a long, hopeful pause, his heavy footsteps echoed down the stairs, slow, plodding, resigned, when she did not answer.

Georgia jammed her hand in her mouth, biting it hard enough to bleed. She pictured him walking down the stairs, out the door, slamming the door of his truck, the engine growing softer as it drove off. It wasn't fair that he wasn't shackled by it, that he could escape it, that he didn't have to carry around the reminder of *her*.

"I hate him." Her eyes fell to her stomach, still swollen, her once taut skin drooping. *Now you've done it. You looked.*

She drove her fists into the door and the pain exploded across her knuckles. They glowed red through the vapor cloud, swollen or bleeding—she didn't care. It might be easier somehow if she could hate him, at least as much as she hated herself. *But I can't.* Slumping against the door, Georgia examined the gritty, choking, greedy pain, felt its weight against the back of her throat, the copper tang blooming cankers on the fragile insides of her cheeks. She swallowed a mouthful and knew it for jealousy. He could walk away; his strong shoulders could carry his share of this nightmare outside of this prison she now lived in. Georgia looked down at her chest—*why did I look*—the steam around her parted and she saw her swollen breasts, hard and painful. Rich pools formed along the underside, dripping down her stomach to the floor.

She couldn't escape this. Not even for a minute.

TWO

HER WHISPERS CUT THROUGH THE DARK-
ness, ragged and choked, a wordless refrain.

Nathan Pritchard was awake, but even in his
dreamless state their bed was heavy with her nightmares.
He held Georgia as best he could, his wife's limbs twitch-
ing as if they were being pulled by a relentless troupe of
puppeteers. She was asleep, but it was the hunted sleep of
wounded prey, fitful and broken. Her lips were curved up
in a grim approximation of her once beguiling smile, her
body now a dead weight in his arms. He shifted in their
tangled sheets and pulled her on top of him, hoping the
steady beat in his chest would calm the racing one in hers.

Their embrace was a cruel mimicry of the casual posses-
sion that years of marriage had forged. Instead of the familiar entanglement, their limbs now seemed at war with each
other. Each night, he tried desperately to hold her together,
all the while her unconscious body seemed determined to fly
apart. His hands searched in vain for the latch on the cruel
snare that held her, but her pain was a relentless, vicious
animal devouring her one small piece at a time. Each night
ended as it began—a maddening, Sisyphean endeavor.

Nathan didn't sleep anymore, not in their home, not in their bed. He'd catch a few minutes in his truck in the street, a leaden, dead-limbed intermission that did little to compensate for his night watch. Then he would unlock the door to their shuttered home, climb the stairs like he had that day, a bleak pilgrim's progress

Her sweater draped over the banister, her shoes kicked to one side.

What else? What had he done? It had been so quiet, like time held its breath, each moment that followed the verse of a dirge.

Stop all the clocks, cut off the telephone.

If only he'd kept his phone with him. That was it. That was the point it all went . . .

Pour away the ocean and dismantle the sun.

Or was it before that? Was it the day before that? The day he hadn't come home, the day he'd . . .

For nothing now can ever come to any good.

Night after night spent studying each moment of that day, trying to find the precise moment that separated everything that came before from everything that came after. And then it would start all over again.

Her voice cut through the dark as she began struggling again in his arms.

"Nathan, please rip the carpet out."

Nathan's heart sank as he reached for her hands. Pulling her clawing fingers away from her face, he laced his fingers with hers and held them to her chest.

"Please. Today. Now. Rip it out, take it away. I can't bear it."

"Georgia, baby, the carpet is fine. Please don't do this again." His voice was a frayed tight rope.

"No. No, it's not." She began struggling again and this time he let her go. "It's not fine. It's wrong. I can still smell it. I can smell it from here. I can see it. Can't you see it? Why can't you see it?"

"See what, Georgia? What do you see?" He pulled her clutching hands from her hair, held them to his lips and kissed her white knuckles.

"I can still see the blood. I can smell it. It smells like rotting flowers."

Nathan pushed her away and stood up fast. "Fine." That one sharp word shocked her wide-awake and he regretted as soon as he said it. He turned in the dark so she wouldn't see the revulsion on his face. Then, softer, "I'll rip it out. Whatever you want. Whatever you need."

"Nathan, are you mad at me?" Her gray irises dilated, black pools with silver rims, searching his like an animal caught in a snare.

"No, I'm fine. Everything's fine."

"Nathan, you look so tired."

"I'm fine, Georgia. I'm not tired." He let out the breath he'd been holding and pulled her to him, kissing her eyes, her cheeks, her lips, each gentle press to her body a silent plea. Come back to me.

"Georgia?"

"Yes, Nathan." She froze in his arms.

"I think maybe we should talk to someone."

"No."

"Georgia, you can't go on like this, it's not . . ."

"No, Nathan." Instead of pushing him away, she grasped his arms, her nails digging into his skin. "No. It's mine. This . . . this . . . and I won't let anyone else touch it. I won't let them reclassify it, rename it, try to twist it into something bearable. I'm not going to let some doctor teach me how to shelve it. It's mine. She's mine . . . she was supposed to be mine. I have to hold on to this or it'll be like she never was. Like she never mattered. And I can't . . . I won't live like that."

Her hands slid down his arms, releasing him. Nathan found himself pulling away from her as his sympathy shifted toward anger. Just a fraction of an inch, but she noticed and her shoulders fell in rebuke.

"I'm taking you somewhere tomorrow. Away from this place. This isn't living, Georgia." His voice was a knife's edge, as close as he'd come in weeks to snapping at her.

She began to wring her hands in her lap, a frantic cat's cradle.

"Please, no. Not tomorrow." Licking her cracked lips, she ran a hand through her hair, tried to smooth it. "Next week. I can't . . . I . . . I'll be better next week, I promise." He could see her pulse racing through the delicate skin of her throat as she stared through tears at the ceiling. "Please."

"No," he whispered in her ear, turning her chin, forcing her to look at him. "Tomorrow. Tomorrow morning, you'll get up, get dressed, and I'll take you somewhere better." He slid a hand over her tangled curls. "I don't want you to have to wait till next week," he whispered. "I can't watch you live like this anymore."

◆   ◆   ◆

Georgia sat motionless while he showered, dressed, and left, frozen by the tone of his voice and the fear of leaving the nest she'd made. The sun continued its crawl, finding its way to the mirror across from the bed. She watched as her reflection shifted from shadow to pastel to sun-lit. Her complexion was peaked and gray, the skin around her eyes dry and cracked, a spindly porcelain doll ravaged by grief and neglect. She smelled her hair, her arms, wincing at the sour, stale odor. *I'm driving him away. I'll lose him.* She tried to imagine a loss like that, compared it to the one she'd been nursing. All these weeks thinking the worst had happened. The loss that had driven her to this sanctuary was almost clinical, numb comparatively; her body pumped full of painkillers and antibiotics to combat any threat of infection or real feeling. The loss of Nathan would be nothing like that. It would be a bloody battlefield amputation; her teeth gripped tight on a filthy stick as her limbs were sawed off one at a time with a dull, rusty relic. The resulting infection would kill her and there would be no respite from that kind of living death. Losing him would be a pain mythological in scale, waking every day to be ripped apart by it, forever.

Georgia staggered from the bed, dragging the sheets with her, stripping the mattress with one vicious jerk, then threw the musty bundle out the bedroom door. *I disgust myself; I must disgust him, too.* The windows now—she flung them wide and let the wind send the curtains flying like ship sails. *I will not drown in this lake of tears, I will sail across it in a shining silver ship.* She pulled her gown over her head and rent it in two—*I will not wear this shroud a moment longer. I will not let this break me*—then jammed it in the bathroom wastebasket.

Not tomorrow. I have to be better today. For him.

THREE

NATHAN'S HOPES ROSE WITH EACH MILE they put behind them. The black ribbon of road ahead felt less as if it were unfurling and more as if it were coaxing them, beckoning them. Nathan's foot grew heavy on the pedal, desperate to escape the past and hurry towards the promise that seemed to wait for them just beyond the horizon. Nathan glanced at Georgia across the truck cab. Oversized sunglasses hid her expression while she gazed steadfastly out the passenger window. Her gaunt wrists stuck out awkwardly from a sweater—a sweater in all this heat—a woolen cocoon that did little to disguise that she had slipped from petite to shrunken. She hadn't really eaten *since* . . . and what pregnancy weight she had gained vanished in the weeks she had spent lying in bed *after*. Every day whittled her down a little bit more, a relentless rasp exploiting each spot where she was worn thin and he had no idea how to stop it. But still, she'd gotten dressed today. That was a start. And maybe this was just the thing. Maybe this hegira would be just the thing to lead her out of the dream world she was trapped in and back to herself, back to him, back to each other.

"Where are we going?"

"It's a surprise, Miss Georgia." He took a chance and reached over, pinching her gently. She jumped and looked at him finally, her startled face slipping into something almost like her old smile.

"Is this surprise in Ohio, Mr. Pritchard?"

He winked at her, watched the smile transform into a heady blush, then reached for her hand. She gripped it and he felt a moment of perfect certainty that he was doing the right thing. *Of course it's right. It's perfect. It'll all work out now. You'll see.*

"No hints. You'll just have to be patient." He raised her hand to his lips, watched the delicate smile widen then fall, a fragile, brief idyll as her hand slipped from his. Nathan looked back to the road, wishing he could have frozen that moment, held that small victory in his hand and fanned its flames until it shone like it used to. Georgia slid across the bench seat and leaned her head on his shoulder, a tepid embrace before she retreated back to her side of the truck. *Still,* he thought, and as the miles flew by he allowed himself to imagine everything the way it used to be.

◆　　◆　　◆

Nathan usually sat in his truck at the university, writing out landscaping quotes between classes. Radio on, air-conditioning as high as it would go. Alone, no chance of yet another unpleasant encounter with either his ex, Cat, or one of her legions of sorority sisters who took her vendettas as their own. Cat had been a blistering, stupid, exhilarating, demoralizing lesson in remembering who he was: white trash of the Youngstown variety. She'd had her fun with him and left him with the certainty that nothing about him would ever be good enough. Certainly not good enough for her, but—and this was more worrisome—not good enough for anyone. So he kept his head low, his eyes on his classes and work, and shut that part of himself off.

Two more months and he'd be out of this shit show. No more spoiled college kids and microwave dinners, no more reeking of two-cycle oil and grass clippings. He finished his degree in architecture in four years to the wonderment of his advisor. He could have taken a job with the firm he'd interned with but he was used to going his own way, used to calling his own shots, and being one of a team of newbie architects at a giant firm would do nothing to take him where he wanted to go. So he'd applied to graduate school and was now just weeks from a Master's in Art History. The books scattered around in his work truck were filled with a world of beauty in architecture and landscape. He'd start his own firm, work for himself, and see how far his own ambition would take him. It had gotten him this far.

Seven years of working two jobs. Dead on his feet with hours of coursework still to do every night while his colleagues were out doing all the dumb, drunk shit that college kids are known to do. Kids who were handed tuition money, who didn't worry about how to pay for their books, like it was owed to them. Planting trees for men with oversized watches and 9:00 a.m. tee times, men who drove hundred thousand-dollar cars but would nickel and dime him about his weekly rates. Years grabbing minutes he didn't have to study and falling bone-weary every night into bed, one step farther away from the shithole *life he'd been born into. He'd finish school, take the money he'd saved and build his own path, one brick at a time. He'd do it his way and he'd do it alone.*

But fate stepped in, in the form of a hot summer day and a broken air conditioner in his truck. He went into the library to study in the precious few minutes between his last seminar and a job across town, searching for a place where none of Cat's vapid friends would ever think to be, and found himself in the rare book room. At a study table. Across from her.

A girl with heavy black lashes over storm-tossed eyes, hair so wild that even as he sat there he could see each raven curl struggling to escape the haphazard bun perched above a pale, pointed face, held in place by nothing more than a series of pencils.

He watched her read a dog-eared copy of The Book of Marvels. And he'd left in a haze, unable to even think about talking to her. He was an hour late to the cross-town job but even as he was getting his ass chewed out for that, he was trying to remember how many pencils it took to hold that tempestuous hair in place.

He went back the next day. And the one after that. And watched the gray-eyed librarian read, marveling how something so commonplace could be so enchanting. She frowned over a stack of dull-looking paperwork, twirling a pencil through her fingers, only to cast it aside in favor of an oversized, outdated atlas. She intently studied Out of the Silent Planet for forty-five minutes one day, the movement of her lips with the words creating a bead of sweat on his temple. He swallowed hard when he heard her sigh, reluctant to set down the well-worn paperback, a small moment of annoyance before she smiled evenly at the student in front of her. He watched her feet as she climbed the narrow ladders and fetched books off of tall shelves, studied her hands as she twisted her wrist to see the time on an infinitesimal watch with a dangling chain no bigger than a cobweb. He watched her navigate the aisles with ease, her hips swinging in a brisk rhythm that his heartbeat raced to catch up with as she walked past him, the air around her saturated with promises of rainy afternoon naps under warm blankets, twilight walks, and fireflies.

Nathan lay in bed that night and wondered what part of Out of the Silent Planet had caught her attention. What was she looking for? He fell asleep reading C.S. Lewis instead of his book on seventeenth century Orthodox icons, and during his exam the next day, saw her enigmatic face in every Russian icon, every saint, every angel.

Afterward, he went to the library, a desperate man with no thought beyond making her look up from her reading, an irrational certainty that the moment she did, a spell would spring to his lips that could bewitch her, too.

So caught up in her book, she didn't notice him for a long, agonizing moment. A moment long enough for him to revisit every parting barb Cat had thrown at him. Long enough to notice he was grass-stained and disheveled. And long enough for him to see that she was eating an apple furtively under the desk, a careworn copy of The Treasure Seekers on her lap. She reached into her hair and plucked a pencil out—it took five, apparently—and used it to underline something with a long steady line of graphite. And in that moment he felt certain that this tableau in front of him was everything about her, that she was an icon of herself at that moment, symbols hidden in everything she did. Symbols he could find if he only had the chance. Her. This girl.

And then she peered up at him with those gray eyes, the confusion on her face vanishing only to be replaced with a blush that made his knees weak. Her book and pencil fell to the floor, the apple rolled away. He thought he heard her whisper "you" and he was done. He fell to his knees in front of her, offering her back the things she'd dropped. With that small gesture he had lain the cornerstone of his future, right there at her feet.

FOUR

GEORGIA'S SUNGLASSES DID LITTLE TO BLOT out the summer sun. With each mile that passed, she grew angrier at a world that had kept moving without her. People raced in tilt-a-whirl orbits, spring had given way to summer, fertile and lush. Life outside her confinement had soldiered on, pernicious and uncaring. Georgia dug her toes into the floorboards and wished she knew the magic words that would bring everything to a grinding halt, force the whole world to show her grief the respect it deserved.

Nathan pulled her toward him and wrapped his arm around her shoulders. She knew what she was *supposed* to do. She was *supposed* to rest her head on his shoulder, she was *supposed* to make some charming comment on the drive or the weather, he *expected* her to show some interest in this unwanted, bewildering trip. Another small plea—a kiss on her temple—and she realized that she felt betrayed, most of all, by him. By the way he expected anything of her, by the way he hadn't fallen apart, by the way he, too, had soldiered on and left her to mourn alone.

She withdrew under the pretext of stretching, then rested her head on the passenger door, not caring what thoughts filled his own silence.

Their destination was a sleepy part of town, the tree line of century oaks broken by slate rooftops scattered on either side of a broad boulevard. A weather-beaten house elaborately crowned in gables and surrounded by a broken sentry line of porches peered back at her through an entanglement of scaffolding.

"What's this?" she asked. "A new project?'

"Sort of. Something I've been working on."

She peered up and down the street. "Where is everyone? This neighborhood looks like a ghost town."

"Close. This part of Cleveland is still a few years out from gentrification. Most of these homes are empty, slated for demolition as soon as the county gets around to it."

Georgia watched Nathan walk around the truck, his straightened shoulders conveying something vulnerable. She scanned the grounds for other contractors. Nothing. They were alone.

He held the door open for her, holding his hand out for hers.

"Come on. I want you to meet Roseneath."

She let him pull her out of the truck and lead her across an overgrown lawn. Swells of roses bulged out of the foundation and surged across the yard, wicked black thorns embedded in the brick clawed their way up to the roofline, the sun glinted on the attic windows. Uneven stone steps covered in moss led to a golden oak door that Nathan shouldered open with an offhanded familiarity. Georgia stepped into the foyer behind him and listened quietly as he gave her a tour. She noted how nervous he was, how he fidgeted when he spoke.

She followed him as he led her down a passage to a dining room, up a staircase that vanished into a gloomy aerie, toward a corridor to the back of the house with a garden visible beyond—Nathan now stood with both hands in his pockets, his voice shaky—into a living room with scaffolding, stacks of paint cans, and a stone mantel with the remains of a discarded fast food meal. Outside, the world seemed frozen, timeless, the riot of vegetation blotting out the modern world, Sleeping Beauty's forbidden castle, replete with a bewitched forest of thorns. The thick walls and heavy wooden doors smothered the modern world outside, conspired with the overgrown garden to create a peaceful haven. She flushed in understanding, angry at herself for being angry at him. This trip she'd been dreading was just his way of easing her back into the world. *I should have known*, she reproached herself. *I know him better than that.*

"Nate, it's . . ."

He cut her off. "I know, it's a disaster. It'll take another year or two to finish, assuming I have the time, and it'll cost a small fortune. But I got it for almost nothing and it's actually a lot better than it looks. Plumbing works—mostly—the electrical is done, the basement is a disaster, but the rest of the work is cosmetic and I think . . ."

She put her finger against his lips.

"Nate, stop. I know a diamond in the rough when I see one."

"I guess you do." He reached into his pocket and held out a set of keys for her.

"Your new home, Mrs. Pritchard. If you want it."

She stared at the keys as he dropped them into her hand, trying to understand what he could possibly mean. Not a visit. A destination. Hers. Theirs. Here. She looked back to the wrappers on the mantel. The ladders and tools. The lack of crew in the yard. Nate was doing this, all of this, himself. For her. For them.

"Baby, don't you like it? I can sell it if you think it was a stupid idea. Please don't cry, Georgia."

She shook her head. "No, it's not that, it's just—"

He cut her off. "I bought it months ago. Before. I wanted . . . I thought I could make it livable before the baby, and then I could give you a house—a real house— someplace we could raise a family and grow old together. I wanted to surprise you. But then everything went to shit and I didn't . . . I didn't know how to tell you. So I just kept working on it, here and there, and I thought maybe—" He wiped her tears with his thumbs. "Please don't cry."

How could I have been so wrong? He hadn't left her alone in her sorrow, he'd sacrificed his own on an altar for her. To give her all the time she needed, time she'd so selfishly taken. He'd protected her as best he could, kept the world outside at bay until she could face it again. And all the while, laying the foundation for a second chance for them both. The key in her hand was his gentle way of daring her to imagine a new future built on the ruins of the old. Reminding her that she was stronger than what she'd become.

She clutched the keys—*ours*—so tight in her hand that the rough-cut edges imprinted their shape on her palm. Rising up on her toes, she grasped him by the back of his head, her fingers tangling in his hair. She kissed him as a sense of euphoria washed over her.

"Wait here," she whispered.

Ducking out of his careful embrace, Georgia ran through the dining room—*wainscoting and sconces*—through a protesting swinging door into the kitchen—*built-in hutches and a deep stone sink*—and down through the back hall, pausing breathless at a random door. She turned the knob, but it wouldn't budge.

Nathan appeared behind her in the kitchen doorway. "That's the basement. I'd skip it for now if I were you. It's a real nightmare down there." He reached out for her but she twirled away, through the back hall past the garden door—*more roses, a carriage house, and a host of broken statues*—into the living room. Two doors flanked the stone fireplace leading out to an enclosed porch. She opened one of the glass doors and let a flurry of wind and leaves in, which swirled around her feet and sent her skirt flaring out around her.

"Well?" Just behind her now, a breath away.

She let the mirth on her face be his answer. Before he could respond, she pulled him down to her, her lips seeking his. He lifted her in his arms as the worry fell from his face and held her tightly. She kicked at him and struggled until he put her down, then she pushed him away and ran to the base of the stairs, skirt gathered in her hands.

"Want me to give you a tour of the upstairs?" That slow burn smile, the one he'd worn so easily before, returned, a beacon showing her the way. Back to herself, to him, to them.

She shook her head and his grin widened at the sound of her unexpected, excited laughter. She flushed, elated at the way the promise of that grin made her toes curl in her shoes. *This. This is how it was. How we were. Before. I remember now*. It was right there waiting for me to see it again. Here. In this place.

"No, Mr. Pritchard, I shall show myself the upstairs, thank you very much. You'll ruin it with contractor talk and a history lesson."

He bowed to her, his green eyes twinkling. "By all means, Mrs. Pritchard. I'll go check on the roof. Come find me when you're done exploring."

Georgia ran up the staircase, pausing at the landing to marvel at the floor-to-ceiling window that framed the backyard. A secret garden, wild and overgrown, the listing remains of a ramshackle greenhouse pitched alarmingly under the graceful arms of a pine stand, buried waist-deep in Queen Anne's lace and thistles. Waves of roses seemed to crash against the entire foundation of the house, a gentle breeze brought them to life, the thorns scratching against the brick and glass below insistent. Another flight of stairs revealed a trio of closed doors, which opened into bedrooms in varying states of disrepair, another set of double doors led to a cedar-lined linen closet. Next to that, a bedroom door stood open, and she knew it had been left like that intentionally. For her.

Fresh paint, sawdust, floor polish. Their bedroom. The walls a soft wisteria, the trim a crisp white, the wood floors newly finished. Across the room a half-open door revealed a clawfoot bath and marble sink heavily scarred and veined with age. Outside, in the yard, she could hear the clattering of Nathan's tools and ladders, the confident rise and fall of his voice. A phone call. Another site, perhaps. *How long had he been working on this for them? For her. Weeks, while she lay there, doing nothing for him, pushing him away.*

"You have to be better for him," she told her reflection in the window, her lips curling up in surprise as she realized the simple truth of those two little words. They were the key, the incantation. As easy as Dorothy clicking her heels, a magic spell that had been there all along, to transport her out of the dark place she'd fallen into and back into the perfect world they'd inhabited together. Two little words.

"For him," she whispered. "For him, you can do anything. How did I forget that?" She peered out the window to search for Nathan, but an enormous holly tree blocked her view. Two startled mourning doves twittered at her from a branch.

Back out of the bedroom to the last door at the end of the hall, behind which lay a steep flight of wooden stairs. She climbed them two at a time, a single light bulb overhead guiding her up the narrow stairs, and she found herself in a large attic. The rafters soared overhead like a cathedral, windows centered on all four walls like a fairytale tower.

She heard Nathan's voice through the roof outside. He was louder this time, as he wrestled with one of his ladders clanging against the copper gutter. "Fucking thorns. Goddamn it all to—" His voice grew louder as he ascended. "Well, that's just fucking great. Who the fuck patches slate like this? Assholes . . . fucking Vermont Blue slate . . . fucking asphalt shingles." She smiled at his indignation. "Jesus Christ, expanding foam? Son of a . . ." His voice trailed off and Georgia made her way across creaking wooden floors to the southern-facing window. Peeking out, she spied Nathan's sandy brown hair as he descended the ladder, muttering to himself, his boots banging out a drum beat of annoyance.

Georgia jumped when she felt something nudge the back of her shoe. A red rubber ball with the image of a lamb pulling a cart. She studied the whimsical artifact, smiling as she remembered the long-ago day she'd met the stranger who would become her husband kneeling before her like some Crusade-weary knight, picking up her apple and offering her all the things she had lost.

✦   ✦   ✦

There had been other boys. Shy boys and vacuous boys, boys whose voices broke when they asked her out, careless boys who snapped the sharp edges of her heart, boys who made no lasting impression at all. But "boys" was always how she thought of them, and, with few exceptions, none of them stood out for long in her memory. Boys she thought of as placeholders, benchmarks for each year that passed without him. Who he was she didn't know, but she was certain that she would know him the instant she saw him. However, with each passing year she spent in her insulated, sterile library world, Georgia grew more and more concerned that perhaps the "he" she was waiting for, the "he" she'd conjured out of a lifetime with her nose buried in books, wasn't ever coming.

And then, one dull day over summer, a shadow fell over her, startling her from her book. A pair of muddy boots and grass-stained pants. Above, green eyes touched with silver. Hands so big and rough she knew that no matter how gentle they tried to be, they would always insist. And then the mud-splattered man smiled at her, the heat of his intense gaze searing the world around her into negative. Her book fell to the floor, the pencil in her hand, too, and in the moment it took him to stoop down and pick them up, in the fraction of a second before he looked up at her again, she recognized him—him—and she wondered what had taken him so long.

"It's you," she whispered, wondering if he knew it was her.

He looked up from where he knelt at her feet, his hands cradling her book, her pencil, and her half-eaten apple.

"Yeah, it's me. I ruined your apple, Miss . . .?"

"Galloway. Georgia Galloway." She plucked the grimy apple from his hands and dropped it in her wastepaper basket.

"Nathan Pritchard."

She tried to pull her book back out of his tanned hands, hands that obscured entirely the gilt edge of The Treasure Seekers, *but he held it fast. She let his warm hands close over hers until they were holding the book together.*

"Well then, Mr. Pritchard." She felt the color rise in her cheeks, roses.

"Yes, well then." He cleared his throat and she felt his hands tremble in hers. "What should we do about the apple, Miss Galloway?"

"I guess you'll have to get me another."

His lips slid into a slow burn smile, his green eyes crinkled. She dropped her book again and he laughed.

"What time do you get off work?"

He had known. He had always known it was her.

FIVE

 INTRIGUED BY THE RED BALL, GEORGIA began searching for more toys. Unfortunately, most of the attic had already been cleared out. The dusty wooden floor was streaked with long scratch marks, possibly where something had been removed. But, in the shadows, where the attic walls sloped down in a graceful curve to meet the eaves, Georgia could just make out a small, lumpy pile resting on the floor.

Getting on her hands and knees, she crept under the eaves, squinting into the gloom until her head brushed the roof decking. She could just barely reach the pile, which turned out to be a bundled-up blanket concealing a number of bulky objects. Behind that, beyond her reach, lay a moth-eaten rug and a crushed bassinet made of wicker.

Georgia pulled the blanket out of the darkness and into the pool of light in the center of the room. Then, gathering her dirt-streaked skirts around her, she sat cross-legged on the floor and examined its texture. The blanket was a heavy doubled crochet, and, although caked with filth and dead moths, still soft and obviously handmade. *It's a receiving blanket.* Her eyes blurred for a moment, but she held herself firmly in check and began to unwrap the dingy cache.

Inside was a small stack of books, a weighty sleeve of old records, a crumbling sketchbook, and a posy of black feathers, sycamore leaves, and rose hips that smelled strongly of incense and vetiver. Beneath these items lay a toy sword made of tin, and at the very bottom of the pile, a small roll of parchment no bigger than her little finger. She carefully unrolled it to reveal a finely wrought painting, a silver boat made of feathers under heavy seas. *I will not drown in this lake of tears, I will sail across it in a shining silver ship.* Georgia set the painting aside to study the assortment of children's books.

Most of the titles were unfamiliar to her, an aged collection of out-of-print children's stories and grammar school primers. One, however, caught the edge of a memory with its vividly colored cover. *A Child's Book of Nursery Rhymes.* She fanned the thick, yellowed pages, enchanted by the illustrations on each page. *Itsy Bitsy Spider, It's Raining, It's Pouring, Little Boy Blue,* all the ones she expected to find and many she'd forgotten. *Lavender's Blue, The Lion and the Unicorn, Oranges and Lemons.*

Setting the books aside, she reached for the sleeve of records. Not the thin, flimsy vinyl she was used to seeing at tag sales. No, these thick, deeply grooved discs of shellac were weighty and nearly a quarter-inch thick. *Maple Leaf Rag, Peter Gink, Wipin' the Pan, Button Up Your Overcoat.* She pulled the last recording from its olive drab sleeve. *You're The Cream in My Coffee* performed by the Colonial Club Orchestra.

A strange urge whispered in her ear, *This is just the place for treasures like these. A wonderland of Ragtime and Jazz, Wynken, Blynken and Nod, and magpie rhymes.* She did not open the moldering book of verse, instead reciting aloud her favorite rhyme from memory, her voice made small by the attic's thick walls.

> "One for sorrow,
> Two for joy,
> Three for a girl,
> Four for a boy,
> Five for silver,
> Six for gold,
> Seven for a secret,
> Never to be told.
> Eight for a wish,
> Nine for a kiss,
> Ten for a bird,
> You must not miss."

The words seized in her throat—movement behind her—and she froze. Georgia scanned the room, but there was nothing.

"Hello? Is someone there?" Her words echoed in the empty room. She twisted to her right as the same noise came again, a gentle, tentative sigh, like something was moving cautiously across the worn floor. Her mouth went dry. "Hello?" But there was no reply, nothing but a profound silence broken only by the sound of her racing heart. Maybe it was Nathan on the roof again. No, the only sound that came from outside was the wind rattling the windows. And yet, there was something else; the uneasy awareness that someone was holding their breath, hesitating.

Georgia held her own breath as she waited to see what, if anything, came next. One one thousand, two one thousand, three . . .

A floorboard creaked behind her.

The moment cracked like ice. Cold wings spread across her back, as if great feathery masses had sprouted there. She turned to look again behind her, to catch a glimpse of the imagined wings, and, finding none, sought out the window instead. It was closed. Dust motes drifted lazily in the waning sunbeams as they disappeared into the clouds. A rumble of thunder, a gust of air and all four windows shook in their frames. She was certain that window, the southern window she'd spied Nathan through, had been open. Studying the shuddering wooden frame now, she saw that it was not only closed—it was locked.

One one thousand, two one thousand, three one thousand, four . . . nothing.

Georgia let out the breath she'd been holding and turned slowly back to the jumbled items piled on the floor. As she did, out of the corner of her eye, she caught a glint in the floating dust, a glamour that made her think of long hair falling over a small shoulder, shining eyes narrowed in curiosity. But when she turned back, it was gone. Nothing.

One Mississippi, two Mississippi, three Mississippi, four . . .

A harsh pelting against the windowpanes, and the entire attic shuddered under a sudden gale. She held her breath, a hum of anticipation heavy in the air, as if she were waiting for the curtain to rise, the players watching in the wings for the orchestra to finish the opening score, poised and ready.

Nothing, and yet . . . there, along one side of the locked windows were three small fingerprints, too tiny to be hers. She unlatched the window again and swung it open, sending a torrent of rain and wind swirling around her. She examined the latch to see if, by some oddity of its mechanics, it could have shut and locked itself. *Impossible.* She closed the window, careful not to touch the prints, and locked it again. Such tiny fingerprints, right where a hand would rest if someone, someone small, had stood on tiptoes to swing it shut. *How old must those little prints be? How long can fingerprints last on glass?*

Nathan's voice broke the spell.

"Georgia? Honey?"

"I'll be right down!" Gathering up the strange assortment of artifacts, she carefully wrapped them back in the grimy blanket and tucked the bundle back under the eaves. Far back, where only someone small could reach it. Satisfied, she crawled out and stood in the center of the attic room, wiping her hands on her skirt, when she spied the red ball. It was now perched on the threshold of the attic door, splattered with raindrops, bits of sycamore leaves and a few downy black feathers, its glossy crimson sheen shining through the bits of garden the wind had blown in. She picked it up, wiped it clean on her skirt and rolled it back under the eaves with the other relics to save for another day.

Georgia raced down the steps, her feet barely touching the treads. Nathan was waiting for her in the living room, drenched from the sudden downpour, once again that rakish smile she hadn't seen in ages lit up his face, sent a delicious tremor through her legs.

"What's the verdict, boss?" he asked.

"It's like something out of a fairy tale." A long-forgotten happiness bloomed inside her, a tiny ember fanned by the light in his eyes. She slipped her sweater off and let it fall to the floor.

"Reminds me of you," Nathan replied. He took two steps toward her then stopped, a cautious pilot testing the waters.

"I love it, Nate, but how can we possibly afford this? I know work hasn't been—"

"We'll find a way." His voice was level and almost convincing. "Work will pick up. Just a bit of a downturn, nothing to worry about. And I want this for us. For you. Just let me do this."

Georgia kicked her shoes off and padded toward him on bare feet. He closed his eyes as she reached up and ran one hand through his damp hair, standing it wildly on end. He surrendered everything as she cupped his face with her hands, ran her thumbs over his lips, then pulled him down to her, blindly seeking her lips. She slid her hands up the back of his shirt, dragged her nails down, felt his skin rise in gooseflesh. The soft touch of his waistband sent a wave of warmth from her fingertips up through her arms and neck, to the tips of her ears. She traced the contours of his hips to his front and slipped into his jeans, her hands now frantic and clumsy, out of practice.

Nathan groaned as she tugged on his ear with her teeth. She fumbled with his belt with one hand then dragged him to his knees.

"Jesus, Georgia, of all the places. Here? Now?" He held her like she was made of glass, those once insistent hands still cautious, tentative.

"Here," she whispered. "Now."

"Are you sure? I don't want to hurt you." His hands seemed to hover just over her, wavering, uncertain after all this time.

"You won't. You can't." She fell backward onto the wood floor, pulling him down on top of her, winding her legs around him. "I want to stay here tonight. I never ever want to leave. I feel like, I . . ."

"Tell me, Georgia."

"I feel alive, Nate. So excited and alive and . . . safe. Like I've finally come home." She pulled him down to her, kissing his mouth, his eyes, his neck, whispering against his chest. "Bringing me here, it's like waking me up from a nightmare. It sounds crazy but somehow I know I can be better here. You've made me a sanctuary, Nate. I don't know how you knew. I can't believe you could love me like this."

His hands gripped her thighs and she unwound her legs from his waist. He slid down her body, his lips landing hot on her breasts, her stomach, her hips, the pressure of his fingertips demanding, needful.

"There is nothing I wouldn't do for you, Georgia. Nothing." Deft fingers slid her panties down her legs, then slipped inside her, the lapping of his tongue so slow, so gently persistent. Tears slid down her face as she remembered what it meant to be touched by his passion for her and not his comfort for their mutual grief. Instead of drowning in them, this time she rose on their tide, sails flung wide, opening to him. Nathan stopped then, his breath hot on her thigh.

"Don't leave me again, Georgia. Don't disappear on me. I think you forget sometimes."

He let her pull him up over her, her hands greedy, her mouth devouring him. She gripped him, guided him, gasping at the moment, filled, whole, one.

"What have I forgotten?" All caution was gone from his eyes, they shone down on her, dazzling, ravenous.

"That I need you more than you need me. That you're the center of me."

She raised her hips, pulling him in deeper, surrendering to the desperate fervor of his need, elated, grateful, determined. His lips, his hands, his chest on hers, the feel of the backs of his thighs under her feet, every single place their bodies met a flickering trail in a dark wood she followed until one candle became hundreds, thousands of steady watchtowers lighting up the dark recesses of her mind.

It was the light from the mirror that woke her, a curious reflection that bathed the floor where they slumbered in a rich wash of silver. All around them, Roseneath, too, slumbered; the wind in the pines outside composed a gentle lullaby that swirled through the windows. A great gust of wind shook the windowpanes, the thorns that covered them a jarring percussion to the soothing melody. Georgia stretched and as she did the house around her settled with a luxurious groan, the wooden beams creaking like aged bones. Dozing, she traced the lines of his lips, his jaw, let him pull her closer in his sleep, heard him mumble in her ear. *Love you.* Whispered back the same in his. In the silence that followed, Georgia startled at a sound from above. She listened, waited, and heard it again. A padded sound. *Pitter-patter.* A pause. *Pitter-patter, pitter-patter.* High above them.

Bathed in the watchful glow of the mirror, Georgia slipped from Nathan's embrace and made her way across the room to the hearth. Taking the flashlight from where it leaned against the stone mantel, she glanced back to be sure she had not woken him. But Nathan's soft snores rumbled evenly across the room; the mottled light from the mirror a mackerel sky shimmering through the darkness he slumbered in. Upstairs, the sound again. In the attic.

Heart beating wildly now, she crept up the stairs. Past the dark landing window, past the empty, silent bedrooms to the open attic door. Frowning, she touched the doorjamb with her fingertips. *I must have left it open.* Silence from above. Minutes passed, long enough for her hand holding the flashlight to cease trembling. *Just an old house.* And then, an impatient groan. *Pitter-pat. Pitter-pat.*

"Bother."

The complaint tumbled down the stairs, punctuated with a frustrated stomp. *Pitter-pat.* Switching the flashlight on, Georgia tiptoed up the creaking attic stairs, apprehension mingling with discovery, an intoxicating combination that spurred her on. *Hair tumbling over a little face, an illusion caught in a sunbeam.* One step, two steps. Three steps from the top, another pitter-patter. A gasp. Silence. Georgia slipped into the lofty room and swung the beam over the floor. A trail of smudges wandered out from the rug under the eaves across the attic floor to the window. Crossing the floor, careful not to disturb the faint marks in the dust, Georgia crouched and studied what she found at the end of the meandering path. The red ball. It, too, was covered in soot. Angling the light, she studied the tiny, dirty marks on both the floor and the ball. She compared them to the marks on the windowpane. *Fingerprints.* Kneeling now, she made a closer examination of the marks on the floor. Bare footprints, no bigger than the palm of her hand.

Pat.

She dropped the ball. Spinning, she shone the flashlight back under the eaves, searched the entire attic with the warm yellow light. Nothing.

"Hello?" she whispered. "Is someone there?"

Silence, the only sound the roaring in her ears, her heart pounding in her chest. *I saw something this morning. I know I did.*

"Honey?"

Startled, Georgia dropped the flashlight with a strangled cry.

"Honey, where are you?" Nathan's sleepy voice drifted up the stairs.

Grabbing the spinning flashlight from the floor, she hurried down the attic stairs.

Georgia reached the landing and called down. "I'm here. I was just in the bathroom." Georgia waited there in the darkness, willing her racing heart to slow, even as her eyes were riveted on the open attic door. Upstairs, nothing but silence. Another gust of wind shook the house and then the pine trees settled back into their lilting lullaby. Walking slowly down the last flight of stairs, she switched the flashlight off and let the shadows of Roseneath hide the exhilaration that lit up her face. *Not something. Someone.*

Slipping back into the circle of Nathan's arms, she felt his lips on her forehead, another murmur in her ear. The light from the mirror flickered once, a brilliant flash of silver, before leaving them in total darkness. The winds blew the clouds away and the stars came out, their distant twinkling a faint accompaniment to the song of the pine trees, a sighing on a grand scale, rising, falling, a vast lament that seemed to come from nowhere and everywhere. As sleep took her, Georgia dreamed she could decipher the song, each verse a symphony of heartbreak and grief, the chorus a gentle refrain reminding her that the miracle of healing was not a solitary endeavor, that it lay instead, as with all good things, in the arms of another.

SIX

NATHAN PLANNED TWO WEEKS FOR THE move to Roseneath, but Georgia accomplished it in one. True to her word, she never spent another night in the condo . . .

Step on a crack

. . . a ruthless, feverish gleam in her eyes as she discarded pieces of their life with abandon. The pile on the street grew with alarming speed, her only grim explanation for this purge . . .

Break your mother's back

. . . a desire for a fresh start, unencumbered by the detritus of college furniture, milk crates, and years of indifferent housekeeping. By the time she'd pared down their things, boxed them and scrubbed the condo clean, only a few trips with Nathan's truck would see them safely ensconced in their new, albeit ramshackle, home.

She groaned as she dropped another box in the living room. "Whose bright idea was it to marry a librarian?" Georgia sank to the floor and stretched her sore limbs out, heedless of the sawdust and plaster dust. Nathan stood over her, his upside-down smile unfamiliar. Squinting up at him, she wondered what her upside-down face looked like to him.

"You have wood curls in your hair," he pointed out.

Georgia reached a hand and found a scattering of wood shavings nestled there.

"Aren't I a fortunate girl? My husband made me a crown." She grinned up at him. "What were you doing anyway?"

His smile shifted, stumbled, his upside-down face shuttered and reopened in an expression she could not name. His lips parted, a tremor there, and then the smile reappeared so completely, she wondered if she'd imagined the whole moment.

"Oh, I was in the basement. Checking on things." His expression stumbled again, his brow wrinkled as if he was confused.

Puzzled, she tugged on his pant leg. The cuff was thick with mud. "I thought you were in the yard, Nate."

Nathan's tongue flicked over his lips. "No."

"I must be more tired than I thought." Georgia stifled a yawn as that nameless look flashed across his face again. "I could have sworn I saw you walking into that old wreck of a greenhouse a few minutes ago."

"No, I was in the basement." But his eyes still gazed steadily out the window, in the direction of the weed-choked ruins. She tugged on his pant leg again, harder this time.

"Fine, you were in the basement. What's going on down there anyway? I thought I heard water dripping down there earlier." She studied his face, wondering what was worrying him.

"Yeah." He ran a hand over his chin, his jaw tight. "It's fine. I'll take care of it." He looked back down at her. "Do me a favor, though. Stay out of the basement until I get it sorted. The wiring is bad . . ."

". . . and the stairs are bad and the foundation is bad and the basement of my dream home is some sort of *hellmouth*. Jesus, Nate, relax. I get it. It's a nightmare and I will stay out." She grinned at him and waited for him to smile back. He didn't. "Nate, cross my heart and hope to die: I will not go down in the basement. Not one toe."

"Promise?"

"Promise," she replied, relief flooding her as he seemed to relax. "I have enough to do up here."

"I just worry," he said. "How—" He broke off, ran a hand over his eyes. It was crusted in dirt, a dark maroon stain on one side of his arm where he must have scratched himself, already dried and cracked. "How long was I down there, anyway?" he asked.

She held her arms up to him. "Ages. Tell me something, do you intend to use those muscles today or am I emptying the truck all by myself?"

Nathan's brow furrowed for an instant before a familiar, wolfish look overwhelmed it. He reached down to help her up, spinning her to face him as he did. She shook the wood curls from her hair.

"You've got a nasty cut on your arm, mister," she whispered, kissing his neck. "You should clean it."

He nibbled her neck and slid one hand down her shirt. "If you're suggesting we move this conversation to the shower . . ."

"No time for that." She pulled his hand from her shirt and pushed him away. "I want to be settled in here today." He reached for her again but she twirled away. "Finish your chores, Mr. Pritchard, and I will find a suitable way to reward you that may or may not involve soaping every last inch of you."

"Yes, ma'am." He glanced back to the hall again, cocked his head and took two halting steps away from her, toward the darkened hall and the basement door.

"What is it?" she asked.

"Did you hear that?" he whispered. "That noise? Like . . ." He broke off, took another step.

Georgia listened carefully, studying the tense set of his shoulders. Nothing. Her eyes slid down his body and saw his dirt-crusted hands clenched in fists.

"I didn't hear a thing." Georgia started across the room, but Nathan blocked her. She tried to push past, a sharp stab of hope in her chest at the thought of hearing that small voice again—

Bother

"You know, it's funny you say that because I—"

But Nathan wrapped one broad hand around her arm and cut her off.

"It was nothing. Just the house settling." His hand tightened, lingered almost long enough to hurt, then he played with her fingertips, a familiar habit of unease. "Why don't you go upstairs and unpack? I'll finish unloading the truck and go back for the last of our stuff. Might be a few hours."

"And then we're done?" she asked, still listening. Silence. No small voice, no small feet, no frightened gasp. It would be silly to mention it and yet she almost had. She looked up to the cracked ivory ceiling and felt that sharp stab again, a needful hunger in her chest. Little fingerprints. Little footprints. *Bother.*

Nathan plucked one lingering wood curl from her hair and held it up between two fingers. "And then we're done. Make a wish."

She closed her eyes, blew the curl from his fingertips, and with it her worries. *You're imagining things again. There is no more in the basement than there is in the attic.*

"If your wish involved my drafting table and twenty minutes of your husband's undivided attention, I can make that happen," he said. She took a step back and shook her head, eyes twinkling.

"Nope. Dinner. I wished you'd bring back dinner."

He growled and reached for her, nibbled on her neck as he whispered several of his own wishes, less virtuous ones, and then whistling, returned to the truck.

With one ear to the driveway, Georgia made their bed with crisp, brand new sheets. She tore the tags off new towels and put them carefully away in the bathroom. There was no point in unpacking their clothes as they lacked any furniture to put them in, so instead she neatly stacked clothes for Nathan in orderly piles: shirt, pants, socks, on the radiator, a week's worth to start. Outside, she heard him slam the tailgate. Heard the truck start. She flew to the front window and, along with the mourning doves, watched him back out of the drive in a cloud of gravel dust.

Abandoning her guise of organizing the bedroom, Georgia tiptoed into the hallway. The attic door was closed. Before she opened it, she laid her cheek upon the smooth, dark wood, held her breath, and listened. Nothing. Silence from above. And yet, the door against her cheek moved in and out, in and out; the attic bellowing. In, out. In, out. *Just the house settling*, she told herself. *Like Nathan said.*

Georgia counted one hundred imagined breaths, then backed away from the tantalizing door, hurrying down the stairs to survey their new kingdom, winding her way through the ladders and tools, the sawhorses and piles of lumber, methodically touching every window, every doorframe. *If I touch every lock on every door and window*, she thought, *I won't find anything up there. Of course there is nothing there. No one. It's absurd. It's just an attic, like any other. You're a silly girl with silly notions, Georgia Pritchard.*

Worrying a spot on her forehead, Georgia knelt by the sun porch door, intrigued by a new detail she found there. Just above the keyhole was a delicate engraving of a rose in bloom. Instead of a fresh pang of grief, she felt even more like she belonged here, that Roseneath had always been waiting for her, that some long dead architect had carved her memories into its very foundation. *Did I imagine it? I swear I saw a little girl up there. And that first night,* Georgia weighed the strange occurrences in the attic against the days and weeks after they lost their daughter. Waking every night to the imagined sound of her baby crying, her entire body wracked with a bone-deep yearning for a child that wasn't there, a little girl named Rose who had been born

too soon only to die. No, this was different. I saw someone peeking at me. I heard a child playing. *Pitter-patter,*
pitter-patter. Bother. Whatever this was, it wasn't grief. It
was something more, and until she knew, knew for sure,
it was best to keep it to herself. Best not to worry Nathan
any more than she already had. Just in case she was wrong.

Georgia stood and quit her game of bargaining with
locks. *No,* she thought, *I am doing better, so much better.*
This house is like a balm, like a womb, I'm better here. She
was holding on—by a thread some days—but she was
holding on. And yet, in the attic, up two long flights of
stairs and behind a thick, old door there had been someone. And if she was honest, the truth was she *wanted* there
to be someone. Someone small with wide eyes

Pitter-patter

. . . waiting for her to open the bundle, uncover the relics and recite the magic words to conjure her, to bring her
back . . .

Bother

Wanted there to be more than *this*, needed there to be
more than a coffin the size of a dresser drawer. She shied
away from the predictable, pat names for what she thought
she'd spied in the attic. Apparition, phantom, shade, all far
too indistinct for the weight of promise that was woven
into that one small exclamation. *Bother.* No, nothing as
clumsy as a ghost. A small messenger from the other side,
tiny hands brimming with unimaginable possibilities,
hiding in the attic, each pitter-pat a signal that there was
something *more*.

. . . just like a fairy tale.

She sprinted back up the sighing wooden steps, jumping over the thirteenth,

Jack be nimble,

Jack be quick

teetering for a moment before grasping the cool iron rail and racing on. Past their bedroom, past the empty guest rooms, the cedar closet, and finally to the attic door. She moved quickly, as if afraid she'd change her mind, bare feet soundless on the treads of the steps before coming to a breathless stop at the top. The attic door jarred in its frame. In, out, in, out, each inhale drawing the door in, each exhale reaching out for her.

Georgia gripped the doorknob and held her breath as she counted to three. Then she turned the knob a quarter of the way. A click in the housing, but she did not pursue. Heart in her throat, she counted to three again, a mad notion that someone else, someone small with delicate fingerprints

Pitter-pat

held fast to the other side, waiting as breathless as she was. Georgia released the knob, heard the housing snap back again as it latched, and then knelt in front of the shuddering door. The lock was faded copper, green with age, and there, another engraving just beneath the keyhole. Scraping at it with her thumbnail, she could make out nothing more than a sword shape, stylized lines like the sun's rays radiating out from it, the detail lost in a thick grit that surrounded it. The door drew in then out. A beat. A soft sigh from the other side, so delicate it barely reached her. Georgia rose to her feet, her lips curved up on the knife's edge of fear and, grasping the knob

click

pushed the door open. Three windows closed. One open. Where there had been three fingerprints there were now a dozen. Georgia stepped inside and closed the door behind her, leaning against it, hands shaking. Silence.

Georgia jumped as the open dormer window swung wildly on its hinges, teetering mid-swing before coming to rest against the wall. *Just the wind.* A steady breeze blew across the attic, anointing her face and sending her hair flying. The bundle had been moved. It now sat in the exact center of the attic floor, surrounded by tiny smudges. She followed the winding trail of prints across the dusty floor, deep beneath the eaves and spied the red ball, the rug, and the bassinet. And in the air, a hush. A pause. The attic held its breath.

Kneeling in front of the bundle, Georgia removed her watch and set it to one side of the attic cache. 11:49 a.m. She cleared her throat. Her hands were shaking. *This is crazy*, she scolded herself. *What am I even doing?*

"You know, I like rhymes, too." Georgia's breath caught in her throat. "Maybe I'll read a few. Would you like that?"

Silence. Not a sound outside of her own beating heart.

"Unless you'd rather not read. Maybe we could play with the ball."

Silence.

Georgia waited. One one thousand, two one thousand, three . . .

"All right then, nursery rhymes it is. We can play with the ball later." She licked her dry lips and swallowed hard. "Well, then. Here we go."

She flipped quickly through the pages, feeling something between silly and afraid. *Elated.* This was absurd. It had to be. She thought of the locks again downstairs. She'd touched seventeen of them. Was that enough? How many had she missed? She shook the thought from her head and began reading aloud.

> *Baa, baa, black sheep,*
> *Have you any wool?*
> *Yes, sir, yes, sir,*
> *Three bags full;*
> *One for the master,*
> *And one for the dame,*
> *And one for the little boy*
> *Who lives*

Georgia broke off abruptly. That feeling crept across her shoulders, great wings of euphoria this time, a rush of delight behind her. No little pattering feet this time like Alice had heard, but perhaps whatever, whoever, was here, perhaps this was their way of announcing their arrival. Georgia flipped through the pages and selected another, her voice shifting to something more animated, as if there were a real flesh and blood child sitting at her feet soaking up every word.

Cold wings, frigid wings at her back, and the familiar words of *Hot Cross Buns* died in her throat. A scratching noise just behind her, as before, followed by a pregnant silence. Georgia's hands shook as she searched for one of her favorites, dropping the pitch of her voice to something soothing and inviting, letting the metronome pace of each rhyme coax her wildly beating heart back into its normal rhythm.

> *Sing a song of sixpence,*
> *A pocket full of rye.*
> *Four and twenty blackbirds,*
> *Baked in a pie.*
> *When the pie was opened*
> *The birds began to sing;*
> *Wasn't that a dainty dish,*
> *To set before the king.*
> *The king was in his counting house,*
> *Counting out his money;*
> *The queen was in the parlour,*
> *Eating bread and honey.*

Georgia continued, page after page, until she reached the last rhyme. A glance at the watch told her that forty-five minutes had passed. She stifled a yawn and rubbed her eyes. The cold tingling at her back had shifted to a sunshine warmth. She set the book down with care and once again studied the attic. Nothing, and yet . . . Georgia reached into her pocket for her mobile phone and tapped the playlist she'd made the day before. *In for a penny, in for a pound.*

"I'd never heard of most of these songs," she called out. "And I don't have a Victrola to play your records, but . . ." She tapped "play" and the air filled with the jaunty sound of a clarinet. "We could listen to them like this." She placed the phone in the middle of the jumbled assortment of child's playthings and waited. The playlist she'd created meandered through the Lost Generation hits. Opera of the 1900s, ragtime from the 1910s, jazz of the 1920s, her best guesses mingled with the titles she'd found in the bundle, a patchwork incantation she hoped might conjure whatever atmosphere or presence she'd felt before.

Before she knew it, an hour had passed, and her feet were now pins and needles. By the time the playlist reached a rather zealous rendition of *Pack Up Your Troubles*, Georgia was yawning. When the songs shifted to more dulcet tunes, like *Tonight in the Moonlight* and *Somewhere a Voice Is Calling*, her eyes grew heavy. Bundling the blanket up into a makeshift pillow, Georgia curled around the mysterious cache. *What a lovely song*, she thought as she drifted off. *How have I never heard this before?*

> *Dusk and the shadows falling o'er land and sea*
> *Somewhere a voice is calling, calling for me*
> *Dusk and the shadows falling o'er land and sea*
> *Somewhere a voice is calling, calling for me*
> *Dearest, my heart is dreaming, dreaming of you*
> *Somewhere a voice is calling, calling for me,*
>   *calling for me*

Georgia dreamed of roses and thorns, fire and falling, dark night wings and stars screaming. She dreamed of Nathan working in an orchard, his arms covered in primitive white scars, waving to her. She dreamed of herself running joyfully through a forest of sycamores, elated because *someone* was coming. Someone more precious than she could express was *coming* finally and the star screams shifted to a rapturous song filled with hope. She fell to her knees in a sycamore forest, felt the wet earth under her nails and stretched out to sleep there, too, a dream within a dream, for ages, time running backward around her until the forest was unmade and she slept in the gauzy vacuum of time itself, sooty feathers floating like dust motes all around her. An epoch followed an age and she floated in a primordial cloud, wishing that she could stay in this time before time, forever.

The sun's relentless march across the attic floor reached her hours later. A kaleidoscope of constellations dazzled their way through the delicate skin of her eyelids, urging her to wake. With a sigh, Georgia blew away the sooty feathers that had buried her deep in sleep and made her way back through the sycamore forest, past the now empty orchard and toward consciousness. The music had stopped and the attic was silent. Yawning, she stretched her leaden arms and legs and rubbed her sleep-heavy eyes. She regretfully opened the door of the dreamland she'd stumbled upon and, crossing the threshold, opened her eyes and saw she was not alone. *It worked*, she thought, elated. *I was right.*

She was little more than a charcoal sketch, the barest hint of a child rendered in shades of ash and dove. The book of nursery rhymes floated impossibly on the hastily drawn lines of her gauzy knees. In one sooty little hand, the almost-girl clutched Georgia's watch. Her brow was drawn in a delicate frown as she studied it; the only sound in the attic the *tick tick tick* of the second hand. Her expressions shifted bewilderingly, as if her artist could not make up their mind, perplexed, worried, rapt, the ticking of the second hand marking each shift. Then, the shade of a child bent to peer at the silent phone. When she tried to poke it with one chalky finger, it passed right through.

"Bother," she whispered. "What ratty luck."

Georgia sat up with great care, afraid to startle the specter in front of her. The girl's black eyes flicked to hers and as it did, the fragile vision rippled, exploding for one brief tick of the watch into a burst of color and clarity before settling back to ashes. A stubborn nose peppered unevenly with freckles, skin like moonglow. Tiny white teeth. The lock of hair that hung over her shoulder was maple syrup, appearing briefly in the spreading ripples before fading once more to shades of smoke. Chubby little hands with dimples clutched the watch; a tattered dress was drawn tightly over grimy knees where she crouched. Her body was pocked with dark wounds, the center of each a pinprick blacker than ink.

Georgia wanted to speak but was dumbstruck by the tender magnitude of the moment. What words could possibly suffice? Instead she held her breath and the girl's gaze. As the watch ticked off the seconds, the child's eyes dazzled in an unexpected maze of heterochromia, ocean salt over mossy stones. They gazed at each other for hours, or seconds, a moment that passed in dreamtime. *How long is forever? Sometimes forever is just one second.* And then, finally, Georgia knew exactly what to say.

Cautiously, she pulled her knees to her chest. Then she fluttered her fingers against the floor, catching the girl's attention.

"Hickory, dickory, dock." Georgia made her fingers dance on the floor, let them scamper onto the instep of her foot. The little girl watched closely.

"The mouse ran up the clock." Her fingers scampered up her leg, alighted on her kneecap. The child's eyes followed.

"The clock struck one." She mimed a startled mouse with her fingers and the little ghost's mouth popped open, surprised.

"And down he run."

Her fingers fled down her leg, hid behind her heel like a frightened mouse. The child moved closer, like smoke drafting across the floor, to see where Georgia's hand had gone. Georgia suppressed a shiver and tried not to flinch.

"Hickory, dickory, dock!" Not a petulant whisper this time. She sang out like a robin in springtime, then giggled, as if charmed by the sound of her own voice.

Georgia crossed her legs, drawing out each movement so as not to frighten the apparition away.

"Shall we do another?"

The girl nodded, scattering ashes around her on the attic floor that curled up and vanished even as they landed. The watch fell through her hand, landing on the attic floor with a clatter.

"Bunk," she complained, studying her own hand as if to scold it. "Have I spoiled it?"

"Not at all. Never mind the watch. It's your turn," Georgia smiled encouragingly at her. The girl beamed at her, then studied the ceiling.

"Mary, Mary," she tried again. "Mary, Mary . . ." She looked to Georgia for help, chagrined.

"Quite contrary," Georgia prompted. Recognition flashed in the child's eyes before she sang out the following verse in a mad, sing-song rush.

"How does your garden grow?" she exclaimed. "With silver bells and cockleshells . . ." Then she broke off and waited, her pert nose wrinkled impishly.

"And pretty maids, all in a row!" Georgia finished, astonished.

The child's face lit up for one prismatic second and then, slower this time, faded back to chalk and shale. Georgia knew she should be afraid. But, sitting there in the sunlight with this little soul, fear felt like a sacrilege, an insult to this guileless visitation. Every shred of sense inside her told her to run, but instead, Georgia crept closer.

"My name is Georgia. I'm . . . I'm very glad to meet you."

The child shimmered once more and floated closer, uncomfortably close to Georgia. Her scent was familiar and oddly comforting, like old blankets and dust. Her wounds blurred, swirled, then vanished. She smiled and twin dimples appeared on her cheeks.

"Edith." A flush appeared on her fair cheeks. "My name is Edith." She extended her hand and without thinking, Georgia reached for it.

Nothing. I feel nothing. And yet there was something in the air that hadn't been there before, like the smell of ozone before a lightning strike. Gingerly, as if handling a cobweb, Georgia shook Edith's vaporous hand.

"How do you *do*?" she chirped.

There was no real substance to it, just a shimmering outline wavering in the spaces between Georgia's fingers. Closing her eyes, Georgia could almost, *almost* feel something petal-light.

"Very well. And how do *you* do, Edith?"

The child exploded again into a supernova of color and detail, burning into Georgia's retinas a whole image of a little girl, complete and shining, filled with life. It vanished almost as soon as it appeared, but the memory floated in her eye, a glamour that lingered on superimposed over the subtle creature before her.

"Georgia?" Her voice was as delicate as a wind chime.

"Yes?" Georgia searched the child's face, wondering what had caused her to look so bashful.

"Are you . . . are you afraid of me?"

Georgia reached as if to tuck a lock of hair behind the girl's ear. She felt nothing, but a moment later, like a slow tide, the hair followed the track her fingers had made, the tousled curl tucked itself neatly behind her little ear. "Why would I be afraid of you, Edith?"

"Because . . . because I'm dead." Edith flushed, a pop of color in her otherwise somber face. She looked embarrassed, as if her whole world hung on Georgia's response.

"Well, that seems like a very silly reason to be scared of such a pretty little girl."

Edith giggled and the curl fell forward. This time, when Georgia reached for it, it ran ahead of her, smoothing itself into place.

"Papa called me Edie," she said shyly.

"Well, then, shall I read to you some more, Edie?"

The child opened her mouth to speak but her reply was cut off by a door slamming downstairs. Georgia whirled her attention to the attic door, listening, her hands instinctively moving to protect the girl. She felt a soft sensation when she reached for Edie's hands, like feathers slipping between her fingers. Downstairs, Roseneath sighed, protested, then settled. Georgia looked back to the ashy child. Edie's eyes were wide, her mouth frozen in a terrified, rose-tinted 'O', the color stark against her gray face.

"What is it, Edie?" she whispered hoarsely.

"Some dead things are very frightening," Edie whispered.

"It was just the house settling," she tried to assure the frightened child. But Edie shook her head. The lines of her face below her eyes blurred. With a start, Georgia realized she was crying. Wounds bloomed again all over her body and she shifted from sketch to smoke again.

"Is there someone else here? Someone like you?"

Edie reached for her bruised throat, her flickering fingers clutching the tattered collar of her dress in a fist. "Oh, no. Not like me. I'm not like anyone, not anymore." Edie's cloudy hand suddenly felt heavy where Georgia still held it, almost corporeal. Then it faded,

lighter

lighter

lighter

and the little girl was gone.

Silence fell on the attic, as did the warmth that seemed to trail in Edie's wake. Georgia blinked, fumbled about for her watch. It was somehow, impossibly, late afternoon.

The day had slipped away from her. *Forever in a just a second. Forever and ever and ever.* She climbed to her feet and noticed the floor was covered in dust and ash and feathery smudges where Edie had sat. From outside came the sound of crushed gravel on the drive. She hurried to the window in time to see Nathan park in front of the carriage house, the truck bed filled with the last of their belongings. She spun around, her eyes lit with a feverish gleam.

"Can we play again tomorrow, Edie? Just you and I?"

"Oh, yes please!" the child's voice danced through the attic air, her sweet laughter dwindling in a joyful spiral. "What fun we'll have, Georgia."

SEVEN

THAT EVENING, GEORGIA WANDERED DOWN the stairs of Roseneath. She danced her fingers against the wrought-iron bannister, trailed her other hand down the thick plaster wall, unable to believe that all this belonged to them. *Ours. All ours. My own fairy tale come to life.* Her bare feet made the wood floors sigh as she crossed the room to the fireplace to admire the botanical carving in the stone surface: roses, leaves, feathers, and vines. *Silver bells, and cockle shells, and pretty maids all in a row.* Rising on her tiptoes, she laid the palms of her hands on the aged surface of the mirror above, the mottled mercury glass distorting her features as if she'd aged fifty years in a moment. *There was an old woman . . .* She smiled and the old woman in the mirror smiled back. A sound from the back hall froze the shared expression on both of their faces. Feet on the basement stairs, a jangle of keys, a door softly shutting.

"Nathan?" she called out. But no reply came from the back hall, only silence.

A flash of light drew Georgia's gaze to the top-left corner of the mirror. There, a gleaming flicker grew to a searing silver flame, engulfing the whole mirror. The aged surface began to twist, distorting the reflection of the room around her. Georgia fell back, caught herself on the arm of a chair, then spun, searching in vain for the setting sun, for the lights of a passing car, something, anything to explain the mirage, but found only the deepening twilight behind her. She turned back to the mirror, drawn by the relentless fire burning deep inside the silvery surface. Georgia held her hand out to it and as she did, took one tentative step closer to the mirror, entranced by this new wonder.

"Edie?" she whispered. "Is that you? Are you doing that?"

But even as she said the words, she knew somehow this apparition was not as gentle as the child's presence. She watched as the horizon line behind her warped, twisted, ripped apart the room around her, even as her own reflection remained unaltered. The awe in her expression was swallowed by fear. A flash of unbearable heat and then the roiling illusion vanished. *Not like me.*

"Georgia? Honey?"

She spun at the sound of Nathan's voice in the back hall and then hurried to him, away from the darkening mirror. *I'm not like anyone, not anymore.* Georgia balanced on the precarious line between fear and attraction, waited until the first passed so she could luxuriate once more in the latter. *Neither am I, Edie. Neither am I. What is this place?*

She found him in the back hall, a tarnished ring of skeleton keys in his hand. Nathan looked at her comically.

"You okay?"

"Mm-hmm," she said. "How was your day?"

Nathan frowned as he selected a key from the chain and struggled to fit it in the lock on the basement door. "Tedious. Met with the accountant."

You need to tell him. About Edie and the attic. And the mirror.

But not just yet. Not until I know more. Not until I'm sure I understand.

"Not like that, I hope." She brushed the dirt off his shoulder. "You're filthy."

Sure, she told the scolding voice in her head. *I'll just say, 'Hey, Nate, there's a ghost in the attic. Her name's Edie and we both like nursery rhymes.'*

The silence of her conscience rang in her ears.

I will, she promised herself. *I will tell him about Edie and the attic and even the mirror. But not just yet. Not until I know more. Not until I'm sure what all this is.*

Frustrated, Nathan chose another key and tried again in vain to lock the door. "Yeah. Sometimes I don't know what I was thinking when I bought this place."

"Where did you find these?" she asked, tapping the keys.

Nathan turned abruptly and looked over his shoulder.

"Find what?" His words were directed not at her but at the window into the backyard, where the long arms of the pine trees swayed in the darkness over the twisted frame of the greenhouse.

Georgia groaned. "The keys, Mr. Pritchard. The ones in your hand. I've never seen those before. They look archaic."

He looked down at them. A beat. The confusion on his face deepened then vanished.

"Right. Yeah, I found them in the basement. Damnedest thing. They were buried in about a foot of dirt."

"A foot of dirt?" Georgia reached for the door handle. "This I have to see." But before she even touched the knob, Nathan dropped the keys and grabbed her hand, yanking her back. Georgia tried to pull her hand free but his grip tightened, the bones of her fingers ground painfully together.

"Nathan, you're hurting me!"

She ripped her hand away. "What's wrong with you?"

"Goddamn it. I didn't mean to . . . I'm sorry, Georgia." He reached for her, but she pushed him away. "Shit, please don't be mad, Georgie."

"Try to remember I'm half your size, you big oaf," she snapped. "I'm not some union contractor you can arm wrestle." Her anger deflated quickly at the contrite look on his face. "Nate, I just think it's extremely weird that you won't let me set foot in the basement of my own house. I've just never seen you this worried about a basement. That's not like you."

"Well, some of it's professional embarrassment." He pushed away from the basement door, kicking it. "No self-respecting contractor, let alone architect, wants to admit he underestimated the condition of the foundation."

"Underestimated by how much?" She let him reach behind her back for her throbbing hand.

"A lot."

Georgia let out a low whistle as he examined her wrist. "Maybe you're right. The less I know the better." His lips lingered on her wrist before releasing it.

"So promise me you won't go down there." He scratched the top of his head and shook off a dusting of dirt and rust. "I got the boiler and the hot water tank squared away and honestly it would be easier on me to just lock it up and throw away the key for now."

"You know, when I married you I thought I'd be living in exquisitely curated palaces."

"Sorry to disappoint," he grimaced. "I'm too busy dealing with that nightmare Colonial in Chagrin Falls to deal with my own." He kicked his boot against the door again and it rattled, echoing down below. "I'll have more time in the spring. I think."

Georgia picked the keys up. They were still coated with a thin layer of earth.

"What if I could put at least one of your worries to rest?" She selected one key and held it up. "Did you notice anything funny about the locks in this house?"

There, on the intricately carved head of the skeleton key, was a small rose detail. Georgia selected another key, this one with a small sword.

"I'm not sure I follow you, hon," Nathan murmured, perplexed.

"I was exploring Roseneath and I found some of the doors—in the house at least— have engravings under the keyholes. The one in the living room has a rose on it, the attic door has a sword on it." She searched through the heavy key ring. "See? The front door is a feather."

"Clever girl. So what's engraved on the basement door?"

Kneeling, Georgia peered at the detail under the keyhole.

"A star or something." Then, pressing her hands against the door, she peered through the keyhole into the darkness beyond.

"It's dark down there," she remarked. Nathan shifted instantly, pressing his shoulder against the door, as if it might burst open at any moment. Georgia noticed his hands balling into fists.

"Yeah," he repeated. "Dark." Nathan gently pulled her to her feet with one hand and took the keys from her with the other.

He studied the detail on the basement key for a moment before inserting it into the keyhole. The lock slid into place and echoed down into the cavernous basement. "*The doors of hell are locked on the inside*," he mused under his breath.

"Jesus Christ, Nate!" Georgia exclaimed. "How bad does a basement have to be to steal a quote from C.S. Lewis?"

"Pretty bad. Anyway, I don't think it's a star. Looks more like a flame. Weird." He bit his lip as he studied it.

"Very weird," she agreed. "What architect bothers with this stuff anymore?" Nathan moved to tuck the key ring in his pocket, but Georgia grabbed his hand.

"Not so fast," she said, slipping the keys from his hand. She found the one she was looking for, slipped it from the ring, then handed the rest back to him.

"What are you up to?" he asked, a quizzical expression on his face.

She held the key up in front of her so he could clearly see the engraved sword on its head.

"What makes you think I'm up to something," she said with a quirky smile. She took two quick steps back toward the kitchen.

"Oh, I know that look, Miss Georgia. You're up to something," his voice, so anxious moments before, was now teasing.

Georgia spun away and tucked the key into her bra.

"How about this: if the basement is off limits to me, the attic is out of bounds for you. Entrance is by permission only. No boys allowed."

"That depends. What are you up to in that attic?" he growled, pulling her back against him and kissing her neck.

Georgia leaned back into him, astonished at how easily the words flew to her lips.

"Nothing. I just want my own space."

"And having the entirety of Roseneath isn't enough for you?"

She avoided his gaze under the guise of examining the scabs on his hands.

"It's not that. I just want my own space, up and away from all the construction site that is my living room. Somewhere where I can think. Maybe work a bit. And you better put something on these cuts, they look infected."

"Sure, Mom, I'll get right on that."

She stuck her tongue out at him. He laughed but that worry returned. "You're not thinking about going back, are you?"

She shook her head. "No, Nate. Not the library. I'm not ready for . . . for that. But I thought I might do some research. I have an idea about something; I'm not sure about it yet. But I think it might be good for me. A project. A secret."

His lips landed on top of her head.

"Say no more. The attic is yours. Do you need me to take anything up there?"

Georgia frowned, worried suddenly that his presence might scare Edie away, and then dismissed the thought. *He doesn't know the spell. She won't come out for him.*

"My desk, if it's not too much. And the old green easy chair in our bedroom? Everything else I can do myself."

"Done." He picked her up, sweeping her off her feet with a laugh. "Now I'm taking you to bed. I think you overdid it today."

"Stop it," she protested. "I hate it when you fuss."

"Liar. You love it when I fuss."

Nathan carried her up the steep stairs and into the bedroom. He laid her gently on the bed and slid her pants down to her ankles. She sat up and he pulled her shirt off over her head. She grabbed his belt buckle and tried unsuccessfully to pull him into bed with her.

"Not tonight," he said, chuckling at the scowl on her face. "I have some work to finish up before my meeting tomorrow morning."

Georgia reached for him again as he pulled the blankets up and tucked her in.

"How dare you reject my advances," she protested, grabbing him this time by his shirt. "I was just getting my second wind."

"I bet you were," he replied wryly, leaning down to kiss her goodnight and untangling himself from her arms.

"Who are you meeting with?" she demanded. "I demand the name of my competition."

"A new client." His tired eyes twinkled down at her.

"I knew it! I knew there was something more than the basement making you act crazy," she laughed. "Tell me."

"Nope. Don't want to jinx it."

"It's a whole house, isn't it?

"Maybe."

"What if you woke me up early tomorrow morning? For luck," she whispered.

Another kiss, this one longer, tender.

"I might be able to manage that." He smoothed her hair back from her face. "But now I want you to rest, okay?" That twinge of worry again. "Please."

She curled up on her side and tucked her hands under her cheek.

"Don't stay up too late," she yawned.

"I won't."

Nathan paused in the dark doorway, a jangle of keys as he worried the ring in his pocket.

"Remember, honey. I love you. More than anything. No matter what."

But Georgia was already drifting off, dreams of lost little girls and fairy tale attics dancing in her head like wisps of smoke.

*   *   *

Nathan waited for two hours in the parking lot that night for her, each minute adding certainty that he'd imagined her, imagined the moment. Every passing moment summoned ever more reasons to roost in his head, twittering to him that his offering was silly, clucking that she'd only laugh at him. Strains from the radio in his truck created a soundtrack to his misery, a torment that only worsened when she appeared, picking her way deliberately across the darkened lot to him, around bike racks and speed bumps, past a kiosk filled with faded flyers from last semester until she finally stood in front of him. She'd let her hair down and it fell in thick, twisted vines past her shoulders like a cloak.

Words failed him, so he held the basket of apples out to her, his face twisted in discomfort. She took the basket from him in one hand and his shaking hand in her other and sank to the pavement, pulling him down with her, the steady look in her eyes allaying the uncertainty in his.

They sat for hours that night in the dark lot as she unlocked, one by one, every single latch on his heart, teased thoughts out of him he never thought he would ever share with anyone. He sat helplessly as her nimble mind and easy laughter captured him like a mist net.

"What will we do after our picnic, Mr. Pritchard?" she asked, taking a bite of her apple.

"Nate."

"Nate," she repeated, lashes fluttering as she fiddled with the basket handle.

"I thought I'd take you dancing."

An expression of unease ran across her face, as if he'd broken the spell. He held out his hand anyway.

"Come on, they're playing our song."

The radio in his truck played a familiar tune, one that would never quite sound so anonymous again. She let him pull her up, then slipped her hand over his shoulder. David Bowie sang about red shoes and moonlight and trembling flowers, and Nathan realized that every verse was nothing more than a love song written just for her.

He cradled her to his chest and wondered if she could hear the galloping of his heart. As they swayed in the dark, he closed his eyes and decided this was all a dream.

"This song always makes me think of you," he said as the music wound down.

She countered, "But we've only just met."

"I know."

Her eyes flashed luminous gray pools in the dark.

"What are you doing tomorrow?" he asked, reaching for her hand.

"It's my day off."

His mind raced. He had a full day of classes and hours of jobs after. He'd fallen incredibly far behind this week with his library vigil, and it would take a miracle for him to catch up.

"I'm off, too," he lied. "Spend the day with me." She slipped her hand from his and began worrying a spot on her forehead between her eyes. She wrinkled her nose, studied her feet, and then peered back at him, eyes narrowed.

"Yes," she said finally.

"That's it? Just yes?"

A long, slow smile.

"Just yes."

"All right then, Miss Galloway."

"Georgie."

"Georgie. Can I kiss you goodnight?"

"Oh, yes. Yes, I think you should."

EIGHT

DAWN WAS JUST BREAKING WHEN GEORGIA slipped into the quiet attic, a carrier bag clutched tight in her hand. On the desk, she arranged the bag's contents: a box of crayons, a pack of markers, construction paper, and glue. A sheet of star-shaped stickers. Safety scissors. Another trip back down the stairs and she added a small digital radio. The hum in the air was palpable when she plugged it in, a bit of adjustment and then the strains of *Glad Rag Doll* filled the silent attic as a blanket of cold settled over the room.

Georgia pulled a chair deliberately across the attic floor to the desk, letting the metal feet drag across the wooden beams, a mischievous twinkle in her eye. Selecting a crayon—orange—she began drawing on a sheet of construction paper. Cold, colder, wings of cold at her back that melted like springtime into warmth. A shadow at her side. Out of the corner of her eye she saw Edie slide up next to her, felt the barest feather-light brush as the child laid her hand on Georgia's shoulder. Georgia pretended to ignore her and continued sketching until a giraffe began to take shape. Neck, legs, tail.

"That looks fun," Edie said wistfully. Georgia's lips twitched as she drew patches and horns on the giraffe. Edie circled her, laid her cheek down on the desk opposite her and sighed deliberately.

"Do you need help?" she asked.

Georgia shook her head. "No, that's okay." A quick glance up at Edie's frustrated face and she added long floppy ears and a bow tie. That did it. Edie planted her small ashy hands on either side of the comic giraffe and proclaimed, "That giraffe is positively *goop*. I could draw better than that when I was *five*."

Georgia laughed. "'*Goop*', huh?"

Edie nodded, twirling one tangled curl around her finger. "The goopiest." In an instant her face fell as if an unseen voice had admonished her. "That was rude. Mama doesn't like it when I use slang. She says it's *common*."

Georgia leaned forward and beckoned Edie closer. The air filled with her heady scent, chalk and lilies, dust and paper.

"I won't tell a soul, Edie," she whispered in her ear. "Want to try?"

Edie leaned back, her pug nose wrinkled. "I don't think I can."

"That's . . ." Georgia squinted at the ceiling, trying to remember the word she'd heard Edie use before. "*Bunk!*" Georgia exclaimed, causing Edie to burst out in laughter, her wispy edges solidifying to solid lines as she did. "I think you can." Georgia clasped Edie's shadow of a hand in hers and placed it on top of a crayon.

"Concentrate, Edie." Georgia withdrew her hand. "Can you feel it?"

Edie fumbled with the crayon—it jumped in and out of her vaporous fingers like a flopping fish as she tried to control it. In a flash, her demeanor shifted from delight to anger, her silver cloud of hair floating above her, indignant.

"No, I *can't*." A sharp percussion in the attic and Georgia realized that Edie had audibly stomped her foot. Taken aback, Georgia watched as Edie's color shifted from ashy gray to porcelain pink. "Applesauce!" Edie slammed her fist on the desk in frustration and three crayons fell to the floor. The crayon in her hand snapped in two and landed on top of the giraffe. Tears brimmed in her shale-colored eyes, fell in a pewter wash down her dandelion cheeks. "It's not *fair*. It's *ratty*. I'm so *bored*," she cried. "You've no idea how bored I am! Bother, bother, *bother*!"

Georgia reached over to smooth Edie's hair, amazed to discover that she *could*. Impossible. She could feel each distinct strand, soft and warm, each stroke of her hand against Edie's hair shifting it from paper white and charcoal to mineral to toffee and amber. On impulse, Georgia tapped the tip of Edie's indignant nose. Even with only her fingertip, Georgia could feel a flicker of dewy, smooth skin. Edie jumped as if she'd been shocked.

"Oh, my. That's new." Edie crossed her eyes to look at her own nose. "Do it again."

Georgia leaned forward and placed a kiss on Edie's pert nose, like kissing a petal in the wind. Edie's eyes flared, jade and amber, and went wide with wonder. "I think you can really do this, Edie. It just takes practice. Let's try again?"

Edie reached out, her hand trembling a cloud of ash as she sought the orange crayon. Georgia held Edie's small shoulders, every molecule in her willing the child to feel the crayon. The ragtime stomp raced ahead and Edie's delicate form began to solidify and intensify. Her skin shifted from gray to white to pink, chestnut hair ran riot where it had been a zinc cloud, and a drop-waist cotton shift where there had only been the hint of a dress.

"I did it! I did it!" Edie cried, holding the orange crayon aloft. Beaming, she began sketching her own giraffe on another sheet of paper with excited, clumsy stokes. "Easy as duck soup!"

Georgia knelt next to her and tucked a long lock of cinnamon hair behind a seashell ear. The crayon slid off the paper and left an orange swath across the desk. Edie laughed, a twinkling cascade higher even than the trumpets. "Giraffes aren't orange, but I don't give a jitney! I can do it! Oh, this is wonderful, Georgia!"

With a flourish, Georgia dumped all the crayons out on the desk, selected a yellow one, and began drawing a bird on a sheet of black paper. Edie scrambled up over the desk, and settled herself on Georgia's lap. Holding Edie was like cuddling a sunbeam or feeling the edges of a cobweb. As they colored their way through all the animals in Noah's Ark, Edie's delicate weight grew and grew so that when Georgia shifted Edie on her lap a few hours later, it was as if she were adjusting a satin bag filled with down.

"Oh!' Edie laughed, turning in surprise. "Look what we did!"

"Oh, my little Edie," Georgia beamed. *Everything that was taken from me is here. Right here in my arms.* "Oh, the things we will do together, you and I."

"Forever and ever, Georgia?" she said, tracing the lines of Georgia's lips with one small finger.

"Forever and ever, Edie," Georgia replied, kissing the tip of her finger.

Edie began tangling their fingers in a cat's cradle, humming to herself.

"Edie," Georgia said. "What if I brought someone else up here to visit you? Someone else to play with. Would you like that?"

Edie's face lit up. "Can it be a puppy?"

Georgia laughed. "Well, I was thinking I'd bring my best friend up to meet you, if that's okay with you. My husband, Nathan. He's so nice." Edie's eyes went wide with alarm. Georgia's voice wavered briefly. "And he'd love you, I just know he would."

Edie grew lighter on Georgia's lap.

"No, I shouldn't like that at all," she whispered. "Please, no." Her edges began to fade, vanishing in the sunlight like wisps of ash.

"But I bet he knows some fun games," Georgia tried again. "What if I—"

"I don't want to play his fun games," Edie snapped. Her body was completely indistinct now, only her face remained vivid. "He sounds *p . . . peculiar* to me."

"I'm sorry," Georgia pleaded, trying to grasp Edie's shoulders. Her hands fell through the air and clutched at nothing. "Please don't go. Please stay with me. I'm lonely, too. Edie and I . . ." Edie laid a vaporous hand on her cheek. It felt warm and soft. Georgia grabbed it, pulled the delicate weight of the slowly distilling child back to her. "Please don't leave me, Edie. I won't bring anyone up here. I won't tell a soul."

Edie's body returned, limp and heavy, in Georgia's lap. Georgia laid her hand on her small chest and she could have sworn she felt her heart racing. *Oh, you poor child. What happened to you to make you so scared?*

"I'm . . . I'm sorry, Georgia," Edie stammered softly, "but I'm tired. I don't want to talk anymore just now. Will you read to me?"

"Of course," Georgia pulled the blanket from the back of the chair and wrapped it around them both. "Let's read about *The Treasure Seekers*, shall we?"

"Oh yes," Edie yawned. "That's my favorite."

Georgia read about the adventures of the precocious Bastable children as Edie slowly fell asleep, fading from pink to white to a silver cloud, the crayon she still clutched tight in one hand falling to the floor before she evaporated into nothing.

"Tomorrow," Georgia whispered into the still attic air. "Oh, the things we'll do tomorrow, Edie. Just you and I." She tidied up the crayons and organized the books into a pile, then reached into the bag for a set of pushpins. A short while later and she had covered an entire wall of the attic with Edie's artwork, a cheerful wash of color in the otherwise gloomy attic. Then she locked the upper attic door with great care, tucking the key carefully in her pocket.

✦ ✦ ✦

The fading rays of the sun cast long shadows through the pines and across the kitchen floor. Singing an unfamiliar, old-fashioned song as she prepared dinner, Georgia hadn't noticed Nathan enter through the back door. He leaned against the doorframe quietly, watching her as the sun continued its descent, the long shadow arms reaching for his wife's bare feet.

"You're the cream in my coffee," she sang, "you're the salt in my stew." She rummaged in a drawer, slammed it shut with her hip. "You will always be," she reached above her, grabbed a can from the shelf, "my necessity, I'd be lost without you." She laughed to herself, some private joke, and for a second, seeing her like this, Nathan almost forgot how shitty his day had been. However, when he looked past her to the open bottle of wine, the lit candles on the small kitchen table, it all came flooding back to him.

"What's all this?" he asked, startling her.

Georgia spun around with a cry, chopping knife in hand, cursing under her breath when she saw him.

"Damn it all, Nate, you scared me."

Nathan raised his hands defensively and took an exaggerated step back.

"Good thing I didn't goose you, you might have stabbed me." He tried to keep his voice light, but he knew it fell flat. He'd never been all that good at disguising his moods with her.

She looked down at the knife in her hand and, with a laugh, set it on the counter and threw herself in his arms.

"It's your celebration meal, dummy. The new job, remember? Tell me everything. Where is it? When do you start?"

She hadn't forgotten. Nathan groaned and gingerly pulled her away from him.

"What?" she asked, confused.

"Might have to be a consolation meal," he said with a grimace.

"I don't understand. You didn't get the job?"

Nathan crossed the kitchen and grabbed the wine bottle. He poured them each a glass and then flung himself down in the chair. If only he were capable of lying to her. That, however distasteful, would be far easier than the conversation he knew lay before him.

"I turned it down." Without looking at her, he downed his glass in one gulp and then poured himself another. Georgia sat down quietly across from him and spread her pale white hands out on the butcher-block table.

"Turned it down?" she repeated carefully. He met her gaze, saw the storm clouds gathering there.

"I met with a lawyer today. Represents some couple with more money than sense. Whole house restoration, Georgie. 1881. Incredible architecture. Ridiculous budget and an advance on top of it all." He ran his hand through his hair as he ticked these tantalizing facts off. "They wanted me to take a look, maybe take me on as lead architect. Design, manage the whole project. It's an enormous undertaking. The scale is massive, Georgie. It's . . . it's like nothing I've ever done before." He drummed his fingers on the table and took another sip of his wine.

"But that sounds wonderful, Nate, I don't . . ." she began, confused. Nathan cut her off.

"It's in San Francisco. That's why I turned it down." He reached across the table and laced his fingers with hers. He studied her wedding ring in silence, waiting for the inevitable, running his fingertips over the constellation of freckles on her wrist.

"Nate?"

He looked up and saw the storm in her eyes on the verge of breaking.

"Why would you do that?" Her voice was tight and clipped. Nathan pulled one hand away and began scraping the waxed table with one fingernail.

"Because I'd be too far away, Georgia. From you and the house. For months at a time. The timing is bad. Hell, I'm not even sure I could do it. Never mind that we just moved in, and anyway I don't want to leave you. Not yet."

"Damn it, Nate, that's not fair," she snapped.

"What's not fair?"

"Putting this on me."

"I'm not putting anything on you," he protested. "I just—"

"Nate," her voice cut through his in a tone he rarely heard. "Stop it."

"Stop what?"

"Stop treating me like an invalid." She yanked her hand from his. He let his hand fall heavy on the table and then fumbled for hers again. He could feel her trembling, furious. He stared at the soft white fist nestled in his palm before facing the tempest in her eyes.

"Georgia, you . . ." he tried.

"No, Nate. It's not fair. I'm *fine*. I'm *better*. Can't you see that? You have to let me be better." Angrily, she wiped away the tears that streaked down her face.

"Georgia . . ." he said feebly, and then stopped, a sickness twisting in his stomach. She jerked her hand from his and blew the candles out. He reached for her but she pushed him away. Crossing the kitchen and switching the oven off with a savage twist, she stood with her back to him, her shoulders shaking. Nothing moved except for the snaking wisps of the snuffed candles.

"I'm sorry," he said finally. Nathan crossed the distance between them and pulled her to him. The clouds had cleared but in their wake was a familiar pain.

"No, I'm sorry," she insisted hoarsely.

"You have nothing to be sorry about," he said, bending to kiss her forehead. "I just love you so much," he wiped her cheeks, "and I know what losing the baby did to you. And I . . ."

"Nathan, what happened to us was terrible. The worst. But," she said, forcing a smile, "life goes on. It has to. It's the only way we can get past this. And I don't want to ever hold you back."

He kissed her lips, knowing that her smile was for his benefit. "You don't."

"Then call them back. At least go look at the house. Please."

"Georgia . . ."

"Do it for me," she said, pushing him backward until he hit the table. The light had returned to her eyes, bright and clear like sunny meadow. Without looking away, she slowly unbuttoned his shirt.

"Are you sure?" he asked. He slid his hands down the sides of her skirt, and then slid them up inside it, a delicious moment when his hands found only her soft skin and nothing else.

She nodded, busy now with his belt.

"How sturdy," she said, her lips on his chest, "do you think this table is?"

A sound beckoned in the back hall, but Georgia didn't seem to hear it. Even as she slipped her shirt off, her skirt settling in a soft bundle at his feet, even as her lips trailed kisses across his chest, Nathan's eyes were trained on the back hall. There, louder now, a voice snaked across the room and into his head.

There's nothing our Georgie wouldn't do for you. She's perfect, isn't she? She wants you to go, wants us to leave.

The words, whatever their origin, felt like truth. Like a reprieve. Like permission. Nathan nodded slowly as if in agreement, and then, lifting her into his arms, he laid her out across the table. *It'll all be perfect. You'll see. You'll do anything, everything, every . . . single . . . thing we want.*

"Let's find out," he said, pulling his shirt the rest of the way off.

She laughed and he knew, just knew, that everything was going to be all right. That he'd said the right things, done the right things. That what she said was true, not just what he wanted to hear. She *was* better. And, somehow, in the wake of this rare argument, they were giving each other a gift: he her dignity, and she his dream. *Everything.* Sprawled across the table, a pale, naked Ophelia shining like porcelain against the dull gleam of the wood, he wondered again how he'd ever been so lucky to find her. Reaching down, he ran his thumb across her jaw to her lips, down her chin. *Every . . . single . . . thing.* Then his whole hand around her neck, down now to her breasts. For a brief moment, the image of his wife blurred in front of him. Her slender limbs and her pale skin disappeared under a mound of wilted roses and crushed leaves, thorns and earth, a spectral funeral bower pinning her to the table, swallowing her whole. Nathan shook his head and as quickly as the image appeared, it vanished.

"You're perfect, aren't you?" he whispered.

"Why," she said, pulling him down on top of her, "are you still talking?"

NINE

 GEORGIA CLOSED THE ATTIC DOOR BEHIND her. "Edie?" But there was no reply. She paced the perimeter of the room, ducking under joists. "Edie, are you here?" As if in reply, the red ball rolled out from the eaves. Georgia stopped to pick it up. Behind her, a sudden burst of heat and a familiar giggle.

"Boo!" Startled, Georgia fell to one side. She rolled onto her back and peered up into the grinning face of Edie, floating just over her.

"Did I scare you?" she asked.

"That's not funny, Edith," Georgia scolded, climbing to her feet.

Edie pooled back to the floor in yet another fit of giggles.

"That was a *gas*," she insisted. "You should have seen your face," she twittered. "Boo! It's Edie the ghost!"

Georgia tried to keep up the pretense of being annoyed but it was impossible. Edie's joy had an infectious quality that transcended her more spectral aspects. She rumpled Edie's dandelion hair and joined in her laughter. *And* she told herself, as she set the elaborately wrapped and berib-boned box in the center of the attic floor, *Edie deserves her fun after all her time alone up here. It's a miracle the girl can laugh at all, isn't it?*

Edie's attention immediately jumped to the box.

"What's that?" she asked.

"Nothing," Georgia replied. "Wanna play with the ball today?"

Edie shrugged. "I guess we can try."

Georgia tossed the ball to Edie but it passed right through her chest, bounced off the wall, and rolled back to Georgia's feet.

"Bother. This again," Edie complained. Her eyes flicked back over to the box greedily. Georgia pretended not to notice.

"I told you. Practice. It just takes practice. Like the crayon. You'll get it." She tossed the ball again, but again it sailed right through Edie's outstretched arms.

"It's no use," Edie chirped in cheerful resignation. "Maybe we should do something else. Like . . ." she licked her lips and jerked her chin at the box.

Georgia went after the ball, sinking to her knees and rolling it back and forth between her hands. "Maybe you're right. Maybe the ball is too hard. We'll find something *easy* for you to do."

Edie gave Georgia a dirty look and huffed, "Only ninnies are quitters!" She stomped her feet, frustrated. "Let me try again." She was flickering again, gray scale to Technicolor, her nose wrinkled in concentration.

Georgia rolled the ball once more and Edie stopped it easily with one hand. In one fluid motion, she flicked it back to Georgia with one finger.

"Applesauce!" she exclaimed. "Aren't I the bee's knees?"

"Yes, you are," Georgia said. "See what you can do when you try?" She underhanded the ball back this time. Edie bobbled it, dropped it, then caught it on the bounce.

"Crickets! You're right. There's no telling what I can do if I keep practicing!" With an impish look on her face, Edie wiggled down onto her belly, lined the ball up with the wrapped box and flicked it hard, like she was playing marbles. The red ball shot across the room, right past Georgia, and struck the box solidly. The top fell off and the contents hit the floor with a clatter.

"Cheating!" Georgia sang out. Edie scrambled to her feet and rushed to see what was inside.

"A stick of chalk and a pebble?" Edie was more indignant than disappointed. "What kind of goopy present is that?" she demanded, holding the offending items out for Georgia to see.

"It's not the least bit goopy, young lady," Georgia admonished, snatching the chalk and the stone from her hands. "Watch."

She began drawing a grid of numbered squares on the floor, only reaching the fourth square when Edie began jumping up and down.

"Hopscotch!" she cried. "Oh, I'd forgotten hopscotch." Georgia threw Edie a teasing look.

"Thought you said it was goopy."

Edie rushed at her, her sudden and markedly substantial weight knocking Georgia off balance.

"I'm a *goose*. I love it."

Georgia rumpled the girl's maple sugar hair and dropped the rock in her hand.

"Yes, you are a little goose. But you can go first."

Georgia watched Edie toss the rock and begin skipping. She had always thought the notion of a ghost was nothing more than silly superstition. White sheets, rattling chains, graveyards at midnight. What happened *after* death, if anything, didn't seem to matter as much as what happened *before*. One turn, one toss of a pebble on a board and that was all you got. She'd never given much thought to an afterlife until they'd lost the baby. Then, suddenly, what came after this world mattered a lot.

"I bunged up," Edie's voice pulled her out of her reveries. "Can I take another turn?"

Georgia nodded and the girl tossed the pebble again. But here, in the stark light of day, in the presence of a being like Edie, the idea of a ghost or a soul or whatever she was, didn't seem silly at all. The very notion that something as arbitrary as death could possibly snuff out a creature as vital as Edie seemed absurd. The spark of life that filled this little girl to the brim, it couldn't just vanish into the ether. That made no sense. And Edie made her wonder. Gave her something like hope for the first time. That maybe there were things like loopholes in the cosmic game of life and death. Possibilities that she'd never dreamed of.

"Stop daydreaming, Georgia," Edie giggled. "It's your turn now."

"Sorry," Georgia said, taking the pebble from her. She tossed it and began hopping down the chalk grid, jumping neatly over the square with the pebble in it. When she reached the end, she turned and hopped back.

"Let's make it harder," she said, reaching into her pocket. "Let's see if you can do two pebbles."

While Edie busied herself with the new challenge, Georgia chose her words carefully.

"Edie, I know you said there wasn't anyone else here in Roseneath, but—"

"No, I said there wasn't anyone else here like *me*," Edie corrected.

"Ah. I see." Georgia took a deep breath and plunged ahead. "So is there someone not like you in the mirror?" Edie froze mid-hop and floated down, landing on one tiptoe.

"Oh, yes. The man in the mirror. But he's nothing to lose your custard over." She continued hopping with vigor.

"Tut-tut-tut," Georgia scolded. "Floating is cheating, young lady." With a pout, Edie dropped back to the ground and began hopping loudly.

"The man in the mirror, huh?" She struggled to keep her voice level. "Well, do you think he would like to come play with us?"

"Oh, no. Not him. He stays in his mirror. The mirror is for him, the attic is for me."

"But maybe if we . . ."

Edie turned and gave her an exasperated look. "It's no use. And anyway, he's shy.

"Shy?"

"Yep. Like me. He's hiding in his safe place until the right person calls him. Like you called me." She gave Georgia a toothy smile and Georgia noticed her upper lip was beaded in sweat.

"Well, why isn't he like you?"

"Because he can leave. He moves about when he thinks no one notices. But I do. Anyway, the man in the mirror won't bother you, not a bit." She handed Georgia the pebbles and twirled away in two tight pirouettes.

"What about your parents?" Edie froze mid-twirl, shimmered, faded, her back to Georgia. "Are they here somewhere, too? Maybe hiding like you?"

"No." Edie's voice flickered like a candle.

"No, they're not here?" Georgia wanted to go to her, to see her face, but something in the atmosphere that was building around Edie locked her feet in place.

"They're gone." Edie's Kodachrome color bled to the floor, leaving her in a wash of smoke. "They left when *he* left." That one word came out of her like a hiss. "When he . . . he . . . he . . . and now it's just *me*." Edie began hiccuping and Georgia realized she was crying. "And I've been all alone *forever* and the mirror man won't play with me and . . . and . . . and it's so boring and I'm so *lonely* . . ." The air around her began to spark and snap as color flooded back to her as if pulled by the child's longing. The bubble of intensity surrounding Edie burst and in its wake was nothing more than the exact likeness of a sad little girl standing in the attic, indistinguishable from a real child in every way.

"But now you've got me, haven't you, Edie?" Georgia said, rushing to gather the miserable child into her arms. Edie's tears were damp on her blouse and when she settled her on her hip, it was impossible to believe Edie wasn't alive. "And I won't ever leave you," she whispered, brushing the girl's tousled hair from her face.

"Promise?" Edie snuffled against her neck.

"I promise, Edie."

"Cross your heart?" Edie looked up and wiped her tears with one dimpled fist.

"And hope to die."

Edie grinned through her rapidly fading tears.

"Will you play me some music, please?"

"Yes," Georgia said, hugging her tight. "Will you let me braid your hair?"

Edie's face lit up and she nodded so hard her curls couldn't seem to keep up.

"You're the jammiest bits of jam, Georgia. The absolute living end."

TEN

THE PAINTBRUSH TRAILED A FINE WASH OF green against the ivory picture-frame molding. Her hand steady, wrist relaxed, Georgia let the brush slide until the trail shifted into little more than filmy eyelashes. The smooth plaster walls of the small room adjoining their own were cool to the touch despite the summer's day, a sultry caress where the meat of her hand slid along it. Someone nearly a hundred years ago had labored here just as she was now, sculpting the very wall that she now painted. Some unknown, unremembered craftsman had applied layer upon layer of thick plaster over a massive skeleton of intricate lathing, a wholly terrestrial version of a god fashioning a living being from little more than sheer will and clay. Another faceless master had followed in his wake, carefully constructing the intricate picture-frame molding she, a hundred years later, now used to guide her brush, his breath and his hands likely as steady and controlled as her own. There was a power in this, not just in creation but also in resurrection. A power that lay in the purposeful task of bringing something once beautiful and perfect back from the ruins, with care and patience and breath.

Hours passed in silence as Georgia edged around every inch of trim on one wall, and then two, finally climbing down off her ladder to stretch her back, replenish her paint, and evaluate her work. The room was small and perfectly square, double-hung windows spaced amidst three doors, one to the hall, one to their bathroom, one to a closet. Thick crown molding over her head mirrored below in the shining wood floors. The diminutive bedroom adjoining their own was like an empty jewel box.

"We could use it for a closet," Nathan had said when they first moved in. "Make you a dressing room, if you'd like."

"Maybe," she'd replied, hoping her vague smile disguised the heartbreak she felt at his clumsy attempt to distract her from what they both knew was meant to be a nursery. Neither of them had mentioned the small room again. They had enough worries to occupy them, and, as far as she knew, neither of them had set foot back into that room since they'd moved in. Until this morning, when she had returned overladen from the paint store, pushed the pointedly forgotten adjoining door open, threw up the sashes on the heavy wooden windows, and began her work.

Georgia nearly fell off the ladder when she heard Nathan come home, the now familiar sound of his truck spraying gravel as he hit the brakes in front of the carriage house, home hours earlier than expected. Taking a deep breath, she began a new line of paint along the fine edge of the old ivory-painted oak. Her hand was less steady now than it had been moments before, and she stopped to shake a cramp out, scowling when she realized she had smudged some green paint on the white trim. Dabbing at it with a rag, she listened as Nathan made his way through the downstairs. She jumped when she heard the basement door slam shut, hard, an uncharacteristically crude gesture for Nathan.

Now she could hear him rummaging around in the kitchen, cursing as he sorted the mail by the front door, an avalanche of bills he would no doubt tell her not to worry over. Her frown deepened even as her brush steadied.

"Georgie? Babe? I'm home early," his voice called out.

The brush froze in her hand for a moment before she gripped it tighter and forced herself to continue. "Up here, Nate," she replied.

"Up where?" More footfalls, in the living room now, rounding to the staircase.

"In here."

"Hon?" his voice echoed inside their bathroom, floated back to her through the open door.

When he finally found her, he asked, "What's this?"

"I'm painting."

"I can see that."

Another long silence and then,

"Georgie?"

"Yes, Nate?" Her brush faltered, steadied, continued.

"Want some help?"

She met his questioning eyes only briefly before removing a second brush from her apron pocket.

"Counting on it." She held the brush out to him. "I think we can finish before dinner."

Nathan set to work next to Georgia, mimicking her graceful strokes against the white molding.

"You're home early," Georgia said. "Everything all right?"

He glanced at her with a side eye but kept the focus on his strokes. "Yeah, everything's fine," he said finally. Then his brush stopped and she heard his boots shift on his own ladder. "No," he corrected. "Not fine, not at all. My day was frustrating and stupid. If I do call that guy back, a trip to the West Coast is going to eat up a week of my time. I got underbid on two small jobs, the goddamn city inspector is giving me shit about the project in Shaker, wasting time and money I don't have, fucking carpenter is AWOL, and the homeowner in Hingetown is all over me. And all I wanted was to be home. So I shifted everything to tomorrow, which I will no doubt regret, but there it is."

Georgia set her brush down, climbed down from her perch and crossed the room to him. Nathan stood on the bottommost rung of his ladder, his back to her, one hand raised just as hers had been a moment before. She caught his free hand with hers, kissed the back of it, and then rose up on her toes to meet his lips.

"Better?"

"Better."

"We don't have to paint. This can wait."

"No, I want to. This is relaxing. With you, anyway."

"Sure?" she asked. He tapped the tip of her nose with the handle of his brush.

"Yeah." She smiled and returned to her own ladder.

They worked in silence, the sound of his breathing steadying until it mirrored her own, the soft rasp of brushes on the smooth plaster, the birds singing outside, the sun making its way across the sky, shifting the color of the room from jade to sea foam to willow.

"It's a nice little room," he said, minutes or hours later, the drowsy afternoon and the lulling sounds of breathing and painting and birdsong muffling the steady march of time.

"Yes. Yes, it is." Her hand gripped the brush tight as she shifted on the ladder.

"I like this color you picked." A tentative nudge.

"Thought you might." Georgia swallowed hard and tried to keep her eyes focused on the thin paint line.

"What's it called?" he asked, when she volunteered no more.

"Dutch Clover."

"Good color for a closet," he said.

"Mmm . . ." she replied. "I'm not sure I need a walk-in closet, Nate."

"Dressing room, then?" he offered. "Sewing room?"

She climbed off the ladder and opened another can of paint.

"Seems greedy to have two rooms of my own," she replied, pouring a steady stream of pale green paint into her container. "I already have the whole attic."

"Maybe I'll make it my hobby room," he quipped. "Take up model airplanes."

Georgia laughed as she climbed back up on the ladder, steadying herself with one hand on the wall as she did.

"Tiny little propellers," he continued. "Glue. Paint. I'll get a magnifying glass; drag my drafting table up here. Before you know it, I'll have some obscure aerial battle from World War Two dangling from the ceiling."

"Maybe," she replied. "If that's what you'd like."

Another pause. "I'm not sure. Maybe not model airplanes. Let's see . . . maybe stamps?"

"Stamps," she repeated with a laugh. "Like Penny Blacks and Inverted Jennys?"

"Yes, that's the ticket. Stamp collecting. And cigars. I'll take up stamp collecting and get me a big velvet chair, sit in here at night studying Philatelic Monthly and smoking big, smelly cigars. I like this plan."

"No," Georgia replied thoughtfully. "I don't think that will work either."

"You're probably right. You already know more about stamps than I do. I have no idea who Jenny is, nor why she is inverted."

Georgia's lips curved up as she tucked the brush into a corner and drew it down the inside edge of the wall.

"Maybe if we decided on the curtains, that would help settle this. What kind of curtains do you think would go well with this color, Nate? I was thinking white, maybe lace. Maybe a dotted Swiss." She watched him scratch the back of his head before answering her.

"I'd agree with you, Georgie, if I knew what the hell dotted Swiss *was*. Sounds like cheese."

He turned then and caught her watching him, a grin spanning his face. She spun around to face her own wall again. "Not *cheese*. It just means white. With little dots." A small dab of the brush and her last corner was done.

"Like freckles," he remarked. "Well, you know I'm a big fan of freckles. Particularly yours."

She wiped her hands off on her rag. "I just thought a little something to keep the morning light from waking . . . anyone who might be sleeping in here."

"Sleeping?" Nathan stopped painting and cast a glance around the room. "I guess it would be a step up from the couch or the doghouse," he said wryly. "Can I have a sleeping bag?"

"I didn't mean you, Nathan." She smirked.

He decided to change tack. "Do they make those Swiss cheese curtains in blue? Blue might look nice with this green. A nice soft blue."

Georgia considered for a minute before answering.

"Not blue," she said slowly. "Maybe yellow."

"Hmm . . .. Yellow Swiss cheese curtains in my Dutch Clover smoking room. Bit froufrou, but you're the boss."

"No," she said, shaking her head. "Not a smoking room. Not a model airplane room, not a dressing room, not a closet." Across the room, Nathan's brush froze.

Her words hung in the air, as suspended as his paintbrush. She studied his shoulders, they were tense, braced, but he did not turn. The birds outside grew noisy. Licking her lips, she tried to think of the right way to tell him, imagining each phrase as a stroke of the brush, filling in the gaps and restoring something long neglected.

Nathan stepped back off his ladder and set his own brush down. "Georgia . . ." he began. His hands fell to his waist, landed on his hips, and he tried again. "Georgia, I . . ." He broke off again. "Damn."

Georgia stepped away from her ladder and inspected her work. "I think you might be right about making it a bedroom. It's not very big, though, is it, Nate?"

"No, it's not very big at all." He met her gaze, worry in every line of his face.

"We'd need a small bed, I think." A smile.

"That's about all that would work."

"I wonder . . ." she said, the words coming easier now. "What would you think of a rocking chair? Just here. Just near the window."

"Yeah . . . . A rocking chair and a little bed. We could put the bed right here." He gestured to the wall behind her, framing the space with his hands. He took a step closer. "What else would we need?"

"I think we'd need a chest. You know, to store things so they aren't underfoot."

"Things like blankets?"

"And blocks."

"Paper dolls?"

"Maybe little trucks, even."

His arms were around her waist now. She let her head fall to his chest.

"The only thing I'm not absolutely certain about is the curtains," she said. His lips landed on her hair.

"Georgie?"

"Nate."

"I don't care what color the damn curtains are." He kissed her. She ran her fingertips over the side of his neck, let them slip into his collar.

"Neither do I."

He began walking backward, pulling her across the room toward the open door.

"We should finish painting," she said, spinning around him to lead the way, walking faster now.

"It'll keep. Everything can wait."

ELEVEN

GEORGIA LUGGED THE BOX OF BOOKS UP THE attic stairs. At Edie's request, she'd unearthed all the books she'd saved from her childhood bookcase. Picture books and chapter books, tattered paperback Newbery Award winners, and yellowed library-bound fairy tales. To this assortment, she'd added a few art books, an enormous photography book, and her old elementary school dictionary; her name doodled on the front cover in a clumsy script . . .

Georgia G.

. . . whatever she could find that might appeal to the little girl in the attic and, as Edie had pointed out, help her wile away the hours she spent alone.

"It's dull as dirt up here, Georgia," she'd groused, her lip set in a charming pout. "Coloring and hopscotch is all well and good but one can only scotch so much. I'm not a *baby*."

Pausing on the top step, Georgia shifted the box on her hip and smiled, remembering, savoring the moment that reality became miraculous, when the mundane became magical. She reached for the doorknob but before she even touched it, Edie yanked the heavy attic door open.

"Finally!" she sang out, pulling Georgia inside and attempting to spin both her and the heavy box. "I've been waiting *ages*, Georgia," she reproached her. "It's nearly *tea* time." She noticed the box and stopped trying to twirl Georgia abruptly. "Oh. What's that?" she purred greedily. With a laugh, Georgia dropped the heavy box to the floor.

"All my old books, as per Captain Edie's direct orders." She snapped off a quick salute.

"Well done, soldier!" Edie exclaimed, tearing the box open. "I shall instruct the Quarter Master to double your rations of chocolate and biscuits!" Georgia sank into the easy chair and watched, delighted, as Edie quickly emptied the box of books.

"*Island of the Blue Dolphins?* Nineteen-hundred and SIXTY?" she sputtered. "And . . . and this one: *A Wrinkle in Time?* Nineteen hundred and seventy-THREE? How long have I been dead for, anyway?" She held up another book. "Now *this* one I know. *Jane Eyre*. Papa and I gave Mama a spanking new copy for her birthday. She said it's better than butter on bacon!" Her face disappeared back into the box.

"I think there's one in there from 2009," Georgia said. "*The Evolution of Calpurnia Tate*. Stubborn little girl from 1900." Edie emerged from the box, clearly intrigued. "Seemed right up your alley."

Edie jumped to her feet and turned a wobbly cartwheel, landing near the radio. She spun the dial, scrolling through the selections Georgia had loaded. As she did, Georgia noticed how easily she was now able to work the little digital radio. She looked back to the towering stack of books and realized how confidently Edie had stacked them, how forcefully she'd ripped open the box. *Curioser and curiouser,* she thought.

Edie pulled her out of the chair and away from her musings.

"Let's celebrate my new books. I want to dance." She fumbled for Georgia's hands, frustrated when Georgia had no idea where she was meant to put them. "Don't they dance in the future?" Edie demanded. "What kind of jinxy future is this, anyway?"

"Well, we do, but not to this kind of music," Georgia confessed, peering down at the radio. "*Blue Goose Rag?* Is it a waltz, or—?"

Edie groaned, but her eyes shone with mischief. "No, ducky, it's a rag! I'll teach you. Easy as apple custard, I promise." She dropped her right hand on Georgia's shoulder, placing Georgia's left hand on her own shoulder. "I'll be the gentleman, you be the lady."

Edie nudged Georgia's left foot with her right and without waiting, began marching her backward. "Eight counts back, six-seven-eight, now you're doing it." She twisted Georgia sideways abruptly so the two were walking side-by-side, "And now eight counts promenade, you see?" She laughed as Georgia tripped trying to keep up. "You're doing *swell*, Georgia, don't worry." She shifted their positions so Georgia was dancing backward again and the two were hip-to-hip. "Now promenade again, two-three-four . . . Okay, when we get to eight, I'm going to pinwheel you."

"Pinwheel me?" Georgia protested, "but . . ."

Edie ignored her. "Seven-eight, now spin!" The hand on Georgia's waist guided her firmly in a circle. "Two-three-four!" Edie laughed as she spun Georgia alone one last time, then wrapped her gangly arms around her shoulders and clicked her heels. "And that's how you dance the rag!"

"You're a very good dancer, Edie," Georgia remarked carefully as Edie led her backward again. "You must have had a good teacher."

Edie nodded and used her foot to prod Georgia to one side. "Like that—little steps. Papa taught me to dance. Mama disapproves of popular music but Papa is just *mad* for it. Spin, two-three-four." Edie paused to toss her curls over her shoulder then resumed promenading Georgia around the attic. "The Victrola in the living room is Mama's, no ragtime allowed. But Papa has a nice little Stentor with a crank in his workshop and a great stack of records." She laughed and pinwheeled Georgia again. "And we just dance and dance, when he's not too busy."

Georgia tried to concentrate on the steps but the transformation the music and dancing had wrought in Edie was distracting, to say the least. Her hands held tightly to Georgia's, and, Georgia realized, with a start, were a bit sweaty. The once vaporous cloud of hair was now a tangled mass of sorrel rag curls that bounced with each step. If she'd tried, Georgia could have counted each freckle on Edie's stubborn little face. Her eyes were hazel and honey and bright as stars. When Georgia lagged, Edie pulled her along with all the spunk and determination of a real little girl.

"Want to know a secret?" Edie whispered.

Georgia swallowed hard and nodded.

"Promise not to tell?" Edie demanded.

"Cross my heart," Georgia whispered back.

"Mama says it's not *seemly* for a lady to dance to ragtime but . . ."

She lowered her voice even further and glanced around as if someone might hear her secret. "One night, I crept out of bed and peeked out the window. Mama and Papa were dancing in his workshop in the middle of the night. Really cutting a rug, too. I'd no idea Mama could dance like that. Sawdust was flying everywhere and Papa laughed and laughed." Her face fell and she dropped Georgia's hands. The music played on but Edie was clearly done dancing. She traced the tip of one shoe in an arc on the floor pensively.

"You miss them, don't you?" Georgia asked gently. Edie looked up in alarm.

"No," Edie shook her head violently. "No, I do *not*. I'm *glad*."

"Glad?" All of Edie's mirth was gone, and, in its wake, something dire. Anger and fear. The air around Edie trembled, her edges faded to wisps.

"Glad they're gone," she whispered darkly. "I don't want to remember. I *won't*." She glanced back to the attic door and as she did, shadows of bruises began to bloom across her paper-white skin.

"Edie, what's wrong?" Georgia wanted to reach for her but was suddenly afraid to.

Edie shook her head, her brilliant cinnamon hair faded back to a silver cloud. "I don't know. I don't remember."

"You're safe, Edie, I promise. I won't let anything hurt you again."

Edie bit her lower lip and wiped her cheeks, then threw her arms around Georgia's waist, the strange mood gone in an instant.

"Would you read to me a bit more? I feel kind of ratty just now."

"I'd love to," Georgia said, leading her to the green easy chair. "Your pick. *Alice in Wonderland* or *The Lion, The Witch, and the Wardrobe*. What'll it be?"

"I'm scared of witches," Edie said with a shiver. "Let's read about this Alice. She sounds just bricky!" She climbed into Georgia's lap and kissed her cheek.

"Well, Wonderland has a Jabberwock," Georgia cautioned. "Fair warning."

"What's a Jabberwock?" Edie asked.

"A monster. Pretty scary stuff. All teeth and claws."

Edie considered, face screwed up as she weighed her options. "If I must choose between witches and monsters, I choose monsters. Monsters are made-up things after all."

"They certainly are," Georgia said, setting the offending book aside. "Very sensible of you," she added, smiling to herself.

"You're so kind to me. I almost don't mind that I'm dead. Now that *you're* here." She wrapped her arms around Georgia's shoulders and settled her head there. With a start, Georgia realized her weight was suddenly exactly that of a real child.

"Edie," Georgia said. "Just look at you today. You feel so . . . so . . ." Georgia struggled to find the words to describe how the cobweb sunbeam of a little girl had turned corporeal in her arms, warmth and weight, breath and pulse. *Resurrected*. The word popped into her head and Georgia examined it even as she examined the child in her arms and felt the rightness of it. She looked down and noticed Edie's legs were longer than they were yesterday, the hands fiddling with Georgia's hair were no longer tiny and dimpled. They were tapered and elegantly long. "Edie, I think you've grown."

Edie laughed and shook her head.

"Of course I have, silly!" she preened. "Isn't it *marvelous*? I've been practicing, just like you told me to. Now read me a story before I fall asleep. I'm worn out from all that dancing."

Georgia pulled her close and began reading.

"'Chapter One: Down the Rabbit Hole. Alice was beginning to get very tired . . .'"

Edie fell asleep before Alice had even reached the bottom of the White Rabbit's burrow. But instead of evaporating as she had before, she remained heavy in Georgia's arms, slumbering peacefully and snoring softly. Georgia held her for a long time, playing with her hair, kissing her temple, and rubbing her slender back. Then she rose and settled little Edie in the chair and tucked her in with a blanket. Edie sighed and burrowed her freckled nose under the blanket, a slight shimmer the only thing marking her as anything other than a real little girl.

✦ ✦ ✦

Georgia carefully closed and locked the attic door behind her. She made her way down the staircase and sat on the last stair tread, a knot of pain forming on her forehead.

She stared pensively into the mirror across the room and, as always, wondered if the little girl she had just talked to was real. What had seemed like a fancy at first had become a game of dare; every day Georgia goaded herself to climb the stairs, certain until the last second before Edie appeared that she had dreamed it all. That the child she thought she'd found in the attic was a dream thing born of grief and no more, hoping and not hoping to find the attic empty. But, every day, Edie appeared, as if summoned by nothing more than Georgia's voice, a beautiful, intricate, enchanting child thriving under her attention. And now this, today.

She looked back up the stairwell and listened but heard only silence. Edie was growing. It was undeniable. The late afternoon sun shimmered softly in the mirror, illuminating the pitted portions and reflecting the view out the windows, so that it was as if an entire wood appeared in the mercury surface, a broken forest wreathed in silver. She watched, entranced by the illusion, as a dark figure seemed to rise in the middle and then stride out of sight. *What magic words would it take to conjure you*, she wondered.

There was a momentum to this. She could no longer deny it. A child? *No, call her what she is. A ghost.* A ghost child, a wisp, somehow now warm and vital, a winsome young girl who was learning, maturing even. Remembering. Growing. *I almost don't mind that I'm dead. Now that you're here. There's no telling what I can do if I keep practicing!*

Georgia wondered how on earth she could ever tell Nathan. A secret like this could not be kept forever. Perhaps should not be. But Edie was so sweet, so gentle. Surely she would never hurt anyone. There was too much Georgia didn't know about this child and what awful act led to her death. *I'm glad. Glad they're gone.* Georgia would tell Nathan soon, but not yet. *He sounds peculiar to me.* Georgia shook the girl's strange words away. Just a frightened child, a little girl afraid of a big, unfamiliar man. Something bad, very bad, had happened to Edie and it was no wonder she was frightened. She just needed time. Time to heal, time to grow. Georgia let her worries fade away. She'd find a way to share Edie with him. Soon. There was no rush. No rush at all.

TWELVE

THE DAY HAD BEEN UNUSUALLY WARM AND stuffy, late summer's last hot breath. After a late night followed by a long day, Nathan slid the transmission of his truck into park in the gravel drive and studied the waves of heat coming off Roseneath's slate roof, making it shimmer like a mirage. The relentless sun washed down the yellowed brick of the third floor, transforming the attic windows into mirrors. The green of the landscape and the buttery cream of the peeling house turned the whole scene into a forgotten Polaroid from another time. Nathan entered through the back door and found Georgia in the kitchen, a sea of grocery bags at her feet and some old-timey music blasting from her radio again.

"What's all this? Dinner two times in one week?"

She spun around and kissed him. "I even made a menu for the week. Be amazed," she called over the loud music. Then she reached behind her and turned the volume down.

"About damn time," Nathan quipped, snatching a bag of chips off the counter. "I was this close to leaving you for total dereliction of wifely duties."

Georgia scowled and snatched the chips back. "I more than fulfilled my duties last night, Mr. Pritchard. If I recall correctly, you said something about my attentions taking several years off your life. I am offended, sir. I demand satisfaction."

He pulled her indignant body to him and reclaimed the bag of chips, holding them over her head, his lips finding hers again.

"Satisfaction, huh? We'll see. Maybe I'll keep you around on a trial basis."

"I might need regular reviews. Keep me up to snuff," she said, pushing away from him as he tore the bag open. "You'll spoil your dinner," she admonished. Instead of replying, he chewed loudly on a mouthful of chips. She rolled her eyes.

"What's with all the Big Band music all of a sudden?"

"It's ragtime, Nate. Totally different era."

"You didn't answer my question," he pointed out.

"No, I didn't," she grinned and promenaded across the kitchen to grab a tea towel. "Speaking of leaving me," she said, "did you call that lawyer back?"

He tossed the bag of chips onto the counter, grabbed her around the waist and spun her in a circle. "Yes, boss lady, I did."

"And?" she demanded.

"*And* I'm all booked to fly out next week and take a look. A look, Georgia, nothing more."

"But . . ."

He pulled her to him and silenced her sputtering lips with his.

"Hush. I'll go have a look and we'll talk about it then. There could be a million reasons why this might not be the right opportunity. The house, the owners, the plans. Georgie, I might go out there and find out the lawyer tried to sell me a bill of goods. Maybe the owners went so far afield because no sane architect would touch their firetrap. Or maybe the budget isn't what they promised. Never mind that no one has mentioned exactly how much they are willing to pay me for turning my life upside down. I'll go look, that's all. Let's not get ahead of ourselves."

Georgia glared at him before giving him a quick, obligatory kiss.

"Fine. Party pooper."

He slipped a hand under her shirt and tickled her. She pushed him, laughing.

"Enough!" she said. "Go find something to do while I unpack all this food. Dinner's going to be late enough as it is."

"Enough for now, Georgie girl. I'm going to get a few hours in on the yard, see what I can do before dinner. I swear, those roses are devouring the entire yard."

Nathan dropped the wheelbarrow with a heavy thump and pulled the secateurs out of his belt. The roses spilled across the lawn, snaking their way up the foundation of Roseneath, leggy to the point of breaking. He stretched, looking up at the sky. Plenty of daylight to do what he wanted. He squatted down and grasped the long stem of the nearest rose bush, grimacing at the sting of the thorns.

Snip.

Reaching for the next, he felt a sting. A thick black thorn had pierced the back of his hand, curved and gleaming, a drop of bright red blood already trailing down to his wrist. Using his thumb and forefinger, he plucked the thorn out and kept going.

Snip.

Snip.

He tossed the rose cuttings into neat piles on the lawn and was soon lost in the rhythm of his work. The piles around him grew higher, sharp mounds of branches that clawed at his legs as he moved across the sweeping back rose beds. After the first thorn, he ignored the others, intent on his work. After a while he didn't even feel them anymore, paid no attention to the blood trailing from his arms and hands, down his calves.

Finally, with the last wave of grasping stems cut into a neat bundle, Nathan stopped to look back at his work. The roses were tidy now, sparse in areas where he'd been ruthless, but even with this first bit of attention, they seemed to stand taller. The air was rank with the smell of cut rose petals in the hot sun, and he was surprised at the sheer number of piles he'd made, the shifting light through the pine stand to the west transforming them into primitive funeral mounds in the waning light. *Beautiful*, he thought, and he found himself wishing he could see them in Roseneath's basement, saw himself carrying the limp remnants in, one at a time, arranging them inside like corpses in a mausoleum. He shook the idea from his head and reached for the shovel.

Nathan began digging, driving the spade into the ground with his boot, deep and hard, then tossed the wedges of dirt and grass into the wheelbarrow, giving the rose beds a nice clean edge. Shovel after shovel, the wheelbarrow began to fill up. He paused, sweating in the hot sun, as a sudden notion whispered in his ear. *They're so beautiful. You should bury them. Bury their arms and legs, their thorns and petals. Cover them with earth and tuck them away safe and sound and see what springs from their rotted corpses.* Minutes passed and still he stared, his eyes unfocused, unable to shake the persistent suggestion—*you should do it, if only to see, to know what could spring from the dead earth, the spent roses, a grimoire pierced with thorns hibernating deep below overwintering in the still darkness, reborn anew in springtime, a third of the stars of heaven, fallen into decay, scattered by His great hand*—only refocusing when a bee buzzed past his face. He swatted at it idly. Then he dropped the shovel and went to the carriage house, returning with an assortment of cardboard boxes.

Nathan sank his hands deep into the dirt and began scattering handful after handful into the boxes, smoothing them out when the bottoms were covered. Then he turned to the rose clippings and gently layered the cuttings over the dirt. He covered that with dirt, too, and continued burying layer after layer—dirt, roses, dirt—until the boxes were full.

He carried each box across the backyard, through the back door. The basement door stood open, the darkness below beckoning. Nathan carried each one down the basement steps into the dark, not bothering with a light. Back,

back into the dark recesses of the root cellar, until he'd brought every carefully arranged box down. *Beautiful. Perfect. This time will be perfect. We're coming along nicely, aren't we?* Nathan nodded. He wrenched open the first box and upended its contents on the damp basement floor, a rush of adrenaline coursing through him as he was enveloped in the scent of rotten vegetation and earth, rose petals and copper. One after another, until he stood over a giant nest woven through with long, thorn-crusted stems, his arms slick with the soil of Roseneath and his own blood. He felt his lips stretch into a satisfied smile and wondered why such a task would please him so, but the voice returned, stronger this time, consoling, soothing.

Just a notion, Nathan, an experiment, a flight of fancy. Nothing surely that would hurt her. Nothing she ever need know about. Harmless. Just some earth. Keep them safe. Lock them up tight and throw away the key.

Once upstairs, he carefully shut the basement door and locked it. Then, kneeling, he slipped the key back under the door and smiled as it tumbled down the stairs. Tears streaked down his cheeks, rivulets that mingled helplessly with the earth that clung there.

"The doors of Hell," he heard himself whimper, "are locked on the inside."

Returning to the yard, Nathan stared at the trench he'd dug, at the scattered mounds of rose cuttings that remained. He stood so long and so still he could have been a statue.

Just one more thing, Nathan, my boy, and we're all done. I'll be you and you'll be me, worlds without end, amen.

Nathan stumbled backward after a sharp pain rent through his leg. He fell to one knee, tore his eyes from the beckoning shell of the greenhouse and toward a thorn-crusted garotte wrapped tightly around his calf. He reached to extract the painful binding from his flesh and, as he did, saw the ruin of his hands, the trails of blood that snaked down his arm. Watched as they twined with the earth only to blur into nothingness. Felt a suffocating blanket of numbness envelop him.

"Why?" The question forced itself out from between his clenched teeth.

Because I found you, kid. And you let me in.

Nathan nodded mournfully, his eyes glazed. He moved then and began piling the cuttings, like tangles of arms with jagged teeth, into his wheelbarrow. He wiped his sweaty, bloody hands on the handles of the wheelbarrow and hoisted it, grunting at the pain in his hands, rolling his cargo behind the carriage house. The greenhouse, sagging and bereft of its glass walls, stood wide open, inviting. The weeds that had grown up around it, the vines that snaked their way through and over its brittle frame, made a kind of mausoleum, and he walked into its skeletal embrace with an offering of blood and roses.

THIRTEEN

"COULD YOU JUST GIVE ME A MINUTE?" GEOR-
gia said. She released his grip and hurried from
the room, her heels padding softly on the worn
linoleum.

*Confused, Nathan watched as she disappeared down the
dark, narrow hall.*

*They'd spent the day together, a blur of hours that slipped
through his fingers far too fast for him to remember exactly
how they'd spent it. He remembered worrying that morning
as he shaved that he'd imagined the night before in the parking
lot. That the astonishing girl from the library who had agreed
to spend the day with him would be altered by the light of day,
little more than a dim reflection of the illusion that had consumed his thoughts for the last week, certain that he'd built up
the ordinary into the extraordinary.*

*He was wrong. From the moment she climbed into his truck
and dropped a small, unexpected picnic basket between them,
she had bewitched him. He had no idea how they'd spent the
day. He knew only that being with her was like a miraculous
visitation. That her every word, every glance, every frown,*

every laugh was a bewildering mystery he wanted only to spend the rest of his days deciphering.

Late that night, when he offered to walk her to her door, she said yes. He kissed her goodnight against the door of a midcentury walk up, told her he needed to see her again, soon. She smiled and shook her head, an infuriating contradiction. Then she fumbled for her keys, the door behind her opening as she asked him to come in, just for a minute. And then she vanished, leaving him standing there alone in her apartment, wondering if he'd done something wrong.

Nathan used Georgia's absence to study her apartment, automatically cataloging each clue about the siren that had lured him to her haunt only to disappear without a word. A sagging couch covered in bright afghans. A sewing basket and some fabric set on the floor within arm's reach. Piles of books operating as both end tables and coffee tables. Beyond the small sitting room, a tiny, spartan kitchen. Mismatched dime store prints on the wall, an ancient percolator on the counter. The basket of apples he'd given her sat in the center of a red and yellow enameled kitchen table. He turned in a slow circle, taking in the tea towel curtains, the few but shabby bits of good furniture, the scattering of cheerful threadbare rugs, and wondered if he'd somehow stumbled into a fairy tale.

His heart lodged in his throat when he saw her emerge from the darkness. She'd let her hair down, her feet now bare. Her hands twisted and wrung themselves, worrying the sash on a sepia robe, her eyes wide, uncertain and meticulously studying anything but his face. Nathan let out a long breath and said nothing, hesitant as he had been last night when she'd appeared in the parking lot, afraid once more to break the spell.

"I just . . ." she whispered, her wringing hands now tangling themselves in one of her long curls. She swallowed hard and crossed the room to him, grasped one of his hands in hers. "I thought maybe . . ." Again she was looking at his hands and not his face. Her cheeks were red.

Nathan tilted her chin gently, watched her lashes flutter shut, and kissed her lips softly. He whispered her name, hoping she'd understand that he, too, lacked the words for this moment.

Once, twice, the third time his lips touched hers, each time more insistent, she began walking backward, pulling him with her. Her lips stretched wide now as she kissed him, clutching both of his hands in hers as she did, hurrying him, both of them laughing incredulously in the dark hall.

Once they managed to fumble into her bedroom, Nathan caught glimpses of lace-covered windows, sills dotted with ferns and geraniums, walls papered in something like a trellis. But the center of his attention was the porcelain enchantress now flashing him an insatiable smile, letting her flimsy garment slip from one shoulder. Nathan felt that he'd chased a dryad into her garden, that there was no catching this creature, no understanding her or possessing her. That she was a wish, a dream that would vanish before he could reach her, that would leave him ever wanting, having glimpsed this, her, now, more.

Standing in front of him was the antithesis of everything his life had ever been. He gripped the bit of her satin tight in his hands and tried to squash the nagging voices in his head, reminding him of how unworthy he knew himself to be. His dismal, poor childhood, his uncertain career prospects, the string of cheap, shiny women that had wandered into his bed and *ultimately out of his life. It all felt something like a sacrilege now. Georgia Galloway was something fine, far finer than he deserved, and yet here he was.*

Time seemed to stumble then and restart, and he looked away from the boon in his hands to her crestfallen face. He saw the moment she realized he had stopped his pursuit and stood, instead, hesitating outside the doorway.

"I'm sorry," she whispered, shocking Nathan out of his brooding. Blushing, she pulled the robe back over her shoulder, fumbled at her side futilely for the sash he held in his hands. "It's too soon, I've ruined things, I . . ."

"No," he protested, dropping the sash and hurrying to her. "Oh no, it isn't that at all." He stayed her hands, then pulled the robe away from her shoulder once more, kissing her collarbone, then her neck. "It's just," he whispered, searching her face, trying to get her to look him in the eyes. She wouldn't.

"Georgia," he whispered, "please look at me."

When she finally did, he saw humiliation where there had been mirth only seconds before.

"This was all wrong," she said, trying to detach her hands from his. "I'm so embarrassed, please . . ."

"No, no, no," he insisted. He brushed her hair back and let his forehead fall gently against hers. "It's just, I was standing there," another kiss and he pushed her robe the rest of the way off, heard it hit the floor at their feet with a whisper. ". . . thinking that," he turned her chin up to him, kissed her long and hard, held her small body tightly against him, ". . . I'm never going to get another chance to make love to you for the first time."

She wove her fingers into his hair, trailed her thumb over his lips, a question in her eyes.

"I didn't want to mess it up," he confessed, kissing her thumb.

She buried her face in his chest, her arms tightened around him. "You can't. You won't."

He laid her down on the bed. Her skin was silkier than the confection she wore. He traced a line down her thigh to her feet and kissed her ankles, let her squirm away only to pull her back. He couldn't tell if she was trembling or he was.

"Are you real, Georgia?" he whispered in her ear. "Am I dreaming?"

She kissed his eyes, pulled his head to her chest and held him there, her soft reply a simple incantation, a benediction that wiped all his insecurities away.

"Nathan Pritchard, you're every dream I've ever had."

FOURTEEN

GEORGIA STOOD IN THEIR BEDROOM, LOST IN thought, idly fanning herself with her to-do list. *Air conditioning would be nice. And we really need another dresser.* She considered the jumble of boxes at her feet. *Ugh. Impossible. I'll have to go shopping again tomorrow. See if I can find some used furniture. And while I'm out,* she thought, a light appearing in her eyes, *I'll pick up some more things for Edie. I'll tell him soon. I'll think of a way. And then it will be our secret. Our secret little girl, his and mine. Nathan will love Edie.* A smile stretched across her face as she recalled her morning in the attic with Edie. *Poor little poppet. She needs more. More than just me, more than just that attic.* Georgia slipped her hand into the pocket of her skirt, feeling for the skeleton key. With the door safely locked, she could take her time, choose the right moment to tell Nathan, the right time to introduce Edie into a wider world, when she was ready. She stooped and gathered an armful of tightly rolled socks, casting her eyes about for a place to put them. *And what would that mean, exactly?* The voice of her conscience was filled with trepidation. *I'll unlock that door when I find it,* she told herself.

Behind her, Georgia heard Nathan's heavy footfalls as he climbed the stairs and entered their room.

"All done in the yard?" she asked, dumping the socks in a shoebox. Without turning, she added, "This is your new sock drawer, at least for . . ."

She jumped when he wrapped his arms around her. His chest was feverish against her back; her skin rose in goose-flesh when his perspiration, acrid and coppery, soaked through her shirt. His arms were splattered in clots of mud, adding sour notes of loam and decay to his sharp musk. She tried to shrug him off but he held her firmly against him. He kissed her neck, his lips a rough trail rasping down her collarbone; she could feel how eager he was as he ground into her from behind.

She fought to move her arms, to pull open the trap of his forearms, but they tightened around her, pinning them to her sides. She wondered what strange new game this was, a wild moment of fright when she saw the mud on his arms laced through with something red and thick. His breath came hot and heavy on her shoulder, his kisses turned to bites.

"Nate? What are you doing?"

Instead of answering, his arms tightened even more as he forcibly lifted her and began dragging her toward the bed.

"Nathan, stop it. This isn't funny. You're hurting me." She was struggling in earnest now, kicking, trying to slow his steady progress across the room, her feet slipping, unable to gain any purchase in the trail of his muddy footprints that crossed the room.

At the bed now, his crushing embrace loosened only enough to spin her around. The room was a blur, a fraction of a second in which she saw his face, a frightening unfamiliar expression, angry and vacant. She saw the mix of red and brown on his face as well, his bare chest smeared with whatever it was that had soaked through her own clothes. *He's bleeding.*

"Nathan, you're . . ."

But he cupped the back of her head, forced her mouth open with his tongue, choking off her protests. They fell heavily on the bed, her mouth filled with the sweet rot of roses, his teeth clashing against hers. A scream rose helplessly in her throat as her lungs tried to inflate but could not. He pressed her harder into the bed, his weight pinning her there. She tore his face away from hers long enough to spit out a mouthful of cold mud. Nathan slackened his grip and allowed her lungs to fill with air, but before she could roll away, he seized her hands and pinned them over her head, holding them tightly in one of his own, her arms and hands now stained with whatever primitive mélange painted him.

She could smell the mud all over her now, bitter petrichor. He lifted her skirt, his fingernails clawed a scalding trail up her thighs. He pressed her face to one side with his forearm, drove her face into the thick muck she'd spat out, and she held her breath, wondered what strange desire this was, wondered what in this world could make her gentle husband ravage her like this. She gasped for air when he shifted his arm, nauseated by coarse spittle that now coated her face, his mouth savage on her breasts, her stomach, pulling her panties off with his teeth, nipping at the delicate flesh of her inner thigh as he did. She wondered if the reserve, the care he'd always shown her had always been hiding this terrifying passion, this wonton need to consume her, his strange silence born of an inability to ask her for this, to take it instead. Torn between pleading with him to stop and begging him to continue, she could only go limp under his onslaught.

"Nathan," her voice a needful sob, a reproaching plea. He released her wrists and wrenched her legs apart. His teeth and tongue on her thighs, and then higher, lapping at her, rough, insistent. He shredded her clothing from her, catching her fragile skin everywhere he touched. As if from a great distance, she heard herself plead with him to stop.

You're hurting me, Nathan, please don't hurt me.

His tongue was hot inside her and she wrapped her legs around his head, drove herself into his face, her pleas turned to demands.

Fuck me, take me, take what you want, every last bit of me is yours.

Something savage inside of her rose to meet him, to match him. Then a horrible, agonizing nothing when he pulled back, leaving her desperate for more, all of him, anything, even this—

Please

Don't

Stop

—aching with the absence of him. The room heaved in deep bellows, the bed wrapped around them like a snake.

The light in the room flickered, drew arcane shapes against his mud-stained skin. She had to keep her focus on his eyes, otherwise she would tumble toward the ceiling. She wanted him, needed him, but not like this. Just a moment, a word from him so she could feel safe inside his merciless hunger. She whispered in a gentle voice for him to stop, but inside she wanted more. So much more. He said nothing.

A pause, the whole room, the air, the light, the two of them poised on the edge of a terrible precipice, a brief eternity that granted Georgia one moment out of time to look down at herself, to see the bloody trails raking crude marks on her breasts, her thighs, to see the same scrawl twine around his naked body, mud, blood, thorns, and something else, *something, no someone, no, no, no.*

My God, what's happening? Please, don't. Stop.

"Wait, Nathan, don't. Stop," she gasped. She fought to sit up but Nathan threw her back. Her teeth jarred in her head and she tasted blood.

The house around her creaked and groaned, drowning out her cries.

Georgia scrambled to her knees, tried to crawl away from him.

"Nathan, no, don't, please stop. You're frightening me, no—"

The house shook as he pulled her to him, spun her around, slammed her facedown onto the bed, one hand holding the back of her neck, pressing her face deep into the mattress, the other pulling her legs apart. A scream died in her throat, lost in the thick blankets. She kicked at him, but he only pushed her face down harder into the bed, so hard she couldn't breathe. She went limp. The hand on the back of her neck tangled itself in her hair, yanking her head backward, one startled gasp as his other hand reached around her hips, his fingers reaching down, slipping roughly inside her again, and then he drove into her, his slick chest crushing her back, releasing her hair to spread her arms, pinning them under his own, crucifying her, each thrust coupled with mumbled words she could not understand in her ear, his saliva running down the side of her neck, finally his seed hot inside her.

Another brief eternity, time stopping, her mind reaching out for reason, her body paralyzed in ecstasy and fear, want and revulsion, her silence now mirroring his own, a scorching mix of shame and desire, need and disgust, rapture and pain.

But it was not her voice that broke the spell this time, it was his own, the strange slurring incantation replaced by pitiful whimpers as he slid off her. Georgia rolled, amazed she could, her body a landscape of bruises and scratches, and saw Nathan stagger to his feet, backing away from the bed, the earth and blood on his body drying before her eyes as he wept, eyes unfocused, hands trembling, held out not for her but as if to push her away.

"No . . . no . . . oh God, no . . . please no . . . don't . . ."

"Nathan, look at me," she whispered. "Nathan?"

Another step back, his feet sliding in the scattering of dry earth on the floor. He fell with a crash against the wall, slid down it and slumped there, senseless.

"Nathan!" She fell from the bed to the floor after him, the earth and blood on her body tight and crusted, falling from her like dust as she moved, her body rejecting it like a poisoned shroud.

His eyes were closed, but his lips were a flurry of whispers.

"No . . . no . . . Georgia, please . . . oh my god, no . . . someone's here . . . someone else . . . no . . ."

Georgia ran her hands over his chest, his face, all the while whispering his name, an incantation to bring him back to himself, back to her. Georgia searched for any wounds and found none. Just a wash of dried, earth-smeared runes that twisted and vanished before her incredulous eyes could decipher them.

And then his eyes opened, the angry man, the weeping child gone. In their place once more was her Nathan, blinking, as if waking from a deep sleep.

"Georgia?' he whispered. His eyes wavered, rolling in his head for one sickening moment only to refocus.

"Nathan?"

"Georgia?" His sleepy voice climbed now into a hysterical octave, his hands reaching for purchase on the wall, rising to his feet, unsteady, pulling her up to him, his fingers shaking, trailing over her swollen face, her dusty body. Georgia looked down from his bewildered face, searching for the bruises, for the scratches she knew should be there and found none. Another fall of dust and she saw they both stood unmarked, naked, the floor around them littered with musty earth. No blood, no mud, no wounds, the only reminder of what had transpired the sting between her legs, the throbbing where he'd wrenched her hair out.

"Georgia?" His head swiveled, wide eyes taking in the dusty bed, her shredded clothing scattered across the deep impression they'd made in the mattress.

He reached for her face, his hands wiping the tears that tracked there.

"Georgia, who hurt you? Who . . . what did I do? Did I do this? Did . . . I don't . . ."

"Nathan?" Her voice trembled.

"Georgia, I don't understand," he whispered, his words thick, choked, tears streaming down his own face. "What did I do? Who hurt you? What have I done?"

"I don't . . . I don't know what you've done."

Uncertain if she was more frightened of him or for him, Georgia led Nathan to the bed and pulled him down with her. He followed, meek as a lamb. Wrapping her arms around his trembling body, she kissed his forehead, smoothed his hair, and held him until he stopped weeping, until his body stopped trembling and his breath was steady, even if her own was not. She pulled the blankets up over them, shushing him, tucking him in like a child, a litany of reassurances and gentle caresses as she tried to erase the memory of what had just happened in this very bed, moments, hours, ages ago, *didn't happen, didn't happen* until she drove it entirely from her mind, locked it up and threw away the key. Her lips found his, soft and sweet, even as he tumbled back into a deep sleep.

"Hurt you . . ." she barely caught the mumbled words as they fell from his lips.

"No one hurt me, Nathan. No one. You could never hurt me. Ever." Her lips fluttered against his ear, repeating the lie until her eyes fell shut and a heavy darkness engulfed her.

FIFTEEN

A COARSE CLOUD FILLED THE AIR AS GEORgia shifted in the sheets the next morning; a film of dry earth clung to her skin. The bed next to her was empty, the hollow he'd slept in already cool.

What have I done?

Throwing the sheet off, she tumbled from the bed, fell to one knee, her hand landing in a patch of dry earth on the floor, the print from Nathan's boots a distinct reminder of . . .

Please,

Don't,

Stop.

Swallowing the bile that climbed in her throat, she rose, stumbling once more, and then steadying herself, one hand on the headboard—

Hurt you

—threw her shoulders back, squared her jaw, and tiptoed around each patch of earth—

Chin up, don't look down.

—circling the bed in a hopscotch pattern—

step on a crack, break your mother's back,

—letting out her tightly held breath when her feet touched the cold tile of the bathroom floor, her weak hold on her churning stomach slipping. She wretched into the sink until her throat was raw, then stretched out across the cool surface until the urge to vomit subsided. A fumbling search under the counter and she crawled back to their bedroom, a small broom clenched in one scrambling hand, a dustpan in the other, and began sweeping up each crumb of earth. As she worked, she forced herself to sing, a long-forgotten nursery song,

> *Early one morning,*
> *Just as the sun was rising,*

to drive away the memories of the night before and hold her sickened stomach at bay until every last bit had been collected. Then, flinging the sash up, she cast every last measure of earth out the window and let the racing winds scatter it into nothing.

It had been mud, slick and sharp, rivulets snaking through it, crimson and black,

a twisting, shifting rune coiling around him,

painting her

Hurt you

"No," she whispered. "No."

Then she stripped the filthy bed, bundled up the sheets, the scattered, shredded clothing, and sang to herself as she did.

I heard a young maid sing,
In the valley below

She tied them into a tight parcel and hurried downstairs, her song climbing in both volume and octave as she descended.

Oh, don't deceive me
Oh, never leave me

Through the back hall she rushed, her feet slipping in a bit of earth near the basement door, and then stumbled out the back door. Her song faltered as she jammed the bundle into the trash bin, slamming the lid on it, and then fell to her knees in the gravel drive, the mourning dove chorus now accompanying her.

How could you use,
A poor maiden so?

Crawling, the gravel biting into the soft flesh of her palms, digging into her knees, she reached the back porch, used the rail to pull herself to her feet. She wiped her face, felt the salt there sting the myriad cuts that now hatched her hands. When she reached the back door, she hesitated, felt the basement door looming beyond in the darkness. Before she knew it, she was climbing the stairs back up to the bedroom.

He was tired. That was all. He was overwrought, that was it, consumed with worry. About the house, work, money, her, her, her. It was always back to her and everything he did, had to do to protect her, no wonder he'd

He'd . . .

He'd . . .

Didn't happen, didn't happen.

She stopped on the landing, swaying, imagined she saw the listing greenhouse sway in time with her as the winds raced gleefully through its splintered arms—

> *Early one morning,*
> *Just as the sun was rising.*

The song fell from her lips as fresh tears tracked down her face, landed on her breasts. She looked down, frightened she'd see those marks, the mud, the blood, the way his hands had—

Chin up. Don't look down. Don't. Just like before. That's how we get through this.

It hadn't really been like that. She was remembering wrong. He'd just been a little rough, that was all. Surely all men were, some time or another. And he'd been in the hot sun . . . yes, that was it, her explanation haphazardly arranging itself. He was not himself . . . he couldn't have been . . . and the way he'd sobbed . . . the way he'd shaken in her arms, weeping. Nathan weeping . . .

Oh, God, who hurt you. Hurt you . . .

His hand tangling in her hair, pulling her back, that voice in her ear as he

> *Remember the vows that,*
> *You made to me truly.*

No. It hadn't happened like that at all. She'd imagined it, dreamed it, a nightmare tinged with just enough reality to make her believe, make her doubt. She was slipping back into that dark place again—

We mustn't go in the dark places, Georgia, ever

—imagining things, frightening dreams shaded with gruesome memories, shadowy memories best left dead and buried, bitter heartbreaks that cut the heart and joy from you,

Not like me

murdered you over and over again forever like a persistent dagger.

I'm not like anyone

She would drive him away with this . . . this . . . this

Not anymore

Georgia barely made it to the sink in time, as wave after wave of a strangely familiar heaving gripped her. She fell into the shower now, her hands spinning the daisy wheel until scalding hot water fell over her, washing the grit and the strands of vomit away with it. Scrubbing her hair over and over, fingers gently probing the bare spot at the nape of her neck where he'd . . .

Remember how tenderly,
You nestled close to me.

He didn't hurt you, not really, she thought, closing her eyes to the pink stain in the water, ignoring the light trickle from between her legs. Curling up into a ball in the heavily marbled tub, she let the water wash her clean.

Nathan, you're hurting me.

No, he *hadn't*. He was just a little . . . and . . . and . . . the way he'd . . . she hadn't seen him weep like that since . . . since . . .

She laid there until the water ran cold and her pale skin was wrinkled and clammy, and then she climbed, shivering, out of the bath and dressed. She remade the bed with fresh sheets, opened all the windows, let the racing winds scour the room clean of any trace of the day before, nodding to herself and humming the tune as she did, reorganizing the tale in her mind until it was something else entirely.

There. All better. Like it had never happened. No, it never did. Nothing happened. I'm better, so much better. And he is, too. We are fine. We are going to be fine. But I think it's best . . . best to wait. Not tell him about Edie. Not until he . . . he's himself again. Until he stops acting so peculiarly. Swallowing hard, she startled when she realized she'd chosen the same word Edie had. *Peculiar. He sounds peculiar to me. He reminds me of someone.*

Furiously, she wiped the stains from her eyes. *No. Stop it, Georgia. You can't fall apart again. Not now. Not when she needs you. Not when Nathan is so . . .*

Peculiar. She turned the word over and over in her head and then discarded it. A child's word, an innocent label for something they couldn't understand. Something darker and more complicated. For something . . .

She turned and forced herself to face the bed. Forced herself to remember the nest she herself had built there, the way she'd hid from him for all those weeks, pushed him away, left him alone in his own grief while she wallowed luxuriously in hers. *Selfish.* She closed her eyes and took one last peek behind the haphazard fortress she'd constructed last night, on that very same bed. *Look what I drove him to.* She opened her eyes and looked around at the enormous house he'd bought her, *her*, an expense that was breaking him, just for *her*. Just to heal *her*. *All while I pushed him away. Neither of us is quite ourselves. Like Edie. Not anymore.* Plastering a smile on her tear-streaked face, she resumed singing and left their bed behind her as she climbed the attic stairs—

Early one morning,

Just as the sun was rising

—pushed the attic door open. She felt Edie throw her arms around her waist, tangle their hands tight, let her spin them both in a clumsy reel around the attic.

"Is that a new nursery rhyme, Georgia? I don't know that one." She paused and Georgia looked down and saw a flicker of worry on the young girl's face.

"What's the matter, Georgia? You look so . . . is something wrong downstairs?" Her voice trembled and a fine cloud of ash fell around her, dusting them both.

Georgia's vision blurred. She squeezed her eyes tight, ran a hand over them, wiped away the dampness there along with the ash, and forced herself to forget everything that existed below the sanctuary of the attic. She let the child's spell surround her and bind her in its intoxicating enchantment, a dream become reality. She opened her eyes and looked down into Edie's unsettled face, found the strength to voice the words to calm the little girl.

"No, not at all. Everything's just fine, Edie. Don't you look pretty today!" Edie beamed and the ash cloud vanished in a soft, shimmering wash. "Would you like me to teach it to you?" Edie laughed and twirled.

"Yes, please, teach me! Teach me everything!"

Georgia swallowed the lump in her throat and forced a laugh for Edie's benefit, finding that after a moment her mirth became genuine. *Impossible not to be happy here. With her. Nothing can touch this happiness. I won't let it.*

"It goes like this," she said, grasping Edie's hands in hers again. "Ready?"

It took Edie only minutes to learn the words to the old song. After another hour of steady practice, she could sing it in three clear octaves, her soprano voice rising higher with each verse. Sinking wearily to the floor, exhausted from the young girl's relentless enthusiasm, Georgia watched Edie dance and sing for yet another hour. Each minute that ticked by in the attic erased the world outside, drew a thick veil over the previous day, more resilient than the one she'd created in her mind that morning. *I have to protect her. Protect this*, she thought, looking around at the small nursery she'd created. *And I have to find a way to make things easier for him, to heal him. I've been selfish for far too long. He needs something. Something more*, she would tell him. *But not just yet. Not now. Not after . . ..* She shook her head and rose to join Edie's dance. It could wait. *Nothing matters*, Georgia thought, as she and Edie twirled around the room. *Nothing matters but this magic. My magic. My sweet little girl.*

SIXTEEN

 GEORGIA WATCHED FOR NATHAN'S TRUCK that evening from the staircase window. He was late, nothing unusual about that, but after, and the way he'd left so early—

Early one morning,
Just as the sun

—without waking her, without any attempt to explain. After.

I heard,
I heard a
young maid

She shook the thought from her head. *No. He'd never hurt me. Ever. It wasn't like that. Didn't happen like that.*

The gleam from his headlights startled her, her careful retelling of what had happened—*didn't happen*—in the bedroom that night a precarious scaffolding which threatened to collapse under its own weight. She ran to meet him, reaching the door of his truck before he'd even slipped the transmission into park.

"Hey," he said, his voice soft and low, pulling her gently to him. Relieved, Georgia let him wrap her in his arms, buried her face in his shoulder. The breath she'd been holding escaped gratefully when she felt his lips land on her temple.

"Georgia." He hugged her tighter. "About yesterday. I . . ."

Georgia took a step back and shook her head, a small gesture.

"No," she whispered, spying the clutch of wildflowers on the seat behind him in the truck. "Got a date?" her voice trembled, fell flat, her smile a crooked mimicry, causing the anxious frown on Nathan's face to deepen.

He reached behind him and handed them to her.

"Yeah. With my sweetheart." A pause in which she prayed he wouldn't continue, but he did. "Georgia, I'm so sorry, I don't know what happened . . . Why I . . ." he broke off, eyes squeezed shut. "I don't know what came over me. I don't remember . . . but it's all . . ."

"Nate, please don't. Don't ask me to . . . I don't want to talk about it. Let's not. Please."

His eyes flashed open. "It's not like me, Georgia, I swear to God. I would never hurt you, ever."

"Nate, please, *don't*. I . . . I can't . . ." she whispered, eyes moistening. "It's fine. I'm fine. You're just tired, that's all. Under so much pressure, and I only ever make it worse and . . ."

Nathan pulled her back to him, crushing the flowers between them as he did.

"You do not make things worse. You make everything in my life better. And I don't want *that*. That won't ever happen again."

Georgia nodded against his chest, counting a dozen beats of his heart before letting it out, drawing in a shuddering breath scented with crushed flowers, letting her body fall against his, part trust, part resignation.

"Did I hurt you, Georgia?" he whispered into her hair. "Tell me the truth."

She shook her head and, looking up into his shame-filled face, lied to him.

"No, Nate. You didn't hurt me at all. It wasn't like that."

"Yes, I did." His lips were an unrelenting line, thunderclouds had settled in his eyes, a furious self-directed rebuke she knew well. "I've got to get my head straight. Everything's all . . . I just haven't been myself lately but that's no excuse and I don't—"

"No, Nate, I'm fine. Really. I'm just so very tired and I can't . . . Please just drop it."

Whether he registered the lie or accepted the truth, she could not tell. He let the moment pass, his forced smile a more brittle facade than her own. He did not speak. Instead, he carried her back into the house in that china doll embrace, kissing her neck, her face, and finally her lips, each kiss a silent plea for forgiveness, for reconciliation. He found it, as ever, in her eyes.

✦   ✦   ✦

Georgia lay on her back, one hand sprawled across his chest, her fingers curled. Her apartment was dark except for the path the rising moon charted.

Nathan watched her, captured a long strand of her black hair and began winding it around his wrist.

"Georgia?"

"Shh . . ."

"Georgia . . ."

She popped one eye open. "I said, 'shh'," and closed it again, her brow wrinkled in concentration.

His soft laugh made the corners of her mouth curl up. He released the long strand of hair and watched it slide off of his wrist. Then, grabbing another curl, he began tickling the end of her nose with it.

She batted his hand away.

"Stop it. I'm busy," she whispered.

"Georgia, I just . . . wait. Busy doing what?"

She fixed him with those luminous gray eyes. "I was reorganizing things. Shifting furniture. I have to make room."

"Room for what? Where?"

"Room for you. For this. I've reorganized things up here," she tapped her forehead, "and given you a cozy corner on the first floor."

"First floor, huh?" He resumed playing with her hair.

"Oh, yes, you're very lucky. I don't often clear things out for guests."

"Is that what I am? A guest?" His hand slid down her cheek, across to her chin, finally to her neck. He rested his thumb on the soft indent of her collarbone, white like a shell in the dark, the scattering of freckles like sand.

"Well, I've given you an entire corner of the greenhouse." Her eyes were closed, her lashes and freckles like diminutive exclamation points. "Oh, you'll love it there. It's always warm, even on a cloudy day, I promise. The air is like perfume from all my flowers and I made sure you have a comfortable chair for naps."

He tapped her gently between her closed eyes. "There's a greenhouse in there?"

She nodded. "It's attached to the living room. But there's no room for you there. Anyway, you wouldn't like it."

"So I don't want to be in Georgia's living room?"

She opened her eyes. "No, that's not prime real estate. That's where all the dull things are. But if you're lucky, I'll move you upstairs one day."

"Could I have my own room?"

She considered, her eyes reflecting the moonlight like lighthouses.

"I can't say. I'm not sure what kind of tenant you are yet. Let's see how you do in the greenhouse. Now, what was so important?"

He had wanted to tell her she was beautiful. He wanted to explain that he had to get up early for work, wanted to ask her when he could see her again, more than anything he wanted to find some magical combination of words to catch this elusive creature, bind her to him with some clever alchemy to fix her, this, them as it was and keep her from vanishing in the morning.

Instead he pulled her on top of him and whispered into her ear, "Nothing has ever been more important than my corner in your greenhouse."

SEVENTEEN

GEORGIA STARED UP AT THE CEILING AS NA-than's voice crackled over the phone line in a rambling stream of explanations. She imagined him pacing back and forth in some foreign hotel room, ticking off the details of the project in San Francisco with a familiar mixture of disgust and delight.

"It's a *wreck*. I mean, forget the fact that the entire thing is boarded up, not a window or door to be seen. How something so shitty is sitting smack dab in the middle of some of the most expensive real estate in the world is beyond me. Jesus, it's got the whole playlist: listing chimneys, rolling ceilings, sloping floors. The basement is worse than ours, if you can believe it. Bricked up fireplaces, cemented-over dumbwaiters, and a partridge in a pear tree. It would be easier to tear the whole thing down and build a new one than to restore this firetrap. The owners didn't even lower themselves to let me in on my own; they sent some lackey to show me the house. Supposed to meet them tomorrow. Richard and Catherine York. Bet that'll be a party. And the timing is terrible. I mean, first of all our house—which is a close second, disaster-wise."

Georgia heard a thump and surmised Nathan had thrown himself down on the bed. She smiled. She hadn't heard him like this in ages—passionate and enthusiastic.

"And I'm still waiting to hear if I got that job in the Heights. I mean, if I got that, the money would almost float us till spring, at least with bills and stuff. We'd have to live like squatters in Roseneath indefinitely. And even if I was dumb enough to take this shit show on, I'd have to cancel everything. Leave you there alone for almost a year. And who knows how often I could come back home. Never mind the fact that I have no clue if I can actually pull this shit off. Might as well just get on a plane in the morning and come home. This whole trip was stupid. But, Jesus, Georgie—1881, San Francisco. Think of it. I mean . . ."

"Nathan, listen. I . . ." *It was so simple. This. Almost too good to be true.*

"I know, I know. I'm not going to take it. It's not worth it. Unless . . ."

"Unless what?" He was on his feet, pacing again, the disgust vanishing under a surge of delight, same as always when it came to her husband and his obsessive love for his work.

"Unless we close up the house there and you come with me. Think about it, Georgia. We could do it. Just put off everything with Roseneath. The damn thing has been sitting for years, what's one more? We get a little studio apartment across the bridge, something dirt cheap, take daytrips every weekend. It'll be like a year-long honeymoon, except at the end we walk away with more than enough money to finish Roseneath. Hell, I might be able to start my own company, hire some full-time employees. Pritchard Construction. How do you like the sound of that?"

Her face lit up, liking not so much the description of the job, but how excited he sounded, a delightful, exhilarating thing that had once come so easy to him, a sound she had not heard for far too long. This was it, almost as if the universe had reached down and set it in front of them both, the answer to everything wrapped up in a big bow. He needed more. More than here, more even than her, and certainly more than what they had become. And this gift, this opportunity, was sparking the life back into him, was shocking him out of the cautious life they had fallen into after the events of the past year.

"Nathan, I think—"

"And it would be good for you. Get away from everything there. The last few months have been so hard. After the baby and . . . And I could use your help, all these details, the research. You're way better at it than I ever was. We do this together. You and me. What do you say?"

"Well, I would say all sorts of things if you'd let me get a word in." A beat and she could imagine him running his hands through his hair and giving her a self-effacing look. She wondered if he was imagining the look of patient exasperation on hers.

"Sorry. I'll shut up. Tell me what you're thinking."

Georgia stared at the cracked plaster ceiling over their bed, wondering now if he was lying again on the hotel bed. She reached one hand out as if she could pull him toward her, across all that space. Her fist clutched empty sheets. Overhead, soft footfalls made their way from one side of the attic to the other. A clatter on the floor. Edie. What was she doing? She smiled, picturing the cozy nest she and Edie were building with the items she'd taken upstairs. Crayons and pillows, music and light. Boxes and boxes of books, nearly every last one in the house. Today, she'd taken up an enormous box of snapshots, pictures of her and Nathan. She and Edie had spent hours pawing through them, then tacked dozens of them up on the walls. Snapshots of their lives, brightly colored glimpses of the world outside and, Georgia had thought, lingering over one candid shot, how they both used to be. Edie had traced the lines of their faces over and over with her elegant, long fingered hands, her luminous eyes wondering and soft. Edie needed her. And he . . . he needed this. And with a moment of wild delight, she realized she could give them both exactly what they needed.

"Georgia? Are you there?"

She sat up and began picking at the little cotton nubs on the old comforter, assembling an argument in her head that he would agree with, a truth he would want to believe. And if it felt like taking advantage, what of it? If they both got what they wanted, who would it hurt? She could give Edie the attention she so needed. And Nate wanted this. Needed it, even. A break in the clouds of juggling half a dozen small, miserly Midwestern jobs. A high-profile, well-paying job that might, just might, lead him to everything he wanted professionally. Hardly a sacrifice at all, for either of them.

"I think . . . I think you should do it. I want you to do it. This job is more than we could have ever wished for. It's almost too good to be true. Not just the money, but the work. I can't imagine how excited you are."

"Georgia, it's everything. It has everything. After this, I can do anything. It's a big gamble, but—"

"You don't have to sell me on it, Nathan. Do it. And everything else will just sort itself out."

"And you'll come out here? Come keep me on track and yell at me when I confuse Deco with Nouveau? Make sure I don't wander around covered in sawdust, looking for my glasses?"

Georgia squashed a pang of doubt before replying. "No." She continued in a rush, cutting him off before he could argue. "Now, hear me out. We can take turns. You fly home, I fly out there, enough that it won't be that bad. We'll see each other all the time and talk every day. I know how you are when you're working. If I were there, I wouldn't see you much anyway. Those weekend trips wouldn't happen until you were almost done, and I'd be bored."

"Bored?" he sputtered. "In San Francisco? How is that even possible?"

"Nate, It's not that I don't want to be with you. It's just that I just started *this* project. Here. And you have no idea how much Roseneath means to me. I'm better here, I feel like . . . this place is *miraculous*, Nate, and I can't bear to leave it. Not right now. If I stay here, we can work on the house a little bit at a time, if they pay you enough. Just think, Roseneath might even be finished when you get home. And we can reset the clock on everything. And, who knows—by then," a glance through the bathroom to the closed door of the adjoining room, "by then there might be three of us." A sound on the other end of the line and she imagined him smiling. She glanced up to the ceiling again, a smile now lifting her lips. *We all get what we want. It's perfect.*

"I don't like it," he was saying, his tone tempted but wavering. "I don't like you alone. No job is worth that. I can't leave you alone, especially if . . . it's too soon, not after everything that happened last time. I'll meet with the owners tomorrow to see what they say, but I'm still thinking I should walk away from this one. Something else will come up."

"Damn it all, Nathan Pritchard, stop treating me like I'm made of glass," she snapped. His protests cut off into stunned silence on the other end. She continued, less forcefully, "I'm not as fragile as you like to think I am, Nate. I know what you've given up for me . . . I know how many opportunities you lost these last few months taking care of me, and I know how little money has been coming in, on top of this new house, and I don't want you to lose another—"

Nathan cut her off. "I'm not losing shit, Georgia. I wanted to be there for you. For us. I didn't give a rat's ass about any of those jobs. Or this one. Don't you get it? *I* couldn't be away from *you*, honey. What happened to our baby girl, it killed me, too. I *needed* to be with you. Even . . . even with the way things were. How you were. I still needed to be with you, no matter how you—" His voice cut off.

The bitterness of his words, the hurt that threaded through them felt like a smack in the face.

"Nate, I didn't mean it like that. I didn't mean to make you feel like I . . . I'm sorry. For everything. For how far I pushed you. How much I took from you." A sharp inhale on the other end of the line but she cut him off, pushed on, and resumed her argument before he could protest. "But everything is so much better now. We're getting past all of this and I want this dream for you. And I want you to let me try to stand on my own two feet again. I told you I'm working again." She thought fast, manufacturing something he'd want to believe, a perfect little white lie that wouldn't hurt a soul. "I . . . I didn't want to say too much before, but I found some papers, here in Roseneath. And a house this age, there's bound to be more downtown at the historical society. I think I have a great idea for a project. Maybe something I can publish, use my fancy education finally. And if I'm busy with that and with the house, Nate, the time will fly. Let me give you this gift, like you gave me this house. After everything you've given me, given up for me, let me do this for you. Let me take care of things here while you chase your dream there. Nothing would make me happier. It's just one year, honey. We have time. All the time in the world."

She lay back on the bed, elated with how easy it had been to lie to him, and listened to him tell her they'd talk about it when he flew home, but she knew they'd both already decided. He'd spend the next year on the West Coast, rebuilding his dream house. And she'd stay here, dreaming her own dreams. With Edie.

EIGHTEEN

NATHAN SANK WEARILY ON THE STAIRCASE of the boarded-up house, covered in soot, cobwebs, and plaster dust, his notes spread out around him, listening to the dense silence all around. Having arrived hours before his meeting with the owners to make a more detailed inspection of the house, he was now able to add significant rot, a buckling south wall, and a complete roof tear-off to the enormous list of work that needed to be done. He closed his eyes and imagined what the mansion would look like when it was built, imagined the smell of fresh lumber, wet plaster, varnish, and polish. He imagined the carved, curling vines in the wooden newel post spreading up the staircase, curling around the gleaming wood bannister so intricate that one could almost imagine it had grown there.

He imagined Georgia coming down those finished stairs, her heels clicking on the shining new treads, face lit up at the sheer enormity of what he'd restored. He could do it. The owners would be happy, he'd see to that, but he wanted to bring Georgia here, show her what he could do. Make her proud of him. And watch those starry eyes light up. He was addicted to those eyes, the way they made him feel that he was the whole world, that he could do anything. He dropped his head into his hands and wondered what she was doing right now.

She belonged in a place like Roseneath, an enormous, rambling old fairy tale that would never quite be done, never quite be perfect. And Georgia, being Georgia, would love it for exactly that reason. She would despair and delight over the state of their unique home, as the handful of children he still hoped for wore down treads and broke windows, their toys slowly filling Roseneath to bursting. And then, one by one, their children would fly the shabby nest and leave the two of them waiting patiently for it to fill again with the ringing laughter of grandchildren. He'd known it the first time he'd laid eyes on the property, like he'd found a tower for his lady. Everything he could ever hope to give her, after everything they had lost, like fate had stopped fucking with his life and cut him some slack. And the way she was already so fiercely protective of it, so unwilling to leave it, made him certain that she was finding her own way out of the nightmare of the last year. She just needed time. And just knowing there was a light at the end of this tunnel gave him the resolve to juggle as much as he needed to. Whatever it took to get them back on track.

The rattle of the door handle jarred him from his daydream. For one wild moment, he thought he'd conjured her, Georgia. That she was about to walk through the door and spend the rest of the day dreaming with him, like old times. Just the two of them.

The door flew open. Silhouetted there was a tall figure, its long hair whipping to one side in the wind. As the figure stepped out of the sun and into the dim light inside, Nathan's mouth went dry.

How did I conjure her, when I wanted Georgia?

Nathan scrambled to his feet even as the woman slammed the door behind her. His boot slipped on one of his legal pads and he caught himself on the newel post.

"Hello, Nate. Long time no see."

It couldn't be. Impossible. Her? Here?

"Cat? What are you doing here?" His voice broke, cracked like an adolescent. *I must be hallucinating.*

But no matter how hard he tried to imagine a scenario where it wasn't her, tried to convince himself he was seeing things, some sort of waking nightmare, it was unmistakable. Cat, as ever, was nothing less than unmistakable. Older, more polished, but undeniably Cat. The woman who had blown into his life one autumn day in college, all legs, confidence and biting wit, crooked her manicured finger and kept him on an exquisitely painful, short leash for three ultimately humiliating years.

"Jesus, Nate, relax," she laughed. "Surprise! What do you think of my house?"

Nathan's mouth fell open; a flush born of shock and adrenaline wiped any trace of professional cool from his expression. Across the dismal foyer, Cat folded her sunglasses and dropped them into a black alligator bag. She fixed Nathan with a smile he remembered well. Confident. Mischievous. Controlling.

Nathan's dream of Georgia descending the stairs vanished. He tried to wipe the shock from his face, replacing it with something approaching his usual confidence, the sweat on his temple ruining the illusion.

"Is this some kind of sick joke?" he demanded, trying to keep his voice from slipping back into that teenaged pitch. *What the fuck is she up to? All this time, it was her on the other end pulling the strings. Just like old times.* He stuffed his papers back in his bag, his initial shock now buried under a flood of resentment. *Fucking manipulative bitch.* He zipped his bag shut and summoned the uncompromising look he'd cultivated over the years that made contractors hustle and workers scatter. He stood defiantly, as if blocking her way back into his life. Across the room, Cat blanched.

"Joke? Oh God, no, no, no. You've got this all wrong, Nate. Shit." She took a step back, heels catching on the rutted parquet floor. "You're mad. Damn it, I thought you'd think it was funny. You know." She threw him a beguiling smile, even as she nervously twisted the enormous ring on her hand, an old affectation he knew meant nothing outside of getting her own way.

"No, I don't. Have a nice day, Cat. I'd say it was nice to see you again, but . . ." He moved to push past her to the door.

Cat stopped just short of grabbing his arm and hurried to block his way to the door.

"Please wait. Hear me out, Nate."

Nathan took a deep breath. "Fine. You've got two minutes."

Cat smiled. "Come on, Pritchard. Look at this place. My husband and I have been buying property up and down the West Coast for the last five years, but nothing even remotely like this. You don't need me to tell you what a gem this one is. Richard and I—"

Nathan turned her words over in his head.

"So this Richard York is your husband?"

"Yes, of course. Five years now. After you and I . . ." Across the room, Nathan's face darkened. "Well, anyway my dad thought it best that I get a fresh start. Sent me out west to work for a colleague." She shrugged. "You know me, next thing I know I caught the eye of one of the best and brightest." Her eyebrow rose, coy. "I seem to have a knack for that. Anyway, this time things worked out. Real estate investor, you know the type."

"All too well." He took a step back and crossed his arms over his chest. "Okay, let's cut the horseshit. Despite how unambitious you always considered me to be, I'm a busy man and I don't appreciate being jerked around. Why am I here, Cat? I'm sure it's not for old time's sake."

"Well, you're half wrong about that—"

"For fuck's sake, Cat, I am not—"

"No," she held one hand up to stop him. "Not like that. Listen, I know this sounds crazy but," she fiddled nervously with one long hank of hair. "I bought this house last year, against Richard's better judgment. And he was right; no one out here will touch it. Not for all the money in his very deep pockets. The property has a bit of a reputation I was unaware of. Anyway, I was considering just writing the whole project off. But then—"

"But then you thought, 'Hey, I remember a sucker from Ohio. I'll see if he's dumb enough—'"

"No," she corrected him. "Not at all. That's where you've got me all wrong. Last time I was home, my dad mentioned you. He sold his firm—you know, the one you refused to work for?"

Nathan ground his teeth together and nodded, remembering the particular way she'd tried to handle him.

"Yeah, I heard."

"He still keeps his fingers in the game, dabbles a bit in the construction scene. He told me you'd made a name for yourself in the restoration world. Drove me past that house you did in Bratenahl. Stunning, Nate. Didn't know you had it in you."

Instead of rising to her bait, Nathan just stared at her in silence.

"Jesus, Nate, will you stop looking at me like that and listen?"

"I am listening. Thirty seconds."

"So I did a little research of my own. Saw some of the other houses you've done, talked to a few people. And I knew it was perfect. You. This house."

Nathan shook his head and started back to the door.

"Yeah, thanks but no thanks."

"Please, Nate, listen," she insisted. "I know this is—" she broke off and bit her lip. "And you don't owe me a thing. I know that. But maybe I owe you."

"No. You don't. There is nothing between us. I can't believe you would—"

"Nate," she said, shaking her head, her voice suddenly gentle, apologetic. Against his better judgment, he felt his shoulders drop, his eyes soften as he peered into her contrite eyes, wondering if maybe, miraculously, this older Cat was being sincere. "I behaved badly all those years ago. To you. The things I said, the things I did. I was a horrible bitch. I can admit that now."

"That's the first thing you've said that I completely agree with."

She laughed and Nathan found himself utterly thrown. The old Cat would not have found that amusing. The old Cat might have smacked him. The woman standing in front of him, here, now, was not only more polished, but more poised. He uncrossed his arms and ran a hand over his head, then sighed, a reluctant grin lingering on his face.

"Fine. Go on."

"Nate, I know how tough times are back in the Belt. My dad sold up years ago but a lot of his friends got pinched when the housing bubble burst." She gave him a knowing look. "I am painfully aware how long these troughs can last and I thought we could do each other a favor. That's all. Nothing more."

"A favor," he repeated, intrigue winning out over suspicion.

"Yeah. You dig my ass out of this money pit I bought so Richard doesn't—" she shook her head, her blonde locks tumbling around her shoulders before one manicured hand swept them back. "Well, let's just say he's not happy. An unhappy Richard is not pleasant."

Nathan jammed his hands in his pockets. "That's not my problem."

"No, of course not, but *my* problem, as you put it, puts *me* in a position to give *you* the chance of a lifetime. You can do this, Nate, I can feel it. You can flip this sad old bitch and make a name for yourself out here. Not just California, Nate, *everywhere*. The cover of *Architectural Digest*. You. Here. This is the one, Nate. You're doing me a favor but you'd be doing yourself an even bigger one."

Nathan studied the newel post and beyond it the sagging staircase, the crumbling walls. He imagined them finished, the entirety of this abandoned monolith resurrected, reanimated. He knew he could do it. Knew that his hunger and his drive would push him to succeed where others would not tread.

"Why won't anyone out here touch this firetrap?"

Cat glared at the ceiling. "Two reasons come to mind. Some mumbo jumbo about it being haunted." She wrinkled her nose in disgust. "Some urban legend crap about boogey men and ghosts. But I don't believe in any of that shit and neither do you."

Where have I heard that before? The sudden jolt of déjà vu was disorienting. The room swam before his eyes as bits of a forgotten conversation slithered in his ears.

Locals think it's full of boogey men and ghosts.

I don't believe in any of that shit.

Nathan ran his hands down the gooseflesh that sprang up at the sound of his own voice echoing in his head, and tried to refocus. "And two?"

"I have a bit of a reputation." She was studying her nails now, cheeks flushed as she bit back a smile.

"Let me guess—difficult to work with."

Cat looked up from her nails and winked at him.

"Creative control?" he asked.

Cat snorted. "It's still my house. I've softened over the years, Nate, but I'm not a pushover. I know exactly what I want you to do to this house and I won't settle for less than that. Got it?"

A shared grin.

"Fair enough. Pay?"

"One-fifty, if you can do it in twelve months."

Nathan shook his head, struggled not to let his jaw drop at the sum.

"Too bad you just tipped your hand, Mrs. York. I understand no one else wants to take on this shit show. Two hundred and I'll do it in ten."

Cat laughed.

"Tell you what, Pritchard. One seventy-five and I pay you to fly back and forth to see your drinking buddies or whatever you have back in Ohio."

He scratched the back of his neck. Something pricked there. Digging his fingernails in, he felt a flash of pain and then a small release. Nathan looked down at his hand and saw a smear of pink, and then it was gone.

"I don't know, Cat. I mean, you and I—" he started.

"Ancient history. And, anyway, you'll hardly see me. I actually have a life, Nate. I'm not too terribly interested in hanging out with a bunch of filthy contractors."

He frowned, studied the splinter in the palm of his left hand.

Think of it—the money. The opportunity. This house could be magnificent. She's right. This could be your ticket to everything. It's perfect, isn't it, Nathan? And after all this time, who cares that it's her?

Georgia would care. The splinter had dug in deep. He could almost pinch the edge of it with his fingernails. As he struggled to do so, he tried to imagine a scenario that ended with Georgia on board with the idea of him spending a year working for an ex-girlfriend two thousand miles away and failed.

Georgia doesn't ever have to know.

His eyes widened at the suggestion. Turned it around in his head as Cat waited, the toe of one heeled foot tapping impatiently. The splinter plunged deeper, out of reach. *What did I tell her?* He closed his eyes briefly and tried to recall. *Just their names. Richard and Catherine York. She'd never guess, never suspect, would she? As long as he . . .*

"How soon do you need an answer?" he heard himself say. *No. Those aren't the right words. That's not what I wanted to say, I—*

"Think about it," Cat said, bending to collect her bag. "Let's say twenty-four hours."

He found his voice again. Found the words he meant to say.

"What else is in this for you, Cat? You're never *not* up to something. I remember that much."

She grinned, a devious expression he remembered well. "Oh, me? Three things come to mind." She held up one finger. "I'll have the most sought-after house in San Francisco. I'll flip it and make Richard a fortune. Two, all those architects who wouldn't take my calls can eat shit knowing that I was the one that discovered Nathan Pritchard. And, three, I get to enjoy the spectacle of Richard's friends falling all over themselves to get a piece of you." He bristled at her possessive tone, but even as he did, the voice in his head cajoled him. *So what if she is the instrument of your success? It's still you. It's all yours. Right there for the taking. Take it.*

"It'll cost a fortune to fix this dump, Cat."

She laughed, as if she knew she had her answer.

"You let me worry about that. Let me know when you decide."

And in a blur she strode out the door, slamming it behind her. The light from the street blinded him temporarily and he slumped back onto the staircase, head in his hands. Time passed in the dark gloom, his phone startling him much later with a message from Georgia. He reached for it, wondering why his arms were so cramped, as if he'd sat motionless for hours. He looked at the time and saw that he had. *Must have fallen asleep. Jet lag or something.* He unlocked his phone and tried to read her words with bleary eyes, but every other letter seemed to slip out of place, her message jumbled into gibberish, nonsense words.

"Come to my arms, my beamish boy! O frabjous day! Callooh! Callay!" he chortled in his joy.

Shaking his head, he watched, confused, as the poem tumbled back into order.

I adore you. I miss you. I believe in you. Hope things are going well. Hurry home to me. Feeling a bit under the weather, going to take a nap. Call me later.

All the tension in his body evaporated and he could almost hear her soft voice whispering the brief message in his ears, burning away the confusion like the sun through fog. It was so like her to reach out to him, like an enchantress who felt his need for her even across this distance. He forgot the persistent pain that radiated from his hands up his arms, snaking across his chest, and replied immediately.

You make me feel like I can do anything. Always have. Love you. Get some sleep.

❖   ❖   ❖

Georgia weaved her way through the stacks, step stool in her hands. Just a peek. She still had a half hour to go on her shift, but Nathan always arrived early and she'd fallen into the habit of allowing herself one look out the window at him. Sometimes dozing in his truck, sometimes reading. Once, and this was her favorite stolen glimpse, pacing, as if he could hurry the clock and make her shift end faster. He'd said, a mysterious gleam in his eyes, that he had a very special evening planned for them. She hoped that whatever activity she caught him in would give her a clue as to what that meant. A specific hope had tucked itself away in her heart, and try as she might to shoo it away and replace it with something practical, it would not go away.

She set the stool down and climbed up, bracing herself on the thick mahogany frame of the triple pane window. She easily found his truck, even from her third-floor perch, but her attention shifted to two people arguing next to it. Nathan, his hair wild, his right hand chopping through the air as words flew back and forth between him and the tall, lanky vision in front of him. Like a silent film, she knew he was yelling, knew he'd lost his temper, a side of him she'd never seen before. That small, specific hope withered at the sight of this unfamiliar, volatile version of Nathan with Cat. Nathan had told her the bare facts of their relationship and breakup, but she'd heard the pain in his voice. Seeing that raw emotion pouring out of him like this was a different thing entirely. She'd thought he was hers, hers alone. But this, this other Nathan, he wasn't hers. The sobering realization that she was the outsider here, that she would never know this part of him, that someone else owned it, dashed all her hopes to the ground.

Cat reached out and grasped his arm. One elegant, long-fingered hand lit on him like an exotic bird and in the long moment that passed between them, Georgia lost her footing on the stool and tumbled down.

By the time she'd regained her composure and climbed back up, Cat was walking away. Georgia watched as Nathan punched the side of his truck. She imagined she could hear it, like a book slamming shut.

Georgia lingered in the library long after closing, hoping he would just leave. But he didn't. She watched as Nathan waited for her. Frowning. Pacing. Checking his watch. Finally she knew she could hide no longer. She hesitated in the darkness of the doorway; wanting this one last moment of pretending he was hers to last forever. But it was no use.

"Sorry I'm so late, Nate. Long day. I . . . I think I'll just go home tonight."

Don't cry. Just keep walking.

She tried to brush past him but he blocked her path.

"Georgia, wait. What's wrong?" The concern in his voice was a brutal, poignant caress. Georgia stared at the ground. Hearing it was bad enough, seeing it would undo her resolve. She sidestepped him.

"Nothing's wrong. I'm sorry, Nate. I just want to go home. Just leave me alone." He grabbed her arm, gently spun her around.

"Georgie, I don't understand. Talk to me. What did I do?" His voice broke and she looked up, a horrible mistake.

"Nate, don't." I am not going to cry.

"Don't what, Georgia?" Now that she'd looked at him, she couldn't look away. She'd thought he would look angry, like he had earlier. Instead he looked afraid, an expression she never thought she'd see on his face. "What exactly am I doing? Please don't do this. Please don't play games with me. Not tonight."

His tie was loose and she wanted nothing more than to tug it back into place, to smooth his rumpled hair, to run her hands across his chest one last time. I'm not going to cry.

"I'm not playing a game, Nate." She put some distance between them in case she lost her resolve and actually did any of those things. "But I won't do this." Her chest burned with the effort of not screaming. "It's cruel and I don't want to remember us like that. You could leave me that, at least."

"What the hell are you talking about, Georgia? You're not making any sense. Honey, please—"

"I saw, all right? Everything." It was no use. She was crying now. She dug in her coat for a tissue. "You and her and—"

"*Georgia, let me explain.*" *He tried to brush the tears from her face but she shoved him away.*

"*You don't need to, Nate.*" *She was shaking now, furious that he was making her say the words out loud.* "*I'm not stupid. Whatever that was with the two of you, there's still something there. Isn't there?*"

He flinched as if she'd struck him.

"*You think that's what I want? You think that little of me, Georgia?*"

"*Yes, Nate, that's exactly what I think.*" *She hated how vulnerable she sounded, wished she could have kept it all bottled up until she was home, alone.* "*How do you go from that*"—*she looked down at herself, gestured with disgust to her jumbled assortment of tag sale clothing, the overflowing bag of books and yarn spilling across the pavement. There was a hole in the top of her sneakers and the sight of the chipped varnish on her toe was more than she could bear*—"*to this. I'm a mess, Nate, and she's . . . she's everything I'm not.*" *She began furiously jamming her books back into her bag.* "*I don't want you to look back one day and think that you settled for this.*"

Nathan jerked her to her feet and sent the bag and its contents flying.

"*Georgia, goddamn it, look at me.*" *His grip on her arms was steel wrapped in velvet.* "*I didn't know what love was until I met you. I didn't know happiness like this even existed before you. I love you, Georgia Galloway, and even if you walk away from me tonight, it won't change that. I will love you till the day I die, and no one else will ever be enough.*"

The rawness of his confession shocked her from her flight of self-pity. What she'd seen, or imagined she had, seemed now little more than a tempest in a teacup compared to the weight of his words. She'd focused solely on her feelings for him and never guessed the depth of his for her. Every moment they'd spent together before this moment was little more than the tip of an iceberg, a mere fraction of the whole. His simple plea in the dark parking lot was an overwhelming glimpse at depths she'd never imagined.

He wrapped her in his arms, gentle now, as if by sheer force of his will he could keep her there. Georgia melted into him, tried to hold him as tight as he held her. He smelled like shaving cream and sunshine. She felt her feet leave the ground, the truck cold against her back. His mouth consumed her purposefully, worshipfully. She fumbled for the door handle and pulled him inside. He fell heavily on top of her and she wrapped her legs around him, the rhythm of his hips generating a current she gratefully drowned in.

"Georgia, I won't settle for anyone else than you."

NINETEEN

"ALL RIGHT, LET'S HEAR IT," GEORGIA'S VOICE chimed over the phone later that night. "How were the owners? What did they say?" Her innocent enthusiasm twisted in his gut like a knife, and for a second Nathan faltered. *I can't do this to her. I won't. What the fuck have I been thinking all day?* He tried to remember at what point he'd called Cat back and taken the job, knew they'd settled on a meeting the next day but could not recall anything specific. The day had comprised a series of confusing events that had slipped away before he could pin them down. However, one thing was certain— at some point he'd scanned and emailed a signed contract back to her. There was a copy of it on his nightstand, his broad scrawling signature at the bottom.

You're just trying to do what's best. There's no harm in that. And it's not a lie, not really. A lie of omission, not much of a sin at all. And of course she'd understand. This is how you give her everything she ever wanted, isn't it?

"I want to hear about your day first," Nathan replied, nodding. He studied the city skyline outside his hotel room. "Did the plasterer show up?"

"Yes, and he left his estimate. As did the mason." Her voice was so clear in his ear he glanced to the other side of the bed, pictured her lying there, picking at the duvet and telling him about her day. He blinked and the mirage vanished. Closing his eyes, he concentrated on her voice and let it drown out the sly, persistent one in his head. "If I had to describe the figures they came up with, Nate, I'd go with 'ruinous.'" She was pacing, he could hear her shoes on the floor, four steps one way, a spin, four steps back. He'd watched her do that particular reel for years, the tempo depending on her level of anxiety. He liked to catch her at one of her turns and give her a twirl. *I need to go home*, he thought, opening his eyes to the empty place at his side. *Right now*. The voice in his head trembled, wavered, like a frightened child, pleaded with the cloyingly sweet persistent one. *Home, home, home, please let me go, I just want to go home*.

"Nate," Georgia was saying, "I know you told me not to worry, but that's just two estimates and we can't afford either of them unless you won the lottery and didn't tell me. How will we ever—"

See? The voice assured the small wavering part of him. *You're doing the right thing, Nathan. The only thing. In a way, you have no choice, do you? Without Cat's money, you might lose Roseneath. And who knows? You might lose her, too. This is a godsend, Nathan, am I right?* Nathan frowned, squeezed his eyes shut and nodded.

"You let me worry about that," he whispered. "I'll take care of you."

"Nathan, it's not about that, I—"

"Georgia," he said, his voice stronger now, the words he chose, a careful paraphrasing of the voice in his head, came easier now. *Just let go, let me guide you. Help you.* "I took the job. It's a done deal."

"Wait, what?" she sputtered.

"I know, I said we'd talk about it but—"

"No, Nate, that's fine. I'm just surprised is all. You seemed so undecided yesterday."

See? You were worried for nothing. She doesn't suspect. She understands. Isn't she just perfect?

"Yeah, well when the owners dangled a hundred seventy-five grand under my nose, I figured you'd forgive me for signing up before they changed their minds." *There. How very like you we sound.*

"What?" she gasped. "Did you say—"

"Well, if I deliver inside ten months. It'll be tight but—"

"One hundred seventy-five—Are you joking? That's . . . that's . . ."

"Almost as good as a lottery win?" *That's it. Make her laugh.*

Peals of delighted laughter rang in his ears. *Well done.*

"My sweetheart. I am so proud of you. All your hard work and all the . . ."

"It'll be rough, though," he heard himself say. "Ten months means I won't be able to come home all that much." *See? So easy. Things don't always have to be hard. And you've earned this, haven't you? All these long years, all the sacrifices you've made, all the . . .*

"No, I don't suppose you could." *Of course she understands. Such a darling girl, so trusting. Perfect, perfect, perfect.*

"But it means we'd be able to get Roseneath done. Way ahead of schedule. With you there—"

"Oh, yes. You give me a list and I will work my way through it. Of course, I'm not sure I can afford you now, Mr. Fancy Pants architect. One hundred and seventy-five THOUSAND?" she shrieked.

"Don't worry about my fee, gorgeous. We'll work something out."

"It's going to be so beautiful, Nate. Our home. And you do what you have to out there. I'll be fine. It'll be perfect, you'll see." Nathan smiled.

Perfect. Beautiful. This time. Oh, yes, my beamish boy, everything will work out this time. Everything I've ever wanted and more. We are perfect, aren't we?

Sprawled out on the bed, he found himself digging his nails into one of the scabs on his arm, felt his anxiety diminish ever so slightly as his mind wandered back to the other night, the night he'd injured himself in the garden, in the greenhouse *No, it was the basement.* Lying on their bed at home, the sky twilight, the world all red and gray. His fingers left his arm and slid to one of the scabs on his chest. He pressed on it, hard, the pain blinding as something sharp shifted inside. Georgia covered in blood, her mouth gaping in fear. *You'd never hurt me.* The greenhouse, a sound, something like glass and . . . *No, the basement.* Shaking his head—no, it was just a dream—he pushed harder. *Hurt you.* The pain erupted like fire in his chest. "I want to come home," he whispered, wondering why he felt so afraid. *Please let me go home.* The words sprang into mind and he wondered whom he was pleading with. *No . . .*

no . . . Georgia, please no . . . someone's here . . . someone else . . . no . . . Someone in the greenhouse, offering him something, promising him . . .

Nathan pushed through the fiery pain, searching for whatever was festering in the wound. Something was still wedged in there, a shard from that day. He pushed his fingers in harder, oblivious to the sweat that now covered his hand, trying to find the edges of it. Whatever it was shifted, and as it did the pain transformed into a dull, numbing warmth that spread through him. *She doesn't have to know.* The voice was little more than a hint of a suggestion, innocuous, almost innocent. *It would be a kindness. She doesn't need to know our business. We'd be protecting her after all. We'd never hurt her, would we?* Nathan nodded, agreeing with the whisper even as Georgia chattered excitedly across the phone line. *But then I can go home?*

Yes, Nathan. And then we can go home.

"Well, you'll be home soon enough," Georgia said. "What did you say their names were again?" Her pacing had stopped, the reel ended, silence in the background as she waited for his reply.

"The Y–Yorks. Just a bunch of big money California types. Nothing special." He held his breath, but Georgia had moved on, unconcerned. *Because she trusts you. Like you must trust me. Trust me, my beamish boy. It will all be perfect.* "Never mind all that. Are you feeling any better?"

There was a long pause on the line before she answered.

"Oh, fine. I just needed a nap. Right as rain now. When is your flight?"

"I'll fly home late tomorrow. I miss you so much. Georgia?

"Yes?"

"I'm doing this for us. You know that, don't you?"

She yawned, a soft, familiar noise.

"Of course I do. And I love you for it."

✦   ✦   ✦

At Roseneath, Georgia fell back on the bed, her eyes fixed on the ceiling as if she could see through to Edie's attic. It was almost too perfect. Nathan landing his dream job. Money to fix the house. And almost a whole year alone with Edie. Everything she'd lost, restored to her. Everything they wanted, handed to them. And Edie was thriving under her attention, blooming like a flower, growing like a weed. Ten months with Edie, and who knew what lay at the end of that journey?

And what then? You'll need to tell him.

She frowned at the familiar, insistent voice of her own conscience. *Or, perhaps*, she countered, *I'll never need to tell him.* Maybe, just maybe, whatever magic was enchanting the attic had a specific trajectory, a terminus. A beginning and an end. Edie, once so intangible, was clearly maturing, day by day. Some incomprehensible metamorphosis was transitioning her into something more than just a ghost. Perhaps the time she was spending with her was the key to whatever lay beyond for her. Some magical combination, not unlike Alice in her Wonderland, but instead of eating and drinking, measures of love and attention that would ultimately free her from this plane. That this lost child needed her to finally move on to the other side, if there was one.

And she'd earned this. She had earned the privilege of nurturing this astonishing, fragile being. *And I won't let her go. Not without a fight.* And it wasn't just because little Edie needed someone to help her on her way to wherever the afterlife was taking her. The stakes, in Georgia's mind, were far higher than that. At some point, the seed of an idea had taken root. What if this was a deal the universe cut people like her? People like Georgia who had had the dream of motherhood cruelly ripped from them. Children like Edie whose life had been cut short. What if this was a secret she'd stumbled upon, a path through grief to a bittersweet kind of redemption. Not just for her, but for Edie, too. And what if some future woman, not unlike herself, stumbled upon her Rose? An unending chain of mothers and lost daughters, reaching across time, life, and death. She couldn't break that chain. She had to see this through.

All Edie needed was time. And Nathan might never need to know. Georgia might climb those steps one day and find Edie had vanished, moved on, transcended Roseneath with nothing to mark her time here but an attic full of memories and Georgia's own healed heart. *I deserve this. And so does she.*

But what if Edie never moves on? she worried. *What then?*

Unable, and even a bit unwilling, to answer her own question, Georgia put the thought out of her head as she slipped wearily under the covers, her eyes drifting shut. *I'll worry about that another day. I have time. Time for her, time for him. Time to think of something.*

TWENTY

HE'D BEEN PACING THE LENGTH OF HIS truck for an excruciating ten minutes. Forty minutes till her shift ended. What the fuck was he thinking? He tugged at his uncomfortable tie, ran his hand through his new haircut. Forty minutes and then he'd blow his whole trajectory off course, rewrite the careful plan he'd made for his career and future. He'd planned on graduating and leaving town. He'd planned on starting his own business, keeping up with sixteen-hour days, moving, moving, moving until he had accomplished what he'd set out to and then, maybe then, looking around for someone to share it with.

What he had not planned was buying this stupid dress shirt with a portion of his nest egg and a small engraved ring with an even larger portion of it. What he had not planned on was his life spinning consummately, sublimely, intoxicatingly sideways all because of a broken air conditioner. What he had not planned on was Georgia.

The fact of the matter was that he didn't give a shit about his plans anymore unless he could get her to promise that she'd be there for them.

"You clean up nice," a familiar voice purred.

He spun around. Cat. His mind blanked out, thrown as it was from now, Georgia and his future, to her, his past.

"Cat got your tongue?" she quipped.

"Not now, Cat. I don't want to fight with you. Not now," he barked, halting her advance with one outstretched hand.

"I don't want to fight with you either, Nate. I want to talk. Can't we just talk for once?" She took a step toward him. He took a step back.

"There's nothing to talk about." He glanced back at the library and saw the lights on the fifth floor go dark. They were starting to close down for the night. She'd be out any minute. There went his careful plans again. He broke out into a cold sweat on the small of his back.

"I miss you, Nate. I hate things the way they are."

"The way they are is exactly the way you wanted them. Can't you just leave it alone?"

She took another step forward. He held his ground.

"Let me guess—your little wallflower is keeping you waiting?"

His slender grasp on his temper snapped.

"Don't call her that. How do you know about her anyway? What are you doing, spying on me?" he snapped.

"Word gets around. I heard that you were so broken up over us that some little starry-eyed bookworm managed to get her hooks into you." She laid her hand on his arm. "This is ridiculous. We belong together. You know that. Let's go somewhere, you and I, and work this all out." She licked her lips and took another step toward him.

He flung her hand off of him.

"*Don't you ever fucking talk about her again, do you under-stand me, Cat? Ever again. It's over between us.*"

"*So it's like that, is it, Nate?*"

"*Yeah. It's like that.*"

◆   ◆   ◆

Nathan studied Cat's face across the makeshift desk. Ap-parently, the panicked confusion of the previous night had evaporated with the dawn, leaving in its wake a resigned sense of calm that made him wonder why he'd been so upset. While he showered, he reorganized his thoughts, skirted the nebulous dread that nagged at the back of his mind. He convinced himself as he took a cab to the project house that making the best of this uncomfortable turn of events would ultimately pay off. *Just my dumb luck. That's all it is. No more.* He had assembled a desk with two saw-horses and an old door, all the while wishing to God there was a way out of this, knowing that the signed contract and the wreck of a house he'd bought back in Ohio meant that there wasn't a realistic one. His pencil flew across the paper, eager to finish up the preliminary pitch for the York house, so he could get to his plane on time and back home to Georgia. *A week at home and I can pretend the last two days never happened. Gear up for the next ten months my dumb ass just got myself locked into. I've just got to get through this. I can do this. I have to do this. Just knuckle under and suck it up.*

He repeated this bleak mantra to himself as he watched Cat study his notes a few hours later. As he sat there wait-ing for her verdict, he felt that familiar surge of annoyance at her smallest gesture, every calculated mannerism angering him disproportionately. He remembered the first time he'd felt that, all those years ago, when she'd finally pushed him too far. When the cutesy affectations that he'd obsessed over when they'd first met had unraveled like a blindfold being removed, and he saw them for what they were: contrived manipulations.

"Mmm . . ." she said, flicking her tongue over her lower lip. She flipped a page, made a notation of her own, then gathered her hair in one hand, twisted it to one side, tucking it out of her way, fingertips trailing across her collarbone. She glanced at him over her reading glasses and gave him that coy smirk he remembered so well.

"Glasses, huh?" he quipped. "It's a drag getting old."

The smirk faltered for a second before she stuck her tongue out at him.

"Just for reading." She chewed her lip again before parrying back at him. "Your handwriting is appalling, Nate."

He crossed his arms over his chest and smiled.

"You didn't hire me for my penmanship, Mrs. York."

She rolled her eyes and scanned the page again.

"Why on earth would you need so many bids on concrete?" she asked pointedly, tapping her pencil on the paper in time with her heel on the floor.

Nathan stared at her levelly, the tapping setting his teeth on edge.

"Because the western wall is buckling like the hull on the Titanic, which means we'll have to raise and replace the whole foundation. Also, I plan on jackhammering that decrepit basement to dust and replacing it."

"Why?" she demanded. "Why not rebuild the whole fucking house while you're at it? I hired you to restore this house, Pritchard, not rebuild it. Any old hack could do that." She glared at him before flipping through the pages to the end, adding, "And did you check your math on this? This number seems high."

Instead of following her lure, Nathan gave her a tight, patient smile.

"I'm advising you to replace the basement floor because it's over one hundred years old and was originally dirt. Some 'hack', to use your term, threw down the equivalent of Quik-Crete in the fifties. As your architect, I would advise you and your husband that it would be shortsighted, with the house already raised, to put in a whole new wall and butt it up against a poorly installed foundation. The decision is ultimately yours, but I doubt the building inspector is going to sign off on anything that undermines the structural integrity of the entire house."

Cat fixed him with an irritated stare, then returned to her reading, dropping her pretense at banter entirely.

Thank God, he thought, relieved that his curt manner had drawn what he hoped was a line she'd be too annoyed, possibly too offended, to cross. He waited in silence as Cat finished her review, wondering as the minutes ticked by what he had once seen in her. Pretty, yes. Smart, too. But her acumen had always been the kind that reveled in pointing out others' flaws, a surgical derision that convinced people she was somehow superior by exposing the weaknesses in those around her. And her looks, while obviously attractive, were the kind of high-maintenance beauty dependent on not just money but also time. And by the looks of it, she had both to spare these days. Her hair was blonder, her lips were fuller. Her bust, too, Nathan thought with a quick glance down. Everything about her was an exaggerated, expensive caricature of the girl he'd known years ago.

He drummed his fingers on the table while he waited for this horse-and-pony show to end and caught sight of his bare left hand. Panicked, he fumbled in his pants pockets. Keys, change, wallet. *Where the hell did I leave my wedding ring?* He flexed his hand, grimaced at the pull of the scab on the inside of his ring finger. *Right. It was rubbing that cut so I took it off. Left it on the sink at the hotel.*

Across the table, Cat faked a yawn and stretched. She checked her watch, an elegant display meant to draw the eye to several of her more notable features. Nathan couldn't help but compare them to Georgia's yawns, the way her mouth always settled into a half smile, her eyes puffy with sleep. He closed his eyes for a minute, let his thoughts drift to her pearly skin, a silky expanse that never tanned. He smiled to himself at the way she despaired over the scattering of dark freckles on her nose and cheeks, unable to ever believe he adored each one of those tiny imperfections. Georgia had a classic, fine-boned elegance that had bewitched him from the moment he saw her. And Georgia was smart, sure, smarter than he was if he was honest, but never one to flaunt it. Rather, her empathy, wit, and warmth were hallmarks of her singular brand of quiet strength. That grace, along with her intense curiosity, was what had first drawn him to her, astonished that someone like her existed in real life. The fact that she loved him, despite every single flaw and failing he knew he had in spades, was a miracle he'd go to his grave unable to fathom. He almost laughed out loud. The differences between Cat and Georgia were, in most respects, like comparing a McMansion to a Queen Anne. One couldn't hold a candle to the other.

He let out the breath he'd been holding and felt, with some surprise after yesterday's debacle, the release of not caring about Cat anymore. *It's all going to be okay,* he thought. *I can handle this. This is nothing, just a job. She is nothing to me, not anymore. And there is nothing I wouldn't do for Georgia. Even smile into Cat's vapid face, take her money, and run back home with it. Build my girl her dream house. Fill it with children and a lifetime of happiness and look back one day and forget all this ever happened.*

Having finished her reading, Cat slipped her glasses off and set them by the house plans. Leaning back in her chair, she studied him for a moment in silence. Nathan held her gaze and waited.

"I want you to start immediately. Hit the ground running. How soon can you have a structural report to me?" she said finally.

Nathan shook his head. "Sorry, that won't work. I need a week, maybe ten days back east before I can start." Cat opened her mouth to object but he cut her off. "But I arranged for Brennan Engineering to begin the structural report tomorrow, pending your approval. That'll take a week or so as it is and doesn't require me to be here. I'll be back before you know it. I do have, as you so charmingly put it yesterday, a life. I'm not just going to drop everything."

"For the amount of money I'm paying you, you damn well will, Nate," she snapped.

"One week," he said simply.

"Fine," she acquiesced. "One."

"It'll take me two weeks after I get the structural report to get a detailed plan together, but," he continued, holding up one finger to silence her again, "demo can start in as little as ten days. If I find the right crew and can get the necessary permits. This state is a right pain in the ass when it comes to historical preservation, so if there's going to be a delay right out of the gate, that'll be it," he cautioned.

"Let me know when you expect to file the plans and apply for permits. I have friends down at the permit office. I'll throw a dinner party, make some donations, grease the wheels," she said, making another notation on the top page.

"Same old Cat," he commented. "Why does that not surprise me?"

She smiled thinly. "Oh, don't worry, I have a whole new bag of tricks. You'll see."

Nathan sat back in his folding chair and picked at a scab on the back of his neck, winced at the sharp prick there. He listened for that persistent voice from yesterday but caught only the edge of whispers, weak and fractured. *I'm just tired, that's all. All this noise in my head. It's just my guilty conscience.* The whispers seemed to agree, and as they did, shifted to a soothing, approving murmur. That panic rose in his chest again, the irrational nebulous dread bloomed anew as the whispers grew louder.

O frabjous day! Callooh! Callay!

Nathan vaulted up straight, almost fell out of his folding chair and, before the rollicking whispers in his head could stop him, blurted out, "One last thing."

Cat looked up, startled by the abrupt departure of his previously professional tone, a question on her face.

"I want notice before you stop by, even if it's just a couple hours," he said, letting out a shuddering breath. His hand rose on its own to the back of his neck again, pressed down hard on the sharp prick there. A painful, exquisite burning that stopped almost as soon as it began, trickling down his shoulders and arms in a strange calm.

Cat sat back and crossed her arms. "Ridiculous. It's still my house. I'm not going to ask for permission to stop by my own property."

Nathan fought against the sudden inexplicable urge to agree with her.

Ridiculous, ridiculous callooh callay, my beamish boy, nothing to worry about she's nothing, nothing, nothing.

"Yeah," he soldiered on, shoving the persistent voice down hard, trying to smother it with the sound of his own voice, "and it'll be a hardhat site for the foreseeable future. I don't need you waltzing in here in your—" he gestured at her heels, noticed her legs and as he did the whispers shot up an octave, excited,

Yes, yes, yes, yes!

No, no, no, someone sobbed, a plaintive wail that fought in vain against the approving onslaught. Nathan swallowed hard and continued, "—in your whatever and hurting yourself."

"Fine, I'll give notice. Maybe get myself some work boots. Will that satisfy you?" Cat answered, pleased. She'd noticed.

Nathan smiled at the thought of her in work boots. *No.* "Yes."

Gathering the papers and straightening them, she rose, her heels clicking on the wood floor. "So tell me, Nate, what's your rush to get back home? Got someone special waiting back there?"

Nathan hesitated, teetering on the brink of a lie so distasteful, he wondered how in the hell it had all gotten so out of control.

"Yeah, I . . ." He stopped. *No, no, no, no, no, can't do that, can't do that, can you?*

"What was that?" she asked, shoving the papers into her leather bag. "Didn't quite catch that."

Can't tell her, don't tell her, doesn't matter, nothing, nothing, nothing.

Nathan's heart sank as he realized he had backed himself into a corner. If he didn't tell Georgia about Cat, if he kept that from her, if he lied to his own wife about working for his old girlfriend, how the hell could he betray her even further by telling Cat about her? Especially considering how Georgia felt about her.

What have I done? He made a fist, frowned at the cut on his ring finger, hated the convenient excuse it gave him. *Usually I put it on my key ring for safekeeping. Why would I—*

The whispers stopped his question before he could even form it.

It's nothing, nothing, nothing, nothing, fret not my beamish boy, let me help you, help you, hurt you, help you.

He had no choice. The persistent thought was right—besides, it was the easiest thing to do. He flashed Cat a wry grin and heard himself say,

"Listen, Cat, we're blurring enough professional lines here. Leave my personal life out of this, okay?" *There, you see? Not a lie. Not a betrayal. So easy it can all be, so easy let me help you, it's nothing, nothing, nothing at all.*

Cat let out an exasperated noise as she checked her phone. "My God, I'd forgotten exactly how much no fun you can be, Pritchard."

"I'm working. I'm not here for a good time." *See? That sounded just like you.*

"Good, then tonight's a working dinner. I have some preliminary ideas I want you to be aware of before you get into the meat of this. I don't want you running off half-assed and wasting my time reigning you in. You're going to be on a short leash, Nate. Design-wise."

Nathan looked down at his watch, saw his hands were shaking. The voice, strangely, had fallen silent.

"I don't know, my flight . . . I have a flight at . . ." he trailed off. *What time is my flight? My flight to where? I . . . I . . . wait.* He shook his head, bit the inside of his cheek hard until his mind cleared. *My flight is at 6:20. I am flying home. Home to Georgia. Home. God, I must be tired.*

"We'll be quick," Cat called over her shoulder. She opened the front door. "I'll drop you off at the airport myself. Still like Indian food?"

No, no, no, no, no, another voice, the plaintive one, the frightened one.

"Why yes, Mrs. York, I do," he heard himself saying as he followed her out the door. *Listen to us! We sound like you.* "But you're buying, boss lady. I'm on the clock."

◆   ◆   ◆

So there was no fancy dinner, no dancing, no carefully contrived proposal. Months went by and he shifted his trajectory to small, local restorations that wouldn't take him too far away from her. He took some more of his nest egg and they moved into a bigger place, together. He kept the ring in his pocket and his intentions to himself until he was certain that every single stain that had blemished his first attempt was washed clean from his mind, unwilling to let anything sully their future.

And then, one ordinary night, Georgia was curled up on the couch with her feet in his lap. She had been sewing, but her project now lay cast to one side on top of her sewing basket, abandoned in favor of a book. Some Dickensian turn of events was causing her toes to curl in response. He was watching a documentary on Eames, blueprints for the mid-century restoration he was working on a few towns over cast to one side. She was oblivious to the three pins she clenched still between her lips, and he thought to himself that never in his wildest dreams would he have dared claim a moment, a life, like this for himself. His own fairy tale. Her. Them. Together.

"Georgia."

"Hmm . . ." she murmured, eyes still racing across the page.

"Georgia."

"What, Nate?" She still didn't look up.

"Marry me, Georgia."

The three pins dropped out of her mouth. He didn't remember much after that but he was pretty sure it was a yes.

TWENTY-ONE

 IT WAS THE PACING THAT WOKE HER. GEOR-gia struggled to lift her leaden eyelids and blear-ily studied the cracked plaster ceiling in her bedroom.

Seven impatient pitter pats north, seven frustrated pit-ter pats south. *Tap, tap, tap, tap, tap, tap, tap.* Seven north, seven south. *Tap, tap, tap, tap, tap, tap, tap.* Edie paced the attic floor, her restless feet echoing in the empty house.

Stretching, Georgia wondered what on earth had made Edie awaken so early, what made her pace so insistently. *I'll have to warn her* she thought, rolling over to see the time, *to be extra quiet when Nathan is home. She's so much more now, my own little girl. He might hear. He might suspect.*

2:10 pm. She sat bolt upright, her arms and legs scram-bling to free herself from the twisted sheets. *I've slept the day away,* she thought, jamming her feet into her slippers and hurrying to the attic stairs. *Nathan will be home tonight and there's so much to do before he does.* She yawned as she climbed the stairs, the indignant feet now tapping directly on the other side of the door that towered above her. The attic stairs pitched and swayed ahead of her as she fought a wave of queasiness that flickered through her stomach, up her throat, her mouth filling with saliva. *Forgot to eat. I have to do better about that. I'm slipping again.* Cradling her hands over her belly, she pressed down gently on the soft roundness there, willed the familiar flitting sensation away. *It's nothing. I overslept and haven't eaten a proper meal in days. Must do better. Don't want Nathan thinking I'm not taking care of myself.* Shivering, her roiling stomach protesting the thought of eating, she clasped the handrail with both hands, pulling herself up the steep staircase. *I could sleep another eight hours.* She turned the handle and pushed the door open.

Edie stood next to a crooked tower of books.

"Finally!" she exclaimed in mock frustration, her dancing eyes betraying her scolding tone. "I've been waiting *hours!*"

"What's all this?" Georgia asked, gesturing to the books as she shut the door behind her.

Edie spun and, humming a ditty, did a little dance with the tower of books as her partner.

"I've finished them, Georgia," she laughed, as her feet shifted nimbly into a Charleston. "Every. Last. One!" Edie squealed, each word punctuated with a perfectly executed step, her heels loud in the cavernous attic. She finished her dance with a spin, then bowed to her imaginary partner with a flourish. As she did, the mountain of books Georgia had brought her only days before tumbled in an avalanche to the floor.

With a groan, Edie dropped to her knees and, with a self-satisfied twinkle in her eye, began gathering them in her hands, clearly pleased by the shocked look on Georgia's face at her new abilities. "I am quite *proficient* with my hands now. Which of course brings us back to my first point about the books. That's where I learned *proficient*. And *precocious*. And *persistent*. Fine words *all*, wouldn't you say?"

Georgia sank to her knees, rubbing her eyes and trying to pinpoint each subtle difference in Edie today. It wasn't just the hands, although the confidence with which she moved was a profound change from the stubborn frustration that had marked her movements in the last . . . *days? weeks? I can't recall exactly the day I found her. Surely not weeks. We moved in mid-summer. Just a few weeks ago.* Georgia looked away from Edie for a brief moment to the dormer window. The leaves in the trees had begun to turn, autumn reds and golds mixed with valiant greens and yellows. Frowning, she looked away from the dying leaves back to Edie.

Edie handled the books with a self-assured ease. But there was something more about her today than just the euphoria of having mastered a new skill. Georgia's eyes ran down Edie's body as she stooped. She was taller again. *She's just about my size now. How tall was she yesterday?* Surely *not this tall.* She looked back under the eaves *how tall was she on that first day?* closed her eyes and tried to remember *maybe the size of a second-grader. But now . . .* She opened her eyes and saw in front of her a gangly adolescent, her limbs long and awkward as a child of twelve might be. Moreover, nearly all traces of the ephemeral, the insubstantial, were gone. Her dress, too, today was subtly different. Even as

Georgia watched, the tattered frock seemed to shimmer, to shift. One moment, it was the same threadbare cotton shift it had been that first day, the next, it blurred, became difficult for Georgia to focus on, the details appearing and disappearing at random, eyelet, lace, taffeta, embroidery, as if the dressmaker could not settle on a fashion.

Georgia grabbed Edie's hands, pulled them to her. Edie squeezed back, tight. Warm.

"I might," Georgia said, "also add *pretty*." She lifted Edie's hands to her lips and kissed them each in turn. "And, of course, *precious*."

She traced the delicate swirls of Edie's fingerprints, the meandering, many-forked path of her lifeline to her slender, alabaster wrist. The weight of Edie's hands in hers was exactly what it should be, heavier even. She looked up into Edie's perplexed face and kissed her worried forehead.

"Did I do something wrong, Georgia? I'm so sorry about the books. But it seems dead or alive, I'm a bit of a klutz," Edie explained with a shrug. "But one thing is for sure: I'm going to need more books or I will go mad as a hatter." The tower at her side grew, the speed with which she stacked them blurring her hands. "I've read all of these *twice*. Even the dictionary. Which was dull—even the P's—until I got to the letter 'V' and I learned something else." Her task accomplished, she brushed her hands together and jumped to her feet.

"What's that?" Georgia's throat felt stuffed with cotton wool. *I wish I'd at least had some water.* At the thought, her churning stomach settled briefly. *Ice cold water. That's it. Just as soon as Edie calms down. Some water to settle this.*

God, I hope I'm not coming down with something. Not now. Not with Nathan coming home. Home. When is he coming home? Today? Tomorrow? She cleared her throat, ran her tongue over her chapped lips, trying to remember what he'd said. *Tonight. That's right. Tonight. Late.*

"I'm *voracious. Vivacious!*" Edie cried, oblivious to her distress. Spinning across the attic, her dress shone with a sudden, blinding light, dazzling Georgia's sleep-crusted eyes. "And if we're being honest," she said, coming to an abrupt stop between two windows, a fetching rose-tinted flush on her pale cheeks. "*Vain*. And if it's not *too* much trouble, can I have an encyclopedia? Am I saying that right? En-cy-clo-peeeee-dia. A whole set of them, I've so much to learn. I think I'll need a thesaurus and all the encyclopedias you can manage if I have a hope of getting through *Jane Eyre*. Here. I've made a list." Her dress shifted back from the shimmering kaleidoscope once more to worn cotton, the too-short skirt exposing knobby, dusty kneecaps. The sleeves, which had been tight to her wrists, Georgia realized, were now barely three-quarter length.

Climbing heavily to her feet, Georgia laughed aloud at the vision in front of her, the young girl's mania infectious. She wrapped her arms around her and whispered in her seashell ear.

"Also, my darling girl, *vivid, vital.* And just now? *Verbose.*"

Edie spun away again and threw her arms up into the air.

"Oh, it's true! I am an absolute *church bell* today! I can barely contain myself. You might want to sit down for this one." Edie gestured to the green chair. "In fact, I insist. Your face is the same color as that chair. Feeling all right?"

Georgia swallowed hard and let out a slow breath, willing her stomach to settle.

"Just an upset tummy. I skipped breakfast and rushed up here because *someone*," Georgia arched her brow at the girl, who promptly flushed again, "was pacing a hole through the ceiling. But it can wait until you've shown me your tricks." Georgia sank gratefully into the chair and watched as Edie twirled her way across the room. The waistband of her pants against her reeling stomach was uncomfortable, so she shifted, slipping them down over her hips. *Better. Much better,* she thought as her stomach settled slightly.

"I think this one is *quite* clever. Ready?" she asked, her words punctuated by an impromptu soft-shoe dance, her heels cheerfully pattering against the worn wood floors.

"As I'll ever be."

Georgia watched as the girl situated herself between two of the soaring attic windows, the afternoon light washing her not only in sunlight but in the brilliant autumn hues of the soaring trees outside. Edie took a deep breath, screwed her eyes closed and threw her arms around herself, spinning as she did on the toe of one shoe. Once, twice, spinning faster with each turn, three, four, five faster still. The air around her shimmered, shifted, and began spinning as well, although somewhat slower, creating a surreal discord in the air, as if the molecules themselves were rearranging, creating an Edie-sized ivory chrysalis. After seven spins she began to slow; the chrysalis of light and air enveloping her drifting away in a softly shimmering fog. As it did, the threadbare dress fell from her gangly body in a piece-meal patchwork, shredding itself into nothing, leaving in its place something new, a waterfall of shining taffeta and lace that seemed to assemble itself as it washed down her into a finely wrought creation.

With a cry of delight, Georgia scrambled to her feet, marveling at what Edie had done, afraid to approach the vision that now stood giggling in front of her.

Edie's dingy little dress was gone. In its place was a stunning Gibson Girl confection of a garment, ivory taffeta and green satin above crimson velvet Mary Jane's. The tea length of the spring green skirt accentuated rather than disguised her gangly legs; the mutton leg sleeves and high ruffled neckline transformed the once raggedy child into a bygone, classical silhouette, a cameo brought to life.

Edie's beaming face fell as she looked down at her new dress. Seeing that one mutton sleeve was lagging behind the other, unfinished, and still a dirty eyelet, she stamped her foot indignantly.

"Really!" she seemed to admonish it, and with one more stamp of her foot, the lagging leg of mutton sleeve length-ened and twirled to match its twin. As an afterthought, a new cherry-red ribbon chased the old tattered one away from her hair; her mink rag curls coiling themselves into place as it did. "I'm not sure the spinning is exactly neces-sary but I thought you'd enjoy the *flair*. I know *I* do."

"My God, Edie, that's . . . that's . . ." Georgia's heart raced in her chest. "How did you do this?" She took one hesitant step toward her, then another, and then froze when the gooseflesh rose on her arms, the hairs on the back of her neck prickled. *She's growing up. But into what? What have I done?* Edie's brow furrowed briefly when Georgia took one small step backward. *What is she becoming?*

"It's still me, Georgia," she said reassuringly. "Just all gussied up. I look rather keen, don't you think? A real dilly!" She gave an elegant shiver of disgust. "I am well done with those rinky-dink *rags*." Running her hands down her new dress, she purred as she preened, "Ooh, *ever* so much better."

As Edie stood admiring her velvet shoes, Georgia took a tentative step toward her, a living breathing, fairy tale— Alice in Wonderland, Snow White, Sleeping Beauty, Rapunzel, every imaginary heroine made manifest here, in this attic, in Roseneath, thriving, evolving through nothing more than Georgia's own constant love and care. *Growing*, Georgia thought, reaching out for the young woman's hand. *Mustn't forget that. She is growing, there is no denying it.* Let herself ask the question she'd been avoiding for weeks. *How can a ghost grow?* Georgia ran her finger down the planes of Edie's maturing face and tilted her pointed chin up. *And if ghosts can grow up, what exactly,* she wondered, her eyes twinkling, *do they grow up into?*

"Please don't grow up on me too fast. I—" but just then her lungs tightened painfully; a volley of coughing replaced her words. Edie transformed, blurred from her sight as Georgia bent over, gasping for air, unable to stop coughing long enough to catch her breath. A firm thump on her back from Edie granted her the respite to draw one raggedy breath before another fit descended. Edie grasped both of Georgia's arms and pushed her back into the chair.

"Applesauce!" Edie's worried face reappeared in front of her as the coughing slowly tapered off. "I never meant to alarm you. Perhaps I did lay it on a bit thick. Next time I'll leave off the spinning. Or do I look as bad as all that?"

Georgia managed a wan smile. "Edie, sweetheart, your dress is lovely. I'm just not feeling quite well today." She wiped the spittle from her mouth and shifted her waistband down another inch, felt the pressure lessen there. Pushing herself back further into the chair, she let out a long breath and waited until she could see clearly again. *I'm so tired. I want to go to bed. I want to sleep. I want some water. But mostly I want to sleep. Sleep, sleep, sleep.* "How ever did you manage it?" *Just another few hours with Edie and then I'll get the house ready and then . . . then . . . I can sleep again. No, I can't. Nathan's coming home. Today? Tomorrow?*

"Well, I guess you could say it's like *practicing*. Just harder. I remembered I always wanted a dress like this."

"Edie," Georgia said with a forced casualness, as the girl resumed her preening. "There's more than just the dress."

Edie looked up from her sleeves and tilted her head at her. "More what?"

"You're taller. A great deal so. Didn't you notice?"

"Am I?" Edie cried. "Am I truly?" She ran her hands down her skirt. "My grief, I'm a bean pole, aren't I?" Another burst of coughing from Georgia and Edie sank to her knees beside her. She gripped one of Georgia's hands and frowned at the stain on her pants.

"Edie," Georgia said, ignoring the sharp glance from Edie. "You're as tall as I am today."

Edie's eyes narrowed. Georgia felt her run a finger tentatively down her pant leg, saw Edie's eyes widen. Then Edie looked up into Georgia's eyes, clearly distressed.

Chin up my dear. Don't look down. Step on a crack, break your mother's back.

"How . . . how tall was I yesterday?" Edie whispered.

"I don't know. I couldn't say, not exactly. I don't remember," Georgia said weakly, pulling her hand free and her knees to her chest. *Everything is fine. Just tired. A little bug. So tired.* Edie draped a blanket over her, then dabbed at the corners of her mouth with a lacey ivory handkerchief.

"It's not that I'm trying to be taller," she murmured, clearly flummoxed by the stain on the cloth. "But then, I'm not sure it's up to me." The frown deepened. "Never mind about me and my silly glad rags. Who gives a wooden nickle about all that when you need to rest? And another thing," turning her head this way and that, Edie seemed to be listening for something. "What in the world is that singing?"

"Singing," Georgia repeated sleepily. "It's lovely isn't it? I can almost catch the tune but then it drifts off." Rising, falling, calling, pleading, the tune in her head seemed to match the twirling and flipping within her stomach, a strange sickening synchronicity. *Must have been something I dreamed. Yes, that's it. I dreamed this song. Rest. Sleep. Maybe . . .* Casting an eye over to her watch, carefully avoiding her stomach, the grogginess evaporated the instant she read the time. 5:37 pm. *That's impossible*, she thought, suddenly wide awake. *How . . .?*

Pushing the blanket off, she tried to stand. Edie gently pushed her back down.

"Please sit for a minute," the girl implored. "I'm worried about you. You look a little punch drunk, Georgia, not like yourself at all!"

"I'm fine, really," Georgia insisted. "And I have some news of my own." She sat up as best she could, raising her voice over the softly fading song in her head. She caught a verse, a jumble of lyrics that were oddly specific.

"But aren't you lonely? Here, all by yourself with only the dead for company?"

Edie laid her head on Georgia's lap, as if for comfort, but Georgia found herself wondering if she was really trying to keep her in the chair.

"Do tell me," Edie whispered. "I'll listen to your news. But then I want you to eat. I'll be perfectly jake by myself today. Go downstairs. Maybe go to bed early. Would you do that for me?" she pleaded, looking up into Georgia's eyes with tears in her own.

"Of course," she said, confused by the girl's sudden change in mood. "But after I go shopping. For you." Worry was replaced by delight on Edie's face.

"For me? A present?" Then her face fell. "I don't need a present, silly," she insisted. "I'd much rather you—"

"Yes, you do. Lots and lots of presents," Georgia interrupted her. "Starting with whatever is on your list." Then she continued, cautiously. "You see, that's my news. I . . . I won't be able to come upstairs for a few days. And I don't want you to be bored."

"You're leaving me?" Edie cried. "Whatever for?" She flung her hands to her face, anguished.

"No, I didn't say I'm leaving you. Just that I won't be able to come up here for a few days. A week at most."

Edie's hands fell, tears sliding down her face in shimmering streams.

"What did I do? Is it the dress? Is . . . is it the growing? I can change it back, I'll practice hard not to change. Did I make you sick? I never meant to! I promise, I'll stop learning how to grow up, only please don't leave me!" she wailed.

"No, sweetheart, of course you didn't make me sick. That's silly. Here, come sit on my lap and let me explain," Georgia insisted, pulling the girl up from the floor.

Edie flung herself miserably into Georgia's lap, her tears popping like soap bubbles as they fell from her cheeks.

"Do you remember when I told you that Nathan was flying far away for a few days?"

Edie nodded solemnly. "Aeroplanes sound like made up things," she whispered.

Georgia laughed and Edie's tear-filled eyes lit up again.

"Perhaps they do. But you see he got a job far, far away. So far away, in fact, that he is coming home to pack. And when he leaves, he'll be gone for days and days. Weeks. Months even! Imagine that!"

"Leaving? Why would anyone want to leave you? That's . . . that's very *odd*. Isn't it?" Concern flitted across Edie's face. She glanced down at the handkerchief in her hands, then hurriedly tucked the crimson and ivory bit of cloth into her pocket.

"Not odd at all. Just the nature of his work, but you see what it means. You and I will be alone together in Roseneath for ages! Just us two! The whole house to ourselves!"

Edie's face lit up only briefly before another, darker shadow ran across it.

"A week?" she asked, wringing her hands. "Georgia—" she started, the light in her eyes eclipsed entirely by a dark thought. "What if . . . what if you forget me?" she whispered.

"Forget you? How on earth could I?"

"People do." The girl nodded, a jerky stilted motion. "It happens." A small cloud of ash fell all around her as she began to tremble.

"When does it happen?" Georgia said gently, pulling her down to rest her head on her bosom. "Tell me."

"I don't remember," she said after a long silence, the ashy cloud enveloping them both. "Not exactly."

"Edie," Georgia rubbed the girl's back, up and down, soothing her, "my dearest, there is nothing to worry about. I just need a few days with Nathan."

Edie looked up at her, soot-colored tears washing down her face. "And then he's leaving?"

"Yes, for ten whole months."

"I just worry," she said, wiping her stained cheeks. Her hands were as soot-stained as her face, just as she had appeared when Georgia first met her—like a dirty, lost urchin. The new dress however, seemed to resist the desolate ash cloud and shone immaculately, the contrast between her distraught face and her pretty new trappings a fragile juxtaposition that broke Georgia's heart.

"Tell me what you worry about," she prodded gently, running her hand over the child's brow. "Tell me and I'll make it all better. I promise."

Edie shook her head, but this time no ashes rained down. She was calming from whatever fevered panic had held her. "I don't know exactly. It's not always easy to remember. And I get so dreadfully confused. Everything is changing so fast. I'm not sure I understand."

"Then you'll just have to trust me. One short week and then just the two of us for ages. Won't that be wonderful?" she asked, twisting a lock of russet hair around her finger as she held her breath, willing herself not to cough.

"Ages and ages, all alone," she mused under her breath. "Alone in Roseneath for ages and ages until . . ." Her eyes darted toward the attic door.

"But you won't be alone." Georgia cuddled the fidgeting girl. "You'll have me and my undivided attention. Every day like Christmas. And you won't be alone ever again, Edie, I swear. Okay?"

Edie shook her head. "I'm not making sense, am I?" Sliding from her lap, Edie stood and ran a hand through Georgia's hair, smoothing it back behind her ear. "You mustn't mind me. Mustn't worry. Back to presents." Her lips curved up in a cheeky smile even while her eyes sought out the attic door again.

"Well, that's just it." Georgia rose on shaky legs, felt Edie steady her with her warm hands. "I'll be very busy when Nathan comes home for those few days. And we don't want him to suspect, do we?"

Edie shook her head uncertainly. "No, but . . ."

"So no jitterbugging up here, young lady," Georgia playfully scolded.

"But are you sure—" The air around Edie trembled.

"Of course I'm sure," Georgia insisted. "There's nothing to worry about. I promise. Tonight I'll go shopping. I'll get all the books on your list. Maybe there's a toy or a game you'd like?" The trembling stopped.

"Georgia," Edie groaned. "I might be getting a bit old for toys and games." She ran her hands down her dress again, studying herself, a perplexed look on her face again. "Crazy, that."

Georgia laughed. "Perhaps you are." Looking away from Edie's bemused face she studied the walls of the attic, at the sheer number of crayon and chalk sketches Edie had made since she'd first learned how to hold a crayon.

The early attempts at animals, one-dimensional and out of proportion, and now the newer ones. Exquisitely detailed renderings of people, places, and things she'd seen in the books, her skill even with such meager tools growing at a rate more astonishing than her ever-evolving vocabulary or her height.

"I wonder, Edie, if you might like some paints?"

"Paints!" Edie exclaimed. The distant expression in her eyes vanished under a surge of delight. "Oh yes, please! That would be so jammy!"

"Paints and canvases, and an easel? And then you won't be so bored," Georgia teased, a cough punctuating her words.

"You're so good to me, Georgia. And if it's not too much trouble?" Edie reached into a pocket in her green satin skirt and withdrew a bundle of paper.

Unfolding it, Georgia found it a neat list written in a gracious, old-fashioned cursive hand. The list covered the front and back of three pages. Topmost on the list was Hans Christian Andersen's *The Galoshes of Fortune*.

"If it's not too much to ask," she said bashfully, twirling her hair around one finger. "I'll need all of these."

Georgia scanned the surprisingly detailed list. "Where did you hear of all these books?"

"I remembered them," Edie said simply.

"Well, I'll do my best," Georgia said with a yawn. "Paints and canvases and an easel and as many of these books as I can find before Nathan gets home. *The Galoshes* might be a trick, though. If I recall, it's out of print." She refolded the list and tucked it into her pocket, that gold-fish flipping in her stomach sending a wash of bile up her throat. *Some hot tea and toast*, she thought. *Just a cold. And I've so much to do.*

"And you won't forget about me?" Edie called out to her as she opened the attic door.

"Don't be silly," Georgia said, pausing in the doorway to see the sun setting outside. "Who could forget you? You're the cream in my coffee." Edie blushed.

"Will you teach me to—what did you call it—jitterbug when you get back?" she sang out coyly.

"Yes!" Georgia's laugh was genuine this time. "We can jitter to your heart's content. Now let me go before the art store closes." As she closed the door behind her, Edie called out again.

"I'm going to be an excellent painter, Georgia! Just you wait and see! And that song we keep hearing? I think I've heard it somewhere before. Catchy, isn't it?"

TWENTY-TWO

CURLED UP ON THE COUCH, GEORGIA watched Nathan fuss in front of the crackling fire. Night had fallen; the firelight washed him in wavering tongues of flames, illuminating one side of his face while obscuring the other.

"I miss you," she whispered.

He turned to look at her, the darkness vanishing as he did, his face now washed in firelight.

"I'm right here."

"I know. Still."

He nodded and slid across the floor, coming to rest against the couch at her side. He reached for her hand and kissed the back of it.

"I'd hoped to take you out tonight. Last night and all that. Someplace swanky." He tucked a curl behind her ear and tapped her on her nose.

Georgia burrowed deeper under the blanket.

"I like this better," she confessed apologetically.

A bit of damp wood popped loudly in the fireplace and he slid back on his knees toward the hearth. Using the poker, he shifted the protesting log safely to the back of the firebox.

"Me too. Feeling any better?"

"A bit," she said, sitting up. The truth was she didn't, but there was no sense in worrying him, not with him leaving in the morning. "I should get up. Do some housework at least. I've been too lazy." She scanned the living room, cringing at the disorder surrounding them. "I've ruined our week together by being sick. Stupid stomach flu."

Nathan gently pushed her back down.

"You don't need to do a thing. I am perfectly capable of shifting for myself, you know. And you are not lazy."

"I am so. I'll get fat if I keep lying around like this," she insisted, adjusting the waistband on her pants until the pressure there lessened. "I feel bloated and horrid as it is."

"I wouldn't mind seeing a bit of meat on those bones," he growled. "Sexy."

"Stop," she protested, her lips curving up as he bent down to her. His lips landed on hers, tender, once, twice.

"Nope. Never."

She sat up and burrowed into his arms. He pulled the blanket over both of them. Outside, the wind howled, swirled around the chimney and gusted down, sending the flames flickering wildly. And beyond that, just on the edge of her hearing, the song played endlessly in her head. Rising, falling, calling, crying. She could almost, *almost* just hum it. The words were too soft to hear and seemed to evaporate before she could discern more than a handful.

This dead place is no place to play.

The words seemed to echo in the room, the song in her head stumbled, faltered, then resumed its meandering melody.

"Fall snuck up on us," she said with a shiver.

"It did," he agreed. "I'll make sure to have more firewood delivered. Drive the chill off for you while I'm gone. Do me a favor, though? Get the chimney cleaned soon. I'll leave a number you can call. Buddy owes me one. Everything else will have to wait, though, until I get that first paycheck."

"You know it's funny, Nate. How suddenly it's autumn. It's like time has no meaning here. Do you ever feel that way?" She searched his face, but instead of finding the bemusement that her fancies usually generated, his expression was blank, his thoughts clearly elsewhere. She tried again. "You know, like the days and weeks . . ." He seemed to finally hear her and his eyes flicked over her, something like annoyance. She broke off and shook her head. *He's already miles away working on that house in his head.* "Oh, never mind. I'm being silly."

He blinked then, rapidly. The annoyed look vanished and, in its place, a familiar concern. Nathan placed his hand against her forehead. "Sure you're not running a fever?"

Georgia shook her head, embarrassed. "No, it's not that. I'm just tired."

He palmed her stomach, his fingers spreading out. He pressed down, just a little, and her stomach lurched. The song broke off, as if someone had jerked the needle across a record.

"Tummy still upset?"

"A little." Georgia shifted, twisted sideways, and swallowed the bile that rose in her throat. His hand fell away.

"I thought I saw the basement door open earlier. Were you working down there?"

Peculiar. No, not like me. The words popped into her head, unbidden. *Why did I think of that?* she wondered.

Nathan's face was lost in darkness as he looked toward the back hall.

"Not really. Just checking on things." He flashed her a quick smile before jumping at the sudden slap of vines against the back window.

"Nate, I'd really like to do something about that greenhouse. It's gruesome," she said as the lightning flashed outside, briefly illuminating the listing structure. "And maybe have the roses pulled back from the house, too. Those thorns are wicked. Just look at your hands." The backs of his hands were crisscrossed with a series of deep gouges, black pinpricks where the thorns had dug in and held on. "Jesus, Nate, let me clean those before—"

A sudden anger flashed across his face, choking off her words. He pushed her away and crossed the room to the glass doors.

"It's nothing, just a few scratches. Don't touch them." He looked down at his hands, staring helplessly at the countless cuts and scrapes. "I was out in the yard while you were napping." He was miles away again, upset about something, something he was keeping from her. *He doesn't want me to worry.* She studied him in silence, wondered where he was, what was troubling him so, trying to find the right words to ask him

"What about the greenhouse? What did you say?" An uncharacteristic grimace twisted his lips.

"I was just saying I worry about the greenhouse. That's all. Nate, I . . . what's wrong?" she asked, bewildered by his mercurial reaction to her request.

He studied her for a long moment, then crossed the room and sat down carefully next to her, tucking her in again.

"Nothing's wrong. You're imagining things. I'm just," he shrugged, "distracted, I guess. Got a lot on my mind. Sorry."

Georgia reached over and grabbed his arm. "Nate?"

But he pulled away from her and her hand fell heavily on the couch between them. "Why are you afraid of the greenhouse?" He drew in a ragged breath, let it out between his teeth in a hiss. "There's nothing to be afraid of. I'd never let anything hurt you." His hands were balled up.

"I . . ." she looked at his face, tried to read the strange expression and failed. "I know that, Nate. I never said I was *afraid* of it. I just worry." He looked as if he'd wandered into a dinner party and had no idea what the conversation was about. "You know, neighborhood children . . . wouldn't want someone to . . ." she stopped, confused now herself. *What were they even talking about? What had she said wrong?*

"Someone to what?" he snapped. "What child? Have you seen a child?" he demanded. "Out there? Where?"

"No, Nate, of course not." She drew back, thrown by his sudden anger, alarmed at how he'd abruptly changed 'children' to 'child.' *He mustn't suspect.* Her eyes drifted to the ceiling but she fought to hold his gaze. "I just meant someone could get hurt out there."

His expression in the flickering firelight seemed to shift as wildly as the flames. He smiled at her, that easygoing grin of his so familiar, so affectionate that she wondered if she'd imagined the angry one entirely.

"Stop worrying about it. I'll take care of everything. The house, the basement, the greenhouse. Leave it all to me. There isn't a thing you can do about any of it. All you need to do is rest. Rest and get better. Okay?" His voice was a knife's edge.

"Oh. Yes. Yes, of course," she rebuked, wondering what she'd said to upset him. She fell silent, unwilling to ruin their last evening even more than she'd already ruined the whole last week. The song began in her head again, the melody seemed to spiral up out of her, louder, something glorious in how it led her thoughts away from her cares about Nathan and Edie. Calling, calling. Up an octave, rising, rising, another octave, words and melody a riotous jumble.

I am no mere angel. I am an archangel.

So incomprehensible she gave up trying to understand it—

Archangel! You've left your post!

—and just let it wash over her.

I thought we were going to be great friends.

Nathan slumped back against the couch and kicked his boots off, then crossing his arms behind his head, dropped his feet heavily onto the coffee table.

"So, how's your work going?" His words broke through the wandering ballad. His eyes were closed, that small, tight grin back in place.

"Work?" she repeated, disoriented.

"You know, in the attic. Your 'No Boys Allowed' club?"

"Oh," she swallowed hard, trying to distance herself from the melody and focus. "Fine. Early stages." Her mind reeled, regrouped. She tried to recall what lies she had told him.

"You never really did explain to me what you're researching. What you've got going on up there," he said, probing. Nathan reached for her and, pulling her toward him, wrapped his arms around her in a possessive embrace.

"Well, it's a lot to sort through," she stammered, shifting in his too tight embrace, her eyes caught by the silvery wash of light that bloomed in the corner of the mirror over the fire. It was soft, just a delicate glow, something reassuring in its steady shine. The song in her head leapt one octave, two, three, four, a pitch impossibly high, the sound of glass shattering.

On your feet, archangel! Teach me to fight!

The light in the mirror flickered wildly in response, and Georgia fought the irrational urge to laugh aloud. *Such a beautiful story, I wish I could understand it all.*

"So much information to organize and confirm," she continued, smiling vacantly at the twinkling mirage that drifted in the pitted mercury patches of the mirror. "I'm trying to create an oral history, something like a first-person account, really, of the people who lived here."

"Here in Roseneath? What have you found?" His arms tightened around her uncomfortably.

Georgia faked a yawn and stretched to escape the uncomfortable embrace, retreating to the corner of the couch. Instead of meeting his eyes, she kept her gaze on the mirror's silver glow.

"Oh, it's all a mess. Very confused. I'll let you know when I have an actual timeline that makes sense. Until then, you'll just have to be patient."

"And you said you found this first-person account in the house? Here in Roseneath? I'd like to see it. Whatever you found. Does it have something to do with that song you keep humming?" Something insistent in his tone. "It's very unusual. Reminds me of something."

Have I? she thought wildly. *Have I been humming it? I don't think I have, but I must be. Edie heard it and now . . .*

"Oh, that. Just something I heard on the radio. And I didn't really find anything substantial," she said evenly. "Just some books and some names. I'm tracking them all back through the census. Honestly, I might just be chasing ghosts," she added with what she hoped sounded like an off-hand laugh. Something in his expression was disquieting, pointed.

"Ghosts?"

"Oh, just a turn of phrase, Nate, really. I mean things like maids, children, staff, seasonal laborers. Who knows? The county records are still in giant ledgers in that old archive over on Franklin Boulevard, for God's sake. It'll be months of work. It may go nowhere." She held her breath, wondering if the wall of half-truth would hold up against his questioning. The melody began again, a new verse this time, lower, no longer in the ear-shattering octave, and she felt a measure of calm settle over her, felt the goldfish queasiness vanish.

Cloud watch with me, Michael.

The gentle plea was heartbreaking for reasons Georgia could not fathom. *Yes, please. Cloud watch with her. Please.* The silver flicker in the mirror dimmed, sputtered and nearly went out.

Instead of questioning her further, Nathan rose to throw more wood on the fire. As he stood there, one hand gripping the mantel, the reflected silver light faded to black, leaving behind nothing but his flickering silhouette in the pitted glass surface. The only sound in the room was the crackling fire and the wind and rain outside and Georgia tried in vain to translate his weighty silence. The tension in his shoulders, the worry in his profile, his terse conversation threw her into doubt. Maybe this wasn't a harmless manipulation. Maybe he thought that by encouraging him to leave, she was really just sending him away. *That's exactly what you're doing. Stop kidding yourself, you are sending him away for your own greedy reasons. Don't try to convince yourself you are being anything less than mercenary. Maybe it's not too late. Maybe I could . . .* But even as she tried to think of a compromise, she realized there wasn't one. *I can't leave Edie. I just can't. Not yet. I have no choice but to stay.*

As if he had heard her thoughts, he turned and gave her a reassuring smile. "I love you, you know that don't you? I hate to go, but it's almost as if I don't have a choice." A wry smile twisted his lips.

"I do. I understand," she replied. Inside, the song trailed off, as if the unseen performer had fallen into a deep slumber. "And I wonder if you'll ever know how much I love you." He returned to her side, knelt there. The room was silent except for the crackle of the fire, the racing winds outside, the discordant settling of the house.

"I'm going to be gone a while, you know, Georgie." His lips sought hers.

"I don't want to give you my flu," she protested, even as she held his hand to her breast.

He pulled her shirt up, his lips finding her nipple, his tongue a gentle rasp against it. "I'll take my chances. Unless you're not feeling up to it."

She pulled him up onto the couch, pushed him back and straddled him.

"Don't be silly," she whispered. "And not give you a proper goodbye?"

He tangled his fingers in her hair; his hands pulled her hips against him hard.

"I should at least make sure you have something to remember me by," she said, pulling her pajama top off over her head. His hands and lips traced patterns on her breasts as she removed the pins that held her hair up, surrounding them both in the veil of her tresses. She yanked his shirt open, heard buttons hit the floor, her hands and his fumbling together for his belt buckle.

"Why, Georgia Pritchard," he groaned underneath her, her teeth on his neck. "I could just devour you."

✦   ✦   ✦

Nathan's flight was early. He didn't wake her; instead she felt his lips on her cheek as she struggled to swim up from a deep, crushing sleep. Georgia finally opened her bleary eyes only to see the bedroom door click shut, sat up and heard his footfalls going down the stairs, each step taking him farther away from her. She kicked at the blankets to go after him, to say goodbye one last time, but her stomach twisted savagely and she ran instead to the bathroom, vomiting the meager contents into the sink, then fell weakly to the floor. Her chest was red and irritated from his unshaven cheeks, legs sore from gripping him, her lips chapped and rough, his lovemaking that had begun so sweetly had shifted over the course of the night to something possessive, demanding, relentless. *Don't be silly*, she told herself, *he didn't frighten you. You're remembering wrong again. Didn't hurt you. He would never.*

She drank from the tap, mouthfuls of cool water, her stomach settling once more as she did, then looked into her own eyes in the mirror. She held her own gaze until she summoned the courage to look down, past her swollen breasts to her once flat stomach. A soft swell in profile. She pushed against it with the flat of her hand. *It can't be. It just can't.* She pushed harder and felt something flutter back.

This is impossible, it can't be that. She ran to the bedroom window to see if his truck was still there. *Chin up, don't look down. You didn't see what you thought you did. Didn't feel . . . that.* Nathan's truck sat idling in the driveway under the massive century oak in front of the carriage house. *I've made a mistake. No. No. This is all wrong. Something is horribly wrong.*

A movement across the backyard caught her attention and she watched as her husband— *Nathan?*—strolled out of the greenhouse, his sure gait now more of a swagger, whistling an unfamiliar tune.

She raised her hand to tap on the glass, to beckon him to wait for her to come down, but she hesitated, her fingers curling away from the glass when the gentle butterfly flutter in her stomach became an angry hornet. She watched as his swagger grew tight and coiled, as if beneath lay something like rage.

Her hand dropped silently back to her side as he—

Nathan?

—climbed into the truck, slammed it into gear, and sped too fast down the drive, as if he couldn't wait to leave.

Something is wrong, she thought, even as she hurried back to the bathroom, making it to the toilet this time. *More than this, whatever this is. Because it's not what you think it is. You're being hysterical.* Call him, tonight. *Make him tell me what's on his mind, what's troubling him. What's making him act so . . . peculiar,* Edie's voice chirped in her head.

But not now. I can't just now. Not until I feel better. Not until I'm well again. She stumbled back across the bedroom *don't look, chin up, don't you dare look, you're imagining things again* and climbed back into bed, wound the sheets around her. *I just need to rest for a few minutes. A few more minutes and then I'll go see Edie. I promised.*

Georgia let her heavy eyes fall shut as verse after lilting verse played endlessly in her ears, a song of songs lulling her into a deep, dreamless sleep.

❖　❖　❖

"Nathan. I need you to sit down." Georgia had been cleaning their cramped condo all day, wondering where they could possibly put a baby.

"Georgia. I am sitting down. You're sitting on my lap, honey. I could not sit down more if I tried," He shifted her in his lap. "Baby, what's wrong?"

She searched her mind for her speech and found it had run off. She looked down at her hands, but they didn't help, they just twisted helplessly in her lap. She tried again.

"Nathan. I . . . oh dear. Remember last week," she frowned, "in the kitchen?"

"Oh, yes. I remember. I can totally do that again." He started kissing a path down her neck.

"No, that's not what I . . .." She slipped out of his arms and stood. "All right, remember the day you had the concrete poured at the new site? You came home and you were so muddy and I told you that you had to take your clothes off by the door." He stood up and reached for her. She took a step back.

"I can do that, too, but, Georgie, it doesn't work the same with you across the room."

"Please don't tease me right now. I don't think I can bear it."

"Fine," he said, then crossed his eyes and stuck out his tongue. "I am very serious now."

Exasperated, she said, "Nathan, what did both of those . . . events . . . have in common?"

"'Events.' That's hot. Listen, Georgie," he began unbuttoning her shirt. "I'll have sex with you any time you want, you don't have to sell me on it like some sort of timeshare."

She grabbed one of his hands and placed it on her stomach.

"Nathan," she whispered. "You're not listening to me."

She watched his face go white as a sheet, saw the teasing expression fall to the floor.

"Nathan? Talk to me. Please say something."

She watched several expressions cascade down his face and she waited, wondering where they would land. "I know we didn't plan this," she said. "The timing is terrible, I get it, but this was bound to happen. And it won't change things, not really. We'll make it work. We have plenty of room," she stammered, "and I'll figure out a way to work from home and take care of him so you won't worry about money so much. We'll figure it out. Nothing will change. I promise. It's just one little baby."

"Him?" he asked. "How do you know it's not a her?"

"I don't. I just thought you'd want a boy. Nathan, tell me what you're thinking."

He ran his hand over her belly, his tan fingers spread out over her white skin. "I think you're wrong, Georgia," he said finally. "This changes everything. Everything." He met her worried eyes. "This changes everything for the better."

TWENTY-THREE

SHE BARELY MADE IT TO THE BATHROOM
this time. After rinsing her mouth, Georgia laid
on the cool tile floor, waiting for her breath to
slow. She hummed along with the song in her head to pass
the time, a smile blooming on her gaunt face. *I've got it
now. Just barely, but I've got the tune. So lovely. The loveli-
est tune in all creation.* Later, minutes, hours, she pulled
herself up and drank mouthful after mouthful of water
from the tap, the cool trickle deliciously cold on her raging
stomach. Carefully avoiding the mirror, she let her soiled
clothing fall to the floor, then padded on bare feet back
to the bedroom, skirting the scattered plates and bowls,
boxes of half-empty cereal, cans of fruit and beans, some
licked clean, others half-eaten, a few discarded entirely.
She kicked aside the pile of soiled, vomit-stained clothing
on her way to the nearest sagging cardboard box, *we never
did buy any furniture did we, Nate?* her hands scrambling
blind in the dark until she felt the familiar texture and
weight of Nathan's old bathrobe. She slipped her arms
into it, knotted the sash high up under her breasts where it
wasn't so tender. Then she turned to face the room. It was

dark. Morning? Night? Roseneath was still all around her. Wind and creaks, familiar sounds all, but beyond these small disturbances, nothing. She tried to remember what day it was and found she could not.

How many days and nights had she burrowed here, sick as a dog, rising only to kneel at the toilet, vomiting until nothing but foam came up, rinsing the burning residue from her mouth, then crawl back to bed? Burrow there humming softly to herself until she fell blissfully, deliriously back to sleep. The occasional trips downstairs to rummage through the pantry, trying to find something to assuage the clawing beast in her stomach. Skirting the handful of calls and texts from Nathan entirely.

Three hang-ups, nothing but dead air on her voicemail. A scattering of texts that came in at random intervals, his full days and the time change likely the reason for their brevity and stilted, distant tone.

Just landed. Busy couple of days on deck. I'll check in when I can, try to call this weekend.

Hope you're feeling better. Resting. My perfect girl.

This weekend won't work out, last-minute trip up north. Got a lead on a mantel the owner wants, had to go check it out. Will call when I can.

Very busy here. Thinking about you. So much to do here so much to plan my days are so busy, nights too but a few more weeks. Just a few more weeks and everything will be perfect.

She scanned her responses, amazed her deflections hadn't aroused his normally overprotective nature. She barely recalled sending them.

My phone went dead. I'll get a new charging cord, this one is unraveling. See? It's a good thing I stayed. I'd never see you if I was out there.

I was working and turned my phone off. Going to be at the library downtown all day tomorrow finishing some research, talk the day after?

I hate that I missed your call. Decided at the last minute to go to the archive, lost track of time. I keep forgetting about the time. Wish you'd left a message. I miss the sound of your voice. But I knew it would be like this for a few weeks anyway. You do what you need to. I miss you so much, Nate.

Wait. Her finger hovered over the phone. *Weekend.* She scrolled up, down, then stopped. He'd left Saturday night. She scanned the messages, once, twice *Weekend* then looked at the date and time. *No, that can't be right. That would mean I've been up here for nine days since his last visit. Impossible. No.* She dropped the phone on the bed. *That' can't be right. He just left, just a few days ago. It's a glitch. The phone is wrong. I'm fine. Everything is fine. Just a day or two, I'm sure that's it.*

Another spasm, violent, like the snap of a fish tail. She gasped and clutched the footboard, panting until it stopped.

When it did, she examined the rotting and molding food again, the scent of syrupy decay heavy in the air. *Days. It's only been a few days. Maybe two, three at the most,* she insisted. *You've just gone a bit too far this time. Look at the state of you, worse than after the baby. Baby,* she thought. *Baby. There's something I've forgotten.* She spun and looked toward the adjoining door across the bathroom. The nursery. The attic.

Oh dear God she thought, racing across the room. *I've forgotten Edie.*

Georgia wrenched open the bedroom door, ran up the stairs, one hand supporting her distended stomach, the other pulling herself up, up, up to the attic by the handrail, calling the young girl's name.

"Edie, oh sweetheart, Edie It's me! I'm here!" At the attic door now, her shaking hands wrapped around the crystal doorknob, a moment of panic. *What if . . . what if she left? What if she moved on never came back while I lay here for*

Hours,

Days,

Weeks.

Heart in a free fall, Georgia turned the doorknob and entered. The attic was dark and still, no sound but the birds twittering beyond the roof shingles. Morning. She stepped into the dark attic, her footfalls waking the still house, waiting for her eyes to adjust. Another step and her foot hit a discarded canvas.

"Edie?" Her eyes were beginning to adjust even as the sun rose, and she saw that the dismal nursery she'd left days—

weeks

—ago had been utterly transformed in her prolonged absence. The sheaves of crayon drawings, sketches, and old photographs that had papered the attic walls were gone and, in their place, a surreal mural surrounded her, a glorious *trompe-l'oeil*. Edie and her paints had reimagined the attic from a hollow aerie to a fairytale forest, so exact, so exquisite, Georgia nearly lost her footing, thinking she'd stumble over the scattering of painted moss-covered rocks at her feet. She stooped with some difficulty to pick the canvas up from the painted forest floor, astonished to see her own face there, rendered in such perfect detail it was like looking in a mirror. She scanned the half-lit room again, then set the canvas carefully against the wall, near the base of a sun-dappled sycamore tree and a small cluster of forget-me-nots.

"Edie?" she called again, but there was no reply.

She located the lamp, which now appeared as a whimsical castoff in the painted wood near a heavy arbor covered in vines, thick clusters of grapes dangling over the worn easy chair so lush Georgia imagined she could smell them. The soft electric glow illuminated the room around her and she gasped. Edie had not only painted the walls and floor, she'd painted the ceiling as well. Graceful pines seemed to sway overhead; a stream ran a meandering course across the attic floor, disappearing under a crush of yellowed leaves deep under the eaves. Dotted stone huts in the distance, woodland animals peeking out at her shyly from behind the mackerel bark of the sycamores.

"Oh, Edie," she whispered. "I let you down, didn't I?" She was gone. *I left her for too long and now I've lost her, too. She made us this glorious paradise and now she's gone. She left and I never got a chance to say goodbye.*

A choked sob from deep under the eaves, near one of the distant stone huts startled her.

"Edie," she whispered hoarsely. "Is that you?"

Another sound, fingernails scratching on the floor. Georgia dropped to her knees and crawled toward the sound, ignoring the burning inside her. Out of the darkness a flash of pale skin, tear-filled eyes. A cascade of burnished rag curls. Edie pulled herself out from the darkness across the painted landscape, over imagined loamy earth, a desperate cry as she threw herself into Georgia's arms.

"You came back!" she wept into her chest. "You came back for me."

Georgia clutched Edie to her chest, shifting her gently away from her stomach.

"Oh my Edie, I'm so sorry. I had no idea it had been so long, I never meant to stay away so long."

Edie burrowed her face in Georgia's chest, her entire body wracked with her weeping. "Edie, everything is all right. I'm here now."

"You forgot me," the girl whispered softly.

"I did not," Georgia insisted, squashing down the persistent image of the disjointed string of messages on her phone. *Nine days. Impossible.* "I was sick. I'm better now." She brushed her hair back, smoothed some soot off the trembling girl's anguished face. "Now stop that, silly. It was only a few days. Like we talked about."

Edie sat up and shook her head slowly, "No, I don't think it was, I . . ." the fall of ash gusted away as she wiped her eyes and gave a startled cry. She placed an uncertain hand on Georgia's forehead, traced the new lines that creased and cracked her ashen skin.

"Georgia, what happened?" she choked. "What's happened to you?"

"I told you," Georgia's vision blurred and Edie's face became a kaleidoscope of concern, "I just had a bout of the flu. Maybe something I ate. I slept and slept, but I'm better now. I'll be my old self before long."

"No, I mean," Edie began wringing her hands, "what's happened to your hair? And your . . ." Another quick, tentative touch to her temple.

"Nothing," Georgia said evenly. "Everything is just fine. Perfect. I'm here and you're here and . . . and everything is just like it used to be." Pushing Edie's hands away again, she struggled to stand, fell back heavily to her knees, falling forward on her hands as a coughing fit wracked her. Edie leapt to her feet, the soot falling in a wash to the ground and vanishing. She waited until the coughing subsided, then helped Georgia up.

"Here," Edie said in a calm voice. "Let me help you." Wrapping one arm around Georgia's shoulder, she led her to the easy chair.

Edie's expression was now something terribly, suddenly mature.

"I'm so sorry," she whispered. "I shouldn't have made such a fuss. I've behaved like a baby. It's just," her eyes went wide as they ran down the length of Georgia's body. "I could hear you down there but you never came up, never answered my calls. I thought . . . I thought you'd become like . . ." She swallowed audibly. "But now that I see you . . ." Running a hand over her glistening eyes, she leapt to her feet and ran across the transformed room for a blanket that now lay near a cluster of rose bushes, hurrying back to drape it over Georgia.

"Thank you, Edie," Georgia said gratefully, a yawn cutting off her words. "But I'm better now. I'll be fine soon enough, you'll see." The tears staining Edie's delicate cheekbones disappeared one by one; the tatters and soot stains on her frock vanished as well. Her hair shifted, spun and wound itself into a charming knot on the nape of her neck. None of these changes surprised Georgia anymore. What was shocking was the look on her lovely youthful face.

Another coughing fit wracked her shoulders. Edie flickered from aghast to concerned, like a celluloid starlet. She grabbed a clean oilcloth and gently wiped Georgia's lips, her brow, then settled one smooth hand on her forehead and frowned.

"Shh . . . maybe you should—" She broke off, her hands falling helplessly into her lap.

"Never mind me," Georgia insisted. She pushed herself upright, shifting against the pressure in her stomach. "Look at all of your work! You were right, you are an excellent painter. I feel like I'm in a living forest. No, no, stop fussing. I want to hear about all this," she said, gesturing one hand about the room, now brilliantly lit up with sunrise. "Tell me about our garden."

Edie bit her lip. When she looked at Georgia, her expression held a gravity that felt aged, mature.

"Well, I thought," she said finally, "as many gifts as you've given me, I'd give you one. A secret nowhere, just for the two of us, all the way up here. As far away from . . ."

she paused, turning slowly as if examining her own creation with a critical eye. "I thought," she turned back to Georgia, "I'd make us a paradise like the one I dreamed of. Up here, drenched in the light." She held her arms up and as she did, gesturing grandly to the sunbeams she'd painted, shining through the forest canopy. "Look at this light, Georgia, how it washes through even the darkest corners of the forest. Don't ever forget it. It's important, I remembered, while you were gone, that we have to try to stay in the light, no matter what." She tangled her fingers under her chin. "Yes, stay in the light. Mustn't tread in dark places. Certainly not the greenhouse. And never, ever the basement," she whispered, in a confused, hushed voice before rushing on. "And I worried when you didn't come back that you'd lost your way. And wandered into the dark. It happens you know, by accident."

Across the room, Georgia could see the girl struggling with a memory. She was on the verge of remembering something so distressing, the air around her began to vibrate.

"Edie." The girl's distress fell to the floor in a blanket of dust. "Tell me about the basement."

"I can't." The dust rose in a cloud and stretched across the horizon of the attic, a dark stain in the air. "Please don't ask me to." Edie began to flicker and Georgia immediately regretted her words, wished she could snatch them back.

The song began to pitch and soar again in her head, the vaulting octaves like a fever in her brain.

I want you to run. Run to me. Run to the Garden and hide. Swear it.

She closed her eyes and began humming along, the next verse a lilting promise that ebbed away before Georgia could understand who was promising what. *It's like a saga,* she thought, *like the Song of Roland or Beowulf. So many verses, I'll never learn them all.*

"Georgia." Edie's soft voice woke her from her stupor. She was kneeling next to her again, resting her hand on Georgia's stomach. How long she'd sat there in silence, Georgia could not say. "You . . ." her tongue flicked across her lips, uncertain, "there's something quite different about you," she finished delicately. "If you can just tell me . . ."

Georgia shook her head. "I can't either, Edie. Please."

Edie shifted, pulled Georgia from the chair and settled her in the nest of her arms.

"That's all right. I'll take care of you," she said, brushing Georgia's hair back. "Like you took care of me."

Georgia settled herself heavily against Edie's warmth, curled up against her soft bosom, the melody falling from her lips as the song shifted to a lower, headier octave.

I watch the turn of the universe. I watch the birth of stars, the collapse of suns.

Don't be afraid.

After a minute, Edie joined in, a soprano accompaniment to Georgia's alto.

Can't we just stay here forever?

"You can hear it too?" she whispered.

Edie nodded.

"I wonder where it comes from," she whispered, Edie's warm hands on her middle, something in her touch soothing the agony inside. "I wonder how it ends."

◆　◆　◆

Dawn was breaking again over Roseneath, heralding a new—

Day?

Week?

Year?

—as Georgia crept down the attic stairs. An eerie silence had replaced Edie's rambled chattering, each movement, each word now chosen with deliberate care.

"Downstairs with you now," she'd said, patting Georgia softy on her bottom. "I want you to eat and rest. Take a few days. Don't worry about me; I have lots to occupy myself with."

Clutching the stair rail, Georgia had turned back to her, bemused, before continuing on her way.

"Such as?"

"Oh, I need to add a patch of stars in the sky. I just remembered. True north. And of course, a raven. Can't have you underfoot." A pause and then quickly, "You should call Nathan, too. Does he know how sick you are? Maybe he should come home. Someone to take care of you. Properly." Another beat. "You said he just left?"

But Georgia had ignored her, continuing down the stairs, shutting the door at the bottom behind her. She paused at the upstairs landing. The window was covered in a thick layer of frost, obscuring the yard outside. She breathed on it, rubbed it, but the frost remained. Once downstairs, she hurried past the trash-strewn living room, skated carefully over the avalanche of mail that had fallen through the snow-crusted mail slot, and finally entered the kitchen.

Every cabinet was opened, every drawer dumped out on the floor. Every surface, the counters, the stove, the kitchen table was covered in scraps of food in varying states of rot. Her stomach lurched at the sight of it and she ran, stumbling to the sink, to vomit a foamy blood-flecked mass, missing when her stomach hit the edge of the countertop painfully and retching instead onto a plate of food so covered in mold it was unidentifiable. She tried in vain to ignore the way her stomach swelled in a hard rise against the edge of the wooden counters, then splashed water onto her face, drank from the tap until her stomach settled once more. *Chin up, don't look down. Mustn't look. Everything is fine. It's not what you think. It can't be. Can't be.*

She gazed out the frosted kitchen window toward the sky, as if she could wish herself up and away from Rose-neath, but instead of deliverance, her eyes landed on a small flake of snow, then another. A gust of wind and the small patch of sky she could see at the top of the window frame filled with a gentle flurry, the house shuddering around her as the north wind hit the side of Roseneath, hard. *No*, she whispered, forcing the frozen window open. A blast of winter hit her face; a curtain of snowflakes filled the kitchen. Outside, the trees were bare and black, their limbs clawing at a sterile, ice-blue sky. Georgia looked then to the ground around Roseneath, her eyes searching in vain for grass, leaves, gravel and finding instead snow-crusted vines and frost-tipped thorns. *Oh God why did I look?* Beyond, in every direction, lay a foot of graying snow,

now newly blanketed with a fresh fall of brilliant white. She spun away from the sight and fell to the floor, her hands finally reaching for her stomach. *Impossible. Don't look. Don't. Step on a crack, break your mother's back. It can't be.* The song in her head seemed to rise and fall on the snowstorm that now swirled through the kitchen, snowflakes skittering across the filthy linoleum, calling, weeping, pleading, a melodic, unending threnody.

No.

Georgia's fingertips touched the hard rise of her stomach, traced the burning tracks of stretch marks that crisscrossed her belly like the frost on the windows, felt the flipping fish jump within. She pushed down on her enormously swollen womb and felt a kick. Then another. Ice-cold tears trailed down her grimy cheeks as she pushed on the other side, felt something push back, almost playfully. She looked down to see, *oh God no, why did I look?* to know, unable to pretend anymore, unable to hide from this anymore, pulling her shirt up and off as she did, her hands cradling her swollen breasts, then falling once more to the tumescent, lush swell of the impossible—*oh God, it can't be, can't be*—child inside her and screamed.

Hours passed. Outside the blizzard raged, sending billowing gusts through the open window, a blissful balm to the feverish heat raging inside her. She rose, each step she took melting the dusting of snow around her, and opened the remaining windows, let the deliciously cold air and snow absolve her. Soon, the corners of the kitchen filled with drifts of thick white snow, the spoiled food on the counter disappeared under a heavy white blanket. And in the middle of it all, Georgia sat in a calming warmth, her fingertips trailing over her stomach as the child within sometimes followed, sometimes led, paralyzed by the rapture of the song in her head until finally the movement slowed, stopped and the impossible child she was carrying fell fast asleep within.

Georgia woke as if from a trance and reached blindly on the countertop for her phone. She dialed Nathan's number over and over again, obsessively, futilely, as darkness fell and the storm subsided, moonlight shining on the snow-filled room around her, bathing her and her extraordinary unborn child in a celestial, beatific glow.

❖　❖　❖

The house stood a little farther back from the tired old street. It was, Nathan decided with a practiced eye, a magnificent ruin. He'd seen dozens like it over the years: beautiful, abandoned, needing far too much to bring them back to what they were. Brick that had once been creamy yellow, now faded to a dingy bone. Oversized stone steps under a sagging porch roof, a greenhouse with more glass panes on the ground than in the frames. The yard a tangle of ivy and Queen Anne's lace dotted throughout with relics of broken statuary and trash. A wilting damsel in distress with hollow eyes that time had forgotten. He knew what lay behind those eyes and it was always more nightmare than fairy tale.

"Why did you drag me all the way out here, Joe?" He came around the corner jangling a set of keys.

Joe laughed and underhanded the keys to him.

"The deal of a lifetime, my friend."

Nathan groaned. "You have got to be kidding me."

"Not even a little bit. City owns it. Colonial Revival, hundred years old, give or take, untouched since the thirties or forties." Nathan's eyes darted back with interest now at the towering house's impassive expression.

"Got your attention yet?" Joe laughed again. "Coming up for auction in another month. City wants to unload it. I know a guy, I can get it for you before any of that happens."

"How much?" Nathan turned the keys over and over in his hands.

"Nothing," Joe said, "or close to it. Anyway, it'll take every penny you have and every ounce of smarts in that head of yours to sort this one out. But . . ."

"But what?" Nathan asked quickly.

"If you can do it, you'll either have the house of your dreams or you can flip it and make a fortune."

"Yeah, and if I can't, it'll be the house of my nightmares."

Joe rocked back on his heels and looked over the house again. "Yep. Anyway, there's the keys. Look it over, see what you think. Personally, I think your missus will love it. And with a family on the way, might be just the thing. Think about it. But don't think too long."

"What's wrong with it, Joe? Level with me. Don't jerk me around."

"Oh, people think it's haunted. Locals think it's full of boogeymen and ghosts." He snorted and turned toward his own car.

"I don't believe in any of that shit, Joe."

"I know it. That's why I thought of you when I saw it. Hey, it's even got a name."

A house with a name. God, Georgia would love that. Maybe, just maybe . . .

"What's it called?"

"Roseneath."

Nathan spent the next two hours exploring the property as best he could in the waning light. Most of the roof was in fair condition, considering. The attic was bone dry, which was surprising. The electrical was as he expected—crumbling knob and tube—it would all have to go. All the copper plumbing had been stripped, more than half of the windows were broken—he'd have to replace them all anyway, but still—and rain and weather had ruined the floors in more than one section. The basement was the worst: low ceilings, crumbling walls wept with seeping run-off from the non-existent gutters, a warren of small rooms, most of them filled with mounds of mud and debris and over it all the familiar rank odor of decay.

And yet. A clawfoot bathtub. The scale and proportions of each room made his mouth water. The walls were thick, unblemished plaster, the woodwork was almost pristine. The yard was overgrown but expansive and choked with hundred-year-old roses. The carriage house roof sagged but the walls were sound and he could throw up a new roof in a few days. A motley crew of the good, the bad, and the ugly that arranged itself into a golden ratio. He decided then and there to buy it the next day. Buy it and work on it in his every free moment and get it livable before the baby came, a surprise for Georgia he never dreamed he'd be able to give her.

He still had a few months before the baby, he thought, as he locked up the back door. He'd get a loan tomorrow and start work right away. Georgia wouldn't notice a few more late evenings, and then, when it was habitable, he'd bring her here and surprise her.

Crunch.

He froze on the porch and listened. Something in the greenhouse. It sounded like someone walking on the broken glass.

"Hello? Anyone there?" he called out.

Nothing.

Boogeymen and ghosts.

"I don't believe in any of that shit," he whispered to himself.

Crunch.

"Who's there?" he yelled. He jammed the keys in his pocket and walked across the backyard, into the twilight. The noise came again from the shadow-drenched greenhouse, but softer this time. He cleared his throat, thinking he should go back to his truck for his flashlight. The last thing he remembered was the slickness of something slithering along his skin as it wound itself around his arms and legs, his throat like vines, dragging him deeper into the greenhouse.

When he woke up, it felt like ages had passed, each of his joints felt atrophied, stiff. He rubbed a hand over his eyes and flinched at the earth that scratched his eyelids. He scrambled upright and looked around. Where the hell was he? Light poured down a set of basement stairs. He was lying at the bottom, covered in mud. It was morning. He looked at his filth-streaked watch. 6:20 am.

Shit.

He stood and felt around in his pockets for the keys. They were right where he'd put them last night. But how had he gotten down here? And why? Georgia would be frantic.

"I must have dozed off," he told himself as he raced home. As the miles ticked by, he thought back to the night before. A noise. The greenhouse. Something in it. But there had been nothing. Nothing he could recall. It wasn't like him to just fall asleep like that.

He looked over at the seat next to him and saw a simple bouquet, roses from the overgrown yard. A dozen of them.

He smiled to himself as he rubbed more dirt out of his bleary eyes and thought about the house. Georgia would be furious. At least he wouldn't show up empty-handed. He'd bring her a surprise from Roseneath.

TWENTY-FOUR

 NATHAN PRITCHARD WAS DREAMING. NOT the Nathan that lay in bed, whose face was twisted in a self-satisfied grin—that creature lived his dreams awake. That Nathan lived out his every desire, wakeful, prowling, unrepentant. The other Nathan, the scared little boy inside, hid from his worst nightmares, his face buried in his knees, his hands held tight against his ears, pretending reality was a nightmare that would soon be over.

That small, true shred of Nathan was dreaming, a dream within a dream, his numb, senseless brain spiraling back inside itself, a pocket in a pocket, searching for respite deeper inside a memory of a memory, a shard so small, so sharp, he wondered briefly if he might not have found a way out of this . . . this *prison* and back to somewhere real.

A place so real he could feel the sun on the back of his neck, smell freshly mown hay and clover. He dropped his hands from his ears and heard birdsong, he raised his face and found he was crouched in a pasture, no nightmare to be seen, on a beautiful summer's day.

I know this day.

He stood and held his hands out in front of him, tanned, broad, turned them over and remembered how gentle, how strong they were.

I remember these hands.

He spun at a sound behind him—footfalls and branches breaking—and saw her emerge from the gloom of a deep wood. A dryad, a nymph, a siren, a woodland elf, his mind searched frantically for the name, the classification of the vision that approached, discarding each of them as they fell short.

I know you.

Her face, pale and freckled, flushed in the sun; long black hair fell in tangled vines that coiled and undulated like snakes around her as she walked toward him. He reached for the memory of who she was, what this was, what he was supposed to do and found an enormous vacuum, a nothingness.

I knew you.

He looked back down at his hands, trying to remember how to fill them, unable to remember what he was meant to do, meant to say to this vision that now stood in front of him. He could feel her peering up at him, saw the white tip of her nose, saw the pink of her lips beneath, curved up at him, a patient, maddeningly familiar smile, but he was unable to look away from his empty, rediscovered hands to meet her gaze.

Empty, he thought, closing his eyes. *I'm empty and I have no offering to give her now.*

Nathan felt a gentle tug of his hands toward her lips, heard her laugh at the incredulous look on his face, her merriment a beautiful ringing that shattered the silence of the pasture and fell on them in a flurry of snow. An isolated snowstorm, each flake a sliver of memory, flickers of moments that played in his head as they melted on his skin.

I've ruined your apple.

Hair, her hair, spread out across a wood floor, a crown of wood shavings nestled in her curls.

Aren't I a fortunate girl? My husband has made me a crown.

Her pensive face in a dark parking lot

Oh, yes, I think you should, her voice low, her face tilted to him as she rose on her tiptoes.

I don't know what you've done.

I don't want to hurt you

You can't. You won't.

The snow fell thick and fast, the images swirled around him in a blizzard too furious to grasp, each one evaporating as soon as he glimpsed it. He reached out with both hands, trying to catch just one flake, one memory, to hold it tight and keep it safe, but they all melted before he could see their shape, remember them, hide each precious moment away from . . . from . . .

"*You're doing it wrong,*" she whispered—that voice, the one he remembered. "Like this." She tilted her head back and caught one perfect snowflake on her tongue. Another burst of laughter, like sleigh bells.

"You chased me here once." Her pink tongue darted out again, another flake. "Tickled me. You try."

Afraid she would vanish, Nathan gripped her hands tightly in his and let one flake land on his tongue. He smiled.

"I love you, don't I? That's the secret I forgot."

Her eyes shone with warmth. A small, almost furtive shake of her head.

"No, don't be ridiculous. You'd remember a thing like that."

"I love you," he insisted, pulling her to his chest. "Oh God, I remember now. I love you best of all, more than anything in the world. Say it. I want to hear you say it."

"No," she whispered into his chest, even as her hands slid around him, as her hair lengthened into a riot of gentle tendrils, a forest of roots wrapping around them, anchoring them both in this moment, this memory. She wove her net around them both until the pasture, the sun, the snow and the dark wood vanished and they were safe inside the cocoon she had made. A pocket in a pocket in a pocket.

His hands slipped to her waist, his fingers fluttered against her soft skin.

"Say it," he demanded, his laugh mingling with her own. "I love you best of all."

Giggling, breathless, she threw her head back, her voice echoing in the small sanctuary.

"You love me best of all."

Nathan stopped tickling her. *My hand, my body, my memories, my wife.*

"How long do we have?"

Her eyes grew wide and serious.

"Until you forget me again."

Nathan's heart fell as her face became the moon, the sun, the Milky Way, a hundred different expressions, a thousand faceted memories, the woman in his arms a universe of intricate constellations he remembered completely.

I know you, he thought. *These hands know all of you.*

Her hair tightened around him in elegant knots and braids, as if she was trying to bind herself to him, to secure herself back inside him.

"I could never forget you," Nathan said, his lips finding hers, remembering how. His hands remembered now, they knew, knew everything she was, they were full once more. *Enchantress*, he thought. *That's what she is, who she is. She enchants me and only me. She is my dream, my reality.* "Never," he repeated.

She sighed, her lips falling to his neck. Her reply was so soft he almost missed the words.

"But you did."

Nathan wanted to protest, to plead his case, but before he could, her body convulsed in his arms, her porcelain veneer shattering like a broken poppet. Something dark, something sharp, a vicious nothing tore into her hair, coiled around her sweet face, her arms, her stomach, slicing, cutting their way through her and into the sanctuary she had made for them. He felt his hands—

Not your hands

—release her broken body—

Oh please no

—a snarl of vines, arms of wickedly sharp teeth. Fingers like daggers from deep inside the wood clawed at her, pulled her from him, wrapped her in their arms, and began dragging her across the meadow. Nathan looked down at his feet—

not my feet

—silently pleading with them to run to her, to cleave her, to save her, whoever she was. *I knew. A moment ago I knew who she was.* The tendrils of her memory fell away as a terrible heat began to build in the meadow, the pasture grasses burst into flames, scorching away every trace of this day, this woman, this truth, this reality.

He found me. He found her.

Across the meadow, the relentless vines continued coiling around her, through her, strangling her. She screamed something to him, but her words were lost in the inferno. His hands were no longer his hands and his feet were no longer his feet. He realized that his head, his neck, were still his, at least for now. He raised his head and sought out her dead black eyes, saw the army of sharp teeth whittle her down to a stick doll, and he knew as he watched that she would splinter into nothing if he didn't find a way to stop it. With the last true shred of himself that he still possessed, Nathan found the strength to call out to her.

"I knew you! I knew you! Oh God, who were you?"

His words seemed to hit her like blows and her face cracked into a spider's web. Helpless, Nathan watched as the grasping claws completed their grim work of shredding her to ribbons. Her broken mouth opened in a silent scream that became the night sky as the terrible forest tore the dryad, the siren, the wood elf, the enchantress, the dream apart, until she was nothing more than a sound echoing in the gutted pasture. The wind caught that, too, and sent it spiraling away from him, leaving Nathan alone again.

An enchantress, a dream, something in between, the little boy thought as his feet—

Not your feet

—marched him through the ruined landscape back to a waking nightmare—

Not anymore

— the sound of her voice forgotten as another one spoke his name in the dark room.

"Nathan?"

He struggled to stop his lips from answering, determined to remember

Her.

The pasture.

I knew you.

But then it was gone and his lips found another's.

"Nathan, are you all right?" she asked, smoothing his damp hair from his forehead.

"I'm fine," he heard himself reply, his tongue thick and foreign in his mouth.

"You were screaming. Nightmare?" she asked. On the nightstand, his phone began to vibrate. *Answer it. Answer it, please let me answer it. I want to go home.* But he lay there, immobile, watching helplessly as she sat up and tossed it across the room with disgust, muttering, "Ugh, not again."

He felt his head shake. "No, not at all. I had the most beautiful dream. Sorry I woke you."

He felt his hands pull her toward him, felt the lead weights begin to pull him down, down, down, his lips fluttering against her skin, speaking the words they chose without his permission, a slow poison.

"The most beautiful dream," he repeated as she pushed him back and slid herself on top of him. Her eyes were not round and wide and filled with the universe, they were almond-shaped and green, calculating cat's eyes that bored into him.

"Then why are you crying, Nate?" Her voice drifted down from his ear to his neck, her hair settling on his stomach.

His hands left the back of her head and his fingertips found his face, following the same trail his tears did as a wall of dark water began to fill his lungs. The thick, vicious silt pulled him down like quicksand, dragging him back to that nothing place.

"Am I?" The words seemed to come from deep in the dark woods at the edge of the lake that he drowned in.

"Never mind," she said, her voice muffled beneath the sheets. "It doesn't matter."

TWENTY-FIVE

WHEN YOU'RE PREGNANT AND YOUR HUS-
band doesn't come home one night, your mind
goes straight to bad places. Dead in a ditch.
Drunk in a bar. It lingers there until about one in the
morning and then moves on to very bad places. It moves
on to attractive ex-girlfriends and unexpected pregnancies,
then it roots around until it finds the key to the door you
keep your insecurities in, adds them to the mix, and by
three o'clock you've convinced yourself that your too-good-
for-you husband has decided he's had it with how fat and
dull you are now, no longer finds you attractive, and by five
you've already resigned yourself to the fact that he's leaving
you for someone tall, leggy, wealthy, and not pregnant.

*This was where Georgia was when Nathan came home,
wild-eyed and filth-streaked, clutching a bundle of roses. He
stumbled through the door and wrapped her in his arms before
she could even utter a word, smelling of decay and dry earth.*

"Baby, I am so sorry."

"Where were you? I was frantic." She ran her hand over his
face, down his chest, up over his arms, her fears evaporating

at the sight of him, her worry surging at the state of him. "Are you hurt?"

He shook his head. "No, no, I'm fine. I fell asleep at the site, I must have been more tired than I thought. Slept straight through till morning. Oh, god, baby I am so sorry. Are you all right?"

She drew back from him, trying to understand the near-evangelical glow in his eyes. There was something off about him. Or maybe it was just that she spent a sleepless night and he spent one, by the looks of him, in a pile of dirt.

"I'm fine, Nate."

"How's my little Rose?" he asked, placing one earth-crusted hand on her stomach. She recoiled, pushed his hand off and held it instead.

"We're both fine, Nate. I was just so worried."

He held out the flowers to her.

"Forgive me?"

"Anything." She took them from him, and then she gasped. The roses fell from her hand to the floor. Blood welled up in a constellation across her palm. "Damn, a thorn."

"Let me see." He pulled her hand from her mouth. "A couple thorns. Hold still, I can get them out."

As he carefully pried each thorn out, she studied his face for signs of treachery. Finding none, she reasoned with herself. He did work too hard. He probably did fall asleep. All things being equal, the simplest explanation was the most likely. And he'd never lied to her before.

He kissed her hands when he finished, then the tip of her nose.

"Just keep a bandage on that finger. I couldn't get that thorn out, it's in too deep. Give it a day or so and it'll work itself out."

"Are you really all right, Nathan?" she asked him again.
"I've never felt better."

✦ ✦ ✦

"Nathan?" After dozens of calls, each one ending in an abrupt click, his phone finally rolled to voicemail. It was nearly dawn over Roseneath, but the sky outside hung dark and heavy, the winds howling around the house as yet another winter storm rolled in from the north. The yard, the kitchen, the house, the whole world was a frozen kingdom around her. The basement door was warm against her cheek. "Nate, I . . ." Inside her the child shifted, settled. The movement, though subtle, took her breath away. Somewhere below, the joists and beams of Roseneath groaned. She reached out to gather another handful of deliciously cold snow. She watched as it began to melt the instant she touched it, cupped her hand to save a few draughts. She scattered the warm water around her, watched as it began to crystalize on the frigid floor, then gathered another handful and held it to her parched lips. The cool trickle down her throat tempered the heat inside her. "Come home, Nate," she said. A fit of coughing splattered the snow at her feet in crimson. "Please, Nate. Hurry."

She peered through the keyhole. Darkness swirled on the other side. *Don't tread in dark places, Georgia.* She traced the outline of the door, ran her fingertips along the gap at the bottom. *Promise me you won't go down there.* Recoiled when she found warm, damp earth. *Never, ever the basement.* Georgia hastily scoured the mud from her hand then pressed her ear against the door again, listening. She could feel the rush of warm, moist air coming up from the basement. Silence. And yet a similar sensation, like that first day in the attic. A hesitation, something sentient and alien, down there, deep in the darkness, was listening, too.

9-1-1. She pressed each button carefully, hesitating only for a second before hitting send. Nothing. Static. She tried again. The line crackled angrily then went dead. She tried every contact in her list but each call ended the same. Static then silence. She tried Nathan again. It rang and rang and then cut off with a click. Across the yard she could just barely make out the shape of her car, buried in the snow, drifts spreading out in every direction.

She studied the melt water where she'd scrubbed her hand clean. Rivulets of red in the dank earth mingled with splatters of her own blood. She felt a profound distance, in that moment, from Roseneath, Edie, Nathan, the inconceivable child in her stomach, even from herself, as if she floated above it all, an impassive observer. It all looked so obvious, so insidious from that vantage. Every decision, every choice she'd made since the day she arrived in Roseneath had led her to this place. Each intention innocent enough, but seen as a whole, madness. Ruin. Trapped.

She dropped the phone into a snowdrift and then dove forward, burying her hands and arms, her feverish face in the snow, the sudden shock of the wintery chill a brief respite. She rolled to her side and lay for hours in the melt of her wake, staring at the ceiling, at the snow trickling through the open windows. Inside the baby hummed and twirled. Upstairs, Edie was dancing. Outside the storm raged, but inside, the silence of Roseneath pressed in all around her.

I'm not like anyone. Not anymore.

✦ ✦ ✦

Georgia had been at work when the pains started. They hadn't been bad at first. She stretched, then rubbed her stomach. She'd had little pains before. This pain was sharp, different somehow. She'd grasped the shelves on either side of her, breathing until the pain passed. When it did, it left a nauseating aftertaste in her mouth. She felt sore and achy, like she had the flu. It almost reminded her of those first weeks spent retching up everything she tried to eat.

Her head spun, trying to decide if this was yet another unpleasant discovery of pregnancy, along with the occasional bizarre discharge, the vomiting, the leaking breasts, the random pains. Pregnancy, she'd discovered, was more graphic than the books told you. She'd asked the doctor about all of her symptoms, feeling silly each time he told her it was all normal. So, she just left work early, concerned but not alarmed. She didn't bother to call Nathan and tell him she wasn't feeling well. He was so busy these days, there was no sense in worrying him. Especially after his strange behavior the night before.

She went home, thinking a nap would fix everything. That she'd wake up and it would all go back to eating and waddling and waiting for their daughter to make her miraculous appearance in three months' time.

She'd climbed into bed, dropping her clothes in a trail behind her because suddenly it all felt too tight. She drifted off instantly, only to be woken up by the feeling that someone was killing her, someone was ripping her in half, her stomach rolled and she felt the horrible clenching pain again and she held very, very still thinking it would stop. Thinking it would leave as quickly as it came if she just lay there playing possum, that the horrible pain wouldn't find her again if she hid from it.

But it did come back, with a vengeance, and without a thought, she fell out of bed and crawled to the bathroom. Her thighs slick with something, her knees sliding; no, no she wouldn't look, couldn't look. After an eternity of crawling, she made it to the bathroom and curled there on the floor as wave after wave broke over her, rocks broke over her, boulders of pain thrown by an unseen giant. They pressed her into the ground and pinned her there under a center of gravity composed of agony and a terrible wetness. Hours passed; she lay there delirious, praying the pains would pass so she could call for help. But there was no time, no space between them until the last wave hit her. She slumped over on her back, breathless at the suddenness of the release, no sound in the bathroom except her ragged breathing. But then, a sound, something moving, something soft. She tried to move her legs, tried to find it, tried to do something, anything but lie there. Instead, she felt her eyes close, so heavy, and the soft fluttering at her feet shushed her gently to sleep.

That's how Nathan had found them. Or so he told her later. She remembered nothing but waking up in the hospital, hours later, long after that little fluttering girl had sighed once in Nathan's arms there on the floor and rushed away from them forever.

TWENTY-SIX

 There was a
book
lying near
Alice
on the
table, and
while she sat
watching
the White King
she
turned
over the leaves
to find some part
that
that
she could read—
"for it's all in some language I don't know . . ."

Edie sat with her long legs crossed, her elbows elegantly poised on each knee. She tilted her head to one side, her eyes rapt as she listened to Georgia read aloud. And she *was* listening, intently. Not to the story, but to the way

Georgia stumbled over the words, to the way her breath caught and wheezed. To the damp cough that punctuated every other sentence. And she *was* rapt, but not in the manner of a child enchanted by a fairy tale, but by how very much effort it was taking Georgia to read to her, studying exactly how much she had changed, trying in vain to understand this odd, unsettling transformation.

Perplexed, Edie looked out the peaked attic window. Ice-blue skies, naked tree limbs. The dead of winter. Back to Georgia now, she pursed her lower lip thoughtfully as she took in the patches of hair missing from the sides of her head, the scabs on her lips, no longer simply pale but now near translucent. And when Edie touched her, Georgia no longer felt warm like Edie remembered bathwater to feel. No, now her skin shifted in a mystifying cycle between scorching hot and, more frighteningly, icy cold. But most troubling and confusing of all was the enormity of her stomach. Ponderous and round, softly shifting even as Edie watched, it was as if some gruesome monster was consuming her from the inside out. And, all the while, her Georgia seemed serenely set that it was not happening.

Why is she pretending? Edie thought to herself, chewing a hank of hair. *She is clearly ill. Clearly troubled.* With a start Edie thought, *Clearly whatever is happening with her stomach is not quite right. She is clearly afraid. But of what?* Georgia coughed thickly into a handkerchief, blanching as she glanced down before tucking it behind her. But Edie's sharp eyes had caught a glimpse of another crimson stain.

She puzzled over this for some time, but at last a bright thought struck her. "Why, it's a Looking-Glass book, of course!

And if I hold it up to a glass, the words will all go the right way again."

The realization of just why Georgia was going to such lengths to deny her appearance shook Edie like the sharp northern winds against the frozen branches of the sycamore outside.

She doesn't want to worry me, Edie thought with a start. *She's trying to protect me.*

"'Twas brillig,
and
the slithy toves,"

Georgia continued to stumble over the words, oblivious to Edie's revelation.

"Did gyre and gimble
in the wabe;
All mimsy
were
the borogoves,
And the mome raths
outgrabe.
Beware
the Jabberwock, my son!
The jaws that bite,
the claws that catch!"

Georgia's voice caught on the last word. She ran her tongue over cracked lips and tried to start again.

"Beware . . ." she stopped. "Beware the . . . the . . ."

"Georgia," Edie said softly, reaching over to pull the book from her hands. "I've changed my mind about monsters. I don't think I care to hear any more today."

Georgia's hands fell limp in her lap. "Neither do I. I hate this story. What child would want to read this?"

Edie rose and placed the book back with her childhood toys. She paused to study Georgia slumped on a mound of pillows against the *trompe-l'oeil* wall. Her posture was so broken, her arms and legs so emaciated, she looked like a marionette dropped by a careless, thoughtless child. Edie looked away from the distressing image and stared thoughtfully out the window.

"You know," Edie said finally, "when I was a little girl, I was frightened of monsters." She cast a swift glance at the attic door. "Papa told me there were no such things."

Another glance at the door. The house shuddered in a sudden gale, the windows rattled and below, far below, the house settled with a prolonged luxurious groan.

Georgia shifted back against the pillows, stretching her swollen feet out in front of her. Her bruised toes slid across a painted clutch of black feathers before coming to rest on a rock so realistic she imagined she could feel the damp moss soothing her mottled feet. "Your Papa was right. There is no Jabberwock, there is no haunted wood in Wonderland. Nothing that dreadful exists, not really."

Edie swallowed hard. "Maybe. Or maybe . . ." She pursed her lips as if considering how to go on, when suddenly her pale brow wrinkled. She leaned forward, listening intently.

They're all gone. He killed them, burned them all.

Georgia's eyes darted up, almost guiltily, from her stomach to meet Edie's steady, knowing gaze.

Cautiously, Edie reached her hands out and placed them on Georgia's burgeoning stomach, spread her fingers out. She felt Georgia go limp under her touch, spent, defeated. Edie left her hands there for a long time, trying to span them wide enough to cover the blooming expanse, when suddenly something inside pushed, kicked, kicked again. Edie snatched her hand back.

"Oh!" she cried.

Georgia's lips cracked in a weary smile. She pulled Edie's hands back onto her belly.

"Wait," she sighed, lips thinly curved in a smile. Another kick, this one harder. Edie gasped, even as tears began to slide down Georgia's waxen cheeks.

Edie snatched her hands away and twisted the lace at her throat thoughtfully. "Well, I guess now we know who's singing. Do they all do that?"

"No, Edie," Georgia replied, running her hands in slow circles over her stomach. "No, they do not."

Edie reached back to touch her stomach tentatively. "Does it hurt?"

"No, not the kicking," she said. "That much, at least, doesn't hurt." She closed her eyes, a wan smile shifting the trajectory of the tears that coursed down her face.

"I remember this feeling," she whispered. "At first it's just a little flutter, you see?" She waved her fingers gently in the air. "You think you're imagining it. But then it grows stronger. Every day. Then one day you feel a foot. A hand. The curve of a little head. It's the most beautiful thing. It's strange and wonderful and . . ." Her tears fell faster now.

Edie scooted closer and held Georgia's hand to her cheek. *She feels so cold now, but her face is so flushed. I don't understand.*

"Please talk to me, Georgia. Please help me understand. I want to help," Edie pleaded. Georgia managed a wan smile.

"We had a baby, Edie, Nathan and I. Before we came to Roseneath. She . . . she . . . but we lost her," she said, wiping her cheeks. "Nathan wanted to name her Rose and that's what we called her. She . . . she was so healthy and we were going to be so happy but she . . . she . . . she . . ."

Georgia swallowed hard and met Edie's eyes, hollow. "It was like something snatched her away from us. Took her for no reason." She struggled to sit upright and Edie moved quickly to help her. "And then we came here, and I found you. A miracle, Edie, my miracle, and I thought . . . it was as if someone had given her back to me. In you. Another chance to . . . that being with you would . . ." she broke off, coughing, then continued.

"And I want to believe that this is a miracle, too." She lifted her shirt. Her belly underneath was grotesquely huge, pale white like an eggshell, thin blue veins like marble. "But it's . . . it's . . ."

Edie licked her lips and finished the sentence for her. "Peculiar."

Georgia pulled her shirt down and nodded. "I can't be pregnant. Not this pregnant, at least. It's impossible for me to be this pregnant," she shook her head. "It's only been days, maybe weeks and . . . I don't know exactly how to explain, you see—"

"Georgia," Edie said delicately, flushing. "I'm not a complete ninny." Her face fell to her hands and with it a scattering of coal-black tears. "And, you see, Mama was . . . Mama said I'd have a brother or sister by summer's end."

She shrugged. "I have some understanding of this sort of thing. I'm not a *baby*."

"Of course you're not," Georgia said with a sigh. "Edie, the fact is I'm bigger now than I ever got with Rose. And it can't be more than a few weeks since—" A shadow crossed her face. Edie decided not to press that point, not now at least.

"Georgia, can you tell me, I wonder," Edie chose her words with care, not wanting to distress her more. "What day is today?"

Georgia's head fell into her hands. She did not reply. Edie took a deep breath and wrapped her arms around Georgia.

"There, there, enough of that. Nothing to cry over." She kissed Georgia's temple, crestfallen to see bare patches where her lovely dark locks had been. She felt the icy coolness disappear as whatever fever burned in her spiked again. "I remember when I was a little girl, when we came to this place." Georgia raised her red-rimmed eyes to listen, her breathing labored. "I thought we'd come to a fairytale castle," Edie said with a small laugh. "A place where time did not exist. One day bled gloriously into the next as I played my games." She bit her lip, considering for a moment. "A bit like Alice in the story, I guess. But then everything changed. And I . . ." she shook her head. "Oh, some of it is so jumbled I'm not sure what I remember. It's been so long. But one thing I do know. One thing I remembered then when I was a little girl and everything went all topsy-turvy and I ended up there," she said evenly, raising one arm to point under the eaves to the rug, "and I fear I must remember now, here, whatever I may be today. Something you, too, must remember and never forget."

"What must I remember, Edie?" Georgia whispered, her voice wet and choked, the spittle on her lips pink. Edie raised her apron and wiped her face tenderly.

"That fairy tales are horrid things. At least the ones my mother told me. Trolls and severed toes. Witches and ovens, the Jabberwock in the wood, wishes made nightmares, reality nothing more than a dream. Handsome princes bewitched into gruesome monsters, ladies trapped in ghastly towers. Papa was wrong, Georgia. There *are* monsters. Horrible monsters who do bad things. Not storybook Jabberwocks but real live monsters."

Georgia's face fell and Edie clutched her to her chest.

"What's happening?" Georgia sobbed against her chest. "What's happened to me? What is this place?" Her legs buckled then as a monstrous coughing fit hit her and the two slid together to the floor. Edie held her apron to Georgia's mouth until it passed, felt the warm dampness soak through with each convulsing hack, looked down and saw red.

"I don't know. But you need to leave Roseneath. Now, while there's still time. You're so sick and I can't—"

"Leave?" Georgia choked. "I can't! Where would I go? What would I say? My God, Edie, no one will believe me, no one will understand . . . and I won't leave you. So help me God, I will not leave you alone in Roseneath. This place is wrong, it's like it's twisting back on itself, swallowing everything, throwing up walls wherever I look until there's no way out."

Edie started to argue, but after looking down again at her ruby-stained apron, reconsidered. "Then you need to call Nathan. Tell him. Everything. Make him come home. I can't help you like he could."

"I can't. I tried but he won't answer. Ever since he left, it's like something is keeping me from him, like he—"

Edie swallowed hard and finished the sentence for her. "Like he can't even hear you."

"E . . . Edie," Georgia stumbled over her name and Edie knew *just knew* that she was struggling to keep her voice calm. "Can you tell me how you know that?"

Edie frowned as swaths of color trailed away from her body, leaving behind patches of gray where there had been skin. "I don't know how I know." She shook her hands out but that only seemed to make matters worse. Her color swirled in the air around her, scented it with ozone and hung heavy, as if the heavens were threatening to crack open above her. Edie hid her face in the crook of her arm and fought to stay present, to push the surge of images back, at least for now. But she could feel her cheeks splintering into cobwebs, as if her body was fighting her efforts to hold back the deluge. *Steady on, Edith,* she implored. *Can't be falling apart now.*

Georgia massaged Edie's shoulders, as if she could will the color back into her face, her clothes, her hair. "We don't have to talk about it, Edith. I didn't mean to push."

Edie looked up and felt the warmth of Georgia's attention burn the clouds that gathered away. Her color pooled back into her features, then settled back upon her like mist. *As hard as she's fought for me,* Edie thought, seeing the toll this charade was taking on Georgia, *I must find a way to do the same for her.* Suddenly, it all seemed so simple. She couldn't *see* the scraps of memory properly because she was standing inside them. And, so, the only thing for it was to hold them at arm's length, to examine them at a safe distance. So Edie held the volatile atmosphere at bay, drew herself back into the circle of safety Georgia created and tried to explain.

"They're not proper memories. I think it's because I remember things as a child would. I'd just had my fifth birthday. I didn't *have* the words then, so I can't *find* the words now. It's like trying to explain a bad dream. You say it out loud and it's bunk. Nonsense." *How funny,* Edie thought. *I sound so grown up now. I wonder if I sound like Mama.* "The closest I can get is this."

She reached for Georgia and clasped her wrists. Then, elbows locked, she began to swing her arms from side to side.

"Do you know "London Bridge"?" Edie asked. Georgia's eyes were red-rimmed and wide. Edie could see herself reflected there, like a doll but all grown up. *Every day, for ages and ages with a thing like me. In a house like this. What have we done to her?*

"Did you fall, Edie? Is that what happened to you?" Georgia asked gently, running her thumbs over Edie's wrists as their arms swung like twin pendulums.

Edie shook her head and began to sing.

> *"Take the key*
> *and*
> *lock her up*

Lock
her
up
lock her up
Take the key and
lock
her
up,
my
fair
lady."

A realization dawned on Georgia's face, prompting Edie to break eye contact. She turned her attention to her own mercurial body, which was now blurring into a kaleidoscope of all her selves—child, adolescent, young woman—each one struggling in their own way to hold the line against the horrible nothing she'd fought her way out of, the darkness that wanted her back. To stand firm in the spell cast by this fragile woman.

"Edie, no." Georgia broke the trap of arms and pulled her close. She was frighteningly cold. Edie heard her heartbeat stumble, falter, and then gallop. "You're safe now." But Edie knew it wasn't true. Knew she was lying to comfort her just as Papa had so long ago. *There are no monsters. Don't be afraid of the dark, Edie. You are safe. I'll keep you safe.* Gentle lies that held nothing at bay. *And look where that got me.*

Edie soldiered on. "It's the basement that I remember . . . and that horrible game. And when I say it was dark down there, I don't mean there was no light. There was light enough to see. I saw everything. I saw what was in the basement and . . . and it was *darkness*. I think it's still here. Trapped. Like me. Like the man in the mirror. And maybe . . . maybe it trapped us. All of us."

Georgia smoothed Edie's hair and tried to work the tangles out with her fingers. But she was trembling so badly that she did little more than entangle herself within Edie's locks. Edie willed her skin to smooth out, her hair to unravel, but the song rang in her ears. *My fair lady.*

"Edie, the basement . . . We don't have to worry about it. Not at all. Nathan locked it. He told me not to go down there. Made me swear." Her breath was coming in short pants again and she bit her lips until they bled.

"But he went down there, didn't he?" Edie ducked her head, forcing Georgia to look at her.

But Georgia continued to avoid her gaze. "He did. Over and over . . . and now . . . now . . . he's . . . he's . . ."

Edie untangled Georgia's fingers from her hair. "Tell me. Please tell me."

"Why didn't I see it?" Georgia's voice cracked and skipped like one of Papa's old records. "All this time. You. The house. Nathan. This child. This faraway, once-in-a-lifetime job that appeared out of nowhere. *I* told him to go. I *wanted* him to. Like perfect little breadcrumbs leading me *here*. I swallowed each one, told myself . . . god, the excuses I made. And now look at us, Edie. I see what it did to you. What is it doing to me?"

Edie could see her pulse racing through the gossamer skin of her neck. Inside, the baby was struggling. Edie could nearly see hands and feet scrambling the more hysterical Georgia became. *It's not fair of me to soak up all the light she casts*, Edie realized with a start. *I have to shine some myself. For her.*

"Well, I can tell you what *you're* doing to you and it's nothing good." Edie used her thumbs to wipe Georgia's cheeks and smooth her hair back. "That's enough gloom and doom for one day, I think, for all three of us. We've upset the baby and that's no good."

Edie rose and easily lifted Georgia in her arms, carrying her to the nest of blankets under the window, laid her down so it appeared she rested upon the stone threshold of a ramshackle stone hut.

"What if," she said, crossing the attic to the bookshelf, "I took over for a bit. Let me read to you for a change."

"I don't want any more Wonderland," Georgia shifted restlessly in the blankets, her eyelids heavy "I've had enough. Lavender's blue, dilly dilly, lavender's green . . ."

Edie froze, chilled by Georgia's rambling. "Of course not. I thought something else for today. Something to give you courage. Ah-ha!"

She spun, a small blue book in her hand. "I've just the thing. *Island of the Blue Dolphins*. The future book from Mr. O'Dell in the year nineteen-hundred and sixty, if you can believe such a thing."

She dragged the easy chair across the forest floor to where Georgia slumped. "It really is a wonderful story. Georgia, listen to me. Do you remember it? It's about a very brave girl, trapped all alone in a beautiful, dangerous place." Then she flipped the book over and began reading the back-cover description. "'This is the story of Karana, the Indian girl who lived alone for years on the Island of the Blue Dolphins. Year after year, she watched one season pass into another and waited for a ship to take her away. But while she waited, she kept herself alive.'" She clasped the book to her chest in ecstasy. "Positively *bricky*, that Karana." Edie settled herself in the chair and then fixed Georgia with a brilliant, relentless grin, trying to coax one out of her as well. "Also, it makes me want a cormorant skirt, but I don't have a clue what a cormorant skirt even looks like!"

That earned her a small smile, so Edie began to read, using the same gentle, coaxing voice she'd heard from Georgia's own lips the day they'd met. Page after page, chapter after chapter, Edie read the day away, and as she did, saw the moment Georgia's heavy burdens lightened ever so slightly. She felt the bittersweet pleasure of taking someone else's pain and carrying a measure of it for them, if only for a little while. She sat up straighter and read just a bit softer as Georgia fell asleep. But even then, Edie read on, tears like crystal dewdrops falling down her face because she remembered something else, something new. *I remember what it felt like to be a little girl*, she thought, as the pages blurred in front of her, *which means I can't be one any longer.*

TWENTY-SEVEN

 THE PHONE RANG AND RANG AND GEORGIA let it. Five rings, ten rings, twenty. The blizzard's fury had spent itself days, weeks ago?

No. Days, she reminded herself, casting a glance over to the piles of mail she'd made, a tidy hopscotch calendar grid on the foyer floor marking each day since he'd left. *You called him four days ago. Edie finished reading* Island of the Blue Dolphins *yesterday. That's days, not weeks. That's something,* she assured herself, head falling back as a frigid blast whirled through the open windows, cooling her. *You have to remember. Keep track. Hold on. Don't let this, whatever it is, in. Don't let Roseneath win.* She swallowed hard, opened her hot, gritty eyes and forced herself to see, to believe, to remember the stark reality of what those piles represented.

One hundred and nine piles. One hundred and nine days. By her estimation, Nathan had left on the twenty-first of September. Today, if she was right, if the vast towering grid was close, was the eighth of January.

One hundred and nine days. A scattering of vague text messages. A handful of hang-ups. Not one trip home, not one message of concern, or anger or guilt. Not a single solitary genuine attempt by Nathan to actually talk to her.

Every message so distant, so bland, it was as if they were from a disinterested stranger struggling to make conversation with her. Someone who didn't know her or care for her. Someone who forgot her as soon as they hit 'Send', as soon as they rang off. *Whatever is happening here, in this house to me,* she thought, dialing again, shushing the baby inside her from whatever had sent her flailing again, *whatever keeps stealing days, weeks from me, somehow it has stolen him from me, too.*

Then the phone in her hand cut off mid-ring with a click. Georgia sighed and redialed, filling her mouth with another handful of slush, a brief moment of relief as the cold numbed the sores in her mouth. She swallowed the rapidly heating water, felt it slide down her throat in a boiling stream. As she did, her thoughts scrolled through the messages she'd received from him, such a small number when compared to all those days, each missive shorter than the last. She gathered more snow, held it first against her forehead, then the back of her neck, let it fall in a wash down her back, felt it evaporate before it reached the base of her spine. She shifted to alleviate the pressure of the baby on her tailbone, closed her eyes from the sudden relief, focusing entirely on the strange message he'd sent her that morning.

Georgie?

That was all.

Georgie?

She'd called him right back but there was no reply. Now, hours later, a new development. The phone was still ringing but instead of a click or voicemail, it rang on endlessly, minute after minute.

Please answer this time, she thought, shifting on the floor, her hand supporting the underside of her stomach. Knees tucked under her, her fingertips dancing gently over the swell of the softly shifting child inside her. *I need you. We need you. I'm frightened, Nathan, please, I don't understand what's happening*, she pleaded silently, imagining her words threaded through each ring, beckoning him. *Please answer. Please come home.*

And then a click. She held very still, certain she'd imagined it.

Silence.

"Nathan?" her voice was hoarse and cracked, barely carrying in her own ears. She cleared her throat and tried again.

"Nathan, is it you? Nathan?"

Breathing on the other end. In out, in out. A hitch.

Silence and then,

"Georgia?" Her name stumbled across the line, as if he'd just awoken.

"Nathan, it's me, Georgia. I need you to listen to me. Nathan?" she repeated, when he did not reply. It was late afternoon on the West Coast.

"Honey?"

"Nathan. I need you to come home."

"Home?" he mumbled. "I can't. Not yet. He said, he said soon, he promised . . . Georgia?" His voice was trailing off, as if he were being dragged away from the phone.

"Nathan," she snapped, her voice strengthening, even as his grew weaker. "I need you to come home right now. Do you hear me? Right now. Today."

A sharp intake of breath, a rough sound as if his hand was gripping the phone tight.

Below, the ancient joists in the basement creaked, a long, agonized sound. The windows all around her shook, the frost covering them shattered and fell to the frozen wood floors, adding a glittery layer to the dingy drifts within, the brilliant light outside flooding the dismal room in grim relief.

"Right," he murmured, "right. Next weekend. I promise, I can't, he promised, he said—"

"Nathan." She was struggling not to scream, her shrill voice a hysterical echo in the frozen cavernous house. She spun at a sound in the back hall. Banging, scratching, a door rattling in its frame. "Now. Today. Nathan, you need to hurry."

"Today? Babe, I can't . . . I . . . I just got out here . . ."

Georgia looked over at the piles of mail. Remembered how confused, how incredulous she herself had been. Sorting the incomprehensible piles, trying to find a reason for it to be a joke, a misunderstanding, the snow on the ground, the dates on the mail, the time stamp on his messages a sickening, unavoidable truth.

One hundred and nine days.

"Nathan, what day is today?" She crept toward the sound in the hall.

"It's . . . it's . . . Thursday, hon," his voice shifted then, his breath quickened.

"Georgia? Honey? Is that you?" He was crying, his voice thick and wet. She felt her eyes fill, tried to keep her voice steady, resolute.

"Nathan, tell me what the date is. Focus. Listen to my voice." The random banging and scratching had become a deliberate thudding. Like someone was using a heavy old knocker. On the other side of the basement door. She hurried back into the living room. The mirror was glowing softly and she sought refuge in the steady glow it cast.

"I don't, I can't," he was fading again. "I've been so busy, he said . . . I . . ."

"Nathan, come home," she hissed into the phone. "Right now. You have to come home."

"What's wrong," he whispered, panting. "What's happened?"

She took a deep breath and let it out, wondering if she was doing the right thing, knowing she had no choice. "I'm pregnant." She slid her hand on her stomach, feeling for the child pressing back, centering her, a delicate assurance.

"You're what?" his voice exploded, suddenly clear, across the line.

"Nathan," she repeated. "I'm pregnant. But it's wrong. It's all wrong," she whispered into the phone. "Please come home. It's all wrong, I'm sick. It's making me sick. I think it's . . . it's . . ."

Something of the old Nathan snapped to attention, his voice thundered now in her ear.

"Get out of the house. Now. Go to the hospital. Get out of that goddamn house—" His voice cut off with a gasp. "Georgia?" the terrified, commanding tone in his voice vanished and he sounded once more sleepy, confused.

Below, the house shifted again, louder this time, a self-satisfied groan that sounded nothing like a house settling, a deliberate, sentient parry. Georgia curled up in a ball around her child, felt the child make herself small within. *I'll keep you safe, I promise.*

"I can't," she said, rising with some difficulty, using the couch to pull herself upright. "I think you know I can't." She waddled as quickly as she could to the bottom of the stairs, a pricking at the back of her neck as the windows vibrating madly in their frames. The basement door rattled spitefully in its frame and she wondered that it did not splinter. Stumbling now up the stairs, the phone slipped from her hand, slid across the landing. Georgia dropped to her knees and scrambled after it, crawling the rest of the way to the bedroom, slammed the door behind her and locked it. She listened into the phone again, heard his breathing.

"Nathan?" she pleaded, pulling herself to her feet, her grotesquely swollen body reflected in silhouette in the windows.

"Get. Out," he spat, something furious, something terrified in his voice. "You. You. Get. Out. Now." His words were a battery of furious shrapnel; she could hear him grinding his teeth.

"I can't," she said softly, turning to the side, watching her reflection in the lead glass shift. She ran her hand over her stomach. "You don't understand. I can't go to the hospital, Nathan."

"Why?" The word came with difficulty, as if through clenched teeth.

"Nathan," she whispered, leaning her head against the frosted windowpane. "Tell me about the basement.

Silence. Below, the determined groaning cut off. Inside her she felt the child relax back into sleep, the song trailing off again.

"Tell me, Nate. Tell me what's down there." She was crying now; her tears ran down the windowpane in a hot wash.

"I don't remember. I can't . . . I won't . . . get out . . . please." He was fading again, mumbling. Georgia swallowed her tears and snapped at him.

"How long have you been gone, Nate? Answer me," she screamed, slamming her fist into the window. "Answer me, goddamn it!"

A loud crash from below made her jump. The line went dead; a buzzing tone filled her ears. Nathan was gone.

✦   ✦   ✦

Across the country, Nathan Pritchard watched as his hand threw the phone across the room. He wondered why he would do such a thing, a furious roaring in his ears briefly overwhelming his senses. He slammed his fist into his thigh, once, twice. The roaring in his voice shifted to laughter, gleeful and vicious, then trailed off into silence. Rubbing his bleary eyes, Nathan turned Georgia's words around, trying to translate them even as they shifted, faded in his memory. She was upset. Frightened. She wanted something . . . something . . . but the fragile thought vanished and he found himself wondering who *she* was. He studied his surroundings as if seeing them for the first time. He was in the York house. In front of him was a desk made of two-by-fours and plywood, an efficient design he remembered duplicating at other sites over the years. But not here. He closed his eyes and tried to remember setting this up but found he could not. He struggled to grab a fistful of the orderly notes spread out across the surface of the makeshift desk. His handwriting, unmistakable. Quotes, deadlines, reminders. Concrete. Tile. HVAC. He studied the handwriting. It was his. And yet

And yet

There in the margins, notes. Comments. In a feminine hand. He tried to read them and watched as they focused—

No,

No,

I would never,

She,

—then popped one by one like bubbles and vanished.

It was nothing, Nathan, nothing at all. Why ever would you worry about that? You don't have to worry about anything anymore. Remember? I promised.

He shook the insistent, cloying voice from his head. He'd been on the phone. His breath caught in his chest, his heart felt like it would explode. *She. Her. Georgia,* he thought, astonished. *I was talking to Georgia. She's my wife. The enchantress. The woman in the wood. She's real. She's not a dream. She's real.* Something about that realization made him so profoundly sad, so heartsick, his eyes filled, blurring the room around him.

He pushed away from the desk and stumbled across the room to where the phone lay. He picked it up, despite the voice hissing not to, and studied the screen.

Missed calls. 56.

Messages. 49.

He opened the messages folder and saw the last text he'd replied to

C. York

then tried to read the endless stream of messages between him and Cat, a confusing, familiar banter that spanned weeks.

Morning

So beautiful

Last night

Hurry

I will

Soon

Now

No

No. He shook his head and tried to read them again, tried to make sense of the gibberish, watched as the letters of each mystifying word linked arms with the next, danced in a square, spun and dipped, then rearranged themselves.

And as in uffish thought he stood,

No.

The Jabberwock, with eyes of flame,

Georgia.

Came whiffling through the tulgey wood,

The greenhouse

I remember now

I can almost—

And burbled as it came.

The groaning. Something. Something that frightened him, called him, wanted him. In the basement.

Come to my arms, my beamish boy!
O frabjous day! Callooh! Callah!

Nathan scrambled for the memories he knew had to be there, somewhere, but they shifted like sand, fell between his fingers.

Blood.

Mud.

Thorns.

Roseneath.

Basement.

Greenhouse.

The true meaning behind each word skipped just out of his reach. All but the one he was able to grab, hold tight, read over and over, burning it into his shattered memory.

Georgia.

He spun, looked around again, saw how altered Cat's house was. Saw brand-new sub floors, new electrical. All traces of demo long gone. Stretching out around him was a forest of studs and doorways. Months of work. He looked down at his phone desperately again, hoping this was a joke, a nightmare. *Please God. No, let me wake up, I want to go home*

January 8.

January.

January.

Georgia. My wife.

No.

He grabbed the papers on his desk again, studied the notes, the handwriting, *not hers* the specific familiarity.

Not hers. Not her. He looked at his phone again, trying not to look at the messages he'd sent to—

No, not her

—past that nauseating, unimaginable dialogue, to the bewilderingly vague messages that comprised his contact over the last—

Months,

No,

—with Georgia.

No.

He said her name aloud, over and over again, pushing everything away but that one thought, that one word, those two syllables fragile fingers that curled tightly around consciousness, sanity. He held her name, pulled himself up over the edge with it, let the sound of it propel him forward.

Coat.

Keys.

Phone.

Cab.

He recited it like a prayer, and did not look back. Not at the mystified crew calling his name, not at the phone that vibrated with persistent calls

Not her.

Not at whatever waited for him at the bottom of that cliff, what lurked in the abyss he'd swam his way up from, at none of it, one thought in his head.

Georgia. Georgia. Georgia.

He called her back, a dozen times, two dozen, but she never answered. Her phone rang endlessly only to trail off as a soft buzzing, whispering. He shut his ears to the cloying voice threaded through the static, coaxing him, cajoling him.

She's not real, never was real, I'm real, I'm the only reality you need, my beamish boy.

He threw his credit card at a startled booking agent. Heard his voice,

No. My voice.

"I don't care what it costs, get me there now. Now," his voice, *my voice, goddamn it,* a jarring mix of pleading, anger. Saw the agent's eyebrows rise in alarm.

"Please," he said, his voice his own again. "It's an emergency. My wife."

The agent's face softened, he heard her say something about a cancelation, an opening in first class, and an outrageous figure he could not afford.

He nodded, trying not to cry.

Why ever would you cry, my beamish boy? We're going home!

The voice pulling him back to the cliff, to the chasm. He peeked over the edge, needed to know.

Home. Roseneath. The basement. The greenhouse. Georgia.

No. Please let this be the dream. Please. Someone please tell me I didn't leave her in that nightmare. Please, God, no.

✦　　✦　　✦

Nathan had hurried home, early for once. He'd been working night and day on Roseneath, and after last night's strange events—so unlike him to fall asleep like that—he needed to

slow down. He'd surprise Georgia, take her out to dinner. When he saw her car in the driveway, he glanced again at his watch. Five o'clock. He distinctly remembered hearing her say she was working till six. He'd grabbed his mobile phone again and double-checked to see if he'd missed a call, a text. Nothing. He tossed his phone back in the car. Later, he wouldn't be able to remember why.

Before he entered their townhouse, he'd laid one hand on the hood of her car. It was cold. Funny how something like that would make him run up the stairs, calling for her in a panic. A panic that crested when she didn't answer.

Through the kitchen, which was empty. Her purse at the bottom of the stairs, left there in a heap with her shoes. Sweater thrown over the bannister. He took the steps two at a time, coming to a shuddering halt in the doorway of their bedroom. There was a trail of clothes on the floor strung together with something like mud, something dried and brown soaked into the rug. His eyes traced the path back to the bed, to her side. Empty. He followed the trail the other way to where it led into the bathroom.

Nathan had always organized everything in his mind like a house. It kept things simple. There was the first floor, where all the day-to-day things existed. A clockwork place where work was done, bills were paid, food was cooked, clothes were washed. The second floor, well, that was all hers. He saw her eyes, wide and starry in each bedroom, beckoning to him, infiltrating his memories whether she'd been there or not, her scent trailing throughout and not one other person could follow where she led him.

The attic, where he stored things he didn't need all the time, things like aunts and uncles, summer lawnmowing jobs as a kid, undergrad classes in astronomy, football. Broken things, discarded things. He shoved all the useless crap up there, under the eaves and ignored it.

The basement was a different story. And it was the difference between them. Georgia filled her first and second floor with everything, a cheerful jumble of her and him, her books and dreams, every part warm and welcoming, messy. She kept one room, locked within her for him, one still secret place for him only and when that door swung wide, he was left breathless every time. But she had no basement, nowhere to hide the dark, the pain. Instead, she put hers in the attic. It shone through the rooftops, hung over balconies, its brittle light sweeping over everything around her, pouring out her gray eyes.

But not him. He shoved it all, every bit of it, in the basement. Let it sit there in the dark, rarely opening that door and peeking down the stairs. He let it gather dust and ash, let it rot. Some days belonged down there. The day he'd come home and found her car in the drive. His basement door had swung open and he'd stared into the darkness and knew that this day belonged down there and that once he put it there, he might never be able to peek down those stairs again.

About a foot before the bathroom door, the brown changed to red, thick and wet. He found himself walking slowly into the bedroom, his legs almost unable to move.

Things like that go in the basement. You lock them up and don't let them near the stairs. He'd taken the image of Georgia on the floor, curled up like a white seashell splattered with blood, and tucked it into the dark root cellar. He took the image of the little purple girl—oh and her hair, how on Earth could she have ever had hair like that?—her skin so thin he could see her veins, so cold. Her hands moved once, almost beckoning him over and he'd slid to his knees in front of his daughter, where she almost seemed to cling to the back of one of Georgia's legs, her little hands held up like a prayer. He'd picked her up, held her against him, frantically untucking his shirt, thinking wildly if he only kept her warm, if he could get to the phone he could save her, it wasn't too late, couldn't be too late. But when he tried to move, he felt the umbilical cord pull, wet and sickening, and he couldn't pull it, couldn't rip it out of his wife. The phone was just around the corner in the bedroom—he could get to it he was sure—but there was no power that could make him set that little fluttering creature down, nothing that could make him put her back on that cold floor in all the gore that spread out around the three of them. He heard someone moaning, heard someone crying, no screaming, and then she opened her eyes, just that once, her infant body spasming against his chest then going limp. He looked then, turned to the mirror, his eyes searching for help that wasn't there, and saw that the person screaming was him.

Things like that, he thought, you dig a hole in the floor of the basement. You dig deep and long until your back aches with it, until you drive every last bit of it into the hole you've made and then you cover it over. Because if you don't, if it finds its way into open air, it will ignite and burn everything down.

TWENTY-EIGHT

GEORGIA WAS ABLE TO COAX A TRICKLE OF water through the frozen pipes, just enough to wash off the grime on her face and neck. She threw the dirty washcloth to the floor and waited as the pipes in the walls clanged, protested, the aged fixture itself shaking until finally another small trickle appeared and she repeated the process with a fresh towel. It took two more attempts to clean herself after the fugue-like weeks that had passed. Then she cupped her hands and drank, each mouthful a delicious numbing reprieve, cool and calming, the song inside her shifting from the frantic, frightened verses to something deeper, more melodic, a re-assuring tenor

Adam's grape vines are still full and ripe. Go and eat your fill. And beyond, there is a small pool . . .

"Shhh little one," Georgia pleaded, pushing herself upright, attempting to soothe the baby inside. "Not now. I need to think. Please, little one."

There is nothing little about me, her child whispered, and then fell silent.

She smiled, imagined the child inside did too, saw the rueful, apologetic face of her daughter in her mind's eye and felt a surge of love so pure, so perfect, that she forgave without question the havoc the poor frightened child was wreaking on her. She tried not to dwell on the shocking sinews in her arms, the burst blood vessels in her cheeks, the way her skin broke open, cracked, bled under the slightest pressure. She brushed her teeth dry, ignoring the pink paste that spackled the sink after the faucet gave one last death rattle, the ceiling overhead raining down cracked plaster from the wildly protesting walls.

She pawed through Nathan's shirts until she found one that still smelled of him, one large enough to cover her. Once the sleeves were rolled, it almost fit. The buttons strained against her burgeoning breasts and flat out refused to meet over her swollen stomach. She gave up trying, then rummaged for a pair of his sweatpants. *There. Clean, mostly, and dressed.*

She had been focusing on her condition in isolation— gaunt wrists, bloody fingertips, cracked toenails, shriveled legs, indecently round, healthy belly. Now she steeled herself to examine the whole. The bedroom mirror reflected the transformation that the last

One hundred and nine, no ten, days,

Had done to her.

There was a manic, evangelical glow to her sunken eyes that might have been dazzling were it not for how red-rimmed they were, if the skin around them hadn't been so cracked and dry. Her face was gaunt, near skeletal, which was hardly surprising considering she hadn't eaten, hadn't needed to eat, in weeks. Shoulders, arms, legs, like toothpicks stuck into an oversized ripe fruit. She saw at last what Edie had seen.

What's happened to your hair?

—She plucked the few wispy bits that still remained on her right temple, then ran her fingers carefully through the long mane that still lay heavy on her neck and felt a sickening tangle come away in her hands. She gingerly gathered the remaining locks and wound them around her head, trying to disguise the worst of it. *You've got bigger problems,* she thought as the child inside elbowed her hard in the spine, *than how your hair looks.*

She took up her watch on the landing. The heat of her hands made short work of the glazing of ice and soon she had a good view of the backyard. Georgia frowned up at the sky, the winter gloom making it impossible to be sure of the time. A quick glance at her phone. *Although,* she thought, reading Nathan's bewildering last message, two lines from the Jabberwocky *I don't trust it much either.* She wavered, wanting desperately to lose herself in the magic of the attic, to hide up there with Edie, knowing she couldn't. *Not today. I have to try. Edie will understand,* she thought with some surprise, sobered by the thought that Edie *would* in fact understand. The young lady she'd grown into would insist, even. Georgia dialed Nathan's number again, let it ring endlessly in her hand.

I'll give him until the sun starts to sink. And if he comes, we'll figure this out together. She pushed on her stomach until the child shifted enough for her to draw a deep breath. *Figure out how to explain this to a doctor without ending up in a psych ward. Find a way to get Edie out. There has to be a way.* She pulled the duffle toward her, cast another glance up the stairs. *Whether he comes home or not, Edie and I are getting out of here today.*

She waited for hours, her fingers compulsively redialing his number, only silence on the other end. After a while, Edie began to pace upstairs, but it was not an impatient march, rather each crisp, steady footfall a steady time signature for her vigil, as if Edie too were waiting in a lofty widow's watch to see which way the tide turned. All around them, Roseneath was silent. The winds had fallen; the air outside was biting and clear, a glittering, brittle winter's day.

The sound of an engine in the distance was faint, but Georgia picked it out immediately. Her heart leapt in her chest, followed swiftly by a fantail flip of the child within her. Louder now, louder still, the crunch of wheels on gravel. A flash of red in the tree line and Nathan's truck sped up the drive, fast, too fast, the wheels churning through the deep snow. *He came back.* The footfalls upstairs broke off. She imagined Edie flying to her own window, watching as hopefully from above as Georgia did from below. The truck door flew open and Nathan fell out, landed on one knee, scrambled clumsily across the drive, eyes wild. Georgia felt the child inside her recoil, felt her entire body do the same a fraction of a second later. Nathan rose, fell, rose again, his body pulled like a marionette away from the house, across the frozen expanse of the backyard, on a trajectory straight toward the dark skeleton of the greenhouse. As Georgia watched, frozen in her lofty perch, she felt her child begin to weep inside her, a pitiful keening—

Mother! Father!

—and she knew that the salvation she'd prayed for, the husband she was waiting for was somehow being stolen from her as well.

Trolls and severed toes. Witches and ovens, the Jabberwock in the wood, wishes made nightmares, reality nothing more than a dream. Handsome princes bewitched into gruesome monsters, ladies trapped in ghastly towers. *Papa lied. There are monsters.*

"Nathan!" she croaked, pounding on the window. Below, he spun at the sound, fell on his back, his eyes meeting hers for one brief moment before he jumped to his feet and struggled on his zigzag course across the yard.

◆　　◆　　◆

Get her out, get her out, doesn't matter what you did, what you promised, what he wants, get her out, you can't have her, I never meant to hurt her, hurt her, save her, save her.

With every mile of road Nathan traveled on his frantic flight back to Roseneath, he did not allow his thoughts to wander back, peek over the edge. He refused to remember, regardless of what life he had lived the last few months. He kept his mind focused on

Georgia

Get her out

Refused to revisit the basement, the greenhouse, held on to the only thing that truly mattered. Not what he'd done, but what he had to do. What he knew *no don't think of it, don't let it back in* he must do at all costs, without fail.

Save her.

He floored it all the way from the airport and felt relief when the truck's wheels bit the gravel of the long drive *I'm here, I made it, there's still time.*

That relief vanished when he broke through the tree line and saw the state of the house.

Roseneath appeared utterly abandoned. The open windows shook in their frames like loose teeth, the sills covered in a fresh fall of snow. The deep drifts in the yard stretched in every direction in an unbroken expanse, the only sign of life a thin track from the neatly plowed street to the front door, mail fluttering in the slot the only thing moving around the house. Fallen gutters were half buried in the frost-tipped rosebushes like pick-up sticks. He slammed his foot on the gas, gunning it through the snowdrifts, slamming the transmission into park under the oak tree.

We're home, my beamish boy! The voice that had been silent the entire journey pierced his head gleefully. *Home, home, home!*

"No!" he screamed. "Get out!" He flung open the truck door and fell to the ground, the shock of the cold briefly driving the voice from his head.

"Georgia," he tried to scream, his words cut off as if a hand had coiled around his throat. *No.* Nathan rolled, jumped to his feet, fell again when his legs tangled in something sharp, something that pierced his calves deeply as he fell in the powdery snow, tightened like a garrote. *Not your legs. Mine.*

A sound, high above him, in Roseneath, someone banging on the landing window. Nathan willed his legs to stand *so close, the house is so close, I can get in there, I can, I can.*

No. You can't.

A blinding wall of pain flooded his body, as if he were pierced—

There's still time, I just have to warn her, tell her, I can do it I can save her

—but he fell backward in the snow, was knocked senseless by the pain that radiated through him, the cold no longer shocking but numbing him. He felt his arms and legs go limp, disappear, as if amputated, fought to roll his eyes back to the house, seeking out the second-story landing. He saw her face *Georgia, I made it, I tried* a diminutive portrait in a small circle of frost, her eyes wide and haunted *what have I done, what did he do* face gaunt and paler than the snow that fell from the sky.

And then her face vanished as he felt his body stand, his head hung low. He desperately wanted to look up, his mouth working noisily, trying to warn her, but he could only watch as his feet—

Those aren't my feet, he thought feebly. *Not anymore.*

—carried him on a stumbling, clumsy path across the backyard, snow crunching under his—

My

—feet to the greenhouse. A brief reprieve, the numbness in his arms dimmed, pain returned, and he felt the control over part of his body return to him. Nathan pinwheeled his arms, trying to throw his weight backward— a futile gesture—grasped the edge of the porch rail, and lost his grip. He balled his hands into fists as he was led through the yard, his stride now more certain, an unfamiliar swagger driving him, propelling him toward *I can't go in there. Not again. There's still time. Time. I can fix this. I can stop it. No, not again, oh God, I forgot, how could I forget, not this, not again* the dark maw of the greenhouse looming, the inside sunk into a greater darkness blanketed with snow and vines. *No*, he screamed, or tried to, but his voice echoed not in the backyard but in his head. His lips had been sewn shut. Two more steps carried him into the shadow of the greenhouse

Mud and blood and thorns

Nathan gnashed his teeth in his head, a flash of pain as his molars chipped. He tasted blood, managed to convince one hand to grasp the twisted aluminum frame of the door, a razor's edge that sliced through his palm, shocking him partially out of the unrelenting grip of this . . . this—

not this

—and he hung on to the pain there, gripped the frame tighter, tighter, the metal slicing deeper, deeper, the pain drilling through the numbness, sense and reason within his reach.

I can still stop this.

No, oh God, no.

Roseneath.

What is this place?

What have I done?

Oh sweet Jesus, the things I have done.

He heard a door slam and Georgia's voice, shrill and raw, but the whispers drowned out her words. Blood was running down both his arms, a fresh scattering of wounds, each one a constellation of gorgeous release so tempting, so insistent that his hand slipped

That's not my hand. I forgot. It's his.

and he lost his tenuous grasp. Her voice was closer now, threaded through the cloying whispers he could hear the crunch of snow outside, running, stumbling. He heard her cry out in pain, all the while his mindless legs propelled him into the greenhouse, one heavy step after another.

Don't follow me, please go back, Georgia, you don't want to know

Feet crunching on fallen glass, crystalline punctuations to the whispers that kissed his ears, caressed his wounds, wrapped him in a gossamer bliss.

It's time to let go, Nathan. I'm here now. So many holes, and I found them all. I filled them all, let go, run and hide little boy, you don't want to watch what happens next. The voice was amiable but resigned. Almost sympathetic. *You don't really want to be here for this part.*

How did I forget this? Nathan wanted to throw his hands up to cover his ears but they weren't his ears anymore, his arms hung useless by his sides. *How did I forget him?*

Yes, the voice whispered, *I'm right here, my boy. Here in the earth and down there in the darkness, and in you, every inch of you. It'll all be easier if you let go . . .*

A delicious blend of pain and release that choked him until he could no longer remember why he'd been so afraid, what had propelled him so frantically home—

Yes

The tips of his boots reached the edge of the dank chasm in the center of the greenhouse, a hole he remembered digging himself long ago in a dream.

How did I forget this?

He gazed down into the grave, felt the moist heat radiate upward, drenching him—

Yes, yes, yes, yes, yes, yes, yes

—a euphoric mix of rapture and terror as he saw the thick bed of thorns and rotten roses, a deep, sharp pool he had only to dive in to be free, finally free of this horrible pain, tumble back into the numb release it delivered

No

The voice was a fragile thing, small and scared, a little boy pleading. For one second, Nathan clung to that voice, a pure, innocent part of himself imploring him to find a way to stop this from happening again.

Please.

His body was stone, unmovable, and yet he fought it, clinging to this last shred of himself, one leg staggering back. The whispers turned to howling, a primitive frenzy shredding his resolve. He pushed through the agony, another step, and the fragile voice in his head began to sob in relief.

I can make it to the door, I can get free of this I can get out grab Georgia and run from this place this damn cursed place I can stop it all it's not too late it can't—

The voice cut off as something wrapped around Nathan's deadened legs and he fell, face first, into the grave of thorns, each prick a vicious wound that bloomed from pain to nothingness.

✦   ✦   ✦

In the attic, Edie watched helplessly as Nathan Pritchard was dragged by unseen hands across the yard and into the greenhouse. A door slammed downstairs, and a moment later Georgia appeared outside, a ghostly waif moving through the black and white palette of winter.

Mama! Papa! No!

"Georgia! No!"

Georgia was running through the snow toward the greenhouse, her stumbling, staggering tracks crisscrossing Nathan's deep prints. Edie pounded her fists on the glass.

"No! Don't go inside!" If Georgia heard her, she gave no sign. She stumbled, crawled, pulled herself to her feet again, blooms of carnation pink snow in her wake. Edie heard her cry out one last time.

"Nathan!"

Before disappearing after him into the greenhouse.

"I remember," Edie whispered, dropping her face into her hands as her porcelain skin faded to shades of gray, her grief made manifest in the air. *Georgia and Nathan, like Mama and Papa.* A thick storm of ash raged inside the fairytale attic, obscuring her from sight.

I remember.

TWENTY-NINE

THE WIND WHISTLED THROUGH THE LIST-ing greenhouse, generating a grating resonant frequency that set Georgia's teeth on edge. Heavy vines crusted in ice smothered the sagging metal frame. The wind fell and a heavy silence with it. A pregnant pause, then the desolate structure bristled in the icy stillness, like a beast shaking water from its back. The frozen vines contracted, expanded, and then they, too, settled.

Don't tread in dark places, Georgia, trolls and toes and terrible tolls

"Nathan?" The wind snatched his name, muffled it. She called again, louder, a visceral instinct warning her not to go inside. But there was no reply. Nathan's tracks were swallowed by the gloom inside. She peered through the window, her breath hung in heavy clouds. Something was moving in the darkness.

"Nate?" But even as she said his name, she knew *knew* it wasn't him. Behind her, Roseneath's windows rattled in their frames as if the house were being throttled, and then nothing. But she didn't look back; she kept her eyes trained on the movement inside. Another step and her pupils adjusted to the darkness enough to see there *was* no inside of the greenhouse. Thick, wet whispers boiled out of the silence. His blood was beginning to freeze on the aluminum doorframe.

Nathan's path ended at the edge of a deep pit in the center of the greenhouse. Georgia stood poised on the edge, every instinct she had telling her to get away from the yawning cataract. But she had to know. Had to look deep down in that awful abyss for any sign, no matter how small, of Nathan. The sides of the chasm were lined with coiling arms of vines and thorns, a spiraling vortex that had no bottom. Gusts of sulphur mingled with the scent of rot. Below, far below, humanoid shapes shifted and undulated. The vines froze as if they were looking at her. One slithered over the edge, its razor-sharp tendril reached for her, a delicate garrote.

I thought you were in the greenhouse, she'd asked him, lying on the floor, wood curls in her hair.

No, I was in the basement.

Georgia fell back, scrambled out of the seething darkness of the greenhouse and into the light. Nathan had simply vanished. The crust of the snow cut into her feet but she ran on. The truck sat idling in the drive but she aimed for the house, the sound of clattering vines chasing her all the way. She spared a glance up at the attic—Edie pounding on the glass, flickering like Morse code, fading each time only to reappear dimmer—crawled up the porch stairs, and grabbed the duffle bag where she'd dropped it. She had to be wrong, Nathan couldn't have disappeared inside that . . . that . . . but she'd seen him with her own eyes, he was there one minute and the next— Inside the house now, she fell to the floor, retching, the sound of the coiling vines slithered in her head, the sound of those teeth snapped in her ears. *There's nothing there, nothing on you.* She used the wall to pull herself up *Something dragged Nathan into that hellmouth* The bile rose in her throat again at the thought of the pit in the greenhouse *and he was gone, gone. He's gone, something else is here, not like Edie, something evil. I have to get out of here. Grab Edie and go, it'll work, it has to, take the truck and*

It was the voice that stopped her. A voice as familiar to her as her own. That amiable timbre a song she'd memorized long ago.

"Honestly, guys, pull yourselves together." He was teasing someone. In the living room. Georgia crept toward the opened door, *his voice*, that dear familiar voice grew louder. *It can't be, he was just in the . . . he*

"A few more weeks? Not sure why you care." He was standing with his back to her, the floor around him crawling with . . . with . . . *something.*

Georgia struggled to understand what she was seeing scattered at his feet—malformed creatures of damp earth rolling and writhing with his every word. "It's not like your lot can experience the concept of time anymore." He crouched down as if to survey the shifting clumps of flesh and wings *dear god teeth and bone, mud and scraps of . . . of* He ran his hand over the horde of eyeless things like pets and they writhed in ecstasy, needle-like whispers manic, discordant, drilling into her eardrums. He sighed and she watched his shoulders settle into resignation, another wholly familiar mannerism.

"Is this mud rat shit the best you can do?" He poked the nearest creature with his finger and the small thing screeched, disintegrated, and fell through the cracks on the floor. He stood up, rocked on his heels *just like . . . like . . . like* and brushed his hands off on his pants.

"I guess when you decide to rule in hell, can't be too picky about the help." The horde drew back against the wall, surged up it, cowered on the ceiling like a colony of bats.

His name froze in her mouth, a primal, prey instinct warned her to hide it away, tuck it deep inside where the thing across the room couldn't find it, couldn't tarnish it. It wasn't until the moment he turned and caught sight of her, that Georgia realized how gracefully, how consummately Nathan had worn his own skin. How the body without the man was just an unrecognizable shell, that his soul had filled that precious frame to bursting and without it was little more than a stranger.

His name bit the back of her throat and she tried to swallow it but it slipped out.

"Nathan?"

In the time it took her to utter that one small word, the floor vanished beneath her feet and she slammed into frigid plaster. She hung there, pinned like an insect, her arms twisted high over her head, legs dangling three feet off the ground. She couldn't move, but her child could. Inside, the baby pinwheeled, fingers and feet attacked her innards. *She's trying to run.* Georgia tried to scream but her lips were paralyzed, all she managed was a strangled gurgle as the child ripped and slashed at her insides. But *he . . . it* took no further notice of her, as if she wasn't even there.

He approached the heavy leaden mirror on the mantel and rapped his knuckles on its shimmering surface. He was singing softly under his breath. An old song, the innocent words of a child's verse imbued with cheerful rancor.

"Frère Jacques, Frère Jacques . . ." Another knock. "Dormez-vous? Dormez-vous?"

The mirror flared; the light intensified to scorching hot white. For a second Georgia, unable to close her eyes, thought she'd been blinded. But then it faded, supernova to starlight, and her vision returned, fractured by sunspots.

"Well, it's nice to see you, too, little brother." He *that's not Nathan* was addressing the mirror, grinning at some shared joke. His voice coursed across the floor, scratched its way up the wall to where she hung, penetrated her skin, nestled in her bones, nailed her to the wall.

"You should see the look on your face!" He laughed again and Georgia's stomach lurched. "Never saw this one coming, did you, Mike? You have to admit," He was rolling up his sleeves, an absentminded habit she'd seen Nathan, her Nathan, do a thousand times, two turns to each cuff, then a sharp push to the elbow. "I've outdone myself this time."

Her mouth was filling with vomit but her jaw was locked in place. Her eyes and nose burned as her stomach acid sought release, any release. The sound of her choking caught the attention of the creature disguised as Nathan. His eyes narrowed in the mirror, flicked over to her, his carefree mirth replaced briefly with annoyance. She felt her jaw loosen, just slightly, but it was enough to allow the vomit to trickle between her lips, drip down her neck to the floor. The mirror rattled in its frame, as if the being on the other side was shaking it, drawing his attention back.

"You have no sense of humor, do you, Mikey? Come on, man, I missed having a body." He was pacing now, kicking his heels playfully against the wood floor. "And you know how resourceful I can be. Can't help it, kid. It's my nature."

Georgia's senses were swamped by the reaction that surged this time from the mirror. To describe the deluge as sound was inadequate. The response, for there was no mistaking that's what it was, surrounded the man across the room in a violent aurora that obliterated her senses, leaving Georgia feeling as if she had been dropped in a fathomless trench or flung into deep space. Her child, however, stopped flailing. Two small hands pressed against her stomach as if the child wanted to touch what her mother could not even understand.

"Oh yeah?" His *it, it that thing is not, can't be . . . what has that creature done with Nathan?* voice cracked like a whip and the eddy of light fell to the floor, inert, and disappeared. "Well, maybe that's because *I* grew up educated in His City and *you* grew up bare-knuckle boxing or whatever it is you jarheads did to kill time in the Land of Milk and Honey."

The mirror splintered, wisps of silver-blue light escaped in hot bursts. The creature held his hands up in surrender.

"Forget I said anything. Listen, can't we just skip all this shit for once? I know *I'm* sick of it, you *have* to be. What if," he pointed his finger as if to silence whomever he was talking to, "what if just this once we did it my way? Come on, you're *moderately* more intelligent than all the other troops. Even you broke ranks, didn't you, Mikey boy? Not as magnificently as I did, but still. You have to see my point. Tell me how I'm wrong."

Shards of mirror boiled into silver parisons, lambent orbs that burst before splashing to the floor, as if the being in the mirror had spat a fiery parry. Georgia could taste hot metal in the air, her ears rang as if she stood under the bells of a great cathedral. The man across the room merely nodded at this strange alchemy before throwing his arms in the air, a mischievous sparkle in his eyes. Her eyes watered, blurred. *Nathan's eyes. Those are Nathan's eyes!* she wanted to scream.

"What do you want me to say?" He flung himself into a chair and stretched out. "Collateral damage, Mike. It sucks that she's your 'treasure—'" He frowned, snapped his fingers. "Nope, that's not it. Sweetheart?" He shook his head. "Damn, I forgot your little nickname for her."

What remained of the mirror shattered. Georgia tried in vain to close her eyes, certain the hot shards would impale her but they froze midair, a host of knives surrounding the man in the chair, before retreating, each fitting neatly back into its proper place.

The creature jumped to his feet with a snort. "Right. *Beloved.* Fuck me. Didn't know you guys were so sentimental." Ignoring the molten wash of silver on the mantel, he gripped it, his teasing voice suddenly serious. "Come on, Mikey, for once in your life stop acting like a dumb grunt.

Use your head. Look around you. We've got that mother-fucker on the ropes if He's letting me get away with this." The raging surface of the mirror stilled. "Got your attention? Great. Now imagine if *you*, Michael the Archangel, switched teams. Disgraced golden boy, banished general of the Divine Armies. Imagine if you stopped playing Switzerland in your little time-out chair and joined me. The rest would follow. And then we'd have Him."

The light in the mirror flickered wildly before retreating to silver-black, the depths of the mirror an endless, hollow expanse. Georgia's eyes burned, painfully dry from being held open by whatever force pinned her to the wall, but she scanned the vacuum of the mirror as best she could, hoping to catch a glimpse of this powerful, furious being. *Michael. An archangel. Impossible. And yet Edie was real. Edie wasn't impossible. A ghost, yes, a real ghost, growing and changing and—* She raced ahead to the inescapable conclusion, looked back to the creature, the man that was not Nathan. *But that would make him . . .*

"See, I've got you there. And once I have her, we win, Michael. You can be my right-hand man. Between you and me," he lowered his voice conspiratorially, "the Fallen are not what you'd call conversationalists." He pushed away from the mantel and plucked one of his minions from the ceiling like rotten fruit. "I mean, look at our brethren. Thousands of years now, right? And this is the best they can manage."

He turned with a grin, tossing the protesting creature back and forth in his hands like a football, then threw it at her. The screaming creature sailed in a perfect spiral across the living room before it hit the wall above her head and exploded. Georgia barely had a chance to register the sound of it bursting like bloated roadkill when the splattered remains slid down the wall and crawled over her face. Disjointed curses sputtered in her ears, a twisted accompaniment to her daughter's fragile humming. *Hurt you, unmake you, consume you yes yes just like we did him down down in the dark and wet, yes yes eat our way inside you, suck the pulp from you* As if aware of her mother's plight, the child in Georgia's womb began humming louder, a harplike vibration that drowned out the worst of the ruined creatures words.

"What if we say this: when I'm done, you can have the pick of the litter?" The mantel cracked, chunks of stone fell in an avalanche on the hearth and he *it* jumped back, laughing. "Fine, whatever. You can have her, too. I don't give a shit. Not sure you'll *want* her back at that point but you've always been a softie for a hard luck case."

A pernicious rumble from the mirror and the stone rubble rose in a cloud. Each fragment drifted back into place, shifting and jostling until the mantel was whole and unblemished.

"Fine, you do that," the creature spat in response. "God our Father, you are such an asshole, Mike. Let me ask you this: how do you know she's still into you? It's been a while since the last Galliana." He ran a finger over the restored mantel. "And after that fiasco in France with the Dauphin," he raised his voice to a falsetto, danced about in a pantomime. "Michael, Michael, help me!" Tears of laughter streamed down his face. "Fuck, man, it was *hilarious*. And then, you *finally* show up and she's already a pile of charcoal. "I mean," he wiped his cheeks with the back of his hand, "I hate to say it, but she *might* be done with you. First you drive her batshit crazy, and then you're late to her bonfire."

The light in the mirror plummeted to black, then deepened to a color that had no name, an intensity that reached across the room, consuming the weak sunlight that shone through the windows. A shade of baleful nothingness swept over Georgia where she hung. The desolation only touched her briefly, but in that instant, she felt herself being stretched across a cosmic rack, her muscles tearing, joints disintegrating, her bones cracking to dust and then it was gone, leaving her gasping. In that terrible wake followed a dazzling wash of silver. It drenched her like a balm, remaking her, scouring away any residue of the Fallen creature and sending the child within her into a manic fervor of humming and twirling.

The creature frowned before quickly crossing the room to where he'd pinned her. Georgia held her breath, forced herself to look at the thing that was not Nathan, braced herself for another assault, but none came. He merely crossed his arms *don't, don't think it, it's not him, no matter how much he looks like him* and studied Georgia's stomach thoughtfully. "Maybe after all this time, 'Precious' here is done with the good brother and wants to take the bad one for a test ride."

The joyful humming and twirling inside her stopped abruptly. The mirror flashed, a warning.

"Why don't we ask her, Mike?" He bent down, his face *his face, that's not your face, that's Nathan's face, no, don't touch me please don't* so close as he draped his hand on her swollen stomach, a gentle pressure. The baby was so still Georgia wondered if she, too, were pinned in place by the horrible sound of that lovely voice. Worried she could hear, as Georgia could, the threats laced through his every light-hearted remark. "Hey, Red," he sang out softly. "Wanna come out and play with Uncle Lucifer?" The hand grew heavier; he was pushing now into her stomach. The child drew back, snatches of her frantic litany filled Georgia's ears with perfect clarity

Teach me to fight, Michael. I'm strong enough.

Why do you want to learn to fight, Galliana?

the baby retreated even deeper until it felt as if she'd coiled herself around Georgia's spine. *Please, don't, you'll kill us, she can't, I can't, don't* but he just pushed harder. "Whaddaya say, sweetheart?" His face disappeared from Georgia's line of sight as he knelt. She felt him kiss her stomach, lay the side of his face against her *like Nathan with Rose, whispering and listening to their poor lost child you are not Nathan, it's not him, it's not, Nathan where are you?* The mirror flared again and she focused on its reassuring brilliance. "Little Galliana and Luc, all alone in the Garden, and your knight in shining armor *late as usual.*" The pressure in the air dropped and Georgia thought her eardrums would burst.

There is nothing little about me.

The voice of her daughter struck like a snake. The weight on her stomach vanished as the parasite wearing Nathan's face stood up suddenly. He narrowed his eyes, not at her but at her stomach, but whether it was in displeasure or confusion, she could not say. The expression was alien, twisting Nathan's once familiar face into something inhuman.

"I think we're done here, Mikey." He tapped her on her nose, his voice a seductive tone that flooded her mind with precious images of tangled limbs, late nights and early mornings. Of Nathan, her Nathan. He winked at her. "See you soon, Miss Muffet."

As he strolled out of the room, the iron grip that held her to the wall disappeared. She fell to the floor, arms and legs filled with pins and needles. *I have to go, get out of here, grab Edie before he . . . in case it . . .* she tried to stand but the room spun; the only fixed point was the serene radiance from the mirror. She crawled back to the stairs, scrambled for the fallen duffle. *Grab Edie and go. Grab Edie and go.* Fighting against the vertigo, she tried to pull herself up when he *that thing* stuck his head back in the room.

Georgia was pulled to the floor, as if the gravity in the room had tripled. She tried to turn her head away from his face but found she could not; her head felt as if it weighed a hundred pounds, her arms a thousand.

"Oh, hey guys?"

The coterie of Fallen took flight, surrounding their master in a cloud of their wings; their clattering teeth landed at his feet, supplicant and cowering. "Keep a lid on this one for me, could you?" He knocked on the doorframe *shave and a haircut* as he threw a smirk at the rapidly fading mirror. The plaintive cries of the Fallen turned to confusion.

"I don't know, be creative." He raised one foot and stomped on the nearest creature. It cracked open like an egg and the others immediately began feasting on the hellish carrion.

"And guys? Fuck this one up for me again and you'll wish you were mud again."

Then, whistling, he spun and jogged out of the house, the door slamming briskly behind him.

The gravity pinning her to the ground vanished so quickly that Georgia thought she would float away from the sudden release. The creatures, having finished their meal, were gathered in a cluster, squabbling and pecking each other, as if conferring.

Mother! Run!

Her daughter's voice pleaded with her. Fast on its heels came another voice, like a legion of trumpets.

Galliana! Run!

Dizzy from the effort, Georgia pulled herself to the bottom of the stairs, the light from the landing window beckoning her. *Get Edie, and go. You can do this.* She crawled up the stairs, the needful chorus below drowning out the creaking of the treads. She made it half-way when she realized the creatures below had fallen silent. *Don't look. Don't.* Something touched her leg. A wobbly weight settled on her thigh, hopped up and down. She tried to gain purchase on the next step but her foot landed in a hot, slippery puddle.

She looked.

They had surrounded her, blanketing the stairs, the walls, the railing behind her, tattered wings beating the air, teeth and claws scoring the plaster walls. The one on her thigh tumbled off, righted itself, and she watched as its mouth swelled, boiled and burst, vomited her name on the floor.

Georgia Georgia Georgia

The words bled down the stairs, her name chasing itself, eating itself. One by one the other creatures followed suit, until her name cascaded down the stairs, scampered up the walls, bits of bone and flesh writhing in the lines of each letter. And then the letters began to rearrange, jostling and blurring before taking flight and painting the air with *his* name.

Nathan Nathan Nathan

Georgia slid down one step, then two, as she tried to decipher the words embroidered into each letter of his name. *Nate? No, he can't be. Not inside that thing, not trapped, helpless . . . you'll destroy him, no one could survive that hell*

Then something new appeared, a scroll through the crossbar of the letter A. Her eyes filled as she reached to scrub it out, to violently erase what she'd read. *He would never. That's a lie, not Nate, please, not my Nate.* She snatched her hand back, horrified that they'd mesmerized her, that she'd nearly buried her hand in that blood-drenched fable. She felt a shock surge through her, something more than adrenaline, like jet fuel.

Mother!

She flew back, the jolt of energy propelling her weakened body. Disappointed cries from the Fallen chased her up the stairs but she kept her eyes shut tight. *Don't look. Stupid, so stupid. They're trying to trick you.* She felt them tug weakly at her feet, but the higher she climbed they seemed to lose interest; their cries fell to chatter and then silence again.

Her fingers touched the bottom of the attic door. *Thank God.* She jumped to her feet, wrenched the door open and fell inside, kicking it shut behind her. The white-hot inertia vanished as quickly as it had come, leaving her exhausted from the effort, grateful for the two stories of stairs and the thick door between those things and her.

But there was little reprieve in the attic. Inside, a storm was raging. Choking, Georgia scrambled to extricate herself from the drift of ash she'd fallen into. The winds raced about the attic, a cyclone of grief that emanated from the weeping form huddled in the tempest's eye. Edie. Each shudder that wracked her slender shoulders sent a tremor through the thick curtain of dove gray soot that fell from the ceiling.

"Edie," Georgia croaked. A sudden wrack of coughing gripped her, the ash at her feet splattered crimson.

Edie turned with a start. The winds dropped but the ash continued to fall. Her skin was a patchwork, Kodachrome and gray scale; tears fell like black ink down her face, pooled all around her.

"I remembered. But it's too late now, isn't it?" she whispered.

"Like hell it is," Georgia scrambled to her feet, stumbled toward the far side of the attic, kicking her way through the drifts. Gripping the rafters to keep from falling, she extended her leg as far as she could, reaching, reaching, until the tips of her foot could just touch the edge of the rug. She dug in with her toes, arms shaking from trying to balance her ungainly body in such a contorted pose, and slid the rug out from the eaves.

"What are you doing?" Edie cried out in alarm.

Georgia ignored her and dragged the rug the rest of the way out, unrolled it. Clouds of ash plumed upward, briefly obscuring the contents. "Edie, honey, don't be scared. It's the only way."

"Don't!" Edie was screaming now. "What are you doing? Don't touch them!"

The ash settled, and spread out before her was the slight outline of a child rendered in bone. Edie pulled at her arm, but Georgia shrugged her off. The skeleton was pristine, vivid white against the dark rug, a tattered eyelet dress draped almost artfully over the ribcage. Edie was whimpering now.

"Don't touch them! Please don't! It *hurts!*"

Georgia hesitated, wondering if she was wrong. But the image of those creatures, those things below coming up here, touching Edie's fragile bones with their poison spurred her into action. She grabbed the feet, the shins, the femurs. Every time she touched Edie's remains the girl screamed as if she were being murdered all over again. Grimly, Georgia kept at her task; pelvic bones, spine, chest, and finally her skull until the entire skeleton was zipped up tight in the duffle bag.

She crawled out from the eaves with her precious cargo and flung the bag over her back. Edie's eyes and mouth were wide as graves.

"What are you doing to me?" Her voice was a broken puzzle.

Instead of answering her, Georgia pulled her to her feet and dragged her across the attic. She cracked the door open and listened downstairs. Silence, broken only by Edie's soft pleading.

Georgia dragged Edie down the attic stairs, through the hall. Then she stopped, pulled Edie to her, and shushed the distraught girl.

"Listen to me, Edie." She kissed her temple shook her, forced her to look at her. "If you've remembered everything, then you know that the thing downstairs is not my husband. And I have a feeling you know what it really is," she hissed.

"Bad. So Bad. He's a bad man. A monster," Edie stammered. "He came out of the dirt." Edie squeezed her eyes shut, but a fresh wash of ink-black tears fell. "Brought those things, I'd forgotten the sound of their teeth. He took them, Mama and Papa and . . . I should have remembered sooner but I was so happy with you I forgot."

"Then you know they're down there. Waiting for us."

Edie began keening.

"Edie," Georgia whispered. "We are going to get past them. Get out of this godforsaken house. I know it hurts, but this is the only way I can take you with me. I can't leave you here."

"But . . ." Edie wrung her hands.

"I don't know what comes next. I don't care. I can't think past getting out of this house." She kissed Edie's forehead, smoothed her hair back. "I'll figure the rest out. That thing wants my baby."

"Oh no," Edie wailed. "Not the baby!"

"Exactly. So you and I are going to get her out of here. Right?"

Edie nodded, emboldened. "They can't touch you. Not really. Can't hurt you. Only with the pictures they make."

"They're lies, Edie. Lies." Georgia could not disguise the tremor in her voice.

"No," Edie placed her hand on Georgia's cheek and shook her head. "That's just it. They're not."

Georgia pushed Edie's hand away with a sob.

"Then don't read them!" she snapped. "Ready?"

She didn't wait for an answer. Georgia pulled the girl by her hand down the stairs, pausing to gather her courage on the landing. *Just keep moving. Walk through them. Don't look too close. Out the back door.* The chattering began to build below, excited thumps, and she imagined the horrible little miscarriages square-dancing. Edie squeezed her hand.

"Don't think of it. Don't feed them," she whispered.

She flashed Edie a grateful smile, hugged her, then walked down the stairs hand-in-hand. *I just have to find a point to focus on*, she thought, as the horde of Fallen took flight, a wall of curses swirling through the air. They'd reached the bottom of the stairs. Wings fanned her face, bumped her head. *Find a point between them so I can keep my bearings, so I can—*

It was hopeless. Their wings and their teeth filled the living room, the gaps between filled with a miasma of sadistic verses. Georgia pulled Edie through the cloud, the girl's trembling causing her own arm to shake uncontrollably.

They can't hurt us, not really. Their breath was putrid and clung to her skin like oil. *It's just words. Words can't hurt us.*

One clawed wing batted Georgia's face, and her disobedient eyes focused. She read the stanza charred into the creature's flesh.

They're lies, she told herself. But Edie's words came back to her.

That's just it. They're not.

Georgia screamed, a hoarse, guttural sound. She wretched a mouthful of bloody vomit on the floor. The flock gathered around the puddle, eager cries, and then they began feeding on the foul mass. This brief distraction opened a path to the back door.

"Edie, run!" Georgia darted around the horde, barely registering the weight of Edie's hand growing lighter, weaker. She flung open the back door and pulled the weakly protesting girl out.

Her car was still buried in a drift. *But if I can clear it enough to get it started, maybe we could . . .* She ran down the porch steps, duffle bag tight around her shoulder, the snow bitter on her bare feet. The cries grew louder behind her, furious, and Edie's hand disappeared from her grasp.

Forget the car, we'll run. Run for help. There has to be someone. Has to be.

"Edie?" Georgia spun, the pounding of her heart drowning out the cries of the Fallen in the house.

Edie stood on the porch, just outside the door. Behind her the Fallen were hurling themselves at the glass, painting it with—

Don't read it.

But Edie, Edie was fading, flickering, her face downturned as she studied her own hands.

"Edie, please!"

Edie looked up, confused. "I can't."

Georgia took a step back. Edie's eyes rolled in her head as she faded, shrank, as if she were being stuffed back into the body of a tiny child, her head now grossly disproportionate, her face a mask of anguish.

"It hurts," she whispered.

Georgia clutched the bones to her chest as she took a step toward the house. Edie flared, cried out, then elongated, like she was being pulled like taffy. Another step and her head and body struggled to resume their former appearance. Another step and she was Edie again, still flickering wildly but—

Edie shook her head sadly and held her arms out for the bag. Georgia handed it to her, ashamed.

"I'm not going anywhere, Georgia." She turned back to Roseneath and squared her shoulders.

"Besides," she pointed to the towering windows, "I'm not sure you can, either."

Oh, but they were cunning. Every one of Roseneath's windows was inscribed, this time not with a story or a riddle, but with a message, just for her. The glass wavered with the intensity of the threat.

I'll hurt him.

I'll destroy him.

And I'll make it last forever, sweetheart.

Georgia watched as Edie walked bravely through the back door, disappeared with her bag of bones into Roseneath, hounded by the creatures he'd left behind. She lifted her face to the sky, felt the wind and the sun for the first time in ages. Wondered if she'd ever feel it again. Edie alone in that house. Nathan tortured by that thing. The two people she loved most in this world martyred because of her. She ran her hands over her stomach. *We'll just have to find another way, little one.* And then she followed Edie back into Roseneath.

THIRTY

"EDIE, TELL ME WHAT YOU REMEMBERED. What is this place?" Georgia finally broke the brittle silence of the attic. The two women had sat shell-shocked for some time after their harrowing journey back upstairs, each lost in their own personal narrative of hell as composed by the creatures from the basement.

Edie didn't reply at first. She placed her bones with great care back under the eaves. Then she waved her hand and the deep drifts of ash swirled, then vanished.

"I don't know what this place is, really." She reached back as far as she could in her memory, to the distant, happy day she'd arrived at Roseneath. "I was so little when we came here. When I—" A quick glance at the door and she continued. *They never have come this far. No reason to think they will now. And yet—*

"Mama and Papa were so happy when we came here, I remember that," she began. "I can't remember exactly where we came from. I remember a great ship. We were ages on the ship. Then a train for days and days, and the next thing I knew we were here."

She gathered a pile of blankets that lay on the imagined forest stream and wrapped them around Georgia before withdrawing to the window. The sun, having barely risen that day, was fading fast. Snow was falling steadily, blanketing the crimson tracks between Roseneath and the greenhouse. *I have to get her out of here. I can't let this happen to her. To either of them. Not if I can stop it.*

"Mama loved the garden," she continued. "She grew the most beautiful things. Flowers, of course, but also fruits and vegetables. I remember picking peas with her in the spring and pumpkins bigger than I was in the fall. She'd let me eat myself sick on raspberries. She taught me how to make pattycakes with sour cherries and huckleberries. We'd bake them and eat them for tea.

"Papa had a woodshop in the carriage house. He made furniture—grand, glorious things—all carved and polished, anything you could imagine. People came from all over and bought them. I remember seeing tables and chairs, beds and curios being crated in hay and off they went. But he had another little woodshop, in the basement, and that was just for him. Down there, he'd make Mama bookshelves and trellises, benches and trunks." She smiled in her reverie, her hands clasped under her chin. "He taught me to dance there. And he'd make me toys, clever little things with gears that wound up and raced about, rocking horses, tiny furniture for my room, just my size."

The wind rattled the windows, sent a shudder through the house. They each froze, listening, bracing themselves for what seemed an inevitable resurgence from the basement. But none came and Edie forced herself to go on, still looking out the back window, finding it was easier to tell this story to her own reflection in the glass than to Georgia's stricken face. *If only. If only there were someone. Someone else here, someone who might . . .*

"But then, one day . . . I remember it was a beautiful summer's night. I'd grown tired of playing with my toys and I wanted my supper. But I couldn't find my parents. I waited and waited." She rested her elbows on the window ledge, settling her chin on her hands as she gazed out into the yard. "That's what made me remember. Seeing your Nathan in the yard, the way he . . ." A quick glance over to Georgia and then she shook her head sadly. "It was just so strange the way I found her. It was full twilight. Long past supper and bath time. But Mama was just kneeling there in the earth, deep inside her greenhouse, her arms buried to her elbows, her face so very strange, peculiar, like she was asleep with her eyes open. I tried to wake her, but she ignored me. It was as if . . . as if I wasn't there at all."

"I thought maybe I was in trouble, that she was angry with me. So I ran off to look for Papa, but I couldn't find him anywhere. Later, I put myself to bed and when I woke in the morning, I thought I must have imagined it. Just a bad dream. I ran downstairs to tell Mama all about it, thinking she and Papa would laugh at the tale, make me my breakfast, the whole frightening thing soon forgotten."

Edie swallowed hard, her eyes flickering over to the attic door, afraid for a moment that telling the tale might be some sort of invocation, curse, drawing him *it* back. *But still, there is someone else. Someone who watches. Someone bright and shining, like a knight. Someone who's been here, like me, all along.*

"But she wasn't in the kitchen. I was too frightened to look for her in the greenhouse. Papa's workshop was locked up tight. It wasn't like them to leave me alone. I . . . I . . ." she cleared her throat and took a deep breath. "I heard a noise. I thought, *Papa is in the cellar. He will know where Mama is.* I ran down the stairs. It was so dark, it took me a minute to see him."

Edie let her eyes fall softly, but she could still see the image of her father, burned in her mind's eye, as if it were happening all over again.

"He was digging. In the basement. Something about him was so very wrong, so very peculiar. He was mumbling words I didn't understand, in a language I'd never heard. He looked like Mama did, like he was sleepwalking. I didn't try to speak to him, he frightened me so. I ran to my room, the little one next to theirs, and that's when I saw her through the window. She was digging in the yard. Her arms, they were . . . were," Edie's head shook in a blur, tears scattering like prisms on the floor, "horribly cut. Blood was running down them. I ran downstairs. I thought she was sick, that she'd hurt herself. I thought maybe they were both sick, that I could . . ."

Edie shook her skirts out to diffuse the rising panic she felt. *It was so long ago. And nothing can touch you now.* She looked over to Georgia and felt her heart break to know the same was not true for her.

"And that's when they came. Those creatures. Out of the hole Papa dug in the basement. Some sort of filth, blood and earth with little bits of teeth and bone, began to weep up from the basement. They oozed out, like rats made out of earth. And then they saw me, began following me, writing things on the floor, the walls, the windows, chasing me. I was just learning to read, of course, and I tried not to read them, not to sound out each word but I couldn't help myself. And then they, those things you saw downstairs, stopped writing words and started making pictures. It was like they knew the words were hard for me, like whatever they did, whatever they said, it was just for me. Terrible pictures. Nightmares in the air. And still my parents kept at their strange tasks. They took no notice of those wretched creatures, didn't seem to care that they hounded me. It was like I'd been orphaned, but my parents were *right there*."

Edie turned away from the window and leaned against the wall, studying the tips of her velvet shoes as she twisted the sash at her waist. Across the room, Georgia moved, the sound of pillows and blankets shifting, her breathing steady if shallow, the baby's song once more lilting and serene, as if she too were listening.

"So I hid in the attic, thinking that whatever this was it would go away if I waited long enough. That Mama and Papa would be themselves again, that I would wake up one morning and those things would be gone. That one day Mama would call for me and we'd all be happy again, like we had been before Roseneath. I waited and waited, oh it seemed forever. I worried sometimes that they'd left me here, alone, with those filthy picture creatures."

"And then, one day, at last, I heard Mama calling me. Papa, too. And it sounded like them, really them, not peculiar at all. So I unlocked the door and ran down the stairs and—" Edie ran a hand over her eyes, studied her own heart-sore reflection in the glittering tear drops as a wash of gray fell down upon her. She looked up and managed a sweet smile for Georgia.

"Some things aren't worth remembering."

"No." Georgia shook her head slowly, remembering what she'd seen downstairs. "I almost wish you hadn't remembered. I wish of all things that I could have given you only good memories."

"Don't be silly," Edie said. "It's all long ago and far away, isn't it? And now the evil in this house, it's taken Nathan, too. Perhaps there's a reason I remembered; perhaps in some way it helps. But remembering isn't *knowing*. Isn't *understanding*."

"Edie, I don't think there is any reason to this," Georgia said, holding her hand out to her. Edie threaded her fingers through Georgia's.

"If only I'd remembered sooner!" Edie cried. "I tried, I did! I grew up as fast as I could! If I'd tried harder, maybe none of this—"

"No, Edie. Don't. None of this is your fault. It's his, whatever that thing is. Don't let him put this on you. You remembered in your own time, in your own way."

"I'd never have if it weren't for you, you know. When I think of the scared girl you found up here, how long I was trapped here, never more than what he'd left me as . . ."

Her face darkened, twisted into something wrathful. "And I'll be," she floundered about for a word strong enough for how angry she now was, "*cussed* if I let him do to you what he did to me." She laid her hand on Georgia's shifting stomach, felt a small push-back and smiled.

"Edie, he said he's coming back. To take her from me." Her voice broke; her breathing grew haggard and shallow. "I don't know what to do. I keep trying to find a way out of all this, for both of us, but—"

Edie jumped to her feet.

"Well, I can tell you what we're not going to do. We're not going to panic. It won't do us any good and you're sick enough as it is. Besides, it upsets her to hear you frightened." She bent down and tipped Georgia's face up to hers. "You need to be calm for her, okay? Remember, it's not her fault any of this is happening. She's just a baby."

She'd intended her words to be comforting, but based on the look in Georgia's eyes, they had the opposite effect.

"But she's not, Edie. She's not just a baby. Not if he's her—what if she's . . ." Georgia's face crumpled even as she wrapped her arm protectively around her stomach.

"Georgia," Edie scolded gently. "You don't really think she's like him, do you? That's the silliest thing I've ever heard." Edie knelt at her side and laid her long fingers over Georgia's stomach. "Listen to her song."

In the silence of the attic, the melody rose again, dipping and swirling in time with the rising winds outside. The lilting words were indecipherable but they seemed to warm the air around them, lighting a spark of gentle hope inside a place as hopeless as Roseneath. Edie watched

Georgia's fears vanish as something wondering and sweet replaced them, as a beatific love shone from her eyes. The child's song paused as if she'd finished her ballad, and in its place came a new song, two notes, two syllables repeated on an endless scale, each escalating octave calling, calling, calling, a hypnotic, soothing meter.

"Nothing evil could ever sing so beautifully. Could never tell a story so lovely. And I won't let him take her from you."

Edie leapt to her feet and began pacing briskly, her heels clicking softly on the painted attic floor. She danced lightly over painted mossy stones, leapt over her imagined fallen trunks and babbling brook as if each woodland feature was actually there.

"We must be very clever and do something he won't expect. Because I for one have had enough of his games," she finished haughtily. "*Mr. Lumpy Porridge* thinks you and I will just *sit* here like shrinking violets. I think not." She spun around to face Georgia, her lips pursed.

"First of all, you're going to use that telephone thing to ring your Nathan."

"No, I can't, you saw what they said—"

"Stuff what they said," Edie snapped. "Stuff him and his stupid Fallen *twice*."

"But," Georgia paled. "It's not Nathan. What if he answers? What if I," her face crumpled. "Make things worse and he hurts him?"

"Listen to me, Georgia: you're the only thing that might bring him back." Edie scowled, indignation making her tremble head to toe. "No matter how scared you are, you can't abandon him. You have to try. I never called to my parents, you see. I hid, just as we are now, up here for the last hundred years and look where that got all of us." She knelt and gathered Georgia's hands in hers, kissed her scabbed knuckles. "I think if I had called to them, eventually they would have heard me." She pleaded now. "Promise me you'll try. Do it for him. Please, Georgia. He's in there. Trapped and alone."

"I'll try," Georgia's voice was thick with emotion. "For him."

"Excellent." Edie jumped back on her feet and whirled across the attic again. "Which brings me to the second part of my plan." She arched her eyebrow at Georgia before continuing, her lips curved up in a manic grin. "I have made a decision."

Across the room, Georgia began coughing again, her body so clearly wracked in pain. Whatever residual reservations Edie had about her mad scheme vanished.

"I have decided to be very bricky. The bravest of the brave," she said, nodding vigorously. "I have decided that . . . that . . . oh!" Her face screwed up in frustration. "I wish I knew a proper curse word or two!" she exclaimed, stamping her feet again. "That bunky *hobgoblin* shan't hurt you or the baby. I won't have it," she cried, each word punctuated with a stomp of one heel. "After all, she's sort of my sister, isn't she? It's all right for me to think of her like that, isn't it? That maybe I could be brave . . . brave for her?"

"Is that another thing you remembered?" Georgia choked, wiping her pink-tinged lips on the blanket. "That you were a brave girl?"

"Oh dear me, no," Edie said with a rueful laugh. "This isn't something I *remembered*. It is something I *decided*." She felt the air around her begin to vibrate, to tremble, but this time, instead of a dismal ash cloud, it was as if the very molecules around her began to spark and snap, each particle falling in a wash of iridescent snow, swirling in a magic gust around her.

"I'm done cowering from that ratty old . . . that *crusty old mustard*. I don't care who that dirty crumb thinks he is. I am going to be very brave. And very clever." Her breath caught in her chest as she realized the depth and breadth of her plan, at once chilled and enamored of her own daring.

"Here's the thing. Remember that man in the mirror? The man who's been watching."

Georgia nodded, the ghost of a smile on her face. Inside her belly, the child's chirping raced along faster, faster.

"I don't think they like each other," Edie added. "And you know what else?" She leaned forward to whisper in Georgia's ear. "*I* think that ugly old Jabberwock is *afraid* of the man in the mirror."

Georgia's face lit up, transformed, as if she'd been restored, cured of what Roseneath had done to her. Inside, the child was laughing, a heady, delighted gale that echoed in the attic stillness.

"He called that man an archangel," Georgia whispered back. "I can't believe I'm going to say this, but I think the man in the mirror is Michael . . . you know—Old Testament Michael."

"Is he now?" Edie's eyes danced. "That's jammy."

"Edie, do you think—"

Edie placed her finger over Georgia's lips, cutting her off.

"Georgia, I feel like making a little mischief."

Georgia followed Edie's pointed gaze back to the door.

"Edie wants to go through the looking glass?"

Edie smiled as she pulled Georgia to her feet and hugged her close. Her laughter rose with Georgia and the baby's, an astonished three-part harmony.

"You know what? I rather think I do."

THIRTY-ONE

 EDIE AND GEORGIA STOOD HAND-IN-HAND in front of the old gilt mirror, their bodies elongated by the wavy glass.

"I look like I had a bit too much to drink in Wonderland," Edie proclaimed with a laugh. "Wherever did you find this mirror?" Despite her jest, Edie preened at her own reflection, stroked her hair, and ran her fingertips over the planes of her face. It was likely, Georgia thought to herself, that the girl had never seen herself before, at least not grown as she was now.

Georgia examined her own reflection with less enthusiasm. "I found it years ago at a flea market. The mirror isn't the best, but I . . . we liked the frame and we . . . I mean—" her eyes burned, and if it was due to the memory of buying the incongruous mirror with Nathan *He'd made Frankenstein faces in the mirror at her until she couldn't breathe from laughing then he'd carried it under one arm to their truck, teasing her with a silly riddle. When is a mirror not a mirror?* or from the bone-deep cramping in her hips, she could not say. *I didn't know then and I don't know now, Nate. I pray this mirror is more than a mirror. I pray to God it's a door.*

Edie studied her with alarm. "And you're sure you didn't have any trouble bringing it up here? The Fallen didn't—"

"No," Georgia lied neatly. "Not a creature was stirring, not even a—" she broke off, knew her attempt at levity had fallen flat. She shrugged and rubbed her eyes, wishing she could wipe away what she had really seen. No more than five minutes. *But it felt like eternity. What if this*, she looked around the attic, *is eternity? For me and Edie. What if this is how it all ends?*

The creatures had been waiting on the landing, a clamoring, shoving assembly, each vying for her attention, mouths boiling over with new tales to tell. *Nathan Nathan Nathan Nathan* She'd read them all, then pushed through them to the bedroom for the mirror, tried to ignore the feeling of rotted leather on her ankles, shut her ears to the sound of her feet squelching in their slick trails. Reread their tales again on her way back, over and over until she was numb. *Lies or the truth or some mix of the two. Anyway, it doesn't matter. It's not Nate. Not anymore.* But Edie seemed to have accepted her explanation and had turned back to the mirror. She leaned forward and placed a kiss on her own lips in the mirror.

"I must say, Georgia, I'm gorgeous, aren't I?"

At least I'm not alone, Georgia thought. *At least I have her.* "Yes, darling, *you* are gorgeous. Whereas I," she ran a hand over her stomach and cringed, "look like someone stuck toothpicks in a marshmallow. If you drank too much Wonderland water, my dear, I must have eaten the whole damn cake." A beat, and then Edie laughed and hugged her, carefully, as if she were handling glass. Then she rested her head on Georgia's chest, laid her hand against her neck and she could have sworn the girl was counting the erratic beats of her heart, listening intently to each rattle in her chest. *I wonder,* she thought, catching the edge of a calculating look from Edie, *who is taking care of whom at this point?* Edie fussed with the mirror, polishing it with the edge of her apron, while Georgia paced, rubbing her back surreptitiously, waiting for the cramping to pass.

"The baby says she's sorry, but it's uncomfortable in there," Edie commented absentmindedly.

"You can hear her?" Georgia stopped her circuit, bewildered.

"Of course, plain as day. Just like that song she likes to sing." Edie studied the mirror again. "Well, that's as clean as I can make it. Not sure if it matters."

The cramping stopped abruptly as the baby drew her limbs in, as if in apology. Georgia sank to the floor. "That's better. I can't always understand her like you can. I can hear her singing but I can't catch the words. Bits and pieces sometimes, but it's all jumbled. Like a story, but all out of order." She followed the child's shifting with her fingers. "Could you tell her I love her? That none of this is her fault?" She looked at Edie. "It's just, I can feel when she's scared, and I don't ever tell her not to be. That I won't let anyone hurt her. Can you tell her that for me, Edie?"

Edie covered Georgia's hand with her own. "Don't be silly. She knows all of that." She listened intently for a moment then rolled her eyes. "Well, *that* time I didn't catch a word." She wagged her finger at Georgia's stomach. "You talk too fast, young lady. Like a church bell." Discomfort flashed across her teasing face "Did you remember to ring Nathan when you were down there?"

Georgia looked away, wondered how much Edie had guessed. "I did. I found my phone where I dropped it on the landing. Fortunately, he . . . *he* didn't answer. So I left him a message. For what it's worth."

Edie pulled her knees to her chest, laid her head on her knees. "You just have to keep trying. I know it's hard, but I think it helps. And remember, we decided to be brave. I can't do it all by myself."

Her sad eyes and gentle urging made it obvious that Edie had guessed most of what Georgia was trying to keep from her, if not everything. She knew Georgia was trying to protect her from the horrors downstairs. *She's not a little girl anymore*, Georgia reminded herself. *My Edie grew up.*

"Right. So now that you have your looking glass, Edie, what exactly is the plan?" She gestured to the mirror.

Edie rubbed her chin. "I've no idea how to summon an archangel," she mused. "But I'd imagine something simple and direct is the best way forward."

She rapped on the mirror three times. Frowned. Waited. Rapped again, louder this time. Nothing. Georgia flinched as Edie kicked the frame in frustration, then glared at her own indignant reflection. "I say, you in there." She continued rapping on the fragile glass, relentlessly. "I'd very much like to speak to whoever you are right this instant." Another glare as she scanned the corners of the mirror suspiciously. "I know you're watching and *we need help*. IS ANYONE HOME IN THERE?" she demanded.

Edie's voice echoed in every corner of the attic, followed by an enormous, weighted silence. Georgia held her
breath, uncertain whether she was more afraid that Edie's
whimsical plan would fail, or worse, that it wouldn't. That
there really was an archangel in the looking glass. A fearsome entity who waited and watched. A being powerful
enough to melt glass and twist reality. Someone whom the
creature wearing Nathan's skin hated, maybe, just maybe,
even *feared. An archangel*, Georgia thought to herself. *And
why not? Angels, demons, it's mad, mad, mad.*

Just then, a flash of light in the corner of the mirror
caught her eye. Edie leaned forward and peered intently
into the surface, clearly self-satisfied.

"Well, that's done it. Something is happening," she said,
casting a nervous glance at Georgia. "Easy as duck soup,"
she whispered.

The baby's two-note melody stumbled, faltered, then
ascended wildly up a lofty scale. Georgia fought against
the thrall of the ballad, tried to focus on Edie and the
mirror. A sudden burst of clarity to the words, the verses
stumbling, stammering over each other—

cloud watch with me
daughter of eve
stain your lips
birth of stars
eden
don't be afraid
Beloved

—as a shadow, a mere spot in the corner of the mirror,
began to move, grow, shift until it loomed behind Georgia's

reflection. She twisted in the blanket to see what was behind her in the attic, but there was nothing. The song in her head spun faster, faster, twirled like a dervish and danced away from her, the words she so briefly grasped lost as the melody left her in its brilliant wake.

Edie was gripping the mirror frame, her eyes locked on the dark shape approaching, an enormous figure that moved closer and closer until its reflection dwarfed her astonished face. The air in the room felt poised to burst into flames. Georgia felt her hair rise up, smelled it singe. The paint on the walls bubbled, the paint on the floor melted into pools, the ceiling dripped a rainbow shower. An oppressive shockwave flowed out from the mirror, drove the breath from Georgia's body, crushed the words she tried to form before they could escape her throat.

"Do you see him, Georgia?" Edie cried with delight, oblivious to her distress. "Oh he looks just like a knight! There's a man in the mirror! It's the archangel! He's coming!"

Edie laid one hand on the mirror's surface. Her hand seemed to float just above like a leaf on a pond, then the silver surface vanished and her hand slipped through the looking glass. Edie let out a small cry as she pitched forward, her right hand flailing to grasp the mirror's frame to arrest her fall, but it slipped, almost as if pulled. She snatched both hands back, even as Georgia was frozen, as if a terrible density had crushed the attic from three dimensions into one, flattening her. A sound filled the attic, a sonic burst that deadened the air around them, vibrations that made Georgia's teeth rattle in her head.

Edie jumped to her feet in one smooth movement, her laughter filling the spaces between the bone-crushing vibrations. Struggling to remain conscious, Georgia willed herself to keep focus on the young girl, on the enormous shadow in the mirror. She watched helplessly as a pair of hands, leather-gloves at the end of leather-clad arms, wrapped themselves around Edie's wrists and pulled her through the glass. One small giggle floated back to Georgia before Edie's cherry-red shoes vanished and the mirror's surface reappeared, wavering for an instant then solidifying. The terrible density vanished, allowing Georgia's lungs to finally fill, and she scrambled across the attic floor to the mirror.

"Edie!" she screamed into the mirror, frantically searching beyond her own reflection for the child, for the shadow, and finding nothing. "Edie!"

But no reply came. Edie was gone.

THIRTY-TWO

"HELLO, YOU'VE REACHED NATHAN Pritchard..."

His voicemail always sounded oddly formal, stilted. Georgia remembered the day he'd recorded it. Long before they'd lost the baby, long before Roseneath, long before they'd lost each other here, in a place that was meant to be a new beginning.

"Georgia, what on earth do I say? I hate this shit," he'd said, tossing her the phone. "Here, you do it. I sound like an idiot."

"...your call is very important to me..."

She'd tossed it back to him. "Not a chance. Pretend you're already a success. Say something confident and sexy." He'd groaned and scowled at the phone, ran a hand through his hair, frustrated. She smiled to remember that mannerism, remembered what it felt like to smooth that hair down.

"...please leave a message..."

"There, how did that sound?" he'd asked.

What did I say then? she asked herself for the hundredth time, the cellphone pressed to her ear. *I can't remember.*

But I remember his face, I remember the room, I remember it was fall. I remember that we felt like us. I remember when he remembered me. Remember, remember, remember.

Beep.

"It's me. Georgia. I know you don't . . . can't . . . Edie says he won't let you remember me. She told me to call you, to try to make you remember, told me not to give up hope. It's hard to be hopeful now. Hard to remember. But she says I have to try. Even if it's only so that one day, when you're back, when you remember me, you will understand what happened. I think I can do that much. Nathan, I should have told you about Edie. I don't know why I didn't. I guess it would be easy to blame him, the Jabberwock, blame the house, blame whatever all this is. But the truth is, Nate, I found a little girl in the attic that first day you brought me to Roseneath. The ghost of a murdered child in the attic and I wanted her for myself. I needed her for myself. And now she's gone. The man in the mirror took her and I don't think she's coming back." *How can he possibly understand any of this? she thought.* She then hung up and dialed again.

He loved me, he did. It was perfect, like something out of a dream. There had been a moment, one she could not pinpoint, when her memories became dreams, when her reality became a dream of memories she could no longer trust. *Then what do nightmares become,* she wondered. *What if he never knows, never remembers? What if he never understands what I have done, what I have become. I should have tried harder to wake him from whatever spell this place has cast over him. What will become of me? What will become of us? My God, what have I done?*

The phone rang twice. But instead of a click, static. Georgia held the phone tight to her ear and listened. *He answered. But who? Is it Nathan? Or is it him?* Her fingers curled tight around the phone. One minute passed, then two. The static faded and in its place, breathing, slow and steady, like someone in a deep sleep. In, out, in, out, she tried to match the steady pace as she waited. And then a sound, soft at first. She held her fist against her mouth, stifling the coughing fit that threatened.

"Georgia?" It was him, him, him, his voice, she was certain of it. A dozen indefinable inflections that no one, not even that thing, could mimic. Weak and confused, but Nathan.

"Nathan, it's me—" she broke off when a rush of angry static overwhelmed the sound of his labored breathing. "Nathan?"

"Please . . ." Just that one small word and then the static returned, erasing his voice, consuming him, and then a click, a dial tone, and he was gone.

Georgia slumped against the attic door, defeated. *He remembered,* she told herself. *If only for a minute. What hell, Nathan* she thought, looking down to her softly shifting stomach, *is yours?*

She crawled her way to the far wall, across Edie's ruined landscape where she'd sought refuge in the days since Edie vanished, to the window. Using the sill, Georgia pulled herself up. Cold rain pelted against the window, ran down it in slushy blotches. Below her lofty perch the snow had melted from the backyard without a trace. She hurried to the north window and looked out. The snow was gone there, too.

Think, Georgia. Remember, she told herself. *How many days since Edie left? How many? You can't lose track. Can't slip. There's no one here to save you, not now.* Making a fist, she drove her hand into the painted wall again and again, the attic stupor fading ever so slightly with each blow. *Remember. Remember.*

The sun rose and set while she burrowed and slept. The child grew, and she dwindled behind it. *Seven,* she thought. *Seven days.* Raising her bloodied knuckles to her lips, she licked them, tasted the coppery tang, felt a surge of adrenaline and panic burn away the oblivion that saturated Roseneath. *Seven days passed like hours. Or weeks. Or . . . or . . . I can't tell anymore. I have to get out of here. No matter what. No matter what he does. I have to try. I'm so sorry, Edie, but I can't wait any longer. I've waited too long as it is.*

Georgia hurried across the attic, scrambled in the nest of blankets for her phone, and then, tucking it securely in her bra, crept down the steep staircase. The upstairs hall was mercifully empty. Down another flight, she paused to catch her breath, a spasm of coughing splattering the landing window, red blotches streaking against the slush outside. Down the main staircase she ran, cradling the ever-shifting weight of her stomach, her only thought to get out the front door. *Keep going, don't stop. Don't think about it, don't feed it, just go. Get out. I have to get out before they*

She kicked aside the towering stacks of mail that blocked her path and then froze, only steps away from freedom, when she saw the cunning barrier Roseneath had created. Where there should have been a door made of lead glass and golden oak, there was instead a towering fetid monolith, her means of escape transformed into a boiling window to hell, the landscape beyond black and red, dotted everywhere with bits of pulp and bone, teeth and gristle. The child inside her recoiled as the creatures oozed out of the surface like weeping pustules, one after another, devils without number. They flapped their wings with glee, conferred with smacking lips and clicking teeth, and then began composing their master's message to her.

Warned you, warned you, warned you.

"No!" she screamed. She shut her eyes tight as they began arranging their next verse. *Don't look. Don't feed them. Run.* Stumbling backwards, blind, across the foyer, feeling for the bannister, she slipped on a scattering of envelopes.

Nathan Nathan my beamish boy oh how I will hurt him ruin him hurt you hurt you

She read the Fallen's chapter and verse, punctuated by the snapping of their broken teeth, the flapping of their shredded wings. *I'll never make it back to the attic,* she thought. All around her, the leathery horde dipped and swooped, followed her up the stairs, tempting her, *look, look, look, look, don't you want to know, don't you want to see? Now you've done it done it made him angry oh so angry Georgie Georgie naughty girl*

Stupid, stupid, why did you look? she scolded herself, scrambling for the railing, *They can't hurt you, not really.*

They can only drive you mad if you look. You can make it, you can make the bedroom at least, the bedroom is safe for now.

With her last bit of strength, she climbed to her feet and nearly collapsed into the bedroom. She ran through the bathroom to the nursery, their frenzied cries louder now, coming, coming, faster, faster, and she slammed the door shut, savagely twisting the key in the lock.

Outside, the Fallen beat their leathery wings ineffectually against the door, their teeth snapping in frustration at the hinges, the doorknob. After a while, they scattered off, leaving the upstairs silent except for Georgia's labored breathing.

"Nathan, I'm so sorry," she whispered, her head falling into her hands. "But I had to try. I have to." Her unborn daughter fluttered inside her, murmured in melody. Georgia laid a hand on her stomach and could feel her daughter reaching out, trying to comfort her in her sorrow. *I have to try again, Nate, and I'm so sorry. But I have to save her. I'll try again and again. No matter what it does to me. Or you.*

She crawled into the closet, then dialed Nathan's number again. Instead of a connection, Georgia heard a click. His voicemail. She tried to picture him, the real him, listening to her on the other end, that intent, affectionate look in his eyes, the one he reserved for her and her alone. *Don't remember him like that. That wasn't him. Remember him the way he was. Remember some part of him is still in there. Has to be.*

"It's me again," she began. She shifted on the closet floor, trying to find a comfortable position. "Georgia. Your wife

Georgia. Was that you today or was it another one of his tricks? Making me think if I keep trying that somehow I can beat him. Tricking me into doing something stupid—" She broke off, coughing, wiped the phone off on her pants before continuing. "And I worry sometimes that he uses these messages to hurt you." She touched her fingertips to her mouth, studied the thick crimson spittle she'd collected. "Edie is gone and I'm not sure she's coming back. I'd tell you where, but I'm not sure what I saw anymore. It's all mixed up in my head, like the story. Through the looking glass, down the rabbit hole, eat me, drink me, pass the tea. Was she ever even here? Is there really someone in the mirror? I can't be sure of anything, not now. It all sounds mad when I say it out loud. Ghosts. Angels. Demons. I should have told you everything, that first day I found her. And now she's gone and you're gone and I'm here and I . . . I . . . I should have done it all differently. I thought I was saving her, sparing you. That's what I told myself. But this is all my fault, isn't it?"

She listened to the dead air on the other end as she drew red hearts on the closet wall and then finally hung up.

THIRTY-THREE

EDIE TUMBLED HEAD-OVER-FEET ONCE, twice, three times before landing with very little dignity on her backside.

"Applesauce!" she exclaimed. "You might have warned me." Scowling, she looked up into the contrite, if very strange, face of the man who had pulled her through the looking glass. Edie saw she had landed on a damp moss-covered rise in a foggy wood. All around her, towering sycamores swayed in a gentle breeze, the ground around her as dappled as the bark on the ancient trees. The air was lush and cool, and smelled strongly of incense and tea.

"My apologies," the man said, holding his enormous hand out to her. "But, you see, I wasn't absolutely sure it would work. All right, then?"

Beaming now, Edie let him pull her to her feet. Then, brushing her skirts off, she laughed.

"Not to worry, sir. That was an absolute gas. I haven't had very many adventures and this one's better than butter on bacon." She squinted up at him again, studying his face, in particular his eyes. They were kind and crinkled about the edges but inside, where there should have been irises, were twin flames, red hot and flickering, set deep in vast black corneas.

"I've never seen someone with fire in their eyes," she proclaimed, nose wrinkled. "Of course, I haven't met many people."

"Well, I doubt you've ever met someone like me," he said, propping one boot up on a rock, his right hand tapping the hilt of an aged sword at his side. "You see, I'm not human. Does that frighten you?"

Edie let out a huff that sent her bangs flying. "I'm dead. Does that frighten you?"

The great man's lips twitched as Edie laughed aloud. She clapped her hands together, delighted by her own joke.

The man reached over and, tentatively, as if still worried he might scare her, took her chin in his glove-clad hands. Turning her face this way and that, he murmured, as if to himself, "You are many things, little miss, but dead is not one of them."

"Curiouser and curiouser," Edie whispered. "Then riddle me this, sir: are you a hatter? I always thought you were just a shy ghost like myself, but Georgia thinks you're a fearsome angel. So which is it?"

He inclined his head in consideration but did not answer directly.

"I'll say this much. I am no hatter. And this is no Wonderland. It is Eden."

Edie gasped in delight. "Eden? Well, that's brilliant! Georgia, we're in . . ." She broke off as she scanned the woods around them. "Bother it all, where's Georgia? Didn't she come, too?"

A look of discomfort passed over the great man's face.

"No, Georgia Pritchard did not come through with you. I think, in her condition, it would be unwise, even dangerous. I thought it best if you and I had a chat. What do you say to that, little one?"

"Well now, that's twice you've 'littled' me," Edie snorted. "Now, really, *look* at me. I've grown so much since Georgia found me. I grew up as fast as I could manage, considering how very long I was a little girl. And I'm quite taller than she is now." She turned back and forth, admiring her velvety shoes, the once sensible round-toed, flat-soled Mary Janes now boasted a small kitten heel and a sparkling buckle. "Although I have no idea *how*. I'm not exactly alive, but I am growing like a weed. It's crazy cakes."

"Yes," he said with a smile. "You are a wonder. You've grown so much since—"

"Since what?" Edie pounced.

He raised one eyebrow but did not reply.

"Have we met before?" Edie inquired slowly.

"Not exactly," was his rather unsatisfactory reply.

"But I'm not wrong in thinking it's been you all this time? Sneaking about in Roseneath?"

His only reply was an enigmatic gesture that might have been a shrug.

Edie pooched her lip out in an exasperated pout. "Well, if she can't come here, let's us go there. I don't like to leave her alone in Roseneath. It's not *safe* there, you see. Which, of course, is why I reached out to you, so to speak. Figuratively *and* literally." Her brow creased in consternation.

The man's boot slid off the rock and he took an earnest step towards her. "Oh, but I *do* see, and that is why I wanted to talk. I might be able to help. But I don't think my going there would be wise. Not yet. I can be a bit frightening, to some."

Edie tapped her lower lip with a slender finger as she considered both him and his words. As tall as she herself now was, this man, this creature, was far taller. His towering stature was accentuated by the tarnished and dented breastplate that spanned his broad chest and shoulders. Beneath, he wore some manner of coarse black linen surcoat and trousers. The boots on his feet were of some archaic design; sturdy, worn, and dusty. He looked, Edie thought, like a lion in the mold of a man, a pilgrim soldier containing the barely restrained vigor of a legion. The air around him crackled with a tightly coiled intensity.

Conceding, Edie nodded. "Fair point. And you're far too tall for the ceilings. You'd have to crawl about and that's hardly dignified. But *I'm* not frightened of you. Not *exactly.*"

"But you're not, as you pointed out, like other girls," he said, one side of his grimly set lips curving up into what might have been a wry smile.

"That's quite true." Then, as if she'd made a decision, she held her hand out. "Edith. How do you do?"

"Michael. I must say, it's nice to meet you properly. Let's take a walk, shall we? I think better when I'm moving. I'll show you a bit of Eden and then we can discuss the matter at hand."

"Are you going to help us? Me and Georgia and the baby? Surely you must understand how bad things are. Back there. If you've been watching like I think you have been."

He nodded once, his jaw set in a stern line. "Yes, I'm going to help you."

"Nathan, too?"

"As much as it is in my power to do so." A sizzling spark in the air as Michael clenched the hilt of his sword.

"And I won't be gone *too* long, will I?" Edie asked as he led her across a carpet of fallen leaves, through the great sycamores that towered overhead.

"Not long at all. At least I don't think so. Time doesn't always work the way I think it does. Certainly not here. And usually not there."

"I understand exactly what you mean. I just don't want Georgia to worry."

"Then we'll be as quick as we can."

Michael led Edie through Eden. Through a great forest, past bubbling brooks and a still, calm pool, pausing briefly in an ancient vineyard where Edie greedily ate grapes the size of plums off the vine. Then out of the woods and across a great meadow, whose center was marked with a ring of roses as tall as herself, were rosehips the size of apples hanging from each thorn-crusted stem. A darkening shadow crept across Michael's face the deeper they traveled, the flames in his eyes flickering, fading, until finally when they reached the last stop on his pilgrim's progress, they were entirely black and devoid of all light.

They'd come to a small stone hut in a clearing surrounded by a ramshackle fence. A path led the way through a neatly tended garden to a smooth stone threshold. To one side of the open doorway was a tidy woodpile, leaning against it an enormous silver axe, clearly scaled for the creature at her side.

"My home," he said, gesturing with one gloved hand. His lips tightened into a flat line as he whispered, "Our home." Edie scanned the clearing, but as was the case throughout their brief tour of the woods, there was not another soul in sight. Eden appeared empty, save for the two of them.

Michael ducked as he entered the ancient house and Edie hurried after. A gentle light flooded the room from a scattering of roughly hewn windows. Each wall was covered in books stacked on long planks of raw sycamore. Over the stone hearth hung a garland of dried rosehips, nearby a pile of neatly folded sheepskins. And that was all—a humble monk's quarters and no more. Edie ran a hand over the soft wool on the floor and watched as Michael surveyed his own home, as if seeing it through her eyes.

"It's not much," he said finally. "I don't even have a chair to offer you. But then, I don't get visitors. I'm a poor host, I'm afraid."

"Never mind a chair," Edie said with a laugh. "You don't even have a bed. Where on earth do you sleep?"

"I don't." A pause. "Not anymore."

Edie threw him a sharp glance, but decided not to pursue an explanation. Instead, she turned to his bookcase and said, "I positively adore books. You've so many." She eagerly flipped through a tattered copy of *The Galoshes of Fortune*. "Oh, this looks *yummy*. It was on my list, but Georgia has been so sick, so she never did get around to locating it for me. I *so* wish I had time to read it." She let out a petulant sigh and then slammed the book down on the table. "Tell me, Michael," she said abruptly, spinning around to face him, "why do you carry a *sword*?"

"Down to brass tacks, is it, Edith of the attic?" That savage, wry look again.

Edie tapped one indignant toe on the earthen floor.

"Enough with all this promenading. Let's get on with it."

"I'm a soldier," he said simply.

"Then where's your *army*?" Edie countered.

"I *am* an army."

"I've never heard of an army with just one man in it," she insisted.

Michael shrugged and ran a hand through his coppery hair. "Fair enough. Your Georgia was correct. I'm an archangel."

"Like in the Bible?" Edie asked, incredulous.

Across the room, Michael visibly flushed.

"Yes and no."

"Are you *the* Michael?" Edie said, taking a step back.

Her question elicited a groan from Michael. "Well, yes. And also *no*. It's vastly more complicated than that cobbled story makes it out to be."

Edie gave a delighted twirl. "My goodness, Michael, why on *Earth* do you bother with all the dramatics? It's all so *simple*." She grasped both his hands and laughed at his disconcerted expression. "We could do with some fearsome archangel just now." Edie tugged him toward the door. "Let's hurry back to Roseneath. You do some righteous *smiting* on that stinky old cheese that hurt me and is hurting my Georgia and we all live happily ever after!"

"It is not that simple, Edith." He untangled himself from her and gave her a sad smile. "I wish that it were."

"Why?" Edie demanded, stamping her foot. "Why is it not simple?"

Michael leaned back against the opposite bookcase, the wall creaking as he did. Instead of answering her question, he asked one of his own.

"Tell me about Georgia."

"But—" Edie sputtered.

"Please, Edith. Tell me about her and then I will answer all your questions. You have my word."

Mollified, Edie pursed her lips and spoke.

"Georgia is *wonderful*. That's the beginning and end of it. She's kind and gentle, never cross, no matter how I vex her. And I must at times. I'm what you might call *relentless*, if I'm honest. But she called to me and saved me from that horrible lonely place and I . . ." Edie's eyes opened, filled now with tears. "But, you see, she's going to have a baby and I think . . . I think it's not all right. I think she's sick, Michael. I think there's a problem with the baby . . . she's too big, too fast, and Georgia says that's peculiar and . . .

and . . . Georgia is so weak now, I don't know how she'll go on, she can barely . . . and she won't tell me much because she wants to protect me." She wiped her eyes and took a deep breath. "And then, of course, there's Nathan."

The air crackled around Michael as his face shifted into something feral, savage. "Tell me. Tell me about Nathan," he snarled.

"The Jabberwock got him." Her voice trembled. "The monster that lives in Roseneath. That horrible beast trapped her, trapped both of us. And he hurt Nathan. Made him *forget* her. Like Mama and Papa forgot *me*. And I'm worried. If he doesn't remember, if . . . if . . ." Edie shook herself and cleared her throat. Then, softly, "I don't want Georgia to end up like me. It's the very *worst* thing ever, you see. To be forgotten."

Across the room, the air around Michael ceased crackling, the unrestrained rage replaced with something raw, grief-stricken. He wiped one hand across his eyes as he nodded. "You're right, Edith. It is the very worst thing. I know a little something about that."

"Then you must see, Michael," Edie continued, using the hem of her skirt to wipe her own eyes, "Why I would very much welcome some good old-fashioned smiting right about now."

The pain on Michael's face lifted and he settled into an acerbic smirk. "All in good time, Edith of the attic, have no fear on that score. In the meantime, I'd like to tell *you* a story. One I've kept secret for far too long. And then I will take you back to your Georgia."

"Is it a true story, Michael, or a fairy tale?"

"A bit of both, I think. It happened, like all fairy tales do, a long time ago and once upon a time. You could even say, the very *first* once upon a time. Interested, young miss?"

He studied her face, gauging her reaction. Edie hopped onto the table, crossed her legs, and arranged her skirts demurely over her knees.

"I love a good story. And a true fairy tale from an archangel in Eden? Chance would be a fine thing if I *weren't* interested."

When his story was all told, Edie wiped her face for the umpteenth time on her sleeve. Michael extracted a small cloth from his surcoat and handed it to her. She loudly and thoroughly blew her nose.

"My grief," Edie exclaimed. "Your brother is the *worst*."

"He certainly earned his reputation. Do you understand now the stakes we face?"

Edie nodded sadly. "I think I do. Smiting at this point would be an absolute *jinx*. "

"It would indeed. We must be patient. For just a little longer."

"Do you think Galliana will remember you this time?"

Michael began prowling the room, fidgeting with the laces crisscrossing the braces on his forearms. "I don't know. Maybe."

"But what if you just *told* her, silly? Told her who you were and, while you're at it, told her who *she* is? And then . . ."

"It won't work," he snarled, the air around him sparked. "At least it never has before. And anyway . . ."

"That's ridiculous!" Edith insisted, scooting back on the table to avoid the shower of sparks. "After all, she's your . . ."

"Be that as it may," Michael said thinly, "that's not something you can *tell* someone. It . . . it doesn't work like that, little one."

Edith chewed her lip as she tried to think of another angle. "Oh, I know! What if . . ."

"Edith, please stop," Michael held one hand up, exasperated. "I've had almost four thousand years to think about this. I'm something of an expert on the subject of how to make a mess of things."

Edith twisted the handkerchief in her lap, chastised by his tone.

"I'm sorry, Michael. I just want to help."

"I know you do, Edith. And I'm sorry if I was short with you." He was pacing again, the books on the shelves bouncing with every step he took. "But you see, Galliana is . . ." The wood floor began to smolder under his feet. "She's . . . she's . . ." Edith could see now that he was tracing the lines of a dent that covered the entire left side of his breastplate as he continued his frustrated circuit of the small hut. "The fact of the matter is, Edith, I don't know what will happen when Galliana really wakes up."

"Are you saying she never has before? In all this time?" Edith asked, incredulous.

" I don't know. Once . . . almost . . . it's just it all happened so fast." He jerked his chin at the open door. "She was right there. Across the meadow. I can see it like it was yesterday. My brother was . . ." Michael seemed lost in some far away moment; the emotion pouring out of him filled the air with static and Edith felt her hair stand on end. "I told her to run but she wouldn't listen. And then she . . ." he trailed off and the walls began to groan and sway.

"She what?" Edie demanded, smoothing her hair down and mapping an emergency path out a nearby window as the heat in the room began to build. "What did she do?"

And then, for the first time since Edith had met him, the dire expression on Michael's face disappeared, replaced with an expression of delight so unique it went far beyond anything as ordinary as a smile. His entire body glowed like starlight and the air in the room became cool and fragrant under the weight of his mirth.

"I think she nearly punched a hole in space/time," he laughed. "I'm not sure, no one ever has before."

"Michael," Edith said, aghast. "She sounds terrifying."

He nodded. "She is. Terrifying and enchanting and absolutely perfect to me in every single way, I'm afraid." He dipped his head and avoided Edith's gaze. "There is literally no one else like her."

Edith couldn't help but giggle at the forlorn look on Michael's face.

"You've got it bad, haven't you? She's got your suspenders all in a knot."

Michael snapped back to attention, glowering. His silvery glow vanished but the perfume still hung heavy in the air.

"Fine," Edith conceded, eyes still dancing. "No smiting or meddling. But there must be something I can do."

"I want you to go back to Georgia. Keep her near you. Tell her nothing of the child, it would only frighten her more. I will find a way to make myself more manageable and, when I come through to Roseneath, will find a way to free you all from his grasp. But I need her to call Nathan."

"She's tried. He won't listen. He can't remember her," Edie reminded him.

"She must keep trying," Michael insisted. "He must be there when her time is nigh, she mustn't be alone. She is strong, stronger possibly than any of her predecessors, to be sure, but to bear one such as Galliana . . ." he trailed off, jaw clenched, eyes flashing fire again.

Edie nodded. "You're right, of course." Then setting her own jaw into a mirror image of his own, a diminutive, charming imitation that earned her the ghost of a smile from the archangel, she knocked her fists on the table. "Right then. I'm off." And with that she leapt down from the table, heels slamming solidly into the earth floor.

"Edith, wait. Before you go . . ."

Edie, already halfway to the door, spun.

"Yes?"

"What if I taught you a few things?" Michael asked. He stretched his broad shoulders under his heavy armor and crossed the room toward her. "A few tricks for your bag, young lady. Tricks that might," he paused to tap her on her nose, "be unique to someone such as yourself."

Edie flushed. "Are they clever?"

"Terribly clever."

Edie's grin widened.

"Well, what are we *waiting* for?"

THIRTY-FOUR

"I KNOW YOU'RE NOT LISTENING TO THESE messages, Nate. And I want you to know I don't blame you. None of this is any more your fault than mine." Georgia leaned heavily on the bathroom sink until the sharp pain in her lower back passed. "Nathan, what happened to us?" she whispered and then hung up.

After the

Days

Nights

Weeks

of drinking handfuls of melted snow from the window ledges, winter's stranglehold on Roseneath loosened. The temperature inside the house rose just enough to thaw the pipes, and Georgia was relieved to discover the taps were working again. It seemed at that moment, more than miraculous, more than serendipitous. It seemed like a benediction. In the frost-edged mirror, Georgia met her own eyes, watched as they appeared and disappeared, each panting breath she took creating a diminutive cloud in the slowly thawing room.

You have no choice, she told her reflection, *not anymore.* Throwing another soiled towel to the floor, she forced herself to stare at the frightening stain that bled across the cloth. She then gently wiped the slow trickle of blood from each thigh, then higher, holding the cloth there as she prayed for the bleeding to stop, her slender hopes shattered when she saw the steady, relentless flow had slowed but not stopped.

I'm so sorry, Nate. Her eyes were dry in the reflection, *But you're gone. And Edie is gone. I can't save anyone but myself. And I will not lose this child. I won't.* Her breath came in sharp pants, her pupils dilated until her eyes were black. *Besides, I don't know if you're coming back. And even if you did, you're not you anymore. And I'm not me. And we may never be us again, Nate. But our daughter, she still has a chance.*

Georgia dropped the towel and coughed wetly into the sink, her heart turning over when she saw the marbled surface flecked with more crimson. *Don't let him in, don't think it. Don't. Don't feed it.* She grabbed her phone and tucked it into the bag she'd strung across her chest.

I can do this. I have to. She caught sight of the silvery flash of her wedding band in the frosted mirror. *It's like the story Edie read to me about Karou. I have to keep myself alive long enough to save her. I have to keep her alive. I can't wait for him to come back. I've lost, Nate . . ..lost Edie. I've lost myself in this godforsaken house. I won't lose her, too.*

She tightened the bag, and leaning heavily against the bathroom countertop, slid her legs into a pair of Nate's pajama pants, her feet into a pair of slippers.

"I won't lose her," she said aloud. "Not this time. He can't have you, little girl."

Inside, the child swirled and spun contentedly, seemingly oblivious to the danger she was in. Georgia cradled her stomach, felt the hands within press gently against her own and let the little one's trust further her resolve to do something she never thought she'd have to do. Choose one love for another. Abandon her husband for her daughter. Risk his life for hers. She knew in that second it was the only choice she'd ever make. That her love for him was only a dim reflection of the love she had for this child.

"I would die for you, little one," she whispered, smiling at the pure truth of her words. "And, somehow, I think he would, too. Your daddy. If he knew. If he wasn't—" she stopped the thought before it took hold, then continued, louder now with a forced cheer.

"And you," Georgia's eyes filled as she felt her child's tentative reply, a foot tapping against her hand. "Mommy needs you to hold still. Can you do that for me? Make yourself as tiny as you can and hold very still? I'm going to get us out of here and I may need to run. If I even can."

The pressure against her hands vanished as the child obediently drew herself up into a tiny ball. This altered her mother's precarious center of balance just enough that Georgia felt, in that moment, that she might be able to run if she needed to. A sudden rush of the child's chirping inside knocked her backward, drove the air from her lungs with her ever-ascending song, as if the child, too, wanted to add to her benediction.

Oh, Mother! Mother is wonderful. Everyone in the well-spring loves her. She's kind and good, never a cross word for all she suffers.

Georgia managed a weak smile for her daughter's words. "I'm not so sure about that, sweetheart. But I need you to—" Her plea cut off when the child's next verse began.

Father adores her. Not many men in our wellspring can claim a love match, but Father can. You have never seen a man more besotted with his wife. Even now, after all these years, he still brings her flowers from the fields . . .

The words faded into a rich soprano hum, and Georgia took a deep breath and tried to continue, tears falling freely down her cheeks, knowing that Nathan did love her like that. Had loved her like that. Even if he was lost to her now. Even if he never could again.

"I need you to be quiet, too, my little songbird. I'm a little bit afraid right now and I need to think."

Inside, as if chided, her song cut off and she drew herself into a tighter ball.

"That's better," Georgia said, nodding as she recited the mantra she'd been ruminating on since she woke. "It's been days and days. At least I think it has been. It has to have been. Edie said they lose interest," she reminded herself. "First, the stairs. Purse is in the kitchen. Keys are in my purse. Back door is closer to the basement but a better choice. Front steps will be iced over, and we can't risk a fall. And if . . ."

She shook her head as she reached for the doorknob. "They can't open doors. If I can just get out, if I can just get through that door, they'll be trapped here. I just have to get to the kitchen. It's not that far, not really. They can't touch me, not really. And *when* I get to the kitchen, just a few steps to the door. If I can just get out . . ."

She turned the doorknob

When I get down the stairs

When I get to the kitchen

When I get out

When

But she didn't make it that far. The Fallen descended en masse at the bottom of the stairs, their laughter rising in vicious gales as they blocked her way to the kitchen, the front door, the back hall. Thick leathery wings, mouths and eyes dripping ox blood gore, they hounded her, herded her, drove her back to the stairs. Georgia fled from their onslaught, trying futilely to hide her eyes, to stop herself before she deciphered each exacting omen. Clinging to the newel post at the bottom of the stairs, she closed her eyes, focused solely on her own thundering heart, on the delicate beating pulse of her daughter inside, a brief respite in which she realized their real strategy. That the evil words they dripped were distractions, entanglements meant to corral, each heart-stabbing revelation meant to control her, herd her, drive her toward the basement door.

No. No, I can't let them, I have to get back up the stairs, this was a mistake, I'm not strong enough, she's not . . . she can't . . . oh God the baby . . .

Inside, the baby began to tremble in a burst of terror that surged through every cell in Georgia's body, as if her frail human form was trying desperately to contain a diminutive caldera. Her fingers lost their grip on the post as she was thrown backwards by her unborn child's fear, flying back into the living room like a discarded rag doll. The drifts of snow did little to soften her impact when she landed, blinded for a brief second by the crack of her head against the cold floor, her mouth filling again with blood as her teeth rattled in her head.

And then silence. Georgia's senses returned to her in a crest of pain that wracked her entire body, as if she'd been shattered from the inside out by her daughter's silent scream. Her eyes drifted open before her short-circuited mind could order them not to.

Don't look don't do it, don't feed them oh dear God no help me someone

Instead, she focused her bleary eyes on the ceiling where his foot soldiers were arranging an excruciating, masterful trap. Hanging there like an offal-drenched colony of bats were thousands of iterations of her husband's name.

Nathan

Nathan

Nathan

Each specimen an exquisite dagger nailing her to the floor, a hellish masterpiece of words and images she was helpless to resist.

The baby's fragile weeping within added a pitiful soundtrack to the creatures' chant, their voices raised in a one-word curse that bloomed in the air, a kaleidoscope of infinite horrors. *Hurt him hurt him break him unmake him until he is nothing nothing nothing* Georgia's lips moved soundlessly in a weaker, desperate invocation, her paralyzed throat unable to give it voice under the onslaught of both the hellish beings and her child.

Help. Help. Help.

The baby's mewling grew louder; so loud that Georgia could no longer hear the leathery wings, no longer hear the bloody oaths as her daughter's melodic grief shifted from sobbing to screaming, a bone-wracking aria. Georgia's eyes rolled in her head as her body spasmed, trying to contain the incomprehensible outpouring of emotion inside her. But the creatures left behind, his grim Fallen, continued to rain down, wet and thick, crawling and skipping as they recreated the pentagram hanging above her on the floor around her, an inescapable binding.

Someone help me. Help her. He's poisoning her. And he's using me to do it. Someone, please. Help us.

And then, in answer to her prayer, she was thrown back in a crushing sonic boom, a sound so vast that it swallowed entirely the cries of her minders, the screams of her daughter, even the groaning, churning of Roseneath beneath her. A resounding vibration, crushing her, unraveling her, her senses stretched out on an infinite, one-dimensional rack. The creatures drew back into themselves, their new message arrested as if they too were frozen in awe. Fast on the heels of the deafening sound wave, a heat surged into the room, followed swiftly by a brilliant white light that mercifully blinded her. The room vanished into nothingness, but just before consciousness was stripped from her, Georgia smelled hot steel, heard a crackling fire, felt the room burning all around her.

When Georgia woke, she was nestled in the firebox under the enormous mirror. Her nose burned with the acrid smell of scorched wood and plaster. Rubbing the ash from her eyes, she scanned the room, bewildered by the havoc around her. The walls were charred, embers still glowing, heavy with soot and smoke that the rising winds caught and chased out the open windows. The moon shone down on the empty living room, revealing a surreal phosphorescence that splattered the walls, floor, and ceiling where the creatures had been. But there was no trace of them anywhere.

Georgia crawled out of the firebox, held her hand up in the moonlight, and saw that it shone with the same soft glow. She was drenched in the same fragrant oil that anointed the room. The charred wooden floors and thick plaster ceilings were scored with deep, vicious gouges, as if something had hacked at the creatures with an instrument of fire, burning them from existence.

Whatever had heard her plea, whatever had driven off her terrible minders and destroyed those horrific murals, left a swath of scorched earth under its feet, and a trail of enlarged, smoldering footprints that circled the room and led to the firebox she'd awoken in. She crawled back into the ash-filled niche she'd awoken in and searched the mirror's pitted surface.

"Edie?" she whispered.

But no reply came, not even a silvery flicker of light. She crawled back into the fireplace, wrapped the blanket about her, and knew, however impossible it might seem, that she was safe. For now.

"It's not much of a hidey-hole, Nate, but I think I'll stay here, where it, whatever it was, put me. I feel safe for the first time in ages. And she does, too, I can tell. I can feel this serenity inside me. It is safe, isn't it, little one? I think whatever took Edie, whatever drove those things away and left those footprints, it's not him. It couldn't be. As above, so below. And why not an archangel? I keep thinking, Nate, if there are devils below us, maybe . . . maybe . . . there really are angels above, watching out for us. The creatures are still here, but they can't seem to come in now. Maybe it was the fire, the oil. Or maybe it's a new game, one I don't understand yet. I'm going to sleep now, Nate. It's better when she's asleep."

✦   ✦   ✦

In the meadow, Edie stifled an astonished cry as Michael strode back into Eden out of thin air, in much the same way he had disappeared quite some time ago.

"Blast it all. Nearly burned the damn place down. Stupid. Rash. Ill-considered and foolhardy. After all this time to be goaded by a *child*." He kicked a large rock near the trunk that Edie perched on. Instead of scolding him for being gone so long, she watched the enormous rock fly straight through the tree canopy, then listened as it fell somewhere deep in the wood with a splash.

"Son of a bitch," he spat, and began patting at the places where his surcoat still smoldered. He swung his gaze toward Edie.

"What?" he barked.

Edie let out a low whistle. "It's just that you . . . you *swore*, didn't you? Just now. Those are proper swears, aren't they? Bully!"

Michael let out another frustrated oath and then ran his hands through his hair, sending a few smoking embers to the ground. They hit the damp moss of Eden and extinguished immediately with a hiss.

"So I did," he snapped. "What of it?"

"But you're an *angel*," she giggled.

He rolled his eyes, the distant flames inside flickering in annoyance.

"*Archangel*," he corrected, grasping both of her hands and hauling her to her feet. "And I'd appreciate it if you could respect the distinction."

"What happened?" she demanded, pushing his hands away to straighten her pinafore. She studied him with a grimace. "Why are you smoldering?"

"I'm *smoldering*," he replied ruefully, crouching down to her eye level, "because a little girl goaded me into trying to cross over again against my better judgment."

"And?" Edie asked innocently, eyes twinkling.

"*And* I made a mess of it. Lost my temper." He took a step back and glared up at the clouds. "Felt good to let off some steam, though." Then, shaking the experience out of his head, he continued. "But as errors in judgment go, it was a timely one. Another minute *there* and I fear all could have been lost. Again." His lids fell over his sparking eyes, his grip tightened on the hilt of his still crackling sword. "But I think I've sorted the problem out. It's clearly this temper of mine. If I can just—"

"See," Edie gloated. "I told you that—"

But it was Michael's turn to cut her off. "We have no time to squabble, young lady. Things are far worse than I imagined and we've little time. It's up to you now. Off you go and steady on. You understand what you need to do?"

Edie nodded fiercely. "You can count on me, Michael. I won't let you down." She spun and took three running steps toward the wood before stopping abruptly and spinning back to him, the determination on her face tempered now with woe.

"Edith, please," Michael implored her. "Whatever it is, it must wait. There is simply no time. If . . . if—" his sonorous voice broke. A distant memory had grabbed him by the throat.

Chagrined, Edie ran back to him. With a little leap, she wrapped her arms around his great chest and, ignoring the smoldering surcoat, hugged him tightly.

"Never you worry, friend. You've got me now!" Edie lowered her voice to a whisper against his collar. "This will all go down easy as peas and carrots, you'll see. Chin up, Michael. You and I have to be as bricky as we can, that's all."

Michael patted her back once, an awkward, disconcerted gesture, then gently untangled her arms from around him and set her back down.

"Well," he said, clearing his throat, his grim expression deepening as he studied her. Undeterred, Edie beamed up at him, her eyes shining with an indefatigable air of encouragement.

"Now run along, friend," he said, his melodic voice gentle. "Remember, it is vital that you stick to the plan. I won't be far behind you." Something in the intensity of his dire gaze shifted, and then, incredibly, the sober archangel winked at her. "And I'll do some smiting. Would that suit you?"

"Applesauce!" Edie cried. "That's the spirit! We'll show that mangy old grouse!" And with that, Edie spun away and raced into the mist-drenched wood.

THIRTY-FIVE

IN ROSENEATH, GEORGIA DREAMED.

The sun rose in the winter sky only to be dragged down by the dark, heavy clouds. At night, the moon shone on the still, unbroken expanse surrounding the derelict house. Relentless northern winds wound a cat's cradle through the open windows, each swirling dervish binding the house and its occupants in an artic spell. The gnashing teeth and leathery wings of the earthen creatures stilled as they slumbered deep in the cellar, the once dank earth there now more permafrost than mud. The reflections in the mirror over the firebox vanished under a delicate needlepoint of ice, crystalline drifts of white blanketed the charred wood floor, illuminated from within by the mysterious balm that now coated the room. Roseneath itself might have been a slumbering, icebound still life, were it not for the way the twisted, thorn-laden vines flourished in the deep wintertide, an unchecked fecundity that writhed and tightened around the very foundation. A host of brittle, vicious arms crowned with determined fingers wove a heavy lace over the windows, blanketing the bleached brick, reaching for the slate roof. And, in this embrace, Georgia slumbered peacefully in her sanctuary under the mantel, warmed from within by her child and the dreams they shared in languid, hushed whispers, her wasted flesh shining softly with a sublime radiance.

They were walking hand-in-hand through a primeval land. The dusty terrain was dotted with rocky outcroppings and threaded with rushing streams, the soft complaints of sheep sounded from distance meadows. Her feet were bare as they strolled languidly under an endless sky. Georgia looked down at their entwined hands and then into the shining face of her daughter, a blinding countenance at once dearly familiar and utterly incomprehensible.

"Are we safe here, Daughter?" she asked, her voice echoing in the still air, "In this secret nowhere?"

Beside her, the shining visage nodded.

"Safer here than anywhere, Mother."

Ahead loomed a dark shadow, little more than chiaroscuro, soft, dark lines broken only by a brilliant light that shone out of the canopy into the very heavens. Her daughter's steps began to quicken, her long legs and towering stature setting a brisk pace Georgia could not keep up with. Georgia felt her hand slip from the child's grasp.

"Wait!" she cried, her voice feeble in the heavy air. "Please, wait for me!"

In the distance, her gangly daughter froze, her face hidden in the reflected brilliant of the sun and the silvery light of the towering grove.

"I *mustn't* wait." A rising wind, hot and needful, scoured the plain, carrying her daughter's broken voice to her. "I must *run* to him. Don't you see?" she pleaded, weeping. "I promised." The shining light of her face disappeared as she turned back to the looming forest. "I remember now."

Georgia's feet pounded uselessly on the dusty plain, but the distance between her and her daughter stretched ever wider with each second. The hot wind fell, and in its place, running footsteps, a frantic quadrille of delicate footfalls. Then a voice calling her name that seemed to come from some far-off place, across a vast, swirling cosmos.

Georgia!

Georgia!

Georgia tore her eyes from the distant image of her daughter. She scanned the landscape, but they were utterly alone. More running footsteps, louder, louder as the voice cried out again.

Georgia, where are you?

Ignoring the voice echoing in the wilderness, Georgia watched as her daughter fell to her knees under the shadow of the towering trees, terror now written in her every line.

"It's time," she wailed. "Time, time, time! Again and again, forever! Oh, Mother," she screamed, "help me! Help me find him! I can't bear it!"

"What do you mean?" Georgia pleaded. "Find who? Wait for me! Let me help you!"

Her feet fell faster but to no avail, her hands clutched at empty air as her weeping daughter curled up in the loamy soil at the edge of the dark forest.

"It's too late," the tattered whisper carried back to her. "It's always too late."

Georgia!

The distant voice shattered the surreal landscape. Hands clutched her shoulders, shaking her, dragging her away from her fallen child, away from the wood, and the dusty plain, a bone-deep cold replacing the arid heat of her unborn child's secret nowhere.

"Georgia?" The pleading voice's delicate lilt was caught in anguish. Georgia opened her eyes and saw a miracle in front of her.

"Edie, you came back." She smiled at Edie's grief-stricken face. She licked her cracked lips and tasted the salty tang of blood, let the pain that surged through her waking body lead her away from her daughter's dreamscape and fully back to this reality, this consciousness. "I knew it. I knew you'd come back."

THIRTY-SIX

EDIE WILLED HER LOWER LIP TO STOP TREM-bling but it was no use. She implored her eyes to stop their crying, but that, too, proved a hopeless task. Her hands shook as she lifted Georgia out of the fireplace, skirting the frighteningly ponderous stomach, praying as she did that the sob she held tight in her chest would not escape.

"Th—there, there," Edie stammered. "I'm here now. Don't . . . don't cry." She addressed her dull reflection in the mirror on the mantel as if Michael, on the other side of time and space, could hear her.

"When you said you'd made a mess," she snapped at her reflection, "I naturally expected some sort of nonsense. But *really*. Stuffing her in the firebox like kindling?" Edie's furious voice broke. "I shall have some words for you, Mr. High and Mighty, when this is all sorted."

Turning her attention away from the mirror, Edie placed her palm on Georgia's forehead, felt the blistering heat coming off her, as if her broken body contained an inferno. *Not far off*, she thought with dismay. "Let's get you more comfortable, all right?" Against her chest, Georgia's fragile weeping interspersed with jumbles of incomprehensible words that the rising wind snatched before Edie could quite understand them.

My dear Georgia. How long was I in the looking glass? Edie blinked away a fresh wash of tears as she looked down at her own wondrously transformed, whole body, a shocking juxtaposition to the broken, senseless woman in her arms. Swallowing hard, she spun in a slow circle, taking in the desolate room. Windows frozen open, each portal guarded with fingers of ice and arms of thorns, soft drifts of snow and a bitter wind the only elements granted access. The floors and ceiling were carved with curious scorch marks, each carrying the acrid scent of a long-extinguished fire mingled with the rich loamy perfume of Eden. She collected all these spectral clues, searching for an explanation to how altered both Roseneath and Georgia were, and as she did this, Michael's words floated back to her.

Time doesn't always work the way I think it does. Certainly not here. And usually not there.

Her frown deepened as she peered at the staircase. More curious scorch marks at the base of the stairs that continued in a vicious swath through the room and into the darkness of the back hall, each crosshatch marked as the others were, with a soft iridescence. And yet, nowhere was there a single trace of the vicious creatures the beast, the Jabberwock, had left behind to torment her. And, again, Michael's words came back to her.

Blast it all. Nearly burned the whole place down. Lost my temper.

"I should say you did, sir," she whispered with a gulp, casting another glance back to the unresponsive mirror. "If this is letting off a bit of steam, I'm not sure I want to be around for all the smiting."

In her arms, Georgia's weeping ceased abruptly and her head went limp against her chest. Edie crossed the room in two quick strides, wiping her cheeks on her shoulders as she did.

"Hang on, Georgia, my little ducky," Edie pleaded as she set her down on the couch. "Georgia?" But Georgia's eyes had fallen shut; her breathing was steady but labored, her skin a frightening shade of parchment. Edie gripped her small shoulders and shook her gently until Georgia's eyes fluttered open again.

"Edie?" she mumbled. Her eyes remained open but they were unfocused, her pupils dilated and unseeing. Georgia's lips continued moving soundlessly as her head briefly lolled back against the arm of the couch only to jerk upright as if she were a doll in the hands of a careless child. The sob Edie held tight in her chest broke free at the sound of Georgia's bones cracking in her neck before a fresh volley of coughing overtook her.

"Stuff his plan," Edie spat, tearing her pinafore off and dampening it in the melt water beside her. As she gently wiped the oil-drenched soot from Georgia's bruised face, she directed her next words again to the mirror across the room. "She's not in *danger*. She's *dying*." Still, no reply came from the mirror. Edie slammed her fist into the couch.

"Son of a . . . Georgia," she pleaded, clasping her shoulders and shaking her. "I need you to wake up for me. Please come back to me, oh please do!"

Think, Edie, think. Be a clever girl. What to do? It's all up to you now.

Georgia's head jerked upright, her eyes focusing sharply on Edie's as if waking from a nightmare.

"Don't. Don't touch the oil," she croaked. "She says . . . she told me . . ..she . . ." Her pleas broke off in a fit of coughing so violent, Edie wondered whether she would splinter like a porcelain doll.

Edie held a palm full of snow to Georgia's cracked lips. *Useless. As is Mr. Arrogant Archangel's plan.* "Better?" she whispered to Georgia. Georgia nodded, a weak gesture, then reached for Edie's hand and held it to her blisteringly hot cheek.

"She . . . she said it's protecting me. He's protecting me. Protecting us. Someone, something was here . . . set the whole room on fire. She said he . . . oh it's all mixed up. It's backwards and upside down. She's trying to tell me something but, we don't remember . . . we can't remember *who* he is. She told me to run to him. Or maybe *from* him . . . I don't know. I—" Georgia's face fell into her hands as she began sobbing again.

Edie threw the soiled pinafore down and flashed the mirror a look of pure disgust.

"'He' *indeed*. The *state* of you. Of course, he *said* he'd made a mess of things but this is *too* much." She smoothed Georgia's damp hair away from her face, her thinly veiled alarm rising when the strands came away in her hand. "He's all thumbs, isn't he?" she continued, trying to hold Georgia's attention and keep her awake. "But then it must be allowed that he's a bit under-socialized." Tipping Georgia's chin up, she fixed her with what she hoped was a reassuring smile.

"Enormous cosmic powers, a bit spare on the social niceties, that one." Her fingers slipped to Georgia's wrist. Her pulse alternated between painfully slow and a chilling, stumbling gallop.

"Who is he?" Georgia croaked, panting. "Please tell me. I can't remember. She said it was important. Or was I dreaming again? This is a dream, too, isn't it?" Her eyes began to drift in their sockets. "You're not really . . . I just want you to be here so much and . . ." Georgia's breathing came in short, damp pants, a terrible hitch punctuating each breath. "Doesn't matter. None of this matters. I need to put her back to sleep, don't you see? Please, I need to sleep . . . we need to sleep." Her eyes drifted shut as she fell back, limp. "She's so frightened when we're awake, Edie. We have to hide. I have to help her get back to the forest . . . the garden . . . she needs to run—" Her eyes flashed open and she frantically struggled back up, looking at Edie as if seeing her for the first time. "Edie? Is that really you? Did you find the man in the mirror?" she whispered. Aghast, Edie clasped the delirious Georgia to her chest, felt the wash of blood and tears soak her lace bodice.

"Yes, oh yes, I did find him, Georgia!" Edie cried out. "And you mustn't despair so! You *can't* give up! He's going to save you. Both of you." A lump rose in her throat as she wondered if, considering Georgia's deteriorating condition, that was even possible anymore.

A fresh wash of blood trickled down Georgia's thighs. "Did he show you the way to heaven?" Her stomach tightened and heaved as if she were being lifted off the couch by the intensity of the contraction. "Is that why you came back? To take us with you?"

Edie's hand flew to her mouth as Georgia's stomach shifted, fresh bruises appearing on her thin, pale flesh under the onslaught of the frantic child inside her.

Oh dear me! she thought desperately. *There's no time!* She pulled Georgia into her arms and held her rigid body tight. "Shhh . . . shhh . . . that's enough of that. None of that matters. All that matters is that you rest." Against her chest, Georgia's breathing began to slow, the ponderous stomach stilled. "Go back to sleep and I'll be right here. I won't let anything hurt you, I promise."

"And you won't leave me?" Georgia's voice, slurred and labored, was poised on the edge of sleep.

"I won't leave you," Edie lied neatly. "I promise. Now go to sleep like a good girl, Georgia. Sleep and dream with her and when you wake up, everything will be right as rain. I promise."

"Promise," Georgia sighed. "Promise me." Her lips rose in a smile. "She remembered that part."

"Of course she did. But don't worry about that now. Just sleep. And I'll tell you both a story." Edie pressed her lips against Georgia's fevered brow. The mirror held no signs of Michael's presence—no flicker or shining ripples of light. Nothing to suggest Michael had any idea of how dire the situation truly was. *It's up to me*, she thought, as Edie's mind raced nimbly ahead, hatching a new plan. She reached down and saw that the child's frantic movements just under the surface of Georgia's belly had slowed to something languid and restful.

"His whole big plan and you know what I think? He left you out of it, didn't he?" she whispered, trailing her fingers in gentle circles over Georgia's belly. "Doesn't seem fair to either of you." The unborn child froze, as if she were listening intently to Edie's words. Edie hazarded a wary glance at the mirror before beginning her tale.

"Someone once told me that the worst thing, the very worst thing, is to be forgotten. That's what the story is all about, I think." Edie paused, her face screwed up in concentration as she carefully considered her words. "Maybe that's why we tell the very same stories in different ways, over and over again, so that no one is ever *truly* forgotten." She gently laid Georgia back, tucking her in as she did and added, "But I have begun backwards, haven't I?" Edie peered intently into Georgia's sleeping face and nodded, satisfied she was fully asleep. "So let's begin as all proper fairy tales do, shall we?" Then, kneeling at her side, she addressed her words not to Georgia but to her unborn child.

"Once upon a time, long ago and far away, there was a girl, the first and last of her kind. She was sweet and fierce, brave and bewitching. Her hair was as bright as the sun and her skin was a map of the night sky." Georgia's stomach rolled and then stilled, as if the infant within had arranged herself face-to-face with Edie, like a child at story time. "One day, while walking in a great wood, the girl came upon a weary, lonely soldier." Edie glanced back at the mirror before continuing in a conspiratorial whisper. "I've met him, you know. He *is* a bit terrifying, it's true, but ever so kind. His eyes are twin universes concealing more secrets than you can comprehend." She wrinkled her nose. "And he's very *handsome*, once you get over the whole not-human business, isn't he, little one? He's sort of savage and gentle and wise and thoughtful and even a little bit funny at times." In her sleep, Georgia smiled, and as she did her translucent skin began to glow, as if the moon shone down on her. Edie's eyes widened at the sight. "But the most important part, the thing you must remember no matter what happens is that he loves you, loves you, *loves you. You're his jammiest bits of jam, you are.* And he'll do *anything* to make sure the Jabberwock doesn't find you this time." A soft humming filled the air in a joyful crescendo. Edie felt Georgia's cheek and saw that her fever had fallen; her chest rose rhythmically in a deep sleep.

◆　◆　◆

As she slept, Georgia heard Edie's voice carry across the great distance between waking life and dream, each word pulling her deeper and deeper into the blissful respite of the secret nowhere. Threaded throughout Edie's strange tale came another voice, softer, honeyed, incredulous. Inside, her daughter was repeating Edie's words rapidly, over and over, faster and faster. They must have been the reason for the delicious hum spreading throughout her body, a tuning fork lulling her, coaxing her away from this consciousness. The once weeping child she had left outside the great dark wood leapt to her feet, a cry of unbridled delight filling the air. The great light in the primeval forest shone brighter, brighter, a magnificent silvery reply that erased the memory of Roseneath entirely.

Georgia sighed as she tumbled deeper under the spell. *She remembers this story. How could we have forgotten? This fairy tale is hers.*

✦ ✦ ✦

"He will take his vorpal sword in hand, long time the maxome foe he sought! He will slay The Jabberwock, snicker-snack!" Edie beamed and placed another kiss on the thin barrier of skin that separated her and the dreaming child. "He's going to ring that ratbag's bell, he is. He promised to *smite* him, you know. Won't *that* be a sight?" Then, laying her head on Georgia's chest, she listened to their alternating heartbeats, one vigorous, one weak, all the while trying to convince herself she was doing the right thing. "So you both just have to hold on, all right? Just a bit longer."

Edie rose and studied the room once more, listening. The child's humming had trailed off and Roseneath was silent all around them.

I won't be gone long at all, she told herself briskly. She shut the windows one by one, her fingertips carefully skirting the thorns that threatened to intrude upon Georgia's small sanctuary. *Just a quick trip to the West Coast. Shouldn't take a moment.* Turning, she cast a wrathful glance toward the back hall but all was silent there as well. *I'll just have to trust they can't cross whatever boundary he's made*, she thought. Hurrying back to the mirror, she placed her hands upon it and focused, imagining her voice ringing throughout Eden, summoning the somber soldier, the archangel who was an army, from his distant post.

"Michael," she pleaded. "Hurry. You have to come *now*. It's time." Her eyes scanned the mercury expanse, thought for sure she saw a glimmer deep in the pitted surface. "I'm going to get Nathan. I know that wasn't the plan, but she's *coming*, and soon, and there simply isn't time to muck about arguing about plans and patience." Edie watched as her eyes began sparkling mischievously, delighted by her own daring. "Besides, I think I know how to scare the devil out of him all by myself."

Edie crossed the room to the nearest closed window.

"Well," she said to her reflection. "Here goes nothing."

She placed her palm on the window and waited just as Michael had shown her, delighted when her hand drifted through effortlessly and disappeared. *Applesauce! He was absolutely right. There's no stopping me now. The world is my oyster.* She glanced briefly at Georgia, still asleep, before diving head-first into her own reflection and leaving Roseneath behind.

THIRTY-SEVEN

THE RESTAURANT WAS LOUD AND FASHION-able; a quartet played its own versions of big band hits that were at odds to the sleek styling of the establishment itself. Nathan sat at a table housed within the restaurant's black glass walls, their cool surfaces like deep mirrors reflecting blood-red Lucite, a fragile glass den in a distant corner of the city. The tempo of the otherwise jazzy tune, "I've Got You Under My Skin," was just a bit too slow, the melody just a fraction off-key.

Nathan shifted his attention from the band to his tapping fingers. The vague smile that had been sewn on his face faltered, stumbled, flat-lined when he noticed he was not keeping time with the beat at all. His hands were an angry swarm, clawing at the table, each knuckle a tight white knot as his fingers dug for purchase on the smooth Lucite surface. The feeling began to return to his body, a wildfire of pins and needles that engulfed him from head to toe, as those fingers—*whose fingers are those?*—continued to dig and gouge out of time with the tune, scratch marks appearing in the transparent red, crimson curls flaking up under the onslaught of his fingernails—*can't be, can't be mine*—something thick and red causing his hands—*are those my hands?*—to slip for a moment before digging in again, pain now supplanting the numbness, radiating up each finger into his forearms, as if he were driving needles under each fragile nail bed, a relentless, determined torture. A fragile, frantic thought swam up through the deep abyss of sedated calm that Nathan's consciousness still floated in, croaking, hoarsely, desperately in his ear.

Wake up.

This is not reality. This is a nightmare.

Wake up.

Nathan—the Nathan that sat in a delicate Lucite chair, not the one struggling to hold his head above the enormous crashing waves of numbing calm—took in a deep breath and held it, listened to the frantic man inside him, tried to resist the waves and the comfort of the deep and hung onto the brutal pain in his nail beds, the reverberation from the amp, the dissonant shift that threaded itself through the music and . . .

Where am I?

There, the second tangible thought he was able to cling to like driftwood, as the song shifted, blissfully, mercilessly to something not from years past, not from the Rat Pack or Billy Holiday or Glenn Miller, but from an incongruous tune, a familiar tune, a tune that could never be anonymous, not to him. Nathan turned in his chair and watched as if through a telescope as the bassist set his guitar down, swung his spyglass vision a few degrees to the right and watched as the drummer took five, the pianist already flirting with the waitress. But the singer sang on, a lonely acapella, a song so out of place in this city, in this club, that for a moment Nathan wondered if he had already sunk beneath the waves again and was dreaming it. It was her song, their song. A tune he'd heard a million times before he realized it was a love song written just for her. Red shoes and moonlight and trembling flowers. It was ages ago, a lifetime ago. They were dancing, just the two of them, empty space all around, a basket of apples at her feet.

Can I kiss you goodnight?

Oh, yes. Yes, I think you should.

The song chewed through the residual wreath of fog that kept his mind so blissfully vacant, each verse an insatiable bite, opening larger holes in the cloudbank, until he could see through to the table, the restaurant. See himself for the first time in ages.

His hands froze, his fingernails wedged into the surface of the table, an unfamiliar suitcoat on his forearms. He rolled his knotted shoulders, tried to loosen a tightness that Atlas must have felt. His stomach churned, a poisonous, bilious mass, as if he'd been filled to the brim with a powerful venom.

The noise of the restaurant shifted from a comforting buzz to a drilling in his ears—this place, these clothes, none of this was him, none of it was familiar. He pulled his fingers from the ruined table and gripped his hands into tight fists. *Something there, something wrong.* A wave of numbness threatened to drown him again—

those aren't your hands

—but he shook it off, and noticed a field of miniscule splinters across the back of his hands. He struggled to remember how to rotate his wrists and found the same on his palms, his weary eyes slipping left, only to find a bare patch on his ring finger. His wedding ring was gone, not even a tan line remained, as if it had never been there at all. As if . . .

He rubbed his eyes against the dazzling lights, the pain in his head staving off the wreath of fog that still threatened him. Images began flooding into his brain, stumbling, starting, over and over again, a shredded film reel of the last few months he remembered as if in a dream.

Cat running barefoot up the stairs of her house, his laughter as he chased her echoing in his ears. Cat sitting next to him in a car, his fingers shifting constantly as he tried in vain to make their fingers fit like puzzle pieces. The coast flying past them, picnic lunch in the back seat, her head on his shoulder, uncomfortable, too high. Cat's face sleepy in the morning, her husky voice demanding coffee, his phone ringing endlessly, his hand reaching over to switch it off.

The churning in his gut sharpened into a host of knives. Swallowing a mouthful of rising vomit, his hands fell from his face helplessly to his lap.

What have I done? What did he do to me?

As the song played on, the singer's eyes closed tightly, as if he were singing lines whispered in his ear by some unseen composer, as if he too had fallen under an enchantment, the song's words a sorcerer's spell only he and Nathan could hear. Moonlit red shoes and flowers dancing the blues and someone's heart breaking in two.

There was something, someone he'd forgotten, someone he'd neglected, locked away in a grim tower, left alone and afraid. Someone precious and gentle, someone whose hands belonged in his, someone whose body fit consummately against his own, someone whose eyes shone like lighthouses, someone his frantic hands had clawed themselves to shreds to get back to.

The waves around him flattened out and he found himself afloat in a sea of rot, flotsam and jetsam, his hands floundering for purchase on dry land, for truth, and finding only guilt.

Georgia.

The enormity of that one small word overwhelmed him. The fragile measure of control he'd regained faltered, and, for a moment, he considered letting go again. *You don't want to know do you, don't want to see, not really, come back to me, you don't need to ever know what we've done break you break you unmake you* He felt her name slip away again, drowned under the deluge of cloying whispers, pulling her name from him even as the waves crashed over his head again. But then a voice called his name, shattering the emptiness of the glass walls.

Nathan!

Nathan!

He used the last bit of his newfound control to search for the source of the voice, finding he could only move his eyes. Sliding them left, then right, he saw the face of a young woman reflected in the deep black mirror of the restaurant wall. A waif of a girl, a silent film starlet. Her eyes bored into him with a shocking intensity and he felt his head clear under the weight of her stare. His eyes drifted back to the singer, to the other couples around him but no one seemed to see her or hear her. His gaze swung back to the girl and he watched as the beautiful siren's image multiplied, surrounded him

Nathan!

Remember!

fair and ghastly, wrathful and insistent

Georgia!

her soprano pleas so deafening it annihilated the voice in his head.

Remember!

Georgia!

Roseneath!

Nathan's lips moved along with hers, the mystery of each word revealed to him the moment she spoke it.

The basement!

The greenhouse!

Jabberwock!

She repeated the words faster and faster

The basement!

The greenhouse!

Each word chipping away at his confusion

Georgia!

Roseneath!

Jabberwock!

Oh God, no.

He felt the thick Lucite crack in his hands. The girl's lips curved up into a winsome smile and she seemed to lean in through the mirrors, closer, closer, so close Nathan imagined he could smell her breath, like lilies and dust, the reality around him and the specter of her supernatural aspect stripping what was left of his stupor, her penetrating eyes sweeping the fog away until all that was left was the truth.

Cat.

My God, I.

And I.

Oh God, no.

Georgia, oh please, no.

No. Not this. Not her.

The girl's head swiveled, a sneer of distaste marring her perfect features. Nathan followed her gaze across the restaurant toward Cat, her shapely legs hugged by a short swinging skirt, lips full and red. She was making her way toward him.

Frozen, Nathan futilely prayed for some sign, some hint, that the images that had flashed through his short-circuiting brain were dreams, fantasies, not reality. *Not this. Not her. Please don't let this be real.*

The infinite number of ghostly girls stared down at Nathan as Cat's hands landed on his shoulders, as lips that were not Georgia's found his ear and whispered into it, words affirming his worst fears, eliciting a host of new images and sensations. *What have I done? What has he done to me? What did I do to her?*

A smothering truth waited for him on the shore he'd struggled to reach.

"Let's get out of here, Nate," Cat purred. "You were right, I'd much rather get room service. Richard will be home this week and we won't have much time together." Her lips on his ear again, her tongue slid behind his ear-lobe as she took it in her teeth.

Nathan's eyes burned and blurred, the girl's face crumpling in something like pity, the singer's voice breaking through the pounding in his head.

Nathan bolted to his feet, knocking the table over, a crash of glassware and cutlery, the smell of alcohol washing over the floor sharp in his nose, and pushed Cat off him, sending her stumbling back, heels screaming across the marble floor.

"What the hell, Nate?" She reached for him, sending him stumbling back. "What's wrong with you?

"Don't touch me," he choked. "Don't ever." His voice seemed to be fighting him, each word he managed a herculean task.

"What do you mean, don't touch you, Nate? Are you drunk? What the fuck happened to your hands?" Her face was a blend of confusion and disgust, but she reached for him again. "Come on, you're making a scene again. Whatever is upsetting you, it doesn't matter. I can—"

His jaw loosened and he realized he was free. His mouth, his thoughts, his words wholly his again and he said the words he'd wanted to say for months.

"I hate you," he whispered. "You make me sick."

Cat's beautiful face splintered, disgust to fury.

"Then what the fuck were the last few months all about?" she demanded.

Nathan let out a heavy breath, his eyes searching past Cat to the specter of the girl. She was beaming at him now, a smile so brilliant, so delighted, so hopeful that it surged inside him like a cloud of strength and he found himself smiling back at her.

"A nightmare."

Around them, the restaurant had fallen still, the on-lookers silent witnesses to a scene. Nathan looked down at his hands, at his ruined fingers, and watched as they seemed to knit themselves back together. On the stage, the man kept singing, lips bared back over his teeth, his voice little more than a whisper, the tune dropping out when he stopped singing entirely and began reciting the lyrics, terse and choked. Nathan looked up from his hands and studied the room. Startled whispers from the other tables, Cat's mouth moving furiously, the mirror girl waving to him as she vanished, her images popping like fireworks.

Nathan ignored it all and focused on the song, focused as hard as the singer seemed to be, fumbling in his pockets for his keys, his fingers seeking the slender gold band before he pulled it out. There, hidden amongst the keys to Cat's house, was his wedding band, tarnished and dented. Fingers shaking, he struggled to free it from the chain. It felt heavy in his hand, a centering density. He slipped it on his finger and found the strength to drop Cat's keys as if they were on fire. They fell with a clatter at her feet.

Go. Move. Now. Run. Before it's too late. His own voice finally registered in his head and his body reacted, like a rusted machine obeying his commands at last. Pushing past Cat, he stumbled from the restaurant, shoved past a sputtering pedestrian to hurl himself into a cab.

"The airport. Hurry."

He fumbled in his pockets for his phone, mouth dry as he scanned his voicemails, his messages. *No. That's impossible.* The phone fell from his shaking hand to the floor of the cab and he scrambled in the trash at his feet, plucked it from something sticky and wet, wiped it off on his pants and looked again, hoping against hope that he could wipe off what he'd seen along with whatever pooled on the floor of the speeding cab.

Two hundred and twelve missed calls. All from Georgia.

Eighty-seven voicemails. All from Georgia.

Seventy-three unread texts. All from Georgia.

He had erected a wall of silence that stretched for nearly ten weeks, a dam wide enough and high enough to hold back the pleading surge of his wife's futile attempts to contact him.

His hand reached over to switch the phone off. Reached back to pull someone to him across crisp white sheets. His stomach lurched again and he fought to keep his own vomit from joining the swill at his feet.

He scrolled through her messages, trying to reconcile her defeated missives with the woman he knew, every text little more than a memory of the two of them, her passive tone framing them as if she was setting them adrift, stripping herself bare of what they had, what they had been, letting him go. *No. No, Georgia, don't let me go. Don't set me adrift. Don't give up on me, on us.*

"I don't want to remember the day we met anymore, Nate, but I keep reliving it, rewriting it. It was perfect, wasn't it? Sometimes I think I imagined it, imagined you, all of it. Like a fairy tale. Too perfect for it to end like this. I'm sorry, Nate. I'm so very sorry."

"It won't be long now, she's so big. I'm better, I think, or at least I understand now. What my role in all this is, how it will end. I just wish—"

"Edie says he won't let you remember me, that by the time you remember me, us, it will be too late. But this isn't your fault, Nate, no more than it was mine. Remember that, if you remember anything. And remember I really loved you. Just like you thought I did."

His eyes filled as he abandoned the bewildering message stream for the voicemails, selecting the newest and hitting play, her voice in his ear, finally. He wiped his eyes with the back of his hand and felt the dig of the thorns scratch his eyelids.

"I know you're not listening to these messages. And I want you to know I don't blame you. None of this is any more your fault than mine," she said, repeating the words in one of her last texts. There was a long pause, a breath in which Nathan could see her, imagine her in front of him, looking up into his eyes, her hand on his cheek, her eyes hollow and dry. "Jesus, Nathan, what happened to us?" A long moment in which he could hear her breathing, smell her perfume, feel her lips on his cheek, felt the moment she let go, a soft click, and then dead air.

Nathan prayed as he dialed her number, prayed for her to answer, prayed for her voicemail, not sure which he was more afraid of: her real voice or her recorded one, but none of those prayers were answered. Instead, the ringing stopped only to be replaced with a dry buzzing, something threaded through with whispers, something so familiar he knew it at once, knew where he'd heard it first, knew the moment he began walking down this fearful road.

That first day. At Roseneath. In the greenhouse. Mud and blood and thorns. The basement. Georgia. Alone. In that house. In that nightmare.

Oh my God, Nathan thought as he pleaded with the driver to hurry. *What have I done? What did he do to her?*

THIRTY-EIGHT

 GEORGIA STRUGGLED FROM THE DEPTHS OF sleep, driven by a thought, a notion teetering on the edge of her consciousness that lured her away from the respite of her daughter's now tranquil dreams. *Edie . . . Edie was here. She came back. She's all alone in Roseneath. Wake up. Wake up. Can't leave her alone.* It seemed as if years had passed before she was able to open her leaden eyes and hours more before she could pull herself upright. Her child was mercifully still inside, dreaming inside a dream. Her fever broken, Georgia shivered for the first time in weeks. Even though the sun shone brilliantly on the frozen landscape of the living room—midmorning—her breath escaped in frigid puffs. All around her Roseneath was still and silent as a grave. She reached down and splashed her face with a handful of slush and snow, shocking her senses until she'd driven off the fugue and was wholly alert.

"Edie?" she called. "Edie, I'm feeling better now. Sort of." She listened carefully but the house was quiet all around her. "Edie, are you here?" Gingerly, she stood on unsteady legs, flinching as she waited for her child to begin flailing again. The child stirred, shifted but did not wake. *Was she ever here? Or did I dream her, too?* A flash of pink and white at her feet and she stooped to gather the discarded pinafore in her hands. She held it to her face and breathed in Edie's lily and dust fragrance, wondered if this remnant was from yesterday or today, or from an age ago.

"Edie?" she called again. Silence. And then a whisper, so soft it was little more than a sigh. From the back hall, just around the corner, just out of sight. A sound not dissimilar to the frightened, desperate cry Edie had made when she crawled out of the attic eaves.

A whisper drifted out of the dark hall, trailed through the frosty air. Edie.

"Mary . . . Mary . . . quite contrary . . ." Edie's lilting voice was nearly lost as a rising wind rattled the windows of Roseneath.

"how . . . how . . . does your . . . garden . . . help . . . me . . ." Then silence.

"Edie!" A great guttural cry broke from her. Georgia ran toward the back hall. The baby woke, frantic, scrambled backward, knocked Georgia briefly off her path with the inertia of her sheer size. Ignoring the clear message her child was sending, she corrected her course and tried again.

Mother! Father! No!

She ignored the voice in her head, pushed against the invisible force that was pulling her backward, step-by-step, until she reached the charred perimeter of the room, her bare feet poised on the unbroken line of mysterious oil. Silence. She took another step, breaching the boundary.

"Edie?" She took another step. The basement door hung open; a tantalizing invitation. Georgia tried to swallow but her mouth was dry as sawdust. *If she's down there, I have to go after her.*

But something tightened around her waist like a slender noose, dragging her away from the dark passage. An invisible embrace pulled her back across the living room floor, her toes barely grazing the snowcapped floor until she came to a halt in front of the fireplace beneath the frosted mirror.

Clouds appeared to flow out of the mantel mirror, swirling, wrapping Georgia in a cool, damp cloak, and erasing the room around her. Then a sickening jerk, the slender noose now a steel rope coiling itself round and round her, binding her, pulling her through the clouds, up, through, beyond. It all happened in a flash; she didn't even have time to spare a breath to scream as she felt her soul cross the threshold of the mirror, her body wrenched from her and left somewhere far, far away. She landed in a heap, her hands scrambling in loamy damp soil and moss, just the hint of an invisible tension reminding her of the tenuous grip she had on the reality she'd been ripped from.

The clouds had traveled with her. Soaring trees, ancient sycamores wept their tea-stained leaves down all around her. It was as if she'd wandered into a literal translation of Edie's attic mural. The very air seemed to be waiting, listening, yearning, a horrible desperate *need*. She reached out with earth-stained hands to grasp the mackerel bark of the nearest tree and pulled herself to her feet, leaning against its massive trunk, disoriented but strangely not afraid. There, in the distance, an opening in the forest, a meadow. She could just barely see soft sunlight through the mist, something—someone—moving. Coming closer. A light. Heavy footfalls. Sparks on the rocky forest floor like stars. And then a voice, gentle and melodic.

"You should not be here." A man. Or something very like one. Someone tall and dark with flashing eyes. She tried to look directly at the creature standing before her, but it was like trying to look at the sun. Her eyes watered, her head grew heavy. So she lowered her gaze to the rocky floor beneath her feet.

"Where am I?" she whispered.

"You mustn't linger here. It's not your time. Not yet." Georgia could just barely perceive his outline now. But every step he took toward her felt like weight added onto her shoulders, crushed under an awesome density. And the smell. Like incense, tea, and autumn leaves, warm and treacly, delicious. *Awe*, she thought. *This is what awe is.*

"Linger where? What is this place?" she asked again.

"You have wandered into Eden. Through the looking glass, as our Edie would say. Tell me, Georgia Pritchard, however did you come to be here?"

And then her child's voice rose in song, a song of songs that seemed to wash down from the heavens and pour out of her.

"Oh, she's singing again." Tears began to stream down Georgia's face as she fell to her knees in the foggy garden and tenderly rubbed her swollen stomach.

"You can hear the song of the stars?" he asked. She felt leather-clad hands grasp hers and pull her back to her feet.

"Almost. I can almost hear it. It's too much, too great . . . I . . . But *she* can. She can hear it and she is singing with them. Calling to someone. I think . . . I think she brought me here. My God," she whispered. Unbidden, Georgia's arms arranged themselves in a contrite posture of genuflection as she felt breath on her face, then fingertips on her stomach.

"No, my lady. Not Him. You'll have to make do with me."

"But who are you?"

"I am the one who would do anything for her. For my Galliana."

Georgia heard a rasp, metal on metal, and then the creature kneeled in front of her, a flash of fire from his eyes blinding her as he bowed his head. He laid a sword at her feet, the edge licked with small curls of flame.

"My lady, may I?" he asked, his melodic voice now more reverent than her own.

"I don't understand . . . I . . ." Georgia gasped as he pressed his lips to the swell of her stomach.

At his touch, the song inside her erupted in a burst of joy so intoxicating that Georgia's head rolled back, dizzy, giddy with it, the creature's voice joining in, a melody so enchanting and overwhelming she would have fallen were it not for the strong hands holding her waist. He was singing to her child. Some melodic, incomprehensible language rose and fell from his lips against her stomach, a song with no words, as if the very skies had opened up and poured out every last measure of love and devotion in the universe. Just as quickly as the being began singing, he stopped. His lips slid from Georgia's stomach and she felt him settle the side of his head against her, listening, both of them frozen to catch the reply from within. There it was, the keenest edge of her hearing, like a harp being plucked on a distant mountaintop, sweet and high and pouring honey balm over a desolate valley.

The enormous being released her and rose, steadying Georgia with one enormous hand.

"Thank you, my lady," he whispered. He bent to collect his sword and slid it back into its scabbard.

"What did she say?" Georgia whispered. "What does she want?" The noose around her waist tightened. The clouds were receding; she was being pulled back through the looking glass.

"Time," he replied, his words punctuated with a rueful laugh. "She wants time, of all the damn things. Oh, Galliana, you do beat all."

The oppressive air surrounding the man lightened as she was pulled back into the mist.

"Wait, please!" she called back to him. "Will I see you again?"

"I'm afraid so," she heard him say, his voice low and mournful.

The silver rope jerked again and the wonderland forest and the shining creature disappeared in the mist. Back, back, back until Georgia found herself alone in Roseneath's living room, her hands stained with moss and earth surrounded by a fairy ring of damp sycamore leaves.

THIRTY-NINE

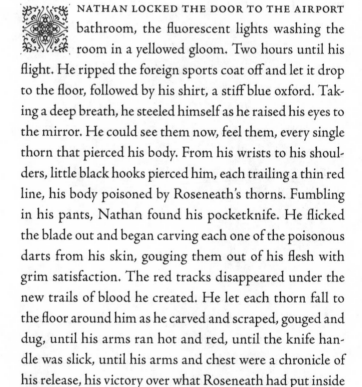 NATHAN LOCKED THE DOOR TO THE AIRPORT bathroom, the fluorescent lights washing the room in a yellowed gloom. Two hours until his flight. He ripped the foreign sports coat off and let it drop to the floor, followed by his shirt, a stiff blue oxford. Taking a deep breath, he steeled himself as he raised his eyes to the mirror. He could see them now, feel them, every single thorn that pierced his body. From his wrists to his shoulders, little black hooks pierced him, each trailing a thin red line, his body poisoned by Roseneath's thorns. Fumbling in his pants, Nathan found his pocketknife. He flicked the blade out and began carving each one of the poisonous darts from his skin, gouging them out of his flesh with grim satisfaction. The red tracks disappeared under the new trails of blood he created. He let each thorn fall to the floor around him as he carved and scraped, gouged and dug, until his arms ran hot and red, until the knife handle was slick, until his arms and chest were a chronicle of his release, his victory over what Roseneath had put inside him.

His mind cleared a little more with each thorn that fell. Months of unremembered time began unraveling, faster,

faster. Roseneath. The garden. The basement. A voice in the earth, sly and convincing. Georgia naked, bloody, covered in his handprints. *Not your hands.* And he'd unearthed whatever it was, whatever had snaked its way into him from the ground, fed it and watered it, nursed it with his own blood, and made it a sanctuary in the basement. Locked it up tight and kept it safe. It wanted *something.* It wanted *someone.* And he had helped it, birthed it, let it send him far away from her, numb and senseless while it waited, biding its time, devouring his life like an insatiable beast.

Nathan set the bloody knife on the sink and leaned forward. His slick hands gripped the rim heavily. As with his hands in the restaurant, he watched as his wounds seemed to close before his eyes, a silvery wash of light flickered over him, a reflection from the mirror, until all that remained were primitive trails of thick white scarring. He closed his eyes against the image, from the scars he knew he would carry for the rest of his life, reminders of what he'd done, what he'd become. His shoulders slumped under the weight of shame as the scared voice inside him matured into a raging man, furious, ashamed, sickened, his fist driving itself—*my hands, my fists, my fault*—over and over again into the mirror, shattering it, shredding his knuckles, unable to look at the one person in the world he did not think he would ever be able to face.

Once on the plane, he waved away the steward and sat, head in his hands, and listened to Georgia's voice crackle through the cheap airline headphones.

"It's me. Georgia. I know you don't . . . can't . . . Edie says he won't let you remember me. Told me to call you, try to make you remember, told me not to give up hope."

A long pause, just the sound of her breathing. "It's hard to be hopeful. Here, anyway. Hard to remember. Remember us. But she says I have to try. Even if it's only so that one day, when you're back, when you remember me, you will understand what happened. I think I can do that much." A crackle. A sigh. "I should start with Edie. Nathan, I should have told you about her. I don't know why I didn't. I guess it would be easy to blame him, the Jabberwock, blame the house, blame whatever all this is. But the truth is, Nate, I found a little girl in the attic that first day you brought me to Roseneath. The ghost of a murdered child in the attic and I wanted her for myself. I needed her for myself. And now she's gone. The man in the mirror took her and I don't think she's coming back."

"Hello?" Nathan could hear her hand shift on the phone, heard her breath catch. "Is it you? Or is it him? Nathan, if it's you, please come home. Please remember me. Me, Georgia." A full minute of silence, shuddering gasps on the other end. "And if it's not, if it's him, whatever you are . . . please don't hurt him. I'll do what you say. Whatever you want. I won't try to leave the house again. I'll do whatever you want, I . . . please don't hurt my Nathan. Please."

Click.

"Nate, I . . . please call me. We . . . I . . . we should talk. Or you could come home, come home now. Please come home now, please hurry. I know you're in there somewhere, maybe you can hear me . . ." her voice choked off in a dry cough, a sickening splatter as he heard her retch on the floor. "Please try to hear me, please call me back, I . . . I'm not . . . something is wrong, she's . . ." A click. Two hang-ups in rapid succession after that.

Soon the messages shifted, became long and rambling, alternating between resignation and pleading, the thickness of her voice telling him she was crying.

"Remember that day at the farm? I've been thinking about that day a lot. Not much else to do, lying here. I'm so heavy now, some days," a choked laugh. "I think she'll be bigger than me." A long sigh. "The first time you told me you loved me." She paused as if waiting for him to nod and, months later, in a plane flying hundreds of miles an hour back to her, he did, his chin jerking down, hands brushing his eyes, "You took me to Malabar Farm." Her voice was labored, asthmatic, "showed me where Bogie and Bacall got married. Remember?" She coughed, cleared her throat, then began again, a terrible wheezing seasoning her words. "And you chased me across that pasture and . . ." He waited an eternity, praying for the next volley of coughing to stop. "When you caught me you kept tickling me, said you wouldn't stop until I said you loved me. Remember that, Nate? Please try." A muffled sound he could not identify "You and me, Nate, please remember us . . . you tickled me and said you wouldn't stop until I told the world you loved me best of all. That happened, didn't it? That wasn't a dream, was it?"

Click.

"I tried, you know. To get Edie out. I thought it was the bones, but it wasn't. She's trapped here and I can't . . . how could I leave her here now? I want to try again but I'm so tired and the baby is so big. But I promise no matter what

I'll try again, think of something. I'll get out and I'll hide somewhere only we know and when you're . . . you're . . . maybe if I leave, he'll let you go, and you'll know how to find me . . . it'll be just like it was before, like none of this ever happened. I can do this . . . I know I can. I can save Edie and the baby . . . I won't let that thing have them. Nathan!" He jerked upright at her sudden burst of anger. "Nathan, listen to me! Goddamn you, Nate, how could you do this to me?"

Click

"Edie is gone. I'd tell you where, but I'm not sure what I saw anymore. It's all mixed up in my head, like the story. Through the looking glass, down the rabbit hole, eat me, drink me, pass the tea. Was she ever even here? Is there really someone in the mirror? I can't be sure of anything, not now. It all sounds mad when I say it out loud. Ghosts. Angels. Demons. I should have told you everything, that first day I found her. And now she's gone and you're gone and I'm here and I . . . I . . . I should have done it all differently. I thought I was saving her, sparing you and this is all my . . ."

Click.

"I can't go upstairs anymore." A long pause, a crackle as she shifted the phone. He could almost see her tucking it under her chin. "It's not . . . safe anymore." She cleared her throat. "I thought, as long as I didn't let them trick me into the basement . . . as long as I stayed inside like he . . . you . . . told me to . . . but they're everywhere now, in every room." Nathan's blood went cold as she started sobbing, and for a long minute her words were indecipherable.

"Please, Nate. I'm so afraid. I don't know how much longer I can . . . please . . ."

Click.

"It's true, isn't it, Nate?" She was hissing, furious, her vocal cords sounded raw. "Every single word. They told me all about it. Every fucking thing. You're somewhere with her. You left me. For her." Nathan flinched as if she'd slapped him. "At first I thought, no, it's crazy, but the monsters, they told me *everything*. And I realized they know too much. Too much about you and her . . . and there's only one person who could have told them, *one person*, Nate, and it's you. Did it all just get too hard for you, Nathan? Was I not fun enough, cute enough for you anymore? Did I just take too fucking long to get over my baby dying for you? You left me here to die, didn't you, Nate? Answer me, goddamn you!"

Click.

"I'm sorry Nate," she was whispering again. "I'm not sure how long I have but I wanted you to know I didn't mean it. They tricked me, didn't they? But the Fallen . . . they're everywhere and they tell me these stories about you and . . . they're so strong now. I don't even have to read the words anymore. I can hear them chanting. It's so loud . . . almost as loud as her song. Can you hear it, too, Nate?" She started sobbing again. "They're telling me about you, please, Nate, no . . ."

Click.

"It's not much of a hidey-hole, Nate, but I think I'll stay here, where it, whatever it was, put me. I feel safe, for the first time in ages. And she does too, I can tell. I can feel this serenity inside me. It is safe, isn't it, little one?" Her voice choked off in a volley of coughing, then a long pause filled with labored breathing, his heart hitching in his chest with each painful draw of breath she took. "I think, I think whatever took Edie, whatever drove them away, set them ablaze, it's not him. It couldn't be. As above, so below. And why not an archangel? I keep thinking, Nate, if there are devils below us, maybe . . . maybe . . . there are angels above, watching out for us." A full minute of silence and he listened to her breathe, struggling to hear the sound in the background. Flapping, clawing, something sharp. "The creatures are still here, but they can't seem to come in now. Maybe it was the fire, the oil. Or maybe it's a new game, one I don't understand yet. I'm going to sleep now, Nate. It's better when she's asleep." Her silence stretched out interminably and then ended with a soft click.

"I don't know what's going to happen, Nate, but I'm not afraid to die. I'm just afraid . . . you'll never know, never remember. Please come home. Please. If not for me, for her. She's so afraid, too, her song is so different now, it's like she knows what's happening, again and again and again and damn it, Nathan, where are you? Please . . ." her pleas trailing off into choking sobs that he felt like punches.

Click.

"Do you ever think, Nathan . . . think that maybe this is all a dream, a horrible dream and we'll wake up together, you and I, just like we used to? Before Roseneath? Do you ever wonder if all this isn't really, can't really be happening? I don't know what's real anymore. Maybe none of it is. This house lies, it deceives. It took Rose, didn't it? Roseneath took our poor baby girl. Gave me Edie . . . only to take her away, too. Gave us back each other only to make you forget me. Gave us this child and I'm afraid, I'm afraid it is only going to take her, too." After a pause, "Promise me you'll love her, Nathan. Swear it." Her voice shook, a furious demand.

One message consisted only of singing. Nathan listened to it over and over, his finger restarting the haunting recording obsessively, letting the eerie music crackle at him through the headphones, something in the register of a sigh on an infinite scale. It was Georgia, he was sure of it, singing a song with no words, just a staggering melody, rising and falling, hunting, seeking, lost and afraid. The longer he listened, he thought he could hear another voice hidden in her own, hesitant, sweet and honeyed. And, surrounding it all, beyond his range, the absence of sound, a black hole that gripped the song tight, a reply so enormous it manifested itself in a vacuum.

When the last message ended, Nathan listened to them all again, and again, until his lips moved along silently with her words, memorizing his wife's strange tale until his plane landed. He tried her phone again, hoping against hope that it was like she said, all a dream, hoping that by carving out whatever had insinuated itself inside him, he had broken the spell that surrounded them both. He listened, hung up, dialed again, then again, but each call was the same. No ring tone, no voicemail, no whispers. Just dead air.

Nathan ran his fingertips over the raised trails of scars that crosshatched his arms, the back of his neck, the palms of his hands. He'd cut it out, dug whatever presence it was that had possessed his body. Nothing remained of him inside, only newly healed flesh and countless scars. His awakened mind followed that truth to a terrifying, logical conclusion. If it, he, him, that beast, that monster, the Jabberwock of Georgia's story was no longer in him, where was it?

His mouth went dry when he landed on the unavoidable truth.

The basement. The greenhouse. Roseneath.

Nathan ran through the concourse to the parking garage, taking the stairs three at a time, slammed the transmission of his truck into drive and drove like hell for Roseneath.

FORTY

ONE MOMENT GEORGIA WAS SURROUNDED BY the deep serenity of the forest of Eden, and the next she lay sprawled on her back within the hell that was Roseneath. She rolled to one side as the house bulged and trembled under her, the wooden timbers groaning as they tried to contain some new, potent arrival, the basement creatures crying out in delighted terror as Roseneath received its host. The sated beast had returned to his lair while Georgia was away. Georgia tried to crawl somewhere, anywhere away from the onslaught surrounding her.

Please, wherever we were, take us back, she pleaded silently with her daughter. *We will surely die here. Please take us back. We were safe there.*

Mud pooled out from the back hall, a slow, wet surge invading the living room, the soft glow of the oily barrier vanishing under the onslaught. Backing away, Georgia turned only to find more thick clots of mud, a winding path of filth that stopped just in front of the oak and glass door, the streaks of sun illuminating the dark wet clumps. And there, dripping down the handle, the lock, seeping through the hinges, was thick black gore collecting on the floor.

"Georgia!"

The voice that screamed her name filled her with dread. She covered her ears and shut her eyes. *No. Please, God, no. I can't. Not that. Not him, not now. I'm not strong enough, not anymore.*

Inside her, the child screamed, a deafening clarion cry.

"Georgia!" Nathan's voice roared again, the brittle sound of glass splintering under pounding fists.

The house trembled beneath Georgia again and threw her off balance. She looked out the window and saw a blood-streaked, scarred man screaming her name with her husband's voice and knew for certain she was mad, knew beyond a doubt that Roseneath had won. *When did he win,* she wondered. *Did any of this really happen or am I long dead, too, a bundle of bones like Edie, with no way out?*

✦   ✦   ✦

Nathan leapt out of the cab of his truck and into the gravel of Roseneath's drive. He missed the shift to park, landing instead in neutral. The sound of the truck slamming into a century-old oak was swallowed by the roaring of the house as it shook in a tremor. He clambered to his feet but was shoved back by the greenhouse windows cracking and bursting, raining shrapnel over him. He ran forward, his boots grinding in the slush and gravel, fell, crawled, rose again with one thought only: to reach the front door. But as he rounded the side of the house, he saw something that made his feet slow until he stood frozen in the front yard.

Roseneath. The roses, the vines, the thorns, all of them black like hardened charcoal wrapped around the base of the porch, arms clawing for each window, each door, as if ages had passed. But this was no natural occurrence, no gentle creep of neglect, this was insidious, the vines constricting even as he watched, as if strangling the very foundation, guarding what was inside, forbidding him entry. His blood ran cold as he skirted those wicked thorns, the deep hedge that had grown up in the dead of winter around the house he'd left his wife in, an impenetrable entanglement locking her inside with the creature he had unearthed in the cellar depths.

There. He spied a gap, a small path through the wicked hedge, the severed edges of each leggy branch dripping with a viscous black bile. Avoiding the glittering thorns, Nathan turned his body sideways and rushed down the narrow path to a living room window. He picked his way carefully through the vicious thorns until he stood in a small clearing against the foundation of Roseneath. Nathan froze in his tracks as the lead glass reflected his own face and body. Crazed eyes, blood-drenched shirt, fragile scabs on his hands weeping blood as he pressed them flat against the grimy windowpane, anointing the windows of Roseneath. He trained his eyes beyond the tattered reflection and into the living room.

Georgia!

There she was, standing motionless in front of a great mirror, her entire body lit up by an unseen source, hands raised as if in worship, her filth and tear-streaked face bearing an expression so profound, so beatific, that for a moment, just a moment, Nathan wondered if she wasn't really there. That she was just another trick in his mind, that she was something beyond reality. Not his wife, not Georgia, but something more. A visitation beyond his understanding.

Before the thought could take hold, she was carried briefly into the air by unseen arms and then lowered, her emaciated arms and legs akimbo, her stomach bloated, coming to rest finally on the floor, as if asleep, her face a gruesome mask of rapture and neglect. A sob fell from his lips as she woke. He saw past this aspect of her to the reality, the one he'd abandoned. She was filthy and battered, her hair a greasy, tangled mass of snakes, bare scabbed patches torn from her scalp. She wore nothing more than one of his old shirts, the tattered stained fabric barely containing her stomach, her arms and legs dangled like a broken marionette from the garment. Her hands where she crawled across the littered floor were bloodied and splintered.

One of his own ruined hands tightened into a fist, and he pounded on the glass, startling her from whatever she was scrambling to, or away from.

"Georgia!" he cried. "Georgia!"

She turned to look at him, senseless at first, then her eyes widened in recognition, recognition that shifted to horror. She screamed, a hoarse sound as if her larynx was shredded, and scrambled backward into the fireplace like a crab, dragging her ungainly body away from him.

Nathan looked down, wondering what awful specter had so frightened her and saw his shirt, his bloody hands, the smears on his face, the tangle of thorns that surrounded him. *Me. She's afraid of me.* He drove his fist through the glass, shattering it, and as he did, the ground-shaking groans from the basement cut off, the sudden silence somehow worse. Ignoring his wounded hands, Nathan punched out the residual shards of glass, creating an opening in the brittle window not even big enough for his head to fit through. She was in the fireplace now, pulling a blanket over her head like a frightened child, wailing, a wounded animal crawling away from a hunter.

He tried to lower his voice, tried not to scare her anymore but his own terror was too great. The words he whispered through the broken window came out in a lower register of her own fearful whimpers.

"Shh . . . shh, baby, no, it's me. Georgia, please don't be afraid of me, please come here, sweetheart, oh my darling come here. It's me, it's me again, it's not him anymore. It's me, Georgia, I cut him . . . it . . . out of me, baby, please." His pleas broke off when she did not respond, and he had a sickening thought that perhaps now *she* didn't know *him*, couldn't remember him. "It's me. Me. It's Nathan." She lowered the blanket, her sunken eyes hopeful even as her mouth trembled.

Nathan let his head fall against the glass. "God, Georgia. What's happened to us?" He turned away, ashamed, unable to look into those wounded eyes. He heard her rise to her feet, her steps slow and obviously painful. *Me. I did this. I did this to her. I let him do this to us.*

Through the small opening he felt her tenuous hand on his head, felt her fingers slip to his chin and tilt his head up.

"Nathan?" she whispered, her battle-worn face cracking into a hesitant smile. He reached up with one hand and wrapped it around hers, brought it to his lips and kissed it.

"Georgia."

Sobbing now, Georgia's breath came in the same fitful hitches he'd heard in her messages. She reached with her other hand through the window, cutting her forearms on the broken edges, wicked fresh trails of his wife's blood mingling with his own, as she desperately tried to climb out to him.

"Help me, Nathan, please. I have to get out. Get me out, please, he's coming, I know it, there's going to be a battle, a terrible battle again and again and again and I'm afraid it will kill her, *here*, Nathan, *here in the garden*, it all started in a garden and it will end in one, too, and she has to live. Nathan, help me, help me."

He tried to push her arms back through the window; the blood that flowed from her pale, blue-tinged limbs made him run cold. She was so wasted, so frail, as if everything inside her had been wrung out, her stomach grossly swollen as if the child was supplanting her, erasing her.

"Georgia. I will get you out. But you have to stop, you're hurting yourself, we have to get you to a doctor, you . . ."

Hysterical laughter bubbled from her bloody lips. She shook her head and began coughing and keening, garbled words barely escaping the fit. 'Edie' and 'mirror' and 'Michael'. 'The garden'. A disjointed, fragmented poem of nonsense.

Alone, in this house. All this time, a prisoner in this evil place. Nathan wrapped his hand around her forearm, pushing it back through the window, even as he tried to coax her out of her hysteria.

"Georgia, I need you to listen to me." She looked at him with renewed interest, her eyes widening, surprised. His eyes blurred and burned to see her so undone.

"Nathan," she whispered. "Is that you? Or is it him? Who are you? Who am I? Am I dead?"

"Don't talk like that!" he sobbed, "Goddamn it, it's me. Nathan. Georgia, honey, you have to focus. Focus on me. I know who Edie is. I listened to your messages. And I think I saw her. Your Edie. She brought me back to you."

That face, that gleeful, indignant Gibson Girl face infinitely reflected in the mirrors, screaming his name, coaxing him, urging him, waking him. Edie. Georgia's fairytale child in the attic. It had to have been her. "She saved me."

"And we have to save her, Nathan," she pleaded. "We can't leave her in this place. I don't know where she is, I can't find her, she . . ."

"We will. I will. I'll get you out, Georgia." Her fingers relaxed and threaded through his. He reached for her other hand through the opening and felt the perfection of the moment as her small hand found its proper place in his, ignored the blood and wounds that stained them both and kissed her fingertips, her touch untying all the knots inside him, burning through any remaining fog, and centering him, finally.

"Georgia," he said with sudden certainty, "I'm sorry. I swear I'll put this all right. I swear on my soul I would never have . . ." His certain voice faltered. "Never. I swear to you." His lips met hers for one brief moment. "It wasn't me, Georgia. It wasn't ever me. I would never."

Her face fell then, and she drew back. In that moment, Nathan saw reflected in her eyes every single way he'd betrayed her in the last few months, ways even he himself could not yet face. Saw the weight of it crush her. Her eyes fluttered shut, her hand went limp in his, broken.

"It's true then," she whispered, pulling her hand back into the house. "Everything he said. All those nightmares he wrote on the walls. It's all true."

"No, no, no, Georgia, please," he began, his confident voice vanishing, the small, scared boy appearing briefly as the air filled with deep, dangerous whispers. An avalanche of groaning promises seemed to flood across the floor, burying them both. Nathan gritted his teeth against the familiar onslaught and grabbed frantically for her hands through the tiny opening, but she stumbled back, now alert. She scanned the room, the air around her as if she were surrounded by an airborne swarm. Georgia pulled herself to her feet with a horrible wail that was nearly lost in the deafening air, her head whipping around, as if someone had called her by name. She took one, two, three stumbling paces through the living room. Toward the back hall. Toward the basement.

"Georgia, no, wait. Come back to the window. Don't listen to it!"

She turned back to him, her ruined, beautiful face lighting up in delirious hope, and he knew then, knew that the creature that had twisted his thoughts, drowned him in blissful release had found his way inside her at last, found the chink in the armor she must have created to last in this house so long, a siren's call she could not resist, now that she knew the worst was true, now that he'd truly taken everything from her.

He knew that she did not hear what he did, a gleeful voice, threaded through with broken glass and charred rot, the smacking of horrible lips against rotted teeth, the slithering pustule-crusted tongue against his ear.

Come on, Nate, let me make it easy on you. Let me back in and you can have it all back, everything you ever wanted. All you have to do is let go, Nathan, and I'll make it all so easy. And if you don't, I'll make it hard. I'll make it hurt, I'll make her hurt, forever and ever and there's not a power in this world that can stop me

"Edie," her voice the thinnest treble piercing the roaring in his ears. "Nathan, it's Edie. I can hear her." Another step.

"No, Georgia, it's not Edie, it's not. It's him. Don't listen, baby. Listen to me, come back here, don't listen to him . . ."

"Nathan, I can hear her. She's in the basement, can't you hear her? She's . . ." Another step backward, both of her hands on her stomach, a grimace erasing her delirious mask. Nathan swore even from that distance he could see her distended belly tighten. "She's frightened, Nathan, she's calling me . . ."

He reached through the glass with both hands, cursing the thick metal frames that would not let him through. "No, Georgia, it's a trick, it's a lie . . ."

"Nathan, I have to try." She cast him only a glance over her shoulder. "I have to. I can't leave her down there in the dark, not again. She's afraid of the dark. Edie! I'm coming!"

"Georgia, don't go in that basement," he pleaded. "Don't go down there, she's not here, he's lying to you."

She turned and leaned heavily against the doorframe into the back hall, letting out one long breath, her face settling into a weary smile.

"Don't you see? I can get her, I know I can. It'll all finally be over and I can rest. We can leave this place, together. She knows the way out, she knows how to get through the looking glass." She stumbled into the back hall like a trusting child, one hand on each wall supporting her trembling legs, called by an unseen piper.

FORTY-ONE

EDIE'S NAME FLEW LIKE A THOUSAND BATS through the air around her, each letter a leathery plea propelling her forward, away from Nathan. Edie's name dripped like scripture down the walls—*Edie, Edie, Edie*—across the floor, a blood-red pool of letters and whispers that led to the basement stairs, flowing over the edge, disappearing into the darkness below. *Edie.* It was the only thought in her head, the only light in her shadow-choked mind. Behind her, she heard a voice she barely remembered, a man calling to her across an endless canyon—*Georgia, Georgia, Georgia*—but before she could recognize it, before she could remember to reply, it was snatched away, erased by the flapping wings of the bats in the air, drowned in the bloody letters at her feet. Piteous whimpers came from the darkness, Edie's, the same whimpers Georgia had heard in the attic when she'd first found her, frightened, timid, her voice one small brittle shard escaping the deep of the basement.

"Lavender's blue, dilly dilly, lavender's green . . ."

Georgia advanced, one slow step at a time, her hands gently cradling the heavy swell of her stomach, refusing to acknowledge how very tight it was, a tightness that came and went like the tides, gripping her, releasing her only to grip her like a vise again, but she persevered. Through the back hall, her breath came in short pants now, her heart pounded in her chest.

"When I am king, dilly dilly, you shall be queen . . ."

She stopped at the top, peering down the steps into the gloom below. A fine-spun cobweb of light illuminated the basement floor, an ethereal gleam that reached like tattered lace into the darkness at the bottom of the steps.

She placed one foot on the top step, the worn treads creaking and swaying as she did, then the other. The dark was thicker down here, and after the fifth step, she couldn't see behind her or in front of her. Edie's voice was louder now. It seemed to come from somewhere just beyond the ever-shifting mirage of flickering light.

"If you should die, dilly dilly . . ."

Edie's voice was muffled and broken. Georgia had reached the bottom of the steps, darkness stretched in every direction except one. A frail light wavered in a far-off corner. *Edie.*

"You will be buried, dilly dilly, under the . . . under the . . ."

Georgia placed one foot on the basement floor. It sank deep into thick, viscous mud.

"You're the cream . . ."

Another foot, the mud tugging her, pulling her.

"In my coffee . . ."

Edie was weeping. Georgia fell to her knees and crawled through until she was slick with it, the delicate light fading as it led her away from the stairs. Deeper, deeper into the basement she crawled, the cavernous rooms echoed with her labored breathing, feathery tendrils of verse guiding her

"I'd be lost . . ."

leading her, the air around her lightening

"Lost . . ."

the narrow windows revealing pockets of dismal light in the fetid basement.

"without you . . .."

A sound behind her, the thick sound of mud slopping on the floor. Georgia froze as the light and Edie's voice vanished. In its wake, the thick sound of mud slopping on the floor. Upstairs, heavy, thudding. Chopping. *A man calling. Calling someone's name. Georgia. Who is that? Who was she? Not me, not anymore. I don't remember her.* The wet sound again, behind her. Closer. Edie's fractured whimpering had been just to the left of her. She had to be there. Georgia reached out in the dark, fumbled for purchase.

"Edie?"

But it wasn't Edie.

"Hey, Miss Muffet."

The sound of that lovely, sickening voice brought Georgia to her senses. She looked up and wished she hadn't.

"Told you I'd be back."

Inside her, the child froze. Georgia fell backward into the earth at the sight of the beast that towered over her.

The creature was vaguely human—a golem of mud and thorns, skin a patchwork of flesh, shards of bone and shattered teeth, bright eyes set deep in a crude mask. Edie's sweet voice had come from the creature's grim mouth, but the laughter that echoed against the damp cellar walls was the one he'd stolen from Nathan. She looked away from the beast's face to the dim light washing down the basement stairs and had no memory of making her way here to kneel at his feet.

Jabberwock. Deceiver. Edie was not here, she'd been tricked into coming down here, propelled by the one thing that could possibly have coaxed her down those stairs. She looked up into the face of the beast that had lured her here, struggling to process the gruesome visage. The branches that stood out of the hideous golem in front of her were covered in thorns, wickedly sharp, glinting in the meager light as it hit them, black like horns, black as hell. The creature's head was wreathed in them as well, a crown of thorns for Hell's king.

She tried to scramble to her feet, but the mud was slick. It clutched at her and pulled her down into it, back into the darkness. She tried to wipe her face off, but her hands were encrusted with the fetid earth. Georgia tried in vain to open her lips, to scream again, but they were sealed, as the gore shifted to something viscous, tarlike. Flailing backward, she felt something like arms pull her back, back, back into the darkness and deep into the basement. Arms that bit and cut. Above, she could hear him, calling her, thundering sounds as he tried to breach the doors to Roseneath. *Is this what he did to you, Nathan?*

Something clamped over her face and cut off her air, strangling her. She couldn't let this happen, couldn't let her child be born under the gaze of this beast. *So help me*

God, I will save her. I will not let this thing take my child again.

Throwing herself forward onto her hands and knees, Georgia crawled. The mud was like a thousand blood-suckers pulling at her from below, the embedded thorns slicing her palms to ribbons. She fought her way, inch-by-inch, to the stairs through the dense, stagnant loam. The room began to dim around her. *How long could she hold her breath?* She had to get the mud off her, had to take a breath. The pain was horrible, but she could do it, had to do it, the sound, the creature, was closer now. *The light. I have to get to the light.* Offal from the creature dripped on her back; it hit her in heavy clumps as it weighed her down, her face sagging close to the floor, too close.

And then, miraculously, she felt the cracked wood of the bottom step. She looked up, her vision no more than a pinprick. The stairs towered above her, swaying back and forth, and light—gorgeous, pure, clean light—shining down on her filth-streaked face, showing her the way up out of this hell. *So many steps, so far to go.* She pulled one hand from the mud and then the other, raising them into the light to see, to know what drilled into her there. Each of her palms was impaled with thorns, the thick black gore that poured from the shattered edges of each glittering black dart a sickening stigmata. *The baby. Under my skin now. This thing, this evil, is poisoning my child, like Rose. Nathan, help me. Help us.*

Behind her, the creature grasped her by the ankles, wrenched her backward, her ruined hands scrambling for purchase on the staircase as his darkness closed in.

"What's your hurry, babe?" His voice swung at her like a scythe. "I'm just getting started."

The golem was pulling her, down, down, drowning her in its mire, his grasp weak but determined, her own grasp of the stairs weaker still. Georgia felt her stomach contract—*oh God it hurts*—as it slid up her shirt, across her breasts. Less than a pinprick now, the light began to dim again as the creature dragged her back into the darkness.

Georgia pulled her hands out of the mud and pried apart her lips, scratching at the fragile flesh there until they finally opened. As air filled her lungs, a brilliant light exploded down the stairs. Edie was at the top of the stairs, gripping a mirror against her chest like a shield. The mirror's reflection allowed Georgia to see, as if she were watching a silent film, the heroine crawling away from the monster, a brave last stand staged in black and white and red. But this was no clever celluloid plot, *there isn't going to be a happy ending,* she realized, as something sliced her thigh, carved a crescent into her back. Behind her towered a nightmare made real and she was going to die here. Her vision was dimming, a small blessing, but there might still be one chance to save her daughter.

"Edie," she pleaded, "Nathan's outside." She was being pulled back down the stairs again. "Help him save her. Don't let him take my baby." She heard Edie scream, a rage-filled battle cry, and then Georgia's vision slipped to black, and she faded into nothing.

FORTY-TWO

NATHAN WATCHED, HELPLESS, AS GEORGIA disappeared into the gloom of the back hall. He clawed the air futilely through the miniscule opening in the window as if he had any hope of reaching her.

"Georgia, no!"

He drove his fist into another pane of glass, shattering it, another then another until he'd broken enough panes to grasp the window by its frame. Wrapping his hands around the thick metal, he pulled, his weakened muscles straining, hands slipping on fresh blood, a rabid, desperate noise from between his gritted teeth, but it did not budge. The ancient casing rattled but did not yield. With a grunt he let go and stumbled backward, oblivious to the vines that had begun to slither around his feet, blind to the new cuts on his arms, legs, and back as he made his way out of the deep hedge that surrounded the house, as Roseneath itself reached for him, tried to draw him back into itself.

Free of the hedge now, he tried to run, but one thick vine wrapped around his ankle, pitching him facedown into the grass. He rolled, yanked his leg free and jumped to his feet, sprinted to the idling truck, no thought in his head except getting inside that house. Yanking the keys from the ignition, he fumbled through them, searching for the lock to his tool chest—*the hatchet, my hatchet, I'll chop my way through*—key after key as he dropped the tailgate and continued to hunt, so many keys, none of them the right one. He climbed into the truck bed, drew his legs to his chest, and drove his boot heel, hard, into the tool chest lock. Again. Again. A third time, but it was impossible. The lock would not budge, the chest's lid too sturdy to cave under the force of his kicks. From the house came a silence so deep, a hollow, resounding despair that Nathan felt as he jumped from the truck, rolling, crawling in the gravel, desperate hands searching again for the keys, scrambling in the gravel. *The truck. I'll drive it though the carriage house doors, there's another axe inside, I'll find something, anything, a sledgehammer, a shovel. I'll drive the truck through the goddamn back porch, that's it, climb over the hood into the house, yes, yes, that'll work, it has to, I can get it, I can get to her before he does, Georgia, oh God, I'm too late.*

From the basement, a scream. *Georgia.* He could see her in his mind, covered in the creature's filth, kneeling at his feet, just as he had, except where he had been senseless, numb, resigned, he knew by the sound of her screaming that she was none of those things. He knew that the sight of it, the evil truth of what dwelled in the earth of Roseneath had shocked her out of the enchantment the creature had lured her with. He knew that she was alone. With it. The beast, the monster. The deceiver. Down there, deep in the basement.

The basement windows. He abandoned his hunt for the keys and began crawling toward the foundation of Roseneath, to the shattered basement windows, desperate to believe he could slip through one, drop down there. The rational part of his mind tried to tell him his chest was too big, his shoulders too broad, the hundred-year-old frames sized for airflow rather than entry, but the sound of her screams drowned that part of him out and propelled him on his hands and knees across the gravel, all reason lost.

The ground began to tremble beneath his feet, the gravel itself quaking faster, faster, as if it would liquefy. An enormous, nameless sound filled the air, the crushing assault on his senses paralyzing him. His eyes dazzled as a shimmering shape bathed in light materialized an arm's length away, the air bending and pleating around it as if this incongruous mass itself was of such awesome density it bent space and time. It flared, white hot, and then dimmed, the sound fading as it did. Nathan's arms collapsed beneath him, even as he struggled to draw air into his constricted lungs. He pitched forward, his jaw striking the still vibrating gravel, the impact restoring his senses, shocking him from his frenzy. He rolled to one side, away from whatever had knocked him senseless, then vaulted to his feet. There, lying neatly on the ground in front of him was an axe. It was not his axe, nor was it in the style of any tool he had ever seen before. The flat, elongated head, wickedly sharp, still glittered silvery white, the handle itself nearly five feet long, the grain of the wood unfamiliar and scored all around in a pattern of flickering runes that spiraled before his eyes. It was an enormous, enchanted weapon, an elegant device more suited for a giant than a man.

Without hesitation, Nathan grasped the weapon in both hands, vaguely admired its weight and balance, then sprinted back to the front of the house. He located the bramble of rose vines infecting the foundation of Roseneath, raised the axe high and swung, over and over, each bite of the sharp blade severing no more than a few inches of the impenetrable vines. Where the axe head touched, the vines seemed to retract, fleeing from their severed limbs, leaving trails of black gore. Each swing of the axe made slow but steady progress through the razor-sharp hedge. Suddenly the world was washed in brilliant light, shining from every window, every crack, *dear God*, even from the chimney of Roseneath, as if the entire house had become a flimsy paper lantern. The light faded and Nathan continued his grim work. Ten swings, twenty, and he reached the bottom step. Fifty swings and he reached the top porch step, another thirty to the front door, his muscles screaming in a horrible harmony with the wrathful groan that came from below, as if drawn by the light, the beast's whispers raging, impotent in Nathan's ears.

The axe head was now drenched in the hedge's black blood, the handle slick with it, and Nathan reached, at last, the looming front door. He grasped the handle but it would not turn. Nathan drove his shoulder into it again and again, but the golden oak and lead glass held firm.

Another blast of scorching light seared his retinas, but he closed his eyes to it and continued his assault on the door.

"Georgia," he screamed helplessly, trying to stay on his feet as the house shook, as if throttled by something enormous, unseen. "I'm coming, Georgia, answer me!"

FORTY-THREE

NOTHING. DARKNESS. AND THEN GEORGIA sputtered, and then consciousness returned in a blinding, exquisite vengeance. The claws that grasped her feet vanished in an instant, a cry of impotent rage from the creature, and then strong hands grabbed her under her arms and the stairs rushed by, the basement vanished. Edie pushed her into the safety of the back hall, then with a grunt, threw Georgia over her shoulder and sprinted up, up, up the stairs, carrying them both away from the horror in the basement. The creature's roars followed them like airborne ghouls, the bleeding walls now dripping with apocryphal incantations of hate, evil, words so unspeakable Georgia closed her eyes to them, but not before she saw the one shining word threaded through all that malevolence. One word over and over again, gleaming and pure, as if the creature's deepest desires could not touch it.

Galliana. Galliana. Galliana.

Bright light now, clouds whipping past, more stairs, and then Edie dumped her into her own bathtub. Georgia was covered in mud and blood, sticks and thorns, the pain so great it was as if she stood outside herself, unable to process the agony. She opened her mouth to tell Edie the sickening truth, *the baby, poisoned, she can't bear it, his filth on her, in her, save her,* when she felt a rush of warmth between her legs. Edie screamed at the gush of bloody fluid that flowed from between Georgia's legs. Georgia reached up with one arm and grabbed her lace shirt.

"The thorns," she rasped. "Get them out."

With a sob, Edie turned the shower knob, drenching them both in frigid water, and began scrubbing her with vicious hands, clawing each thorn from Georgia's wracked body and scraping the filth from the basement from every inch of her. Georgia arched her back, the pain incredible. It was cutting her from the inside out, the baby was coming, no time . . .

But then Edie began to chant, her voice loud and clear, a lyrical spell that cut through the pain.

> *Saint Michael, Archangel,*
> *defend us in battle.*
> *Be our protection against the wickedness and snares*
>   *of the devil.*
> *May God rebuke him, we humbly pray;*
> *and do Thou, O Prince of the Heavenly Host -*
> *by the Divine Power of God -*
> *cast into hell, Satan and all the evil spirits,*
> *who roam throughout the world seeking the ruin of*
>   *souls.*

Nodding, satisfied her plea would be answered, Edie grasped Georgia firmly by her upper arms and submerged her in the ice-cold water. Georgia screamed noiselessly, stiffened as she choked on the water before Edie yanked her back up. As Georgia retched a vomitus mass of mud on the bathroom floor, Edie jumped to her feet and turned the water off with a savage jerk. Then she raised her face to the sky and screamed, loudly, her voice a sweet arrow piercing the demonic roar that still shook the house.

"Michael! Hurry! She's coming!"

Georgia reached for Edie's warm hand and clung to it. The pain in her abdomen was crushing, she was being torn in half; the hot gushes between her legs more frightening than what the creature had conjured below.

"Edie," she managed to whisper, "I saw him. I saw it."

Edie knelt to smooth Georgia's wet hair back and kissed her forehead.

"Yes, my poor Georgia. You tread in the darkness, you bricky girl." Her eyes twinkled down at her. "But remember, there is light, too. Always one to temper the other. And *he'll* be here, soon, any moment. He'll save us all."

Georgia struggled out of the tub, her wet clothes falling in tatters.

"The archangel." *Blood on the floor. Don't look, Georgia, don't look. Just like before. Head up, my dear, don't look down. Step on a crack, break your mother's back.*

Edie nodded. "Oh yes, a proper archangel, sword and all. Positively *fearsome*. And let me tell you, he is *wroth*. Heaven help that old cabbage head once Michael gets ahold of him." Her determined expression faltered as another hot rush flowed between Georgia's bare legs. Laying her hand on Georgia's stomach, she began to whisper, her words an eerie approximation of her daughter's song, the child inside fell still, the sundering pain diminished. Georgia's head swam with the suddenness of the release from pain as a jolt of adrenaline flooded her.

"Don't worry," she whispered to the baby. "This time, it will all work out. You've got me." She whipped her head around as she released Georgia. "He's here!" Georgia tried to listen, to make out the voice in the hall, but all she could hear was the light, a blinding flare that washed over Edie's profile. And in the light, the archangel. Michael.

"Edith?" The baby leapt at the sound of that great voice, jubilant.

"Stars and stripes, take a gander at you! You're almost *incognito*! Maybe tone down the light show a bit and—"

"I'll ask you to keep your japes for later, young Edith, we've no time for it now. What news of my brother?"

"He's made some sort of nest." Edie's voice was low, urgent. "In the basement. He's made golem, Michael, all mud and blood and thorns. I'm frightened."

"Don't be. I'm here. Remember, I promised you a good old-fashioned smiting. " Although teasing, each word the archangel spoke was threaded through with rage.

"But what about the baby? What about Galliana?"

"They must run with her. And never come back."

The light vanished in a flash; the melodious voice with it. In the sudden quiet that followed, Georgia heard Nathan screaming her name over and over again, heard the sound of something striking the front door as he tried to get inside Roseneath.

"Georgia!" *He was so close.* So close. "I'm coming, Georgia, answer me!"

Her throat still burning with mud and water, Georgia tried to call to him, her strangled voice carrying no further than the bathroom.

In a flash, Edie was back beside her, hurriedly shoving her into a thick robe. She placed her hands on either side of Georgia's face and kissed her forehead.

"You have to get out of Roseneath right now. Michael is going to smite that muddy old . . . that muddy old *barn licker* and I mean to help him."

"Edie, don't go back down there, please . . ."

Edie wrapped her arms around her and whispered in her ear. "Don't worry, I'll be safe. I know the way through the looking glass. I take the attic mirror straight to the cellar; I've already scouted it out. I simply haven't time to explain how it all works. Once Michael has routed that *scoundrel,* he and I will go where it can't follow. It'll be trapped here. But you need to get out. And you can't ever come back." She pushed Georgia toward the stairs.

"Can you make it down?" Edie asked. "I think Nathan is almost through. And Michael needs me."

Georgia nodded as she took two slow steps down the staircase, clutching the railing with both hands. The whole house shook as a noxious bellow of rage erupted from below, like shearing metal. Voices rose in argument, one a glorious fury, the other a baneful obscenity. Edie wore a mask of dread.

"You can't understand what he's battling. It's him, you know. The Jabberwock. He's a real thing, after all. Please go. You have to *hurry*, Georgia."

Georgia managed another step, her legs trembling but steady on the steep staircase, the child within holding perfectly still, as if she knew that she must.

"Edie, I love you so much . . ." another step as Georgia searched for the words to say goodbye.

Edie turned and stomped defiantly up the final steps into the attic, her smile lit up with joy, the once lost child now hopeful, brilliant. Georgia knew this was how she'd remember her always—strong and brave. Fearless.

At the top step, Edie hesitated. She turned and said, "Don't you dare start blubbering again, Georgia. We'll see each other one day. He promised. And if I've learned anything about Michael, it's that he always keeps his promises."

Roseneath rocked beneath their feet, vibrating with bitter screams from below.

Damn you, Michael! You ruined everything! She's mine, you dumb fucking grunt!

Georgia froze on the staircase, rapt, as the melodious voice, clear and distinct, snapped with tightly coiled rage.

"I already am damned, brother. And Galliana belongs to no one—least of all to you."

Another great rumble and time seemed to stop. Georgia's foot suspended in the air, poised over the steep staircase. Edie, eyes wide with an almost preternatural horror, arrested in mid-air as she tried to run back to her, her vaulting legs spread like a ballerina frozen in motion. And then time restarted when a thundering cry shook the foundations of Roseneath, and as it did, the staircase vanished under Georgia's feet and she fell, head over heels, down the staircase like a broken doll. Her temple struck the wrought-iron railing as mad laughter exploded all around her. A scream from above—Edie—the sound of Nathan's fists hammering on the threshold of the front door, as her ungainly body, battered and twisted, settled in a limp heap at the bottom of the stairs.

The pendant light suspended above her scattered prisms to every corner of the house, tinted in green and brown, then red. The pain was so great, she couldn't move. Her right eye was blinded, full of something, a coppery tang on her lips as she opened them. One of her hands floated to her head and came away red. Something was pooling in her mouth, coppery and metallic, the taste of her own blood.

Nathan was pounding on the door again, somewhere far, far away and she wished she had the life in her to stand up, to go to him, to open that door at last and fall into the sanctuary of his arms. He was so close, just across the hall, on the other side of those lead glass doors, but he might as well have been on the other side of the looking glass considering her state. Her short-circuiting mind whispered a song. She closed her eyes as her mind replayed a reel of memory against her eyelids, dancing, moonlight, stars, his arms around her, a long time ago.

It wasn't fair, Georgia protested silently, *for it all to end like this*. It was supposed to be a fairy tale; she was supposed to get her happy ending here in Roseneath. *I should have remembered*, she thought, as the song in her head slowed, as the images disintegrated like sand on the beach, *that fairy tales are monstrous things. Wolves and woodsmen, glass slippers and severed toes, witches and ovens. I forgot about that part. It's not all knights and ladies in towers, like Edie said. It's reapers and trolls, unholy bargains with terrible tolls.* And with that final thought, Georgia floated away, the world around her spiraling as the song wound down to silence.

FORTY-FOUR

BEHIND THE GLASS DOORS, NATHAN'S FISTS froze around the axe as he saw a figure in white tumble down the stairs. He could see her pale skin, her black hair as she fell forward, her head striking the rail, before coming to rest at the bottom of the stairs. And then silence. He threw his shoulder against the door once, twice. Rammed the butt of the handle against the lock, tried again in vain to shatter it, to get to her, but the door to Roseneath was impenetrable. He gripped the doorframe in his hands, wishing he possessed the power to wrench it from its hinges, then let go, spent, knowing he could not.

But the door handle began to turn, the mechanism screaming in protest as it did, painfully slow, as if it were being wrenched from an iron grip. The door swung open, the hinges cracking as they teetered between two determined forces, to reveal a young woman dressed in ivory lace and green silk, with hair the color of cognac, a vision in porcelain and pink, the young woman from the restaurant. Edie. She reached out with hands far stronger than his own and pulled him inside, forcing the door open wider, the hinges keening one last time as they yielded to her.

"You . . ." The word barely left his lips when he caught sight of Georgia crumpled lifeless at the bottom of the stairs.

"Nathan, hurry! No time for chitchat," Edie pleaded.

He raced past her to Georgia's still body, reaching for her with trembling hands. A sudden flash of the last time his hands—

Not my hands.

—touched her arrested their path and he hesitated, afraid to let them near her.

"Get her out of this house, Nathan," Edie insisted. "There is no time. Please, you must hurry!"

Nathan fell to his knees beside Georgia. The voices from below were deafening; one enraged, one wrathful, arguing. Beside him, Edie's voice rose and fell, low and insistent, but all he heard was the sound of water dripping off Georgia's face. Her hair was wet, trailing in curls across the blood and dirt-stained floor. Nathan leaned forward, his lips near hers. A soft breath on his face. She was still breathing.

Edie knelt across from him, her hand on Georgia's forehead.

"Nathan," she pleaded. "You need to listen to me. Run and run and run and don't ever come back here."

"I saw you," he whispered. "In the restaurant. In the mirrors, you called my name. Are you Edie?"

She nodded, her eyes never leaving Georgia. "Yes, I'm Edie. Georgia's Edie. She . . ." Using her skirts, Edie gently wiped the streaks of blood and mud from Georgia's face. "She found me, Nathan. In the attic. And she saved me. She brought me back to life. I don't know how or why, but . . ." Edie's lip began to tremble as one sooty tear streaked down her face. She leaned across Georgia's unconscious body and gently tapped Nathan's scarred forearm.

"I knew you could do it, Nathan," she whispered. "I knew you'd be able to dig that monster out. Michael said so. You're a good man. Never forget that, no matter what happened in this house, no matter what Roseneath did to the both of you. Heaven and hell and a looking glass world in-between. None of this was your fault. It all started long before you."

Nathan clutched Edie's arm. "Edie, who did I put in the basement?"

Edie's wide eyes darted to the back hall before she answered, and in his bones, Nathan knew even before she spoke.

"He . . . he was cast down into the earth, at the beginning of time, Nathan, and he . . ."

Edie's reply was cut off as the voices in the basement grew louder and a light, that perfect light, brilliant and scorching, began to flare through the cracks in the floor, washing them all in pure silver. Georgia's head rolled to one side, that strange humming escaping her lips.

A voice, his voice, like ghouls crawling up from the grave, snaked up through the cracks in the floor, blotting out the brilliant light.

"I'll burn her again before I let you take her, Michael. What's another thousand years to me? I have forever to wait. And she'll come again. Again and again forever, isn't that what Father said, brother? And God our Father knows you and I have forever to wait. So why don't you just go back to your garden and brood for another millennium? I'm stronger than you, you know this. You and that stupid, fucking sword."

The silver light flared, wrathful and righteous, bleaching Edie's face into negative. Nathan heard another voice, this one a melodious dagger of noble wrath that shook Roseneath, sending chunks of plaster falling all around the three of them. Edie and Nathan both threw themselves protectively over Georgia.

"I'll destroy us both, Luc, before I let you hurt her again." A terrible heat began to build in the room as the celestial voice called out to Edie. Nathan felt his eardrums burst, the pressure in his head unbearable under the onslaught of that great voice. "Edith, get them out now!"

Edie's sweet voice twisted into a wrathful hiss in Nathan's ear. "Now. Take her and run. Flee, Nathan. *The fire can never be hot enough*. Don't let him find her. *Watch the mirrors*. Michael will warn you, and then you and Georgia have to keep her moving until it's time."

"What do you mean?" Nathan pleaded, "Tell me! I don't understand!" The air began to crackle all around them, the mirror over the mantel cracked, and he slipped his arms under his wife and drew her to his chest.

"Your daughter, Nathan, the child Roseneath gave you. Watch for him in the mirrors. Michael will do anything, *anything* to keep her safe from him."

Then Edie screamed, her voice a shattering clarion, louder than any human voice could be. "Now! Nathan. Go!"

He staggered to his feet, his arms clenched around Georgia's limp body.

Hang on, baby, he thought, ignoring the excruciating pain of his wounds, the blood running hot again under his shirt as he ran, stumbling through the living room to the front door, Edie on his heels. She pushed him through the doorway, then stooped and grasped the gore-drenched axe with a cry of delight. "Ha!" she cried, "Well done, Michael!" then slammed the heavy door shut behind them.

FORTY-FIVE

"MICHAEL, I'M COMING," EDIE CRIED AS SHE ran toward the enormous mirror over the fireplace. Across the scorched wood floors she flew, shining silver axe in hand, leapt atop the coffee table, then hurled herself at the mirror, a moment of panic as she worried if this mirror would take her where she wanted to go, or, for that matter, anywhere at all. Her shoulder hit the shimmering surface, a frightening moment in which she feared she had in fact miscalculated her new skills, and then elation, inertia as she breeched the silver barrier and tumbled through the looking glass, falling, falling until there, just on the other side of a no-man's land wreathed in fog, she spied it. A light shining in the darkness. The back of a mirror. Willing herself to stop falling, *patience, Edie, steady on* she repeated to herself, *like he said, picture where you want to go and go there, hold it in your hand tight like a rope and pull. Easy as banana cream pie* felt herself slow to a stop, hovered in the darkness for a fraction of a second before she let the light pull her through to the other side. Something brilliant and silver flickered violently as she emerged into the dark cavern of Roseneath's basement.

The floor was awash in something so foul, so unspeakable that Edie decided immediately not to make too careful a study of it. The quick, timid glance she did give her surroundings was dire indeed, as if she'd tumbled into hell itself. Thick mud mixed with bones and pulp, shattered teeth and wicked thorns, branches covered with razor-sharp bramble, like thousands of sharp, wicked hands, a mire of horrors that seemed to be boiling up out of the earthen floor, as if drawn to the creature in the center of the room. Across the room Michael prowled like a lion, sword drawn, circling his brother, now an enormous dark shape that towered over him and Edie. His sword was ablaze, the silver fire that flickered down its length a twin to the searing light in his eyes. Edie gripped the axe tight, raised it over her shoulder and waited, unobserved in the dark.

"Look what you've become, brother," Michael snarled. "Once the most beautiful, the most noble, the most powerful among us. Father's favorite. And now look at you." He slashed his sword at a gore-crusted vine that snaked out from the beast across the floor toward him. It exploded into flame and fell back with a hellish scream. The creature in front of him roared in furious frustration. Michael smiled, his lips drawn back over his teeth, predatory and feral. "At least now your body matches your soul," he spat. "It ends here. Now. She's gone and I'll make damn sure you never find her."

The creature spoke, this time in his own voice, a velvet rasp, like a lion licking a dead gazelle. Standing once more in his lair, as she had an age ago, Edie remembered her final moments in the dark basement of Roseneath. Felt every single minute she'd refused to revisit, the very moment of her death, the moment hope, life, and reality was stripped from her.

"Oh, don't be such a fucking bore. I'll find her, Michael. I always have and I always will. And if I don't find her, the Fallen will. Remember, we are legion. I have Dad to thank for that."

That voice, I remember now, he said I was weak . . . said I was . . . was . . . he made Mama and Papa hurt me Edie nodded faster and faster as the memories of those last seconds piled atop each other in tight ranks, *and then it hurt so bad, he hurt me so bad, it was him, him all this time.* Edie felt a spark inside her, an unfamiliar, powerful sensation. Then one spark became two, became a multitude, each flicker a righteous fury welling up inside her, indignant, crackling to get out.

"I'm never going to stop, Michael. And the beauty of our unique situation is that I don't have to. I'll get her eventually. And if she ends up on another woodpile," the creature's enormous trunk-like body slithered toward the archangel, a wild panic joining the fury in Edie's chest as it did. "I'll be sure to get front row seats for us both this time."

Across the room, Michael's eyes snapped, enraged, his entire body now glowing in a liquid wash of blinding silver, a contained supernova in the dark gloom, brighter even than his sword.

"How very fitting that a pestilent craven such as you would hide behind our Father's ignorant, sadistic priesthood," Michael snarled, drawing his sword back. He then froze; his eyes shifted past the laughing creature to Edie, who was trembling in fury in the dark. He shook his head, a tight restrained gesture, his eyes warning. Edie ignored his silent admonishment and charged at the creature from behind, a shrieking dervish.

"I won't let you, you smelly old skunk!" she cried, swinging the axe wildly at the back of the beast. "I won't! I won't! I won't let you hurt her like you hurt me!"

The creature turned in a slow circle and as he did, Edie looked up into the crude features of its face, the simple approximation of a mouth, above that eyes that burned down at her, amused, annoyed. *I remember.* He swung an arm at her, thick as timber, but Edie ducked, rolled, jumped to her feet again and continued chopping madly away at the gruesome golem.

"Not you again," the creature spat, vines snaking toward her. "Annoying little brat."

"I remember," she screamed. "I remember what you did! You're a villain! A white-livered cad! I won't let you hurt her! I won't!" Sobbing now, each chop sending a splatter of filth over her, Edie ran around the flailing creature in a blur, the air crackling around her in powder-blue sparks.

"I won't let you," she cried, her axe severing one arm, then drawing it back for another blow, "hurt anyone ever again!"

She swung again but the creature parried and snatched the silver axe from her small fingers. Edie fell backward, bracing for the eternal fall into the fetid earth, but a powerful hand grabbed her, and Michael threw her across the room. As she sailed through the air, Michael slid to one knee and drove his sword into the thick legs of the beast, an incredible burst of heat filling the room like venting lava. A wick of fire coursed up the creature, his screams a slow agony. The wicking flame grew to an inferno and devoured him before Edie's eyes. As the pyroclastic flow engulfed the entire basement, Michael launched himself across the room, caught Edie in mid-air, and dove head-first into the looking glass, just as Roseneath erupted like a volcano behind them.

Edie lay very still in the grass where she landed, tucked up tight in a ball, afraid to open her eyes.

"Edith," she heard Michael say softly. "It's all right. You're safe."

Edie sat up and looked about her. She had fallen into the tall grasses of Eden, just outside of the great wood, dappled sunlight scattered all around her. The beast, the basement, Roseneath, and every minute of time between her death and unique rebirth lay far away on the other side of the looking glass. She looked up at Michael, concern still etched on his face, and burst into a storm of unrestrained tears, incomprehensible words blubbering from her lips. Michael patted her awkwardly.

"There, there," he stammered. "It's not as bad as all that, is it?" He lifted her up from where she'd fallen and settled her neatly on a stump. She hiccupped loudly, looked up into Michael's uncomfortable face, and resumed crying with abandon, each plaintive sob punctuated with its own corresponding hiccup.

"Horrid, *horrid* thing! And he . . ." she blubbered, ". . . and I . . . and I . . . moldy old turnip! And I . . . I . . . wasn't so very frightened a moment ago," she blew her nose into her skirts, "but I sure am now. Like a big baby!"

"Hush, little miss," Michael said, uncertain. "Here." He handed her another bit of cloth and she snatched it miserably from his hands. "Dry your tears, Edith. Be a good little soldier. Chin up."

Edie's terror dwindled into a sparse array of hiccups. "Thank you," she whispered.

"You were very brave, Edith," Michael said, crouching down awkwardly. "You did well." She beamed at him and he seemed to take courage from that. "I don't know of many angels who would be brave enough to take on my brother as you did." The ghost of a smile softened his grim, inhuman face. "Though she be but little, she is fierce."

Edie sniffled and stared thoughtfully at the handkerchief for a minute. Then she looked into his eyes, something like mischief in her smile.

"I *did* do rather well, didn't I? I don't know what came over me," she said thoughtfully. "I think it's because I heard his voice, that monstrous voice, and I saw what he was and I remembered something very important."

"What's that, Edith?"

"I remembered," Edie said, jumping to her feet and shaking her skirts out. "How very *angry* I am. I think I showed that blasted old cow pie a thing or two!"

Michael rolled his eyes in a wholly un-angelic expression and Edie laughed.

"So what happens now, Michael?" she asked, looking in despair over the state of her skirts, her hysterical breakdown forgotten the moment she saw her lovely frock was ruined. "Is it all over?"

"No," Michael said grimly, crossing his arms over his chest and staring past her. "No, it's not. I'm afraid it's just beginning. Again."

FORTY-SIX

NATHAN LAY ON THE FRONT LAWN, stunned, a loud ringing still pounding in his ears. The explosion had sent both him and Georgia through the air. The last thing he remembered was watching Edie charge back into Roseneath, the axe held high over her head, with the eyes of a warrior going into battle. He crawled on his hands and knees, dragged Georgia to the shelter of one of the sycamores, away from the terrible inferno behind them. He wrapped her in his arms, the blood gushing between her legs now washing down his. He looked back at Roseneath. The house was gone, leveled; the splintered remains engulfed in silvery white flames.

By the time the ambulance arrived, there was nothing left. Nathan cradled their newborn daughter in his arms. Her hair was the color of fire, her eyes silver discs staring up at him with perfect trust. As he wrapped her in his shirt, taking care to tuck her long, spindly arms and legs in against the cold, he plucked her tiny, wrinkled hand, kissed it, and tucked that in as well. Edie's words rang endlessly in his ears. *Keep her moving.*

FORTY-SEVEN

GEORGIA TRIED TO CLAW HER WAY TOWARD consciousness, but each handhold she found felt like a thousand knives digging into her, driving her back into the dark crack in the sidewalk she was trapped in. Voices surrounded her, an incomprehensible cacophony.

"Over here."

"No, goddamn it."

"We don't have time. Get the cart in here."

"You have to wait in the hall, sir."

"Get him out of here."

A crash, arguing.

"Get him out."

Another crash, metal falling.

"Someone get him out of here."

"No time."

The pain coursed like lightning through every inch of her, unmaking her, a crescendo with no end.

"I need a crash team here now."

"We're losing her."

"Losing her."

"Losing her."

And then a low cry broke through the din, thick and filled with despair. She thought for a wild moment, as the pain vanished, as she felt herself float away on the bubble as it burst, that the cry came from Nathan. His voice, raw and thick, like he was talking through water, like he was crying, like that night they lost Rose, the same thick, chest-deep sobbing . . . except now he was calling her name—*Georgia, Georgia, God, please no, Georgia, please*—begging her for something and she couldn't guess what it was and then she was gone and she knew whatever it was she couldn't find it where she was going. The pain faded and the fog around her cleared. She looked out through the looking glass and saw him, pinned to the door by two men in hospital scrubs, and above it all a long, mournful wail contained in one unbearable note. She floated, watching from above, the shrieking electric note filling her until a man in blue scrubs streaked with blood reached over her lifeless, broken body and turned it off.

Through the fog she hovered, slow at first. Flying now, her heart light, Georgia realized that she was back in Eden, the ground soft with leaves and moss, the sky filled with towering sycamores, the air filled with incense. She ran through the fog until it parted and found herself standing in the same meadow the looking glass had taken her to. Two figures waited there. A man, with hair like copper and eyes like fire, his hands resting on the hilt of a sword, a war-weary soldier clad in leather and tarnished armor. And beside him, diminutive, was Edie.

Georgia stopped a short distance from the pair. She felt the dew settle on her cheeks, ran her hands over the gentle grasses of the meadow. Bird song and babbling brooks, gentle breezes in the trees. After what she'd just left behind, paradise. And yet.

"I've lost them," she said, each word filled with sorrow. "And this, all of this will never be half as beautiful as what I lost, will it?"

Edie hurried to her side but the man met her eyes, the set of his mouth and his steady gaze a silent, mournful agreement.

Edie grasped both of her hands and kissed them. "What a load of bunk. You haven't lost a thing. Just got a bit turned around, I think." She glanced over her shoulder. "Michael can sort that out. But you can't stay here. You have to go back. Nathan and Galliana need you. And we'll meet again. I promised, remember?" She threw herself into Georgia's arms and whispered, "In time."

Georgia held Edie tight, her heart torn in two, wanting to stay, wanting desperately to go back. She took one last moment to smell the girl's lily hair and placed one hand on her porcelain cheek. "I love you, Edie," Georgia said, pressing her lips to Edie's forehead. "Forever and ever. Don't ever forget that."

Michael crossed the meadow and, slipping his gloves from his hands, cradled Georgia's face. A glorious sensation, like being bathed in starlight, as her body was knit back together in a surge of euphoric healing. Enraptured, she fell into his arms. Michael carried her back through the fog, his broad chest rumbling with laughter, whispering so only she could hear.

"And they call *me* a saint, Georgia Pritchard. I think the miracles you've managed surpass them all." He laid her down on a bed of moss, as the fog grew thick all around them. Michael stood then and turned, walking slowly away, sparks flying as his scabbard struck the mossy rocks, and vanished.

Forever. In just one second.

And then her lungs filled painfully with air, her chest exploded in agony. Struggling to open her eyes, she heard Nathan's voice, felt his arms wrap around her.

"Georgia, you came back."

She met his eyes—his own eyes this time—dear and familiar once more. His arms left her for a moment and the next she felt a small weight against her chest. Georgia gazed down at her daughter and breathed in her intoxicating scent, like milk and honey and tea and time, a smell as exotic and familiar as the one she left behind in Eden.

Nathan searched Georgia's eyes, and was met with a steady stream of love and forgiveness. He kissed her forehead and then her lips, long and soft, and rested his hand on their daughter's alabaster brow.

"Galliana," Georgia whispered. "That's her name. I know her name." Tears now falling freely down his face, Nathan smiled and nodded.

"My little Galli. Our little angel."

FORTY-EIGHT

GEORGIA ASKED NATHAN TO DRIVE BY ROSE-neath, one last time.

"I need to see for myself that it's gone. All of it. And then we'll go." She kissed him again, the intensity of her unwavering love burning away all his fear and guilt, if only for a moment.

Georgia would never be the same again, a truth that remained unspoken between them. Despite Michael's healing touch, the toll of Galliana's conception and birth had aged her prematurely. The doctors themselves were at a loss to explain exactly how a woman of barely thirty had the musculature, the bone density, the vitals of a woman twice her age, her body ravaged as if she'd been exposed to some undetectable radiation. While her face retained its youthful sweetness, one large swath of her dark hair had gone white overnight; her steps now were halting, hesitant, her joints swollen with the sudden onset of arthritis, a limp in her once girlish stride from a broken hip. No one was able to definitively say if that injury was due to her fall or to the traumatic birth of such a large child. But it was not the physical price she'd paid that frightened Nathan the most. It was the emotional one, the hunted, haunted look in her eyes when she thought he didn't see. But he did see it, he knew who had put it there, and he knew he would spend the rest of his days desperately trying to heal that wound, even if he could do nothing about the others.

As for Nathan, the face he saw in the mirror was the same as ever. The toll Roseneath had taken on him was evident only in the abrupt loss of his once easy smile. It was tinged now with a subtle grief that never really left his face, confidence supplanted by remorse, as if his thoughts were never far from his actions during those three lost months. His body was another story, every inch of his arms and torso covered in a web of fine white scars. How Georgia could let him hold her, let him touch her was beyond him. He was sickened with himself, sickened to see his hands on hers. She said she loved him. Said she forgave him. And that might have been true but he knew even if he spent a lifetime trying, he'd never be able to forgive himself. He woke most nights screaming, pleading with Georgia to tell him who he was, to tell him none of it had happened, that his nightmares were just that and not his unconscious mind struggling with the truth.

As for their daughter, Galliana, she was large for her age, her gangly arms and legs more suited to a toddler and hinting of a towering stature to come. Where her mother was now wan and wasted, Galli's cherry-red cheeks boasted a vigorous health. Her temperament was calm and winsome for one so young. Georgia and Nathan rarely saw her cry, despite the fact that she hardly ever slept. Watching her lie awake all night, eyes searching the heavens, they told themselves it was just a testament to her sweet nature, and refused to ascribe it to anything more.

The car was loaded down with all their things. Considering it was now all they had in the world, it was a meager collection. Moreover, the way Nathan had resigned abruptly from the York project, it might be all they'd ever have. Standing just outside a ring of caution tape, Georgia let out a long sigh as she stared at the ruins of Roseneath. There was nothing left but scorched earth, even the remaining trees that surrounded the property were so badly burned, it was unlikely they would survive the coming season. Nathan gripped her hand; she could feel his worry returning so she turned to him and smiled. "I'm relieved. I was worried there would be something left behind. But it's all gone, isn't it? Every last bit."

He nodded, but she felt his hand tremble.

Georgia glanced at Galli in Nathan's arms, the infant's brilliant red hair a small cap against her pale white skin, a fairy child covered with a galaxy of freckles. Georgia smiled and bent to kiss her nose, humming the strange melody that had filled her during her pregnancy, wondered if the child remembered it. Galli laughed and Georgia looked up into Nathan's sad eyes, kissed his lips, tried to ignore the way he hesitated before wrapping her in his arms, as if he were afraid to hold his own family.

Over his shoulder, a flash of light caught Georgia's eyes. Something shining in the rearview mirror of their car, a silver, insistent flickering. And there, in the corner, a being with eyes of fire.

"Let's go, Nathan," she said, plucking Galli from his arms. "Hurry."

Nathan slid into the driver's seat as Georgia fastened their child into her car seat. "Go, now. Hurry," she pleaded.

In the mirror, Nathan watched Georgia throw herself over Galli. Behind them, in the corner of the mirror, a silhouette rose from one knee and stood, holding out a sword of fire brighter than the flames in his eyes.

"Do you see it, Nathan?" she whispered. "Do you see him?"

Nathan punched the accelerator to the floor and nodded grimly. In the back seat, Galli gurgled and laughed. Nathan drove faster; the man in the mirror seemed to recede as he did, growing smaller and smaller until he vanished entirely.

"Where will we go, Nathan? What have we done?" Georgia was crying now. Nathan reached back for her and she took his hand.

"I don't know, Georgia. I just don't know." Nathan felt her head fall against the back of his seat, heard her sobs mingle with their daughter's laughter as he drove them far away from the beauty and horror, the heaven and hell of Roseneath.

In Eden, on the other side of time, far away and through the looking glass, Michael sheathed his sword and extinguished the wicking flames coating the blade. Beside him, Edie rose on her tiptoes and grabbed hold of his arm.

"What happens now, Michael? What do we do?"

He flashed his eyes in a solemn grin, his twin blue flames, his countenance gentle but determined.

"She asked for time, little one. And now that I have found her, you and I will see to it that she has it. All the time in this world and the next. And, perhaps this time, one day, my Galliana will find her way back to me."

ACKNOWLEDGEMENTS

Sydney Kalnay: your enthusiasm, support, suggestions and midwifery encouraged me and challenged me from the moment this story was born. Thank you for loving this story and characters enough to create an entire universe for them to live in (with slightly less drama) alongside the characters from your own wonderful stories. You are the Jane Eyre to my Helen Burns, oatcakes and Lowood forever.

Megan Alabaugh, who suffered through every horrible draft, called me out every time I was lazy about details, and never, ever gave up on me even when I gave up (hourly) on myself.

All my beta readers over the last ten years: Camille Nice, David Genzen, Amy Russell, Lindsey Emery, and Matt Wilson. Your thoughtful commentary helped me hone this book into the creation you hold in your hands. Thank you from the bottom of my heart.

Lakewood, Ohio, for being filled with beautiful old homes and populated with thoroughly enchanting people. I am proud to call you home.

Peter Gaskin: you pulled the best possible work out of me by using equal parts big brother mocking and Star Trek memes, and elevated this story in every possible way.

I never would have nailed Satan's voice if you hadn't reminded me that he's the ultimate older brother. You are a brilliant editor and I feel honored to have worked with you. Excelsior, my friend.

To my dogs, Zyk and Seymour, who were with me every step of the way, usually snoring on my feet while I was researching and writing. Your endlessly positive feedback and insistence on naps and snack breaks was invaluable.

Henry and Anne: I forgot dinner, I forgot your names, I was late picking you up from school, and I spent way too much time typing in a dark room and crying. Thank you for giving me the space to be both your mom and a writer. You both make this world a better place and I love you more than words can say.

To my husband Winston, who has given me many dream homes, only one of which was haunted. I can't be me without you. Let's get married again forever.

Dana McSwain grew up on the shores of the Great Lakes in the shadow of the Rust Belt. A graduate of Kent State University, she lives in a 106-year-old house in Cleveland, Ohio with her family and two dogs. *Roseneath* was written during the ten years she spent restoring an abandoned 1921 Tudor Revival in one of Cleveland's inner ring suburbs that locals believe to be haunted. Learn more at danamcswain.com.

CPSIA information can be obtained
at www.ICGtesting.com
Printed in the USA
FSHW022242210820
73188FS

9 781735 286044